Imaginary Playmate
Magdalene Breaux

Imaginary Playmate

All character names, descriptions and traits are products of the author's imagination. Similarities to actual people—living or dead—are purely coincidental.

Real events and physical locations related to New Orleans, Louisiana and Atlanta, Georgia are scattered throughout the plot to capture the ambiance of each city's unique culture. Similarities to dates, events or circumstances related to the lives of actual people—living or dead—are purely coincidental.

This book is intended for mature audiences and entertainment purposes only. The author assumes no liability for loss or damage that occur as a result of the content contained within this book.

Copyright 2002 by Breaux Books, LLC
First Edition
Library of Congress Control Number: 2002090860
ISBN: 0-9701709-1-2

Editor
Sharron M. Nuckles
SMN Editing
P.O. Box 139
Atlanta, GA 30303
404-754-4074
smnediting@msn.com

Cover design by Keith Saunders
E-mail: m_asaund@bellsouth.net

Breaux Books, LLC
P. O. Box 67
Fairburn, GA 30213
770-842-4792
E-mail: **magbreaux@mindspring.com**
Web: **www.familycurse.com**

Explore the phantasms of psychology with unexpected twists and turns. *Imaginary Playmate* makes you look over your shoulder and wonder – is someone really there?

~Vincent Alexandria
Author of *Postal Blues, If Walls Could Talk, & Black Rain*

Acknowledgements

I'd like to thank the many book clubs, bookstore owners and managers, organizations and thousands of readers who made my first book, *The Family Curse*, a success.

Special thanks goes to:

- My two sons, Larryn and Obi—just because
- Author Shelia Goss for pushing and prodding me along the way with helpful advice to make *Imaginary Playmate* the best it can be
- Dr. James R. Sowell—Professor of Astronomy and Physics, Georgia Institute of Technology—for verifying key facts of astronomy and for ensuring that "heavenly" and "out-of-worldly" scenes are scientifically accurate
- Author Roy Glenn for providing key industry facts (you know what they are)
- Sharron Nuckles—with her keen eye for detail—for taking time out of her busy schedule to edit *Imaginary Playmate*
- Keith Saunders for designing such a sassy, seductive cover

Now, with all that said, I'd like to present to you, *Imaginary Playmate!*

Sit back, relax and allow each word to bring you many hours of pleasure. Enjoy!

M
☺

Table of Contents

Prologue
Retrograde Motion

The last three months are a blur. If I didn't know any better, I'd say I'm suffering from amnesia. I can't remember half the things I did. I don't where I've been or what I've done ... or with whom. It's all so fuzzy. My sanity is slipping—and fast.

Do you know who I am, Demeter?

Yes, you're Dr. Iverson.

Are you sure?

Yes, you're Dr. Iverson.

Do you know where you are, Demeter?

Yes. I'm in your office, Dr. Iverson. I like this black leather recliner. It's so soft and cozy. I need to get one like it.

Are you sure you're in my office, Demeter?

Yes. I know what you're probably thinking.

What I'm I thinking, Demeter?

You think I've forgotten about you because I haven't made an appointment to see you since September. I've been meaning to ... honest. Especially since ... Anyway. I'm not holding back on you.

Did I say you were holding back on me?

No, but I hear it in your voice. I've told you everything to catch up on the last three months. Let's see, I told you about the people at work and all the stuff they dragged me into, that stunt Percy pulled, Tish and Fern. I know you don't believe me about my mole, but it's true how I got rid of it. Yep, that about covers it. I've told you everything that happened to me over the past three months. Really. Oh, yeah ... can't forget about him ... you know ... him.

Do you know how you got here?

I drove.

Are you sure?

I guess.

You guess?

What's with the questions? And why are you sitting over there in the dark, Dr. Iverson? You always sit in the dark. And what's wrong with your voice? It sounds hoarse, like you have bronchitis or something. Is that why you're over there, because you have a cold and don't want me to catch it?

Are you ready to go through with this, Demeter?

Yes.

Are you sure?

Yes! I can't go on like this, Dr. Iverson. I don't know if I'm coming or going, or going or coming. This is no way to live. Do whatever you can, something, anything … this craziness needs to stop. I can't control them anymore. Please … Please … just make them go away! I just want to be a normal, thirty-eight-year-old woman again. Is that too much to ask?

Good. You're a brave woman. Remember, I'll be right here by your side guiding you to find answers. Drink the cup of coffee on the table to your right. If you're holding anything back, it will come clean now.

Ummm. This is good coffee, Dr. Iverson. Café au lait—really sweet, really creamy—almost as good as Mr. Chap's. You know, Mr. Chap made the best coffee around. Did you know Mr. Chap, Dr. Iverson? Well, did you?

How do you feel, Demeter?

I feel really, really good, Dr. Iverson. I feel all tingly all over!

What day is it?

Uuuhhh … it's Friday, December 31, 1999.

Are you sure?

Yep. It's awfully warm for this time of year. Must be eighty degrees out. It's kinda overcast though.

Good. Continue to relax, Demeter. Now, start at the top of your head and imagine a brilliant, white light flowing to every cell in your body. Feel your arms and legs get heavy—heavier and heavier. Now take in three huge breaths. Now blow them out really fast. Again. Three long breaths in, blow them out. That's it, Demeter. Good.

Now, Demeter, direct your mind to go back to when it all started. Remember, you are the observer. You know all. You feel all. You tell all. On the count of three. One ... two ... three ...

September
A new world
Realm of possibilities to explore
Clouds in heaven
Streets of gold
Imagination set on high
At last!
Away mundane!
Say good-bye

Chapter 1.
A New World

Bright, white clouds appeared as giant balls of cotton against a backdrop of the sparkling, clear, bright, blue sky. The leaves had already begun to change to brilliant earth tones—deep sienna, goldenrod and burgundy—and quietly rustled to the rhythm of the gentle September breeze.

I sped along Highway 74, racing to get to Underground Atlanta. I flicked through the tracks of my CD player, anxious to find that one special selection. Relaxing, mellow sounds of jazz filled the air as I enjoyed my drive along the scenic route.

It was my thirty-eighth birthday, so my long-time friend, Letitia Hollinger, and my sister, Percy, wanted to take me out to Sunday brunch to celebrate. Heck, we would have celebrated the opening of a bag of potato chips as an excuse to go out some place special or try something new.

***

What were you thinking? What were you feeling?

***

I thought about how my dear, sweet sister would have scolded me if I'd arrived late. Percy was always a stickler for time and always went on and on if anyone ever violated her strict code of punctuality. She would say something like, "I've been waiting here a very long time for you. What took you so long anyway?" When asked how long she had been waiting, she'd snap, "About five ... ten minutes! What difference does it make, anyway? You need to learn how to be on time ... that's all there is to it!"

She really, really irritated me and got on my last nerve sometimes. When she made me mad, I got back at her by saying her full name—Persephone Echo Pickens. That really ticked her off. She was soooo prissy—sort of anyway. Everything had to be just so for her. But, she was still my sister, and I loved her. *I think.* If it weren't for her, I don't know how I would have got through this ordeal.

Lucky Percy—she never got married or had children, but that's a whole other story. Anyway, she moved in a small two-bedroom high-rise condo on the fourteenth-floor. It was practically across the street from my office in Buckhead, so we met for lunch when I was free. She was the vice president of marketing and product development of a major pharmaceutical company, or so she said. She told everybody that her office was in New York, but she telecommuted—you know, she worked from home.

***

How about your friend, Letitia?

***

Oh, Tish had been divorced three years and got plenty of alimony. She probably got more in alimony than my take-home pay each month. Some folk got it easy and don't even know it. Hnnn. I had to work for everything I got. Ain't nobody ever gave me nothing!

Tish's twins went off to college, so she had the house to herself. Even when the children were growing up, she had the house to herself anyway. Her husband was away on business most of the time, or so he said. So, Tish just ran the streets and left those poor children with a sitter. She never had time for them. That's why they didn't like to come home on weekends. Between you and me, Dr. Iverson, one of the reasons her husband, what's-his-name, left her was because she was never at home. I told you the other reason why he left.

***

Resfresh my memory. Why did her husband leave?

Because she couldn't ... you know ... satisfy him in bed. She didn't ... you know ... like it. Do you think she preferred women back then too?

***

Anyway, Ms. Percy had the audacity to tell me that I was jealous of Tish. I wasn't jealous of her even if she never worked a day in her life and was a housewife. So what if she had that nice, big house in Alpharetta courtesy of her ex. I have a nice house in Peachtree City that I bought myself, thank you very much. Sure, she wore six hundred dollar shoes and five thousand dollar dresses and had a car even nicer than mine, but who cares, right Dr. Iverson?

If you went over to Tish's house and it was a mess, she would say something like, "It's the maid's day off," and meant it too. She had a full-time maid and a nanny before the children went to kindergarten! Talk about lazy! I worked full-time and still kept a clean house.

***

Enough of that. How about you?

***

You know the routine, Dr. Iverson: I've been divorced over ten years. Till this day, I still don't know why I married that no-good, low-down, good-for-nothing, trifling n …

***

Stay focused, Demeter.

***

Anyway, I chose to live in Peachtree City—period. I don't think I have to explain why I live in Peachtree City. So what if not too many black folk live there.

Anyway, moving right along. When I was promoted to Director of Software Products and Development two years ago, I just knew I had *made it*. I always wanted that job, but now it's way more demanding than I had expected. A staff of about fifty people now reports to me. If someone or something falls short of the schedule, guess who's responsible? Me … Didi. I'm responsible for everybody else's screw-ups.

Then, on the home front, my two boys, Keston and Kevin, are something else! I'm telling you, even though they're fifteen and seventeen, they act like they're five and seven. They always want something. They never give anything back in return! All they do is take, take, take. It's always, "I want this, I need that. I want to go here, I want to go there." They never care about what I want.

So, between driving forty-five miles one way to work, the drama that went on at work, and my boys, I'm just stretched too thin, Dr. Iverson. I need to slow down … and fast.

***

Get back to your birthday. What else did you feel?

***

All these damned traffic lights, I complained. *There's one damn near every mile! I hate to wait, especially when I'm in a hurry.*
Wait a minute!

***

What is it, Demeter?

***

I noticed a large, black bird perched on a tree stump on the side of the road. It almost seemed to have been watching me in anticipation of the green light. As

I began down Highway 74 again, the bird darted in front of me so fast that I had to jam on my brakes to avoid hitting the thing! As it flew past the windshield, its wings spanned at least ten feet across, I swear, Dr. Iverson. It completely blocked any hint of sunlight. The creature stood over four feet tall. Its shiny feathers were the purest, deepest, darkest of black, like voids that led into nothingness.

The bird touched the hood with its large, gripping brown claws and secured a transparent veil that surrounded my car. It disappeared into the myriad of trees that lined the road, as the veil dangled in the wind. For real!

***

Get into the moment, Demeter, with every sight, sound and smell. Look around. Experience the moment.

***

The sky changed to a brighter shade of blue. The clouds looked whiter and more illustrious than ever. A strange tune spewed endlessly from the CD player that became sharper, clearer and more defined. Lilting sounds of saxophone, piano, trumpet and bass hypnotically blended as one, yet each retained its own uniqueness, its own quality, striving together to achieve the crescendo, the moment of perfection, the peak.

For a moment, all became hazy and gray, as though I had been captured into an old black-and-white movie of the 40's. I heard a loud splashing sound. In a flash, a fine mist engulfed my entire body. I thought that I had run into a fire hydrant or something.

I don't believe it, Dr. Iverson.

***

Believe what, Demeter?

***

I must have been losing it, I mean really losing it! So much ran through my mind. *Swell*! I thought. *This new silk suit is ruined! I won't be able to find another one, especially in this color. Honeysuckle is a hard color to find because it has to be specially blended.*

Shit! I just got my hair done yesterday! Now it's ruined.

It's going to cost a fortune to fix the car! I know that the insurance company will try to fight it! They fight anything!

I don't believe that I could have been thinking about my suit and hair. I must have been losing it, I'm telling you!

***

That's all right, Demeter. Don't judge, simply recall. Judging won't help you resolve your current issues. Recollection will. Keep talking, Demeter. What else did you feel?

***

A warm, thick, soothing substance covered my feet. When I looked down, deep, dark, black mud was up to my ankles. My long, lush curls were lost to the warm, moist atmosphere. "What the …" I realized that I was completely nude, but my vanity quickly faded. In an instant, an intense feeling of peace surrounded me. Oooo, it felt sooo gooood, Dr. Iverson. *So, this is heaven,* I thought.

I was too out of it to realize that anything was wrong or out of the ordinary!

***

Go on Demeter. Remember, if you want to solve your riddle, you must experience every nuance as a casual observer. Don't judge. Now, continue… recall every detail.

***

When I turned to my right, the lush landscape changed into a vibrant waterfall that cascaded over a steep mountain, then flowed into a crisp blue river below. The sun appeared as a giant splat of glowing white paint across the way, a prism bouncing colors off misty air, as a giant rainbow filled the silver-blue sky. The smell of jasmine and honeysuckle permeated the air, as exotic birds sang in the distance. Exotic trees painted the landscape; sundries of flowers dotted the scene with specks of color—lilac, pale-blue, canary-yellow, pink and white.

A strange energy pulsated through my veins, which brought a sense of peace and tranquility. I took a few steps and looked in awe of what I beheld. In the distance was a large white structure that peeked over the river. It was square with a small glass-enclosed steeple on top. Soft, yellow lights sparkled through the five large French windows on the first level.

I saw a shadowy figure of a man who seemed to have been admiring the view from the second level balcony.

***

Tell me about the man. What was he doing?

***

He spread his arms across the railing as he took two long, deep breaths. I watched as he slowly made his way to the spiral staircase to the far right, disappearing behind the massive, white columns that hid its view. A few seconds later, he emerged and began his leisurely stroll along the white cobblestone path through the garden. He stroked the foliage ever so gently as he passed by, like the tender touch bestowed upon a favored pet. For a moment he paused, as large white petals floated delicately around him. He plucked a yellow rose from a bush and cradled it close to his heart, as a mother adorns her newborn babe. A smile lit his face as he took one long, deep inhale to capture the aromatic essence the flower poured into the air.

He continued his stroll along the path and admired the view of the waterfall and rainbow. Several large rocks tumbled down the cliff and splashed into the river, one by one. He turned to observe the occurrence and appeared startled to see me watching him. He began to run down the hill toward me and waved his arms like a wild man. Each of his movements resembled fleeting droplets of paint—white, black and red—that rippled gracefully in the wind. The immediate surroundings vibrated to his rhythmic gait. He called to me, but his words were mumbled and gargled, as though he called from the depths of the sea.

I panicked, but could not run fast enough or far enough away to escape the rapture of that mysterious stranger. My legs sank deeper and deeper into the mud with each step I took. The air began to thicken as he approached—closer and closer—until he was almost in sight. Terror saturated every cell in my body as I sank deeper and deeper into that hot black mud.

He reached to me. His body was a blur of white, black and a hint of red, one indistinguishable from the other. The air began to ripple as he touched me ...

***

Two brief toots of a horn reminded me that the light had just changed to green. I felt myself falling from great heights to the great unknown below. Air quickly filled my lungs, jolting me in my seat. Two more toots sounded from behind, but that time longer. I looked in the rearview mirror and noticed a balding, gray-haired, middle-aged man and younger female companion seated in a red convertible Corvette.

Several cars sped around me. I was too shaken to move and was in a deep state of confusion. My heart began to pound, and my breathing became erratic.

***

What else happened?

***

Mellow sounds of jazz filled the air at the point of decrescendo— saxophone, piano, trumpet and bass—only a few seconds advanced in the song than I had remembered. I looked at the dashboard and noticed ten-forty-seven, one minute since the last time I checked the time.

I must be working too hard, I tried to reason, but my whole body trembled by the thought of what had happened.

***

You said that you were meeting your friend and your sister? Did you meet them as planned, or did you decide to go home?

***

I was shaken, but decided to meet them anyway. I thought that being in good company would ease my nerves.

"Eleven-thirty reservations for Pickens," I told the hostess. "Didi Pickens."

"One of your guests has already been seated," she informed me. "Right this way please."

Percy must be here already, I thought as I followed the hostess, but Letitia was seated at our favorite patio table. *Letitia is early,* I thought. *What a first!* She looked a bit distant, like she was daydreaming. I didn't think anything of it. What a big mistake.

Letitia looked like a schoolgirl from a distance with that long, bouncing ponytail; smooth caramel complexion; and long, flowing pastel-blue dress. Looking at her that day took me back twenty years to the day we first. I was a freshman at Spelman, and she was a junior. Tish wore a long, curly ponytail and pair of Chic jeans that hugged her shape just right. She was always a very attractive woman, no wonder I …

Anyway, Michael's was our favorite brunch spot.

***

Our?

Yes. Percy's, Letitia's and mine.

Oh.

***

It was on the third level of Underground Atlanta. When the weather permitted, we often requested a balcony table that overlooked Alabama Street. We savored the clear view of the water fountain and life-like bronze statutes where street-side musicians often performed on a makeshift stage.

Each table was adorned with a crisp white linen tablecloth; sparkling, crystal water goblets; and formal place settings. A single pink and orange floral linen napkin—which was folded to resemble a rose—was carefully placed on top of each salad plate.

I sat down and unfolded my napkin. Letitia continued to stare into space, not even noticing me.

"Hello," I said.

Letitia must have been deep in thought because when I spoke, she spilled water all over her dress. "I got here a bit early," Letitia said as she tried to dry her dress with a cloth napkin.

One of the waiters came over to assist.

"Where's Percy?" I asked then took a wheat roll from the basket. I was still shaken, and my hand was trembling. Letitia didn't seem to notice though.

"She must be running a bit late," Letitia answered in a flat tone.

"Percy?" I laughed as I buttered my roll. "Late? Something important must have really detained her. Has she tried to call or leave a message with you, Tish?"

"No," Letitia said as she checked the time on her cellular phone. "I guess she hasn't tried to contact you either."

"No," I said. "I hope she's all right."

"Sorry I'm late folks," Percy said as she sat down to join us and unfolded her napkin onto her lap. "I had to drop Victor off at the airport." She eagerly took a roll from the basket as the waiter poured water into her goblet. "He's going to Israel for a few weeks."

She wore a brown linen dress that reached her ankles. The long split on the right side revealed her slim, shapely, toned legs. The low V-cut front did justice to her ample 38DD cleavage and svelte, curvaceous figure. Long ringlets of curls flowed down her cheeks. Percy was always the pretty one. She was tall and slender like our mother, with that deep ebony skin and heart-shaped face. I took after our father with his long, ugly, pointy nose and big square box head.

***

Unnnn.

***

Well, anyway. She looked so youthful, yet so elegant. Her forty years of life were a well-kept secret that hid deep beneath the surface of her flawless complexion.

Letitia perked up when Percy came, probably because she knew that Percy would have had tons of questions about why she was looking so distant. Letitia was a good actress. Well, she had to be a good actress because she was married to what's-his-name for so many years. Their marriage was a farce, but that's not my concern, now is it Dr. Iverson?

Anyway, I, too, tried to hide my nervousness. It was something. Percy made Letitia and me feel like we needed to behave properly in her presence. Come to think of it, ever since we were kids, she'd always been bossy. She was forced to play the role of mother to my two brothers and me. Even though she was two years older than me, Percy was more of a parent than our mother could have ever dreamed of being to us.

Through the years, Percy could walk into any room anywhere and instantly command respect. That attitude was the reason why she rose to the rank of vice president. That's what she always thought. If you ask me, I think her 38DD cleavage got her what she wanted through the years.

Anyway.

"How are you ladies doing today?" our usual waiter asked as he flashed that

million-dollar smile. The white cotton shirt; burgundy and black vest; and black
wing-tips complemented his tall lean physique. Ummm, ummm!

"My, my," Percy said as usual. "So young, so tender. You know what I'll
have," she said as she handed him the menu.

"Yes, ma'am," he said. He just laughed as usual.

I think he actually loved it when sweet Miss Percy flirted with him.

"You know what I'm having," Letitia said.

"Ditto," I said.

"Can I get you ladies anything else while you wait for your meal?" he
asked.

"I'll have a plate of you, please," Percy teased and then winked at him.

How embarrassing. She always embarrassed me by flirting with strange
men. But do you think she cared if she embarrassed me? Nooo! That could be
dangerous too. But do you think she cared? Nooo!

Anyway. The waiter let out his usual boyish giggle. His deep bronze skin
and shiny baldhead gave him a sense of maturity that his twenty years of life
couldn't possibly. Umm, umm.

***

Enough of Percy. Now stay focused.

***

"How's Victor doing?" Letitia asked.

Percy flashed a big three-carat diamond solitaire in our faces. "He asked me
to marry him."

"What!" Letitia and I exclaimed.

"When are we going to meet him?" Letitia asked.

"You've dated for a year, and we have never met him," I said. *Yeah, we
haven't met him because he doesn't exist. Victor is her imaginary playmate.
She's making everything up and probably bought the ring herself,* I thought.

"Let me see." Letitia said as she held Percy's ring finger to get a closer
look. "Wow! We have a lot to celebrate today!"

"Did you say yes?" I asked. "When's the date?"

"I have to think about it," Percy informed us. "I've been single so long that
I'm not sure that I want to commit to any one man."

Yeah, right! She didn't want to get married because she screwed every man
she met and didn't want to screw just one man.

***

Stay focused, Demeter. We'll talk about your sister later.

***

"What!" Letitia exclaimed. "He's a multi-millionaire tycoon. What do you
have to think about?"

"I need more than status," Percy informed us. "I've been by myself so long, that nothing short of the very best will do. I have to make sure that he's right for me."

Whatever, Percy, I thought. "Well, you've been dating well over a year now," I informed her. "Isn't that enough time?"

I was still shaken from the earlier incident, but managed to hide my feelings from them. Focusing on Percy's engagement was the perfect escape. I had tons of questions. Just tons!

"Not really," Percy said.

"Not really, Percy," I prodded. "If wealth and status are not what you're looking for? Then would you feel better about marrying a man of less means?" *He probably can't satisfy her libido,* is what I thought. Percy more than made her rounds, if you know what I mean. I told her on many occasions that she was just too open. She had the nerve to tell me, "I have a body and enjoy my sexuality. I don't see how you can be celibate. That's unnatural."

***

Stay focused, Demeter.

***

"Hell, no!" Percy shouted, catching the attention of practically everyone in the restaurant.

Please don't embarrass me Percy, I thought. *Not today, Please.*

"I only date educated men of means," Percy continued, then slammed her fist on the table. "I have an undergraduate degree from Spelman and a master's degree from Howard University. He doesn't have to have attended Ivy or Ebony Leagues, but he must be educated."

One thing about Percy, she made sure that the world knew about her accomplishments. She always had to be the center of attention. But that day, her unpredictable behavior worked like a charm by taking away thoughts about this morning. I wasn't the least bit embarrassed about being with Percy in public—for a change.

"Ebony Leagues?" Letitia asked.

"Well, Morehouse, Howard, Tuskegee, Fisk ... you know," Percy said.

"Oh, really?" I teased. "Then how about that basketball player, two football players, and rap singer you dated some time ago? They weren't well educated as you say. In fact, they didn't finish college."

"Yeah," Letitia said with a laugh. "They were college drop-outs."

"They had culture and class. They wanted to explore life to the fullest. That's something that you can't get from any school. That comes from within."

"You're shallow," Letitia said. "A poor man can give you just as much happiness. It's what's on the inside that counts, not the outside."

Oh no! I thought. *Why did Tish have to go there?*

Percy was huffed. "Oh no she didn't!" She put her hands on her hips, narrowed her little, beady eyes and lips and said, "Your ex isn't doing so badly, now is he, Tish?"

"Well," Tish tried to answer.

Percy was fuming.

"Be good, Percy," I tried to butt in, knowing that something was wrong with Letitia, but Percy wouldn't have it.

"No, no," Percy said while circling her finger in the air. "Mrs. Susie Homemaker-never-worked-a-day-in-her-life-getting alimony wants to tell me about marrying a man of less means?"

"Well," Letitia said. "It just happened that way. I didn't ask for it."

"Bullshit!" Percy informed her. "You went after that man. See, I knew you when. Don't come acting like Ms. Sweet-and-Innocent with me," Percy said as she buttered a roll. "See, I knew you. He moved away to New York and got a big promotion. What is his title now?"

"CEO," I butted in. I couldn't resist. Adding my two-cents worth really took my mind off of my troubles! What an escape, focusing on other people's hardships. Whew!

"But still," Letitia said. "Maybe if I would have married from the inside out, and not the outside in, I would have selected a better husband. Perhaps a poor man can really satisfy your true needs."

Tish dropped her head and looked a bit sad. Percy probably thought that Tish looked sad because she had lost the argument, not that anything was troubling her. But do you think that Percy eased up? No. She probably got a thrill of winning an argument with Tish.

"No, he can't!" Percy informed her. "We are every person, place and thing we've ever been. Where you live, work and play is an extension of your personality. Men of less means just aren't attractive to me. They don't excite me!"

"You two need to stop," I interjected between gulps of lemon water. "I've been divorced over ten years and have not really dated during that time. I know how to make myself happy. I don't need a man to make me happy."

Well, what Percy didn't know was that I didn't need a man to make me happy. But, Tish knew all too well how a woman brought many smiles to my face.

***

All right, enough of them. Look around. Examine the scene. Do you notice anything peculiar, out of the ordinary?

No.

Look again. This time focus harder. Remember, you see all, you know all.

***

A cool breeze rushed through the patio. We needed the breeze too, because the sun was shining really bright that day. The other waiter, besides *our waiter,* of course, who served *our* table was so overly enthusiastic and helpful. I ordered the usual blueberry crepes, but something was different. The once subtle flavors of cinnamon, lemon and vanilla were suddenly more vibrant, more exciting than ever. The blueberries were more moist and plump than usual and seemed a deeper shade of purple. I looked around at the crowded room, and the parties at each table seemed festive, exciting.

Street musicians played two levels below. Every note, every tone—the sultry tenor saxophone, the cello, drums and trumpet—took a life of its own.

"So, Demeter," Letitia said. "How's that new class coming? What are you taking now? First, it was belly dancing, then horse back riding, then Tarot, then Feng Shui, now what?"

"Lucid dreaming and meditation."

"What?" Percy asked. A look of concern crossed her face, but I didn't think much of it. Perhaps I should have.

"Lucid dreaming. It's the ability to take control of your dreams. According to our teacher, Dr. Iverson, you can live out your wildest fantasies in your dreams."

What I told them was somewhat true. I said that you were my teacher, not that I had been seeing you as a patient every week for the past year and lucid dreaming is a stress reduction technique.

"Is that so?" Letitia asked sarcastically.

"Dr. Iverson gave us these tapes, and I've been playing them. They're just so relaxing, especially after a hard day at the office."

"What are the tapes supposed to do?" Percy asked. She seemed a bit jittery. Again, I dismissed her reaction.

"They're supposed to aid us in merging the right and left sides of our brains. According to Dr. Iverson, both hemispheres of the brain are active in people who are lucid dreamers. But for the majority of us, we use only a fraction of our mind's power."

"So, how long have you been taking this class?" Percy inquired. She leaned in closer to me. A serious look crossed her face.

"Four weeks. The last class was Tuesday."

"Well, have you been able to lucid dream," Letitia inquired further.

"No, but Dr. Iverson says that it will come with time." Then, I realized that the incident that I had earlier was perhaps a lucid dream, only I was awake. *Perhaps I need to learn how to control it,* I thought.

"Who's Dr. Iverson?" Percy asked.

"You've never heard of Dr. Iverson!" Letitia exclaimed. "Where've you been, Percy? She's the *one* whose picture has been all over every newspaper, not to mention all over the news. The one who has a Ph.D in quantum physics or something from Harvard, Yale or some place. She got her undergrad from Spelman. That's probably why she returned to Atlanta. She's a real brainiac and real pretty too. She can't be over thirty years old. She's a psychologist or parapsychologist or something like that."

"Oh, you mean the one who *supposedly* proved that life not only exists in *outer space*, but in some hyperspace, innerspace or something?" Percy asked sarcastically.

"Yes. That's her," I said.

"If I were you, I would be careful. One of these days ... " Percy said as she shook her head. It seems like she wanted to say something else, but decided not to.

"What's he staring at?" Letitia asked as a man at the next table just stared endlessly at me.

"If he's interested, he needs to speak up!" Percy said. "One thing I hate is a shy, timid man!"

"What is he anyway?" Letitia asked. "Is he black, white or something else? It's hard to tell."

"He's a mutt," I said.

"He's not all that handsome, either," Letitia observed.

"He's a mutt just like our grandpa, Didi," Percy said. "I couldn't stand that moth' fucker."

"You couldn't stand your own grandfather?" Tish asked.

Percy never forgave Grandpa for how he treated us, especially since he favored our cousin, Juanita, over us. I wrote the asshole off as being a cantankerous, old man.

***

Focus on the man. Was there anything unusual about him?

***

That was him, Dr. Iverson, the one I told you about. Only he was different somehow. I can't explain it, but he was different.

He continued to stare, without as much as blinking an eye, completely motionless, almost like a statute. His eyes were deep, dark and mysterious. That wavy, low-cut, jet-black hair contrasted sharply with his tan complexion and full, pink lips. His cleanly shaven face made that stoic expression much more pronounced. The heavily starched blue-and-white plaid shirt, khakis and loafers he wore seemed awkward for the casual elegant atmosphere Michael's offered. But he seemed so familiar, Dr. Iverson.

"Something seems familiar about him," I said. He wasn't the most attractive man I had seen, but something about him was particularly fascinating. "Maybe I seem familiar to him, too, and he's trying to figure out where he knows me from."

"Why don't you make the first move?" Letitia asked.

"I don't care what you say," Percy said. "He should come over here like a gentleman and introduce himself. That's all there is to it! If he's too scared to talk to you, then he's not worth your time!"

We looked to the table one more time, and the man was gone. We looked in all directions, but he was nowhere in sight. The table was clean and set, like no one had been there all morning.

"Excuse me," I got the waiter's attention. "Where did the gentleman go who was sitting at the table next to us?"

"What man?" the waiter asked. "At which table?"

When we looked to the table again, it was no longer there. We looked all around the patio, but no table. There were three other tables nearby and at least three couples crowded each one.

"Never mind," Percy said as the waiter walked off. "Thank you."

"He was probably waiting for somebody," I said.

"I guess the waiters moved two tables together because that's such a large party over there. We just didn't notice them move them together."

***

Did anything else happen that you considered unusual?

No.

Are you sure?

Yes. Yes, I'm pretty sure, Dr. Iverson.

What happened after brunch?

***

After brunch, Letitia and I waited with Percy until she boarded the train at the Five Points MARTA Train Station. We always thought that it was ironic that someone like Percy—you know, uppity—would even consider using public transportation. But she was environmentally conscious and did her part to combat air pollution. Oh, sure!

"The two of you should drive to one of the MARTA stations and catch the train. It sure would help with the smog problem," she often nagged. But Letitia and I failed to see how our choice of transportation could impact air quality or anything else for that matter.

***

Look around the station. Describe the scene.

***

Hundreds of people walked here and there after leaving the train. The old, the young, the have and the have-nots, all melting into one sea of humanity.

"How y'all ladies doing?" a strange old man asked. He startled us as he approached from behind. Letitia and I were too surprised to respond.

He wore an old brown tweed suit with a brown-and-white striped tie, and brown-and-white wing-tip shoes. His white felt hat with brown trim was slightly tilted to one side, like something out of an old gangster movie.

"Y'all ain't married, heh?" he asked.

"No," we answered, then looked curiously at each other.

***

Describe the man. What was he like?

***

The man was short with a faded caramel complexion. The years had taken their toll on his wrinkled skin and thin, white hair, that's for sure. A thick, gray film covered the irises of his eyes. Amazingly, all of his pearly-white teeth were intact, though.

He turned to Letitia and looked her straight in the eyes. "You divorced, ain't you? And yo' husband got his own bid'ness, too, heh? Yo' husband was a fool to let you get 'way," he said, then feebly shook his index finger in the air. "But he gone get his own. God don't like ugly! Just be careful."

Letitia had that *how'd he know that?* look on her face.

He looked back and forth between Letitia and me, then briefly at the pavement. "Not many folk would stop to talk to a old man like me. Some folk miss they blessin' like that. But the Lord be with y'all, that's why y'all stopped."

He got really close to me, as if to examine me in some way. "You ain't had no man in a real long time," he told me. He laughed an eerie laugh. "But you wait and see..." he shook his feeble index once more."Where you work at? At that electric company over there, heh?"

"Yes," I answered, but was too baffled not to reply.

"You just wait and see," he told me. "Somebody at yo' job been watchin' you fo' 'bout two years now. You don't know who, but he been watchin'. You won't be alone no mo'."

Letitia and I looked in amazement at each other. When we tried to look in the direction of the old man, he wasn't there. We turned and looked all around Five Points, but he was nowhere in sight.

"Where did he go?" Letitia asked.

"He was awfully old. He couldn't have gone far."

***

This could be important. What happened next?

***

We looked toward a pizza parlor near Peachtree Street at the far end of Five Points.

"How'd he get there so quickly?" Letitia asked.

"Are you sure that's him?" I asked.

"Yes," Letitia assured. "He was carrying that old brown bag. I hadn't seen one like that since the late-60's when I was in elementary school. My grandpa had one just like it; worn and torn brown leather with that wide shoulder strap with the buckle at the bottom. That was the ugliest, most raggedy thing you ever wanted to see!"

***

Then what?

You don't even want to know, Dr. Iverson.

Chapter 2.
Realm of Possibilities to Explore

What was your day like on Monday?

It was pretty normal. Nothing unusual.

Are you sure, Demeter? Focus harder.

***

Well, I worked late ... again. Year 2000 project, you know. I'd been at work since six that morning and my eyes could barely stay open. Mr. Chap always stopped at six-thirty before he closed his shop downstairs to bring me some coffee. He always seemed to know when I was working late and delivered the coffee right to my desk. It was served au lait style, with just the right amounts of cream and sugar.

"I'm going to marry you," Mr. Chap would always say right before he gave me the coffee.

"You're so silly, Mr. Chap," I always told him. He would just laugh and walk away.

***

Did you ever take him seriously? He could be the one, you know.

Naw. Get real, Dr. Iverson. Mr. Chap was almost ninety years old! He was just a flirty, old man. That's all.

***

Well, anyway, it was ten-thirty on Monday night, and I had just left the office. But, I had to stop at the store to get some female products, if you know what I mean.

***

Did you always work so late?

***

About two years ago, our company, Georgia Power, started to downsize. I took the package that they offered me. Then, a few weeks later, Georgia Power outsourced some of its staff to a consulting firm. And guess what? I became one of those consultants. I'm doing the same job, in the same building, working with the same people, only I get paid more.

Keston, my older son, started driving about that time. He ran errands for the family and got himself and his younger brother, Kevin, to places they needed to be. I was then free to work long hours to earn the type of money I needed to send them to good colleges. It's funny, though.

**

What's funny?

Even though I made more money, it still didn't seem to be enough.

Are Kevin and Keston good children? Did you feel guilty about leaving them alone?

**

No. I never felt guilty. They are teenagers! Besides, I always call home to check on them at eight-thirty. Keston, who just turned seventeen, is usually at football practice. Kevin, the fifteen-year-old, plays tenor saxophone in the band. I cook meals for the entire week on Sunday afternoon and store them in the freezer. When Keston and Kevin get home, all they need to do is heat their dinner in the microwave and do their homework.

You know, a lot changed in my life two years ago. I started seeing you, I became a consultant, Keston started driving and Mr. Chap took over the café downstairs and made the best coffee and muffins.

**

How about your drive home?

**

Whew! It's a forty-five mile drive home—one way—from my office in Buckhead to Peachtree City. I always play the tapes you gave me to make the drive easier. In fact, I usually listen to the *Sounds of Sea* tape at night, especially right before bed. The soothing sounds of the ocean's waves sweep away over fourteen hours of stress. The sounds of seagulls that bellow in the background remind me of the family vacation to Destin, Florida last year. The sand was almost as white as snow. The ocean was so clear that I was able to see the bustling life contained within—starfish, colorful schools of fish and coral—all the way to the bottom of the sea floor.

**

Did you make it to the store?

***

Oh ... sorry ... I got off on a tangent again. Yes, I made it. Eleven-fifteen and I finally reached Highway 74. The road was unusually quiet. I began to panic because this really strong, intense feeling of loneliness came over me. The road was cold, lonely and isolated—a living soul was nowhere in sight. I was relieved to see two dots of headlights reflected in the rearview mirror. A red sports utility vehicle passed me on the left a few seconds later.

I don't feel too good, I thought. *It's that time of the month. I better just run in the store and get what I need. I should be home in less than thirty minutes.*

The parking lot was full, but I was able to get a spot fairly close to the door. I looked around the parking lot and thought that it was strange.

***

What was strange?

The other stores in the strip mall were opened. That was strange because they usually don't stay open late except during the holidays.

Did you decide to go into the store anyway, Demeter?

Yes. I needed the products, if you know what I mean.

What was the store like, Demeter?

***

The store was unusually still as I picked up the little green, plastic shopping basket. The dairy section was unusually cold, like an arctic blast had just passed through. The store felt lonely, devoid of life. Classical music always played over the sound system, but that night, it was mute. Only sounds of the refrigerators and cooling systems filled the air.

The meat department was normally bustling with laughter from cheerful workers. That too, was still. I passed the deli and customer service desk on the way to the checkout. They both were still, cold and dark.

Suddenly, straight-ahead to the rear, silver metal doors that led to the employee's lounge swung to and fro. Clattery squeaks echoed throughout the store that sent a sharp pain through my head.

I'd better get some aspirin, I thought as I neared the health aisle. My head was beating, beating, beating! I could barely stand the pain, but the door squeaked louder and louder. The pain was so bad that I wanted relief, and I wanted it fast. So, I decided to pay close attention to the labels of pain relievers to find the right one. *Forget it. They're probably all the same anyway. This bargain brand will do nicely,* I thought as I threw the silver and blue box into the shopping basket.

I finally reached the checkout line. The cashier's pale ivory skin and brilliant, curly auburn hair looked ghostly. Deep violet veins throbbed near her temples. Her well-defined nose was over three-inches long, which brought attention to the pronounced concave shape of her face and full, shapely pink lips. Her large, almond-shaped eyes were shimmering specks of green, goldenrod, gray and chestnut-brown that sparkled like freshly shined windowpanes. The tiny, black pupils expanded and contracted as the overhead light swung back and forth like a giant pendulum, as air blew fiercely from a vent in the massive array of silvery ducts that lined the ceiling.

I noticed the young woman's hands as she scanned the milk. Numerous large green veins ran the length of her thin fingers, all the way up her arms.

"Six sixty-six please," the cashier said. Her deep, raspy voice vibrated through my body.

I gave the cashier exact change. Her hands were ice-cold and slimy.

"Ouch!" I yelled.

When the tiny blond hairs on the cashier's arm touched me, a fiery lavender and white light ignited.

"Static electricity." The cashier giggled.

Her voice became deeper and raspier. Her words were spoken in slow motion. When she smiled, only big pearly-white teeth were visible that seemed too large to fit into her tiny slit of a mouth. In fact, her teeth were half the size of her entire face, like something from a cartoon. When I looked again, her smile and teeth appeared normal.

***

What went through your mind?

***

I've been putting in sixty hours each week for the past month. It must be finally catching up to me. Only one more week until this phase of the project is over, I thought as I walked away from the checkout lane. *It's a wonder I've been able to squeeze that lucid dreaming class in.* That was the only thing that kept me going! Well, that and the lucrative overtime pay. *I'll be glad when it's over!*

As the automatic doors opened, a gust of wind entered that almost knocked me to the floor. The cashier's hair became razzled, and a few of the plastic grocery bags flew about. The hair slowly rose on my arms as the outside air thickened to the consistency of a giant cluster of hot, foamy bubbles—the kind my children used to make with sudsy water and a blow hoop. My heart began to race, and my breathing became more difficult. I was overtaken by an eerie nervousness that crept along my neck, then up and down my spine thrice over.

***

Look for clues. That's it. Stay with it.

***

The massive harvest moon filled the horizon, surrounded by large gray and violet clouds. Giant gray craters populated the vast white surface. Its illumination was almost as bright as daylight.

There were only two other cars in the parking lot besides mine. The entire strip mall was dark and deserted. Only minutes before it was bustling with activity. An old soda can and several pieces of paper danced around the ground—at the wind's mercy—prisoners of circumstance.

I felt a strange presence behind me. I gripped a can of mace that was hidden deep in my purse with one hand, while I secured the two white grocery bags and car keys with the other.

I hastened my pace. In a flash, I turned around, expecting to find a mugger or something. No one or anything was in sight. The feeling of the presence had dissipated.

I got in the car and sped out of the parking lot. The streetlights along Highway 74 that shined brightly only moments earlier suddenly became dim.

The feeling of the strange presence returned, only that time, it was next to me on the passenger side.

It emanated warmth similar to that generated by body heat. I noticed a silhouette from the corner of my eye. I swallowed deep and hard then turned to look. Nothing was there except the shadows of trees cast by the moonlight.

"Let's see," I said to myself as I nervously flicked through the radio stations. My hands trembled with each movement. "I earn eighty-five bucks an hour. Multiply that by forty, then add the extra twenty hours. I guess it pays to be a consultant, even if overtime pay is straight time and not time-and-a-half…"

What felt like a warm, soft hand caressed my hair as I turned onto Kirkley Road. That's the road leading to my subdivision. The presence was upon me!

Must be the air conditioning, I thought as I lowered the settings and turned the vents away from my face.

Thick, shapely clouds of fog rose high into the air from the pitch-dark road. A loud symphony of crickets drowned out the radio. Fireflies appeared as specks of light in the thicket that lined the road.

Let's see, I thought in a desperate effort to ignore my immediate surroundings. *I should get a bit over five grand. Then, account for taxes, and I should expect to see roughly three grand. We're paid every two weeks, so multiply that by two. I should see roughly six or seven grand on my next check. Of course, good old Uncle Sam may take even more out!*

"Gullatt Ridge," I sighed. "Almost home! Just turn at the …"

***

What is it, Demeter?

***

A large swarm of insects sprang from the wooded lot next to the stop sign. They buzzed aimlessly around my car for a few seconds then quickly vanished into nothingness. The night wind splattered over a dozen strays onto the hood of my car. But they, too, soon vanished into nothingness.

The presence became stronger and stronger. From the corner of my eye, I saw a dark shadow seated to the right that was slowly moving closer and closer to me. My heart pounded faster than ever, as an intense burning sensation engulfed my body.

"Our Father, who art in..." I prayed. "Hallowed be thy name, thy kingdom..." I activated the remote door opener. "For thine is the kingdom, and the power and the glory..." I became less anxious when I saw that the children had turned the garage lights on.

As I turned into the driveway, a black cat ran across my path. My skin began to crawl as the headlights shined into its deep golden eyes. It stood there for a moment, then quickly dashed into the stillness of night. *That must be one of the neighbors' cat,* I tried to rationalize and hoped that I was right.

I drove into the garage and quickly flicked the remote control, closing the door behind me. Kevin was practicing his saxophone in the basement. Knowing he was near eased my nerves.

***

What did you make of that night?

***

I need to get some sleep, I thought. I quickly dismissed my drive home as being a typical experience of driving down a dark, lonely road.

***

A typical experience?

Yes, typical. I now realize that I was out of it. Anything seemed normal then.

***

Anyway, I grabbed my bags and headed inside. "Oh!" I rushed back to the car then ejected the tape. "Can't forget this. How else am I going to get some sleep?"

***

Did you have trouble falling asleep that night?

***

At first, I was overcome by a nervous restlessness as I tossed and turned, trying really hard to fall asleep. Soothing sounds of ocean waves that spewed endlessly from the cassette player soon put me at ease. The mahogany sleigh bed became a cradle of comfort. The thick, firm mattress felt softer. The lilac fabric softener from Sunday's laundry remained fresh on the green and white plaid comforter and hunter-green linen sheets. All was dark and still, as the ocean waves rustled through the night, gentle as a mother's lullaby, until I was fast asleep.

***

Did you dream that night?

***

I became enmeshed in a thick, gray cloud. Occasional white specks of light sparkled from the midst. As it gradually faded, I was on the second level of a crowded shopping mall looking over black wrought iron railings to the crowd below. A group of teenage girls giggled playfully to the right as they pranced down the way. One of them, a brunette with a long, bouncy ponytail, wore braces.

"Excuse, me ma'am," a young man about my children's age said as he accidentally bumped into me.

It was all too real. I actually felt his physical body. I looked into his eyes and he seemed real—that faded haircut, those loose fitting blue jeans and baggy, white pullover sweater. The soft, cottony fabric of his clothing was unmistakably real.

The air was thick and frothy, yet clear and sharp.

People of all ages: families with babies in strollers, the old, the young, all going about their daily routine of shopping. Wait a minute … come to think of it … there were no old people, but I didn't notice back then.

I strolled further through the mall, ending up in a gigantic food court. The floors were black-and-white, diagonal tiles. All about were tiny, square, white tables surrounded by four black, plastic chairs; on top of each one was a tiny, black metal napkin holder.

I decided to take a seat and admire the new dreamland. Far to the right were glass doors that provided a grand view of the outside world.

"Wow!" I said then decided to take a closer look at the great beyond. "What a treat."

The sky was a deep violet with scattered twinkling stars. Brilliant colors layered the horizon now that the sun had set. Soft melon and yellow hues flared up from a vast sea of deep orange, then blended together as one magnificent glow. Low in the eastern sky was the bright, white harvest moon with its many craters that, from my view, was the size of a cantaloupe.

The northern sky was most spectacular. Far into the distance was a giant, dimmed planet, about three times the size of the stars, surrounded by five glowing ringlets.

"Beautiful isn't it?" a deep voice resonated behind me.

That was him! It was the man from the restaurant on Sunday. Only, he appeared different … more handsome … more real. I was too awed to become alarmed.

"Yes," I said. "Yes it is."

"Marcellus Angelell." He held out his hand for me to shake.

His handshake was firm. I noticed that his hands were that of an aristocrat—well manicured and soft—like he'd never done any manual labor in his life. He emanated a soothing energy that penetrated the depth of my being. I looked deeper and deeper into his dark, mysterious eyes. He seemed so familiar to me like we'd been acquainted in another time or another place perhaps.

"I'm..."

"Demeter," he finished my sentence. "Why don't we have dinner. I know this quaint bistro at the far end of the mall where we can sit and chat for awhile."

"All right," I agreed and was completely at ease in the presence of the mysterious stranger.

In a flash, we were seated in a restaurant near two large white French windows. The place was crowded with festive diners—eating, drinking, talking. It was small, yet charming. Rich burgundy and navy-blue paisley borders contrasted with the antique-white walls and white ceiling. A single six-foot tall palm tree, planted in a golden pot was found in each of the four corners of the room. To the rear, adjacent to the rich mahogany bar, was the band. Each table was round and adorned with a deep burgundy and navy-blue paisley tablecloth and formal setting. Matching paisley napkins were folded to resemble accordion-style fans and placed on top of the matching salad plates. The floor was a deep, earthy stone that was unrecognizable to me. Its dull sheen faintly reflected light from four earthy sconce fixtures that lined the walls. I admired the beautiful twilight sky, as delicate sounds of jazz played softly in the background—saxophone, trumpet, cello and piano.

I looked at the menu, but everything was foreign—indecipherable. The water goblet was filled with a pale blue substance that I dared not to try.

The waiter interrupted my fascination with the *new world*. He was a tall man of about twenty. His thick, black mane and deep, dark eyes set against his olive complexion gave him an air of distinction.

Marcellus listened attentively to the young man as he listed choice selections for the evening, but everything was so strange to me.

"Why don't you order for me," I told Marcellus.

"We'll have the kikkipao in noni," he said as he handed the waiter the menu. "We'll have two glasses of tikti, please."

"Yes, sir," the waiter said as he headed for the kitchen.

"What's a kikkipao?" I asked him.

"You'll like it," Marcellus insisted.

"But what is it," I insisted. "What type of animal is it? Is it fowl, beef, pork, seafood or what?"

Couples at nearby tables heard my question and looked at me in horror. One woman grabbed her stomach, covered her mouth, and quickly ran to the restroom near the hostess station. Another woman at her table gave me an angry look and accompanied her friend. The two men turned around and looked at me in disgust.

Marcellus chuckled, then whispered soft and low in my ear, "People don't eat meat here. In fact, we don't eat anything that comes from any living being. What you know as dairy products, eggs, honey..." he shook his head as if to say no and looked me straight in the eyes, "we don't eat that stuff. It's taboo."

The waiter brought two crystal wine goblets filled with a golden translucent drink.

"Let's toast," Marcellus said as he raised his glass.

As I raised my glass, I noticed that the drink had a strange aroma of lemon, honeysuckle and rum mixed together.

Marcellus took one long gulp, while I hesitated.

"Go on, drink," he urged.

I still hesitated.

"Go on," he said with a laugh. "It won't harm you."

Heck, this is a dream. Nothing can harm me in a dream. Enjoy! I reasoned. I took one tiny sip. Instantly, a warm, tingly sensation flowed from my lips throughout my entire body. I instantly felt at ease; relaxed. My senses were heightened. The harvest moon seemed clearer, the band sounded more alive, and Marcellus looked more handsome than ever.

I took another sip. The concoction reminded me of lemonade sweetened with honey and a hint of rum.

"Woo!" Marcellus cautioned. "Slow down. Tikti is strong. Sip it slowly."

He's a dream. How dare he tell me what to do! I thought. That's funny, Dr. Iverson. Thinking in a dream! "What is tikti?" I asked him.

"It's a wild flower that grows in the wineyards here. It looks like a giant honeysuckle."

"Wineyards?" I inquired. Just then, the waiter served our meals.

"Where you come from it's vineyards. Here, it's wineyards. They rhyme."

I was skeptical about my meal. *I thought portabellas were large,* I thought.

It looked like a gigantic, sliced mushroom covered with brown button-mushroom gravy. One of the side dishes resembled crumbled pieces of feta cheese, and the other looked like green and brown long-grain rice. Oddly, it smelled like roast beef and mash potatoes.

"Go on," Marcellus insisted. "Eat!" He chuckled yet again between bites of kikkipao.

I slowly cut the kikkipao like I would cut a steak and took a bite.

This tastes like steak, I thought and proceeded to sample the side dishes.

Marcellus pointed to the one that resembled feta cheese and said, "That's pikke," then took another bite of kikkipao. "The other one is genee."

I tasted both. The pikke tasted like garlic-roasted potatoes and the genee tasted like a mixture of broccoli, wild rice and cheddar cheese. I wondered what the heck. It was all a dream, a fantasy. Dreams can't harm. Right?

"Ummm," I mumbled. "What is all this made of?"

"The pikke grows on a pikke tree. The genee grows wild in genee fields, kind of like what you know as rice."

I ravenously finished my meal and didn't notice that Marcellus had ordered dessert.

When the waiter served dessert, I was still hesitant about trying anything else new.

"Go on." Marcellus chuckled. "It's poapuu. Before you ask, poapuu is extracted from the gengou fruit, which grows on the gengou tree. You can drink gengou, eat it frozen, add it to other foods, or make desserts like the one in front of you. You can compare it to milk where you come from.

"The thick brown sauce on top is doce. Doce is extracted from the nut of the froppa tree. Doce can be made into a powder, an oil or a sauce like the one on your dessert. You can compare it to cocoa where you come from."

I tasted the poapuu and was amazed. It was almost identical to the brownie cheesecake that I loved so much. Only the poapuu was richer, creamier. The doce was richer and sweeter than any chocolate I had ever tasted. I never knew that you could taste anything in a dream!

"Ummm," I mumbled. "This is so, so good," I told Marcellus. *What a nice experience,* I thought as I finished my meal. The band continued to create exotic melodies through the night, which further heightened my dining experience. The music was so beautiful, like nothing that I had ever heard before. Unearthly.

Marcellus and I sipped endless glasses of tikti as we conversed about anything and everything through the eve. We were both completely fascinated by each other.

***

Tell me about Marcellus.

***

Woooowww! Marcellus was ... I mean is, well was ... well whatever, six-two and one hundred eighty pounds of solid, rippling muscles. Ummm! His baritone voice and articulate style made his conversation that much more fascinating. I was completely charmed by the red T-shirt, blue jeans, and gray and white cowboy boots he wore. With the exception of the deep, dark ebony eyes; that jet-black, wavy hair and tan skin, Marcellus looked like a younger version of Maynard Jackson, you know, the former mayor of Atlanta. His gleaming, white teeth were long and straight as arrows, and hid just inside of those full, pale lips.

***

What was he thinking? Get inside his head.

Dr. Iverson, he was a fantasy, a dream image. How can I get inside of him?

Trust me, you can. Unlocking all of your experiences, whether real or imagined, is the only way to get at the root of the problem. Now try again like I suggested.

***

"You're so feminine, Demeter," he said. He stroked my face with his fingers and gazed deep into my eyes. "You carry yourself so well." He took my hand in his and continued, "You have a beautiful, round face and smooth skin; your eyes are so big and beautiful. Your lashes are so long and pretty. That teeny-tiny waist and curvaceous hips—oh, man—you're everything a man could want. You excite me to the maximum extent. How tall are you?" he asked. "Five-four, five-five?"

"Five-four," I said. He had seized my heart, so I barely got the words out.

"Let me guess. You weigh about, say one-twenty?"

"Yes," I said.

"I'm six-two," he said then sipped more tikti. "You're petite and tiny, just like a pretty, little babydoll. You're just right for me," he said.

Yeah! I thought.

***

What's wrong, Demeter?

I got so much feeling from him.

That means that he's not simply a dream image. He must be real.

Real? I don't remember any of this happenening before. This can't be real.

Yes, real. You cannot feel anything from an image, because an image isn't real. That night was the start of your lucid dreaming phase.

Then what?

***

Well, we decided to spend the remainder of the evening outside on the patio, which was just beyond the massive white French doors to the rear. A crisp, cool breeze circulated the scent of wild flowers all about. A strong chemical bond existed between us, as we looked deep into each other's eyes.

Marcellus moved closer and closer to me and kissed my lips ever so softly. I welcomed his strong, masculine hands around my waist as passionate balls of fire pulsed to every cell of my body. Wow! I felt safe and protected in the comfort of his arms; no one or nothing could harm me.

Marcellus pulled me closer and closer with his big, strong arms. I felt his lips against mine as he softly, but gently ...

***

Three long shrill tones followed by two quick, sharp beeps echoed repeatedly in my head. The tones became louder and more penetrating with each repetition. I began to fall from great heights into a deep, dark pit. "Marcellus! Marcellus!" I called, hoping that he would rescue me. "Marcellus, Marcellus!" I called again. My voice echoed throughout the void as I fell faster and faster ...

I jolted up to a sitting position in bed as I hit rock bottom. A gush of air quickly filled my lungs as I gasped for breath. To the right I turned, and there it was—the little black alarm clock—beeping to its four-thirty daily ritual.

October

Dare to wish upon a star
By faith or chance
There you are
In the mind's eye to behold
The heart's desire to unfold
A point in time when dreams come true
And reality fades before the eyes

Chapter 3.
Clouds in Heaven, Streets of Gold

What happened later in the week, Demeter? How did your day start, especially after such a beautiful night?

***

Every day was uneventful, no dreams, no drama. Well, except Friday. That day even started off rough. It was Friday, October 1, but it sure felt like it should have been Friday the 13th. That was the start of the roughest weekend in my life.

"Oooo!" I moaned. "I-hate-traffic!" I said to myself as I clenched the steering wheel. "Can you say grid-locked?" I grunted and flipped through the radio stations. "No traffic reports! Almost two hours on I-75/85 and no traffic report! Unfrickenbelievable!"

I looked around the endless sea of cars that surrounded me—old cars, new cars, luxury models and jalopies. Some drivers bounced to the tune of music, while others talked on the phone, probably to call work to inform their bosses of their pending tardiness.

I left several messages with everyone on the team after I noticed the time. *Maybe they're stuck in traffic too!* I tried to reason. Eight o'clock, only thirty minutes away from the most important meeting of the project. "Ain't no way," I grunted. "No way, I'm going to be on Peachtree Road by eight-thirty! Damn!"

What's the use in being stressed out, so I reached over to the passenger's side and dug deep into my purse. "Where is it? Where is it?" I was panicky because I couldn't find the tape! I continued to rummage around. "Now I know that I packed it this morning. Ahh!" I sighed as I put my hands on the *Sounds of Sea* tape. "Found it."

I popped it into the cassette player. Soothing sounds of seagulls and the ocean's waves eased my razzled nerves. I became calmer and more relaxed with each rush of water, as if it washed all of my cares and worries out to sea. Each splash became longer and clearer until I pictured the tides rushing endlessly, relentlessly against large, dark rocks that lined the seashore; as flocks of large, white seagulls flew into the distance. The air became cooler, thinner and crisper.

All of my stress was gone. I was at peace.

***

I savored a chilled glass of tikti, as I enjoyed the mellow sounds of piano and saxophone that bellowed from the band on the level below. I wore a long, satiny, pearlescent dress with open-toe pumps and purse to match. My hair was done in an elegant French twist. Tiny ringlets of curls cascaded down my right cheek.

I looked around the dim setting. Several sterling silver bar stools lined the silvery blue bar enclosure. Hundreds of upside-down wine goblets and brandy snifters decorated the ceiling. Bottles of all shapes, sizes and colors lined the shelves to the left. To my right were other bar patrons who laughed and talked, while two bartenders satisfied their liquid desires.

The bar sat in the center of the restaurant, high above the sea of elegantly set tables, down the golden spiral staircase to the left. Gentle, white lights peeked through the transparent, white panels that lined the circular interior walls. The exterior walls were made of clear glass panels.

"Beautiful flowers for a flower," a deep, soothing voice said from behind me. It was Marcellus who presented me with a large bouquet of exotic roses—deep red, muave with touches of white, orange, purple, violet and white. He wore a dark burgundy silk shirt with the first two buttons open that exposed his massive hairy chest. The pleated, black pants fit so well, and the wing-tip shoes perfectly complemented his look.

"Oh thank you!" I said as I smelled each and every flower. I looked deep into his eyes, "You're so wonderful! Just ... just ... sooo wonderful! Thank you so much, Marcellus."

"Delicious doce-chocolate for a delicious chocolate," he smiled as he presented me with a large golden box of exotic doce-chocolates.

I placed the bouquet on the bar, passersby smiled and pointed in my direction as they walked by. Marcellus made me feel special, and he wanted to show the world just how much I meant to him.

"I'll put these in water," the waiter said as he placed the flowers in an opalescent, oblong vase just behind the counter. The bouquet seemed to overpower his diminutive stature and slicked-back, blond hair.

I carefully untied the golden, laced bow that protected the heart-shaped box and was awed when I looked inside. Large doce-chocolate truffles, each decorated with a small dark doce-chocolate bow.

"Truffles are my favorite!" I said, biting into a rich chocolate truffle. "Oooo," I moaned. They were so smooth, so sweet, what a chocolate delight. "This is sooo good." I looked Marcellus straight in his deep, dark eyes. "You are sooo good, Marcellus."

With his strong, masculine hands, Marcellus redirected my hand into his warm, moist mouth. He ate the remaining piece of candy from my hand then proceeded to suck remnants of doce-chocolate off my fingers.

His warm, inviting tongue twirled again and again around my hand ever so gently, and sent chills up my arm, then down my spine. Intense lust covered his face, as I looked deep into his dark, dreamy eyes.

"Your table is ready, sir," the waiter said as he broke the hypnotic trance we shared. "Right this way, please."

Damn! I thought in my annoyance with the waiter. *That felt so good.*

We headed down the stairs, then across the dimly lit room toward the revolving restaurant ahead.

"Watch your step, please," the waiter warned as I noticed the floors move.

The room came to life as we were seated. Far to the right, in front of the band, finely clad couples danced to the soothing sounds of piano and bass. Several men dressed in suits hovered around the bar drinking spirits and laughing, as jolly diners enjoyed their meals and each other's company.

Our table, which was next to the clear glass shell of the building, overlooked seventy-two stories over the city's skyline. Occasional rectangles of light peeked through mammoth office buildings, as dots lit the streets far below. In the distance was a long, flowing river over which several bridges spanned. Hundreds of stars populated the night sky, as two crescent moons smiled through the night in the western sky—gatekeepers to the ringed planet far in the distance.

The gentle rotation of the lounge was so relaxing. *What a beautiful evening,* I thought as I admired the view and Marcellus. It reminded me of the Sundial here in Atlanta. I loved it because it was so relaxing and took an hour for the lounge to rotate a full cycle. You could see all parts of the city just by sitting still and enjoying the view.

"Two glasses of tikti, please," Marcellus told the waiter. "We'll have the soup du jour for starters."

I was lost in thought admiring the skyline—short buildings, tall buildings, structures designed to look like rockets. The city was filled with magnificent edifices.

"Let's dance," Marcellus suggested.

"All right," I agreed.

Marcellus walked around to my side of the table and helped me with my chair. He held my waist with his big, strong, masculine hands all the way to the dance floor, which was the only stationary part of the restaurant—well, that and the bandstand and bar.

We danced the two-step, gliding to sultry sounds of bass. Marcellus held me tighter and tighter with his strong arms, and pulled me closer and closer. He sang soft and low in my ear, sending balls of fire to every cell of my body.

I felt a big, firm bulge rub against me as Marcellus inched his hands slowly across my rear. *Oh yes,* I thought as he began to nibble every niche of my earlobes, then began to softly kiss every inch across my face. *Please don't stop,* I thought as I gently closed my eyes. I inched my hands up his strong, masculine chest then gently wrapped my arms around his neck. Being in his strong embrace moistened my loins below. The warmth of his body was so comforting, so soothing.

He gently licked my lips as he …

***

I was jolted in my seat as screeching sounds of brakes and tooting horns flooded the air. My heart began to pound and an eerie nervousness crept along my arms. I quickly glanced at the clock.

"Eight-fifteen!" I was surprised. I immediately retrieved my cell phone from my purse and tried to call my boss, Patricia. I got her voice mail greeting, so I left a message. I tried calling two other people on our team, again I got voice mail. "I'm late for sure! Traffic is starting to move, but I probably won't get in until nine o'clock. I sure hope that somebody got my message!"

***

"What happened to yo' hair, Demeter?" Trevor Mason asked in his usual loud, boisterous voice as I walked into the crammed conference room. The meetings usually lasted all morning, and I was lucky to have arrived during the first break. "You should o' curled it or somethin'. They is somethin' called perm'nents, you know," Trevor informed me.

"Whatever," I said to myself. I was so busy scrambling around for a comfortable spot that I just turned him off. I found a cozy spot against the back wall next to one of the three large windows. I nestled on the six-inch deep windowsill, rested my back against the glass, and placed my notebook next to me. Two other people followed suit and used the remaining two windows as chairs. As usual, I left the office at two-thirty that morning and was back again for the meeting. So, I slicked my hair back with styling gel and gathered it into a ponytail. My ends were in need of moisture, but working extra hours to provide for my family far outweighed my vanity that day.

"You sho' is late today," Trevor commented. "I ain't gone even tell you what you missed, so don't even go axkin' me nothin'."

I spurned Trevor as usual, especially after waiting in traffic close to three hours. It was nine-thirty in the morning, Friday morning, but still morning. I just wanted to get the meeting over with. I was always too tired or too busy to even dignify his comments with a response. Being ignored over the past year just encouraged him even more. Everyone else often ignored his unpredictable mood and honored his words with a grain of salt, if that much. No one took anything about him seriously.

The room towered twenty floors over the Georgia 400 freeway. Other stragglers filled the room, one by one, until it was filled to capacity. Some carried hot coffee from Chap's, the building cafe on the first level, while others pulled in those blue, cushiony chairs from the cubicles down the hall. The large, shiny, rectangular, wooden table occupied the bulk of the room. On the wall near the front door was a large white board. Near the rear door, several worn staff members propped against the large wooden bookcase as they chatted and drank coffee.

"Shit!" someone yelled. It was my dear, sweet friend D'Angela. She yelled as she spilled coffee on her white silk blouse and the floor. It was a good thing that the Berber was a deep blue in color and concealed the stains.

"Nobody is gone even notice that stain," Trevor told D'Angela. "Just cover it up with yo' jacket. Look, Angie," Trevor continued. "Yo' dizzy girl is having a bad day with that frizzy curl. She can't cover that up!" He giggled. "Oh, Lordy! I just rhymed! Dizzy girl and frizzy curl. I'm just beside myself. I'm just too much."

They both laughed. I ignored them. Everyone else was too busy stuffing their faces with pastries from Chap's or talking about the project.

"My wife could get that stain out," Marcus told D'Angela. "She can get anything out." Marcus was the manager over software development. He was one of the best on the team, but he talked about his wife too much ... way too much. It seemed that to him, the world revolved around his wife. Anything that happened, like D'Angela spilling coffee on her blouse, would somehow be tied back to his wife.

"Hey, Angie," Trevor said. "What did you do last weekend? You wasn't up in here was you?"

"No!" D'Angela exclaimed. "I got a boyfriend, I got a life. People who work on weekends don't have a life."

I wished that I could have fired D'Angela and Trevor, but they were both good, dependable workers. Having a nasty personality wasn't grounds for termination. But I sure tried hard to find loopholes to relieve them of their duties.

D'Angela Webber was the manager over the administrative staff. She was tall and slim—well, she was actually skinny, emaciated—with a wavy, honey-blonde, shoulder-length weave and store-bought hazel eyes. The burgundy suit she wore clashed with the loud pink circles on her cheeks. Her fingernails were long with leopard print designs. She wore open-toe shoes, even in cold weather, to show her leopard print design toenails. Bags had begun to appear under her eyes, no longer hiding her forty-year-old secret and fast, promiscuous lifestyle. Many days, I came real close, I mean real, real close, to slapping that bitch right upside the head.

***

Oooo, Dr. Iverson. Oooo, that Trevor.

What's wrong, Demeter? What about Trevor?

Trevor is a thirty-eight-year-old quality assurance engineering manager. His job is to make sure that the software works the way it should. He has been with the company over fifteen years and attended Georgia State at night while he worked his way up from the mailroom. He is of average height with a deep bronze complexion and shiny baldhead. Many a day, I wanted to go Postal on him. But then I realized that he's worth it. I would be rotting in jail, probably on death row, because of that fool. He's just not worth the time of day.

Let's examine this Trevor character. Tell me about him.

He is nothing to write home about, Dr. Iverson. Really. Trust me.

This could be important.

Oh. You don't think that he is the one, do you? You might as well take my soul right here and now if it is him.

Anything is possible.

I don't think he is the one. I sure hope he isn't the one! Besides, Trevor and I view the world differently. His work is of mediocre quality, and he does the bare minimum, if that much, needed to get the job done; I, on the other hand, often exceed the call of duty. Well, that's not completely true, he is one of my best managers. He knows how to keep his QA team in line and makes sure that everyone does the work that needs to be done. I must admit, he is good at bossing, but not at working.

Anyway, he is a simple man. He drives an old Ford; I drive a new Acura 3.5 RL.

He lives in Decatur, in South Dekalb County; I live in Peachtree City, Fayette County.

He drinks and parties in his spare time; I go skiing, hiking, to wine tastings, enjoy the art of fine dining, or escape to some weekend getaway.

His finances are always strapped, so he often borrows lunch money from coworkers. He says things like, "Gimme fi'dy cents fo' a coke," or "Lemme borra fi' 'ollars fo' lunch," or "I need fi' 'ollars fo' some gas," or some other mess.

On the other hand, my pockets are always full. I invest heavily in mutual funds, fine art and the stock market. That's just the way I am.

***

"Allrightythen!" Patricia said as she entered the room. She was tall and slim with a smooth heart-shaped face. Her brilliant shoulder-length, auburn hair and green eyes blended with the bright red sun that started to shine brightly through the large windows behind me. "Let's get this meeting started again."

***

I was up for her job about eighteen months ago, but didn't get it. If you asked me, Dr. Iverson, my background was far better suited for Vice President than hers. I graduated Cum Laude from Spelman, then got my master's in Computer Engineering from Tulane University. She, on the other hand, graduated top of her class at MIT and later completed her doctorate at Princeton, I think. All I know is that the subject of her dissertation was Cognitive Science, which has nothing to do with developing software whatsoever. But that's my opinion.

Patricia was too hard and aggressive, I guess that's why she got to that— you know, Vice President of Product Development position. Frankly, she didn't go on dates after husband left her. She was just too intimidating for most men to handle. So, at forty-five, she remained a spinster …

Oh, my goodness! Hmmm, almost sounds as if I'm talking about myself, Dr. Iverson. I'm not like her, am I?

***

Anyway. Ms. Ph.D-in-Cognitive Science insisted that everyone call her Patricia. "My name is Patricia," she would always say. "Not Pat, not Patti, Patsy, not Trisha, Trish or Tish. It's Patricia. If that's too hard for ya, then just call me Dr. Owens!"

That Patricia was a piece of work, Dr. Iverson.

***

Anyway. Moving right along.

I felt someone tap me on the shoulders. It was little Ms. D'Angela Webber. She went through the trouble to squeeze her li'l boney tail through a crowd of people just to get to where I was sitting. By the way she hustled to get to me, I *thought* that she had something urgent to tell me. But when it came to her, I should have learned not to *think* so much.

"Final product testing is over," D'Angela got really close to me and whispered in my ear. "What you gone do with yo'self since you won't be working late nights or weekends no mo'? You don't have a man or nothin'."

I looked that bitch straight in her weary eyes and said in that nonchalant manner that irked D'Angela, "Whatever," then listened attentively to Patricia.

"Chil', my man is …"

That bitch came over here for this shit? I whispered in her ear before she could finish, "Tell you what," I paused then looked her straight in the eyes. "Why don't you let me borrow your man? Then, I'll send your man back to his wife when I'm done with him. Then, when his wife gets through with him, she'll send him back to you. Is that all right?"

Apparently, a few people who were squatted on the floor in front of me heard my comments, looked back at us and starting giggling.

Patricia was still speaking and looked in our direction as if to motion for us to *hush*. I didn't feel bad because there were other conversations and giggling going on about the room, and two other software engineers were tossing little rubber balls to each other across the room.

***

Dr. Iverson, I'm telling you, that some of our meetings were like being in a high school classroom.

***

Well anyway, D'Angela rolled her eyes so hard at me; they got really narrow. She squeezed her li'l, boney behind back to her seat then whispered something to Trevor. They both rolled their eyes at me, but I didn't pay them any attention. They were lucky that I didn't have my automatic with me that day! I'm telling you, Dr. Iverson.

I started to feel a bit light-headed. I thought it was because of letting D'Angela and Trevor get the better of me. *I'd better go downstairs to Chap's*

and get some coffee after the meeting. I don't know what that old man puts in
that stuff, but everybody buys it like crazy. It sure does get me through the day!

Patricia walked around the room and handed everybody a small mauve
envelope. Everyone was surprised by what they saw. It was unexpected and
completely out-of-the-blue. All that hard work and effort, the gratitude for
which was nestled inside that tiny envelope. Twisted facial expressions filled the
room. Some screamed, while others cried into each other's arms.

So this is the thanks I get for working sixty- and seventy-hour weeks, I
thought as I and all the others held that precious two thousand dollar bonus
check in our hands.

***

It was noon when the meeting finally ended. I walked off the elevator and
headed straight for Chap's when I noticed a large crowd gathered around the
shop. I wondered what was going on. I didn't see any flyers around the building
for any events in the lobby.

I was greeted by fresh basil and oregano as I neared the shop. "That's what
going on," I said as I noticed the white poster board with the big, bold, black
letters. *Pasta Primavera is the special today. I'm just too hungry!* I thought as
my stomach growled over and over, like a baby in need of a bottle. *Nobody bet'*
not eat my helpin' of Primavera! I mean nobody!

People came from neighboring office buildings because Chap's had the best
food in the area. Mr. Chap was very amiable and made sure that each customer
was treated special. He was of average height, but as a young man, he was
probably much taller. His sparse, slicked-back, wavy, white hair was always
neatly trimmed and contrasted nicely with that deep bronze-tan complexion. At
eighty-nine, he had a full set of healthy, pearly-white teeth that were as straight
as arrows. He was sharp and alert.

Mr. Chap was not only the local Italian chef, but he was counselor,
surrogate father and friend. The customers admired his wisdom and had a deep
sense of respect for him. Some afternoons, he would serve free fudge-pecan
brownies and café au lait. The customers would sit around the lobby and listen
to his World War II stories like children who eagerly awaited their parents'
bedtime tales. Those who came for the free food often stayed for the rich history
lesson.

The shop was sparkling clean all through the day. The black-and-white,
diagonal check floors were always shiny and unscathed. To the right was the
deli counter, where all the weight-watchers flocked for the fine selection of
meat, cheeses and homemade bread. Straight ahead was the "Hot" line, where
the freshest vegetables, sauces, pastas, entrees and desserts were served. Next to
that on the right, was a large, red-and-white canopy that announced in big blue
letters, "The Grill." That was where Mr. Chap served the biggest, meatiest
burgers; longest, plumpest, juiciest hot dogs and barbecue delights. Straight to
the back, red and white booths lined the walls. When the weather permitted,
white, plastic chairs and tables welcomed customers outside on the patio. Near

the front door were two cash registers. On the counters were two large bins that held napkins, plastic cutlery, straws and condiments. There was something for everyone.

"Pasta primavera, corn, broccoli and a roll please," I told Ms. Mabel, who worked the "Hot" line. "Ummm," I moaned. I smelled every herb and spice as the food was being placed into the white Styrofoam container.

"No coffee today?" Ms. Mabel teased. Ms. Mabel was about sixty-two. She was petite with knee-length, thick, wavy, gray hair that she pulled back into a bun. Her soft olive complexion looked so soft and smooth. She worked at Chap's to supplement her retirement income.

***

Say, I know it's my imagination, Dr. Iverson, but Ms. Mabel reminds me of a shorter, paler, older version of my sister, Percy. She looks like she could be related to us, especially since she, too, is from New Orleans. Ms. Mabel is part Choctaw and according to Daddy, we are too.

***

"Oh can't forget my coffee," I told her.

"One café' au lait coming up," Ms. Mabel said.

Mr. Chap was standing right beside Ms. Mabel. "I told you I'm going to marry you," he said as he prepared my favorite treat. "Here ya go, sugar," he said as he wiped excess coffee from the sides of the tall white Styrofoam cup.

As I retrieved my wallet from my purse, I felt Mr. Chap watching me. I turned to my right, and he was smiling right at me, leering almost.

I looked around Chap's, but all of the booths had been taken. I walked around the lobby, but the few tables near some of the other shops were also full.

"Shake it, shake it, baby," Mr. Chap said as I left the shop.

I pressed the *Up* button on the elevators, then turned around to face the lobby. I saw Mr. Chap walk into the lobby, just outside of his shop, hands on hips, as he continued to stare after me. "Ummm, mercy! If this body were fifty years younger … um, um, um, mercy!" he said.

Dirty old man, I thought as I gulped some coffee. A crowd of people left the elevator, then I got on. Mr. Chap continued to smile and stare after me.

I noticed subtleties in the lobby that I had never paid attention to before. They looked so pretty that I decided to stay and eat my lunch in the lobby. I pushed my way through the crowd to leave the elevator.

Tiny white, brown and gray specks highlighted the black marble, diagonal floor tiles. *The floor is really shiny today,* I thought. I noticed the water fountain in the center and decided to sit for a spell to enjoy my lunch. *Wow,* I thought. *Look at all the pennies in there.*

The fresh tomatoes used in the sauce were zestier than ever. The basil, oregano and other spices sent chills through my body. *Oooo,* I thought as I savored each morsel. *This is sooo good!* With each bite, I closed my eyes, shrugged my shoulders, held my head back and moaned. I enjoyed my meal so much that I caught the attention of passersby. But I didn't care.

The cascading water fountain was so relaxing. Droplets of water splashed in my face, so I decided to run my fingers in the cool water. *That feels really, really good.* I continued to stare into the fountain and admire its beauty …

***

Melodies of birds echoed in the distance as the sun welcomed in a new day. The room was cold, but I was securely wrapped in the warmth and tenderness of Marcellus' big, strong …

***

"Hello!" Trevor yelled. "Anybody home!" he said as he knocked on the back of my head as he would a door.

I was jolted once again to reality as air quickly filled my lungs. I should have slapped Trevor, but I was just too relaxed to care. How dare he touch me! I should have bopped him upside the head.

"Boss lady had wanted me to tell ever'body that we havin' a get-together at Antoine's af'er work at five-thirty—sharp," he said. "I ain't wanna tell you, but she would o' got pissed if I ain't invite you. 'Member like she did the last time?"

"All right," I said as I continued to run my fingers back and forth through the water, not looking up once at him. "I'll be there."

"You a'ight?" Trevor asked sarcastically.

I glanced up at him briefly, as he gave me a curious look.

I saw him walk away from the corner of my eye, as I continued to run my finger through the water.

He shook his head and said, "Chil', you be trippin' up in here!"

I continued to run my fingers through the fountain as I drifted away, completely oblivious to the world around me.

Chapter 4.
Imagination Set on High

Five-thirty on Friday afternoon and Antoine's was starting to fill quickly with spirited patrons. The old brown brick building sat alone far into a corner off of Lenox Road and Peachtree Road, nestled between two skyscrapers in the heart of the cosmopolitan Buckhead District. Lanterns shined from the four pointed steeples that decorated each corner of the structure and cast shadows on the four-foot wide simulated moat below. The wooden drawbridge with its two sturdy chains welcomed guests into the foyer.

The band became louder and livelier as I strolled along the winding white cobblestone path from the parking lot. All was dark as I entered. The small, white candles that adorned each table glimmered in the darkness. Straight ahead were four wooden steps that led to the elevated dining areas on the left and right. Far to the back was the band—saxophone, trumpet, piano and bass. The musicians held their instruments as a man holds his wife, and spewed soothing notes to share with the world.

"Demeter!" a voice called.

I climbed the four steps and looked around. No one was in sight. To the left, a couple sipped wine as they enjoyed the band below. To the rear, several couples overlooked the golden rail to the bank below. No one looked familiar.

"Demeter!" the voice called again.

I looked to the right, and several people were walking around, while others sipped wine and enjoyed the band.

A cold, clammy hand touched my arm from behind, sending chills through me.

"Demeter, we're behind you."

It was Marcus Williams, the software development manager on my team. He stood at a proud six-two and weighed a whopping two hundred pounds of solid muscles. His thick moustache and faded hair cut gave him an air of distinction. Too bad he was married.

"Marcus," I said as I placed my hand over my heart. "You startled me."

"This way," Marcus said, gesturing with his hands for me to go before him.

The company rented the section of the pub opposite the band. Along the golden rail that sat over the entrance was a long table with a white linen tablecloth. Meatballs, quiche squares, exotic cheeses and other delectables were for the taking.

I noticed Louisa Bertrand sitting at a table far into a corner niche.

"Well hello, darling!" Lou said as I neared the table. "We ordered some vegetable fondue. It should be out in a minute. Come on ... sit!" Lou insisted as she moved her navy-blue leather purse from the chair to her right and placed it on the floor. Marcus sat to her left

Louisa Bertrand was the Marketing Director. Sure, she had an outgoing personality and never wore the same outfit twice, but she was just way too bubbly sometimes. She had been with the company over five years, ever since she retired at the ripe, old age of thrity-three as a runway model. She was tall and slim with a deep copper complexion. Her short tapered hairdo complemented her heart-shaped face and high cheekbones, giving her that aristocratic look and bourgeois air.

She wore a navy-blue, ankle-length, cashmere dress; opaque, navy-blue hose with coordinating navy-blue, suede pumps. The tiny lavender specks in her navy-blue neckerchief matched the pattern of her small navy-blue, oval eyeglass frames. Lou still was in contact with clothing designers who shipped clothing to her free.

***

Boy, some folk got it made, Dr. Iverson.

***

"This Chardonnay is just excellent!" Lou said as she nibbled another piece of smoked Gouda and sipped white wine. "Umm, umm, this is good! Here," she said then poured me a glass. "I ordered one bottle of white wine and two bottles of Port—one tawny and one ruby—for the table. But nothing compares to real Italian wine from Italy. When I lived in Milan in '88 ..."

***

Lou was nice, but that woman talked too much ... I mean too, too much about the past, Dr. Iverson. Well, I felt sorry for her because that's all she had to hold on to. She didn't have much of a present and her future looked dim. That's why I kept that secret I told you about back in November. I was a fool for not speaking up, especially since I lost my self-respect and sanity in the process.

Besides, no one would have believed me anyway if I had spoken up. Besides, Lou had much more to lose than I. Besides, she was my friend. *I think.* I did the right thing didn't I, Dr. Iverson? Am I making too many excuses?

If I had known then what I know now about Daniel and Lou, I would have run the other way when she invited me to the table. How did I get so deeply involved in their personal affairs? It all happened so quickly that I didn't see it coming. Why did I let them draw me into their ... you know ... stuff?

***

Have mercy! I thought as I sipped a glass of Chardonnay. *Not another long, boring story again, Lou. Shut the fuck up! Please! No one cares about your life as a model! That's the past! Get on with it!*

"Hi, gang!" a voice said. It was Dr. Daniel Batchelor, the Director of Earth Science Projects. "May I join you?"

No! Go 'way! I thought, but I guess my smile welcomed him to the table.

Dan was tall with a soft olive complexion and thick, dark hair. The small black oval wire rim glasses that he wore concealed his deep, dark, penetrating eyes. No matter what he wore—from blue jeans to a business suit—his hard, muscular body accented his clothing perfectly. Dan was a well-renowned geophysicist in the scientific community. He had an IQ and income well into the stratosphere. However, his accomplishments often posed barriers to building successful relationships. At thirty-eight, he had never been married, but dated frequently. Because he found it necessary to flaunt his genius and question the mental acuteness of his dates and others around him, his social life was virtually defunct.

***

You think I'm crazy, Dr. Iverson, but I still believe that Dan has been involved in my condition from the get-go. I can't explain how, but he is.

***

"Yes, yes!" Lou motioned. "Here, have some wine, Danny boy!" Lou poured Dan a glass of wine as he sat next to her. "Here, try some of this tawny Port, Demeter," Lou insisted as she poured me a glassful in a red wine glass.

"My wife and I went to Milan five years ago," Marcus said. "She is quite a lady."

Now Percy would have a fit if someone were to pour anything except red wine in a red wine glass, I thought. *I can just hear her now,* "No, no, no! The bowl of a red wine glass is large and shallow. White wine glasses are taller with a thinner bowl!"

"You've finished the Chardonnay, try some of this. It's a 1974 vintage ruby Port," Lou insisted. "Notice the deep brick color," Lou said as she twirled the glass then inhaled the aroma before sipping. "Ummm," she moaned. "Ah! This is just wonderful. Just wonderful!"

"I have to get some gas after I leave here," Marcus said between sips of wine. "If my wife wants to use the car, it'll be full."

"It's better than breaking down at night, I'll tell you that!" Lou said, then gulped more wine. "My Benz only takes the good gas. The cheap stuff'll probably kill the engine."

"I know," Marcus agreed. "I can't put cheap gas in my car either."

Dan's face became sullen. "I don't believe it!" he started. "Gas is gas! Don't you get it? There's no difference between one formula and the other!"

"But if the engine konks out because of using the cheap stuff, the factory will not honor the warranty," Lou explained.

Dan always wore nice sports coats—even if he wore blue jeans—for the purpose of toting nice Cross pens and a small spiral-bound notepad in his inner pocket.

"Now here's the formula for petroleum," Dan retrieved the notepad and pen from his pocket and proceeded to write not only the chemical formula for petroleum, but diagramed the molecular structure of the compound as well.

"Hey y'all!" I turned and it was dear, sweet D'Angela. *Swell … another one of my favorite people.*

"Shit," Lou complained. "I broke a nail! I can't get a nail appointment until tomorrow afternoon."

"My wife is like you, Lou," Marcus said. "She always gets her nails done."

"You talk a lot about your wife," I told Marcus. "When are we going to meet her?"

"Don't nobody want hear 'bout his wife, Demeter," D'Angela interjected. "Don't nobody want to meet her neither."

D'Angela couldn't have said it better.

Umm! I thought as I sipped the tawny Port. Marcus and D'Angela began to argue, while Dan continued his lecture on petroleum. *This almost reminds me of tikti.* I nibbled on a few pieces of smoked Gouda and finished the tawny Port trying hard to block them all out. Lou quickly poured me another glass probably in an effort to tune Dan out; I gulped every drop. Images of Lou, Marcus, D'Angela, and Dan began to sway back and forth, as other members of the team joined the table. The laughter, band, and myriad of conversations blended into one sea of confusion. I looked around the room, but everything and everybody began to sway back and forth, as the noises melted as one.

A strange figure stood in the far-left corner of the room, watching me as I became oblivious to the world around me. It remained stable in the corner with its arms folded, as all the other images began to melt into one giant pool of fleeting paint. The figure's dark oxblood skin, long pointed ears, and deep, dark eyes sent an eerie, creepy chill through my body as it continued to stare at me.

The room swayed faster and faster, as I struggled to keep my composure. In a flash, all of the images and sounds blended into one giant gray ball of confusion that engulfed me into its midst. Tiny, white lights sparkled intermittently from the clouds until they gradually faded into darkness.

***

A soothing warmth emanated behind me as I sipped a chilled glass of tikti. I turned to the right. *Wow! What a beautiful fireplace!* I thought as Marcellus poured another glass of titki.

It was twilight. The huge golden, crackling fireplace provided a gentle orange tinge to the dimly lit room. Marcellus and I sat alone in the den sipping endless glasses of tikti. Straight ahead through the large French doors was the balcony, with its massive, white, Roman-style columns. To the right was a white grand piano trimmed in gold. Sundries of books filled the tall bookshelves to the left. In the middle, three white marble steps led to the sunken seating area of a square, white, suede sectional with royal-blue and red, overstuffed pillows.

"Let's go outside," Marcellus suggested as he placed his wine goblet on the built-in white marble counter that surrounded the rear of the seating area. He took my wine goblet and placed it next to his, then helped me to my feet.

Mercy! I thought as Marcellus placed his strong, masculine hands around my waist. Powerful electric pulses radiated throughout my body. As I walked up the three steps, Marcellus ran his hands up and down my rear. When he gently squeezed, I almost reached the peak of ecstasy, as my loins became saturated with every touch he gave me.

A gentle breeze gushed in as Marcellus opened the French doors that led to the balcony.

Beautiful! I thought as I admired the landscape's magnificance. The western sky was layered in brilliant colors. Deep burnt sienna layers covered the distant land to the horizon, which gradually faded into delicate hues of goldenrod and canary yellow that dittered into the palest sea of silvery-blue at the pinnacle.

Scattered twinkling stars dotted the deep violet eastern sky. In the center was the faded, gray planet that dazzled its glittery rings. The bright, white harvest moon shined across the way, as it cast its light on the cascading waterfall down the valley to the right. Sundries of exotic flowers and trees appeared as phantoms of dusk, shadowy figures that swayed endlessly to the wind's rhythmic gait, like dancers in a choreographed stage show. The gentle breeze caressed my face, stealing my cares and concerns.

Marcellus eased his strong, masculine arms around my waist again, pulling me closer and closer until I felt the warmth of his body, lost to his embrace. We stared deeper and deeper into each other's eyes as electric shocks penetrated the depths of my being.

Marcellus gently kissed my cheek ever so softly, then worked his way to my lips. He held me tightly in his arms, as I awaited his gentle touch.

I slid my hands up his chest, then around his neck. I felt safe and secure in that moment in time and wished that it could have lasted throughout eternity.

He eased his hands up my back, to my neck, then ran his fingers through my hair.

Ooo, that feels soo good! I thought as I closed my eyes. Tiny beads of energy pulsed from his hands and ran rampant through my body. I began to moan soft and low. I yearned for Marcellus to take me and fulfill all his manly cravings. The thought of my body giving him pleasure made my womanhood throb with anticipation.

Marcellus began to suck my lips, first the top, then the bottom. I tried to pull away, but his strong arms pulled me closer. Then it came—the moment that I had been waiting for—our tongues engaged in a quiet interlude, as they stroked each other up and down. I wrapped my left leg around his hip—his cue to squeeze and tantalize my rear.

He broke our kiss long enough to pick me up by the waist and put me on the balcony's edge. The two side slits in my long, flowing, cottony, white skirt allowed me room to wrap my legs around his thighs.

I watched his facial expressions, which told me that he savored each second as he nudged his big, firm bulge against my clit, rubbing it up, down, and around—over and over again—in a circular motion until I reached the peak of ecstasy.

I finally felt like a woman again nestled in the warmth of his tenderness. I moaned deep and hard from the gut, as I looked deep into my lover's dark, mysterious eyes.

"Demeter," Marcellus said as she sucked my lips. He held my face close to his. "I want to spend all of eternity with you … be my wife," he said with a serious look in his eyes as he eagerly waited a response. "Say yes," he groaned in that deep, sensuous tone that sent balls of fire to every cell in my body.

We turned away for a moment as a large ball of white light caught our attention. A giant shooting star, with its long, trailing white tail, shot up from the eastern horizon like a firecracker on New Year's Eve, as its brilliance dashed across the sky on its journey into infinity.

Without hesitation, I panted as Marcellus captivated me with his eyes, "Yes! Yes!" I said, but the fire that burned deep within me wouldn't dare dishonor his wishes.

Marcellus began to …

***

Three shrill chimes sounded as Patricia tapped her knife against an empty wine goblet. I was tossed back to present time, present place. For a moment, the room twirled around in one giant sea of confusion. All sounds, colors, aromas, and images blended as one pool of reality—one indistinguishable from the other. In the far corner, the strange figure of a man took one backward glance at me, then faded away into the corner shadows. In a flash, the room twirled into the world that I had grown accustomed—that ominous place called life.

I looked around in a stupor. As Patricia spoke, her words and movements were in slow motion. The crowd applauded and roared, returning the room's tempo to normal.

To my right, Lou, Marcus, and Dan laughed and drank wine, while Trevor, who seemed to have appeared from nowhere, gobbled a hefty plate of finger sandwiches. D'Angela walked over to the bar.

"Are you all right?" Marcus asked me. He probably noticed me staring off into the distance.

"Yeah," Dan said between bites of cheese. "You don't look too good."

Trevor must have overheard their concerns for me and decided to walk over. "She always be trippin' like that," he said between hungry bites of finger sandwiches.

From the corner of my eye, I saw that one of the men couldn't take his eyes off of my red cashmere sweater. I admit that it was a tad low-cut, and Victoria was working her secret with the double padded push up bra, but he had no right to come and stand right over me and look down my blouse. From his angle, he probably had clear view of my cleavage.

***

This could be a break, Demeter. Get inside of his head.

I don't know, Dr. Iverson.

Come on. You've come too far to turn back. Now get inside of his head!

***

"Fuck you, moth' fucker!' Lou told Trevor, almost out of nowhere, startling me further back into reality.

"What!" Trevor said. Lou's words jolted the man's long fascination with my bust line. "Now, I know you ain't talkin' to me," Trevor told Lou.

"Go on 'bout your business!" Lou told him. "You know what's good for you!"

Lou gave him that evil-don't-mess-with-me stare with her dark, beady eyes, so he decided to leave. Trevor irritated everybody except Lou. There was a past of sorts between Trevor and Lou, but nobody knew the complete story. Some speculated that it had something to do with that C-shaped scar across the front of Trevor's throat, but those were only rumors.

By their facial expressions, everyone at the table seemed surprised by how quickly Trevor retreated. I didn't care because I was still puzzled and tried to make sense of the world around me. It was like I was still on the balcony. My entire womanhood was still ablaze from Marcellus' tender touch. The liquid that seeped from deep within had saturated the cotton crouch of my panties. I could still feel the breeze caress my hair and smell the scent of exotic flowers in the air.

Trevor walked away and then joined a group of men against the golden rail. "Good God almighty. Umm, umm, umm! Her titties look so tight and so juicy! I wouldn't mind gettin' my hands on 'em boys!" I heard one of the men tell Trevor. From the corner of my eye, I saw that it was the young fellow from the mailroom.

"Oh, her? That's Demeter. Don't go botherin' her. Don't even waste yo' time," Trevor told the young fellow as he nibbled on a Buffalo wing. "If you ain't got no money, she don't want have nothin' to do wit' you."

***

Eleven-thirty on Friday night, and I had just driven into the garage. I was greeted with the sweet smells of basil, oregano, and fresh tomatoes soon as I stepped through the basement door. I always removed my shoes in the garage before entering the house.

***

Why?

Just an old superstition that I blindly followed that warned of how the evils of the world get tracked into the home by wearing shoes indoors.

                                    ***

"Why are you just getting home?"

I was startled by the sudden voice behind me. It was Keston, my older son who, at seventeen, towered over me by over ten inches. He had the face of pure innocence—deep caramel complexion; faded hair cut; full pale-pink lips and piercing hazel eyes like his pa—but a hard, tight, muscular body, pure evidence that manhood was upon him.

"You could have called or something! Where have you been all this time? You have people all worried and stuff like that!" Keston rolled his eyes at me in sheer disgust of my late arrival.

"We had a celebration at the office," I explained. "That smells good," I said as I walked up the perfectly polished mahogany stairs to the right.

"We cooked some linguini with clam sauce," Kevin said as he emerged from the study to the right. He looked like his older brother, only a few inches shorter and a few pounds lighter.

They followed me upstairs. The scent of fresh herbs and seasonings became more intense. Straight through the door was the large L-shaped kitchen. The bright, white cabinets illuminated the dark room with their golden oval knobs. All of the countertops were done in black granite with specks of white and sparkling silver. The white appliances blended into the scenery, except for the refrigerator, which was fashioned to blend into the woodwork and built into the wall.

"Oooo!" I yelled as my feet touched the diagonal, black-and-white linoleum tile floor. "It's freezing in here. Why didn't one of you turn on the heat?"

"It's burning up in here," Keston said, then removed a plastic platter full of reheated crescent rolls from the microwave, which was also built into the wall.

Straight ahead in the center was the island, which was surrounded by four white bar stools trimmed in gold, where we enjoyed most of our meals. Kevin prepared the place settings. Keston arranged the rolls in a white wicker breadbasket lined with a red-and-white checkered cloth, then placed them on the island along with an imported bottle of extra virgin olive oil for dipping.

I tossed my purse on the countertop closest to the entrance door that led to the garage, then sat down at my usual middle bar seat. Kevin served me an ample serving of tossed salad covered in raspberry vinaigrette. Keston served the linguini covered with hot, steamy clam sauce with big, juicy clams; chunks of fresh red tomatoes in a rich tomato sauce; fresh basil and oregano picked from my indoor herb garden; and savory bits of green peppers.

"Umm," I moaned. "This salad is so good!"

"I made the salad," Kevin bragged before he bit into a roll.

"I really appreciate dinner, guys," I told them.

"Thank you," they said in unison.

"We better get to bed by midnight. We have to be at the school by seven-thirty for the bus ride to Valdosta," I said.

"I talked to coach today," Keston said between bites of food. He and Kevin made direct eye contact, a secret signal that they probably didn't know I saw, when I was enjoying the linguini. "He said that we already have enough chaperones. Some of the teachers are volunteering so we don't need as many parents. Right, Kevin?"

"Yeah," Kevin said, "besides, Valdosta is a long drive, about four or five hours. It's near Florida. You've been working so hard all week, and the trip will be tiresome. You may want to just rest tomorrow."

"It should be a good trip. I don't want to miss seeing you play, Keston. And I don't want to miss seeing you in the band, Kevin. So what if it's a long ride, I don't want to miss a game."

Keston and Kevin gave each other that secret look again.

"Besides," Keston said, "the bus will be filled with loud, noisy teenagers. How are you going to rest with all of the racket going on anyway?"

"Yeah," Kevin agreed. "You're going to have to keep everybody in line. That's what chaperones do you know."

"You need to relax," Keston said as he poured me a full glass of Cabernet Merlot. "Why don't you get a movie or go shopping with Percy and Letitia or something and all that different stuff like that."

"We'll be gone until Monday afternoon," Kevin said. "You can go out on the town or something and stay out all night without worrying about us. The teachers'll be watching us, so we won't get into trouble or all that different stuff like that."

Keston cringed when Kevin mentioned staying out all night.

***

To him, Dr. Iverson, I am Mom, which means that my whole life revolves around working, cooking, paying bills and taking care of the home front. I can't date or even let a man within two feet of me, unless the extent of the relationship involves some business-related activity.

***

"Well, Coach Reeves asked me to chaperone," I told them. "He always complains that parents don't volunteer enough. What do you want me to tell him if I back out? I gave him my word, and he's expecting me to fulfill my promise."

Keston rolled his eyes and arched his upper lip in disgust, probably because he knew that the Coach was seriously attracted to me.

"We already *have* enough chaperones," Keston insisted as he edged closer to me. "If you don't believe me, ask Coach yourself," he said then sat back, folding his arms. "You can call him right now. I have his phone number in my book bag."

"All right, all right," I said. "I won't go. Staying here and going out sounds good."

"People are crazy out there," Keston told me. "You don't want to stay out too late on a Saturday night. We have satellite TV and you don't ever get to watch it. Tomorrow would be a good time to curl up with a good book," he said then cradled his chest, "light the fireplace and sip some wine," he cupped his hands as if to drink, "then go to sleep."

"Yeah," Kevin agreed.

Keston and Kevin never agreed on anything. I knew for sure that they were up to something.

***

I ended the day with a nice hot shower then rubbed eucalyptus massage oil all over my body. Then, I put the *Sounds of Sea* tape in the cassette player and snuggled between the soft, lavender fragrant, fluffy downy comforter. Sounds of the ocean's waves grew louder with each beat. Intermittent cries of seagulls echoed in the distance, as I became more relaxed. A deep gray cloud engulfed me, as tiny silvery specks glowed in the darkness ...

Chapter 5.
At Last

Did you dream that night, Demeter?

Yes, I did. At first, it wasn't lucid though. It became lucid later, I think.

How so?

***

I drifted deeper and deeper into slumber. A soft, barely audible hum filled the air. Hmmm. Hmmm. Hmmm. I suddenly found myself engulfed in a thick, gray cloud. Tiny, white lights sparkled intermittently about as I floated through its midst.

The humming grew louder and louder. The cloud began to thin as a soft, white sunbeam peeked through, almost welcoming me home to the great beyond. When the cloud finally dissipated, I was overcome by a deep sense of love and peace. The hum became louder and louder into a thunderous acappella that ripped through my very being.

In a flash, I was dressed in a long, silky, white dress, holding a small white bouquet of flowers. My hair was gently curled beneath a silky, white veil.

Everything was white, silver and sky blue. I looked around the magnificent edifice where I stood and was in awe of what I beheld: pentagon-shaped, stained glass windows lined the antique-white walls. The white marble floors were speckled with silvery blue dots. Straight ahead was a silvery alter that overlooked hundred of pews that stood behind me. The white light that had welcomed me continued to peek through the small glass dome above, providing a hint of softness to the room.

The acappella gradually faded into a quiet whisper of a hum. I noticed three figures slowly walking from behind the altar. Each wore a long white, flowing tunic. Silvery blue Druid robes covered their hands and faces. They soon stood directly in front of me, and a gentle chill suddenly brushed through the building. I was frozen in position, unable to move, yet I felt at peace.

The figures began to chant over and over again, sounding like what some church-goers refer to as "speaking in tongues." As they approached me, the chanting grew louder and louder. I still couldn't see their faces, hands or feet. Their bodies emanated a deep chill that rushed through me. I was frozen in position, unable to move or respond in anyway. Yet, I wasn't scared; it was as though I was becoming one with the universe—one with the Creator.

I felt the warmth of a presence approach from the back of the room. It walked slowly down the long aisle, getting warmer and warmer the closer it got to me. As it came nearer and nearer, my body became charged with a static energy that crept along my spine. Still, I was frozen in place, unable to move. Yet, I had a sense of ... knowingness ... yeah ... if you will, that everything was in divine order.

A familiar hand caressed my back down to my hips, then pulled me closer. It was Marcellus, who looked ever so handsome in that white suit and silver double-knotted tie. His deep, dark penetrating eyes and gentle smile melted my heart, and other parts of me too.

I looked deep into Marcellus' eyes, piercing his very soul. At that moment, the three figures began to circle us waving silvery wands as they continued to chant over and over again.

A tingly sensation radiated in the center of my chest that grew hotter and hotter with each fleeting moment. In a flash, golden lights rushed from my and Marcellus' solar plexus. For a moment, the two twirled around into a small fireball; tiny, white lights pulsed from its core. It quickly grew larger, as the figures chanted louder and faster.

From the corner of my eye, I saw two of the figures run to opposite sides of the room. The remaining figure threw his arm up and roared like a wild lion. All the windows chattered as the sound vibrated throughout the room. The figure then smashed a small white crystal on the floor; the broken pieces transformed into two sparkling rays of light. The golden-orange light twirled around Marcellus as he seemingly beheld its splendor. It was as brilliant as fresh sunshine at the crack of dawn and as vibrant as a raging wildfire. The pink light, with all its majesty, twirled around me. The tiny silver lights that sparked from within felt like tiny snowflakes against my skin. Marcellus and I were frozen in the moment, unable to move as we stared deep into each other's soul.

The figure cast another crystal to the floor and again chanted with great force. The two lights that surrounded us exploded into a fiery, red aura. The energy that it emitted saturated every cell of our bodies as we stood there, frozen like statues; it was so warm and soothing, like being wrapped in a cozy, soft comforter on a cool winter day. Then I realized that I had no body. Marcellus had no body. We had metamorphasized into one giant ball of fire.

The light waved through us both, bringing with it powerful feelings of love and passion unparalleled by any earthly experience. Every molecule, every cell ... no ... no ... every subatomic particle of mine and his were intertwined. We made love on the most profound level imaginable—at the very core of existence—transcending time and space. It was like Marcellus and I had always been together. There was never a beginning—and there won't be an end—to our union. We were flames in that moment in time—multidimensional beings confined by flesh and blood imposed upon us by some unnatural phenomena. That foreign world, that ominous place called life, diverged our souls until they reunited.

Seeing and feeling became one. The sensation was one of floating through a giant whirlpool of carbonated water, immersed in a warm, soothing liquid surrounded by fizzling bubbles of varying sizes—from inkling dots to massive boulders.

Memories of my college biology professor came to mind. Memories that lay dormant, deep in the burrows of my subconscious—old lectures of sodium bicarbonate.

***

Akasic Records.

What?

Akasic Records. Everything that has ever happened, is happening, or will ever happen exist in akasic records. All universal knowledge is contained in these records. You were accessing them in your dream that night.

***

Well … ahhh … anyway, his endless lectures about his theories on evolution and life all came to mind.

Marcellus and I were at the center of creation itself, immersed in a deep crimson sea of matter, sizzling with a brilliant, white light shining above. We were shapeless, shiftless forms drifting through eternity—mind and body indistinguishable from the other. Every proton, electron and neutron of our forms were joined. I had become him; he had become me. In that point in time, I knew that Marcellus and I would never part; I was his, and he was mine. Souls forever united, never to be put asunder.

***

A shrill whistle continued to sound. Though my eyes were closed, all I saw was crimson, like I had fallen asleep with the lights on.

Time to get up, I thought. I tried in vain to reach for the alarm clock, but all I could feel was a big empty void. I assumed that I had tossed and turned in my sleep and rolled to the opposite side of the bed, away from the nightstand where the alarm clock sat. *Okay, Demeter,* I told myself. *Stop being lazy and wake up. You have to take the boys to school for their trip to Valdosta. You don't want them to miss their trip because of you, do you?*

I pried my eyes open. Everything was a blur. All I saw was a deep shade of crimson. I blinked a few times and rubbed my eyes, but still, all I saw was crimson. Uh, that whistling, that annoying whistle had became a quiet whisp …

"Hello, Mrs. Angellel," a voice echoed to my left. It was as though I were in a giant pool. The air was moist and fluid. Every image, every color oscillated to the rhythm of the whistle. I noticed wavy specters of colors go between what appeared to be a narrow aisle with double seats on either side. All movements, all sounds were in slow motion.

I looked to my left, and it was Marcellus. As quickly as I had turned, the scene hastened pace. My vision came into focus. I saw his gentle smile as he kissed me gently on the cheek, then stroked my hair.

"You were sleeping mighty soundly," he said. "I let you sleep. It's been a long trip, twelve hours, but we're almost there now."

I looked all around and noticed that I was on some sort of craft, an airplane perhaps. Straight ahead was a golden door that appeared to open to a cockpit of sorts. Ten rows of double seats lined a wide aisle. Each seat was white velour, with ample room—in front of and behind each one—for comfort. The oatmeal-colored carpet was deep and plush. The windows were larger than what I was accustomed to seeing on an airplane; they were at least six feet tall by four feet wide, giving clear view of the heavens above and landscape below.

It's a good thing this is a dream, I thought. *I'm acrophobic, afraid of heights.*

Marcellus put his arm around me and pulled me closer. The warmth of his body sent shock waves through me. "We're on our way to the Honey Moon," he informed me. His ultra-bass voice resonated through me like a potent aphrodisiac.

"We're on our honeymoon?" I asked.

"Yes. We're on our honeymoon and we're going to the Honey Moon," Marcellus pointed to a moon far into the sky. "That's the Honey Moon over there. The blue-and-white one with all the craters."

The moon looked like pictures I had seen of Earth taken from orbit, only with craters. *A moon wouldn't have an atmosphere, would it?* I asked myself. *Heck, this is a dream. Anything is possible.*

"Come," Marcellus said as he stood up and reached for me. "Let's explore the sky."

"All right," I agreed.

We walked to the back of the craft, which was the dining area. Three men stood around a window drinking a steamy drink—probably coffee—and talking. A group of five sat at the rich mahogany bar trimmed in gold to the left-most corner of the room drinking spirits and nibbling a shared bowl of snacks. Immediately to the left was a set of French doors trimmed in mahogany and gold that led to an observatory.

As we approached, one of the doors was ajar. A cool breeze—like that on a cool spring day—razzled my hair a bit. I noticed tables set with white china trimmed in gold and silverware. When we entered, every cell in my body came to life. The sky was a deep shade of crimson with amber and sienna fading in at spots. Far to the right was the ringed planet. We were so close, yet so far from its surface. Glistening ice crystals that reflected blue, violet and white were trapped within its rings. Tiny, white fragments, probably debris from a comet or planet, floated all about. Several picture windows lined the outside walls, two of which were open. A couple sipped spirits and held hands by the first opened window, so Marcellus took me to the one at the rear of the room.

The quartet played a soft jazzy tune. The combination of notes that bellowed from the saxophone and trumpets were like nothing I had ever heard before. They were lively and very beautiful.

Wait a minute, I thought. *We're on a spacecraft. We're not supposed to breath without* ... Then, I realized that it was all a dream, a figment of my imagination. Anything I wanted to happen could happen, even if it defied the laws of physics known to mankind.

I looked deep into Marcellus' deep, mesmerizing, dark eyes. We talked for hours and hours about everything and anything, as the gentle breeze caressed my skin. Oh, the breeze felt so soothing, so relaxing. Marcellus walked away to get drinks. I wondered how it would feel to fly through the sky, so I went to the door marked *Emergency Exit* in the far corner of the room. There wasn't a visible way to open it. All four sides were lined in steel. Two diagonal bars crossed at the middle, with a giant silver dial that looked like a steering wheel at the center. I tried to turn the dial, but the door wouldn't budge.

"Here, let me help you," a voice said to my right. "Press there," it said and faded as quickly as it had appeared. It was the same shadowy figure that I saw the night of the party—the one that remained clear as the scene faded.

Down the left side of the door was a long black lever that read in bold white letters down its length, *Push here for Emergencies.* So, I pushed the lever and an alarm was tripped that reminded me of a fire engine siren. The door started to slowly push out. A violent wind rushed the cabin that knocked me to the floor. A wine goblet at a nearby table fell to the floor. As I scrambled to my feet, a shard of glass pierced my skin. *Ouch! That hurts. I'm not supposed to hurt in a dream.*

The waitress and the couple she was serving screamed in horror as I started for the door again. They caught the attention of others in the room. The music stopped as screams and excitement filled the air. I tried and tried, but the cabin pressure was too great for me to stand up. I ignored the people in the room as they screamed in horror. *They're all dream figures,* I reasoned.

"She's crazy," someone yelled. "What is she doing?"

"She'll get us all hurt," another woman yelled. "Someone stop her!"

"What're you doing?" a man yelled as he struggled against the cabin pressure to pull the door close. He was tall and tan with dirty blond hair and baby blue eyes. "You want to hurt yourself?" He seemed annoyed.

Hurt myself? This is a dream. You're part of my dream. I can't be hurt.

"What were you trying to do, Demeter?" Marcellus asked, then gave me a curious look.

A crowd surrounded me. Everyone looked at me curiously.

"I wanted to …" I started.

"Is she with you, Marc?" the man who rescued me asked. "You need to tell…"

"It's all right," Marcellus told him. "I'll handle it from here."

"You got to tell her …" he tried to tell Marcellus something again, but was abruptly cut off.

"I said, I'll handle it!" Marcellus huffed.

Marcellus pulled me by the arm back through the double doors and dining area as curious onlookers witnessed. When we arrived back at our seats, I felt like a two-year-old who had been scolded by her parents for committing some terrible act. Marcellus looked at me in the eyes and whispered soft and stern, "Don't you *ever*, I mean *ever*, try anything like that again! Do you understand me, Demeter?"

"What … I just …" I started, but he interrupted me again.

"Don't-you-ever-try-anything-like-that-again! Do-you-understand-me?" he again asked in that stern whisper.

"Yes, Marcellus," I said. "But why?"

He didn't answer, but gave me the most sinister look that sent an eerie chill down my spine.

My arm continued to hurt. "Oh no!" I yelled.

"What!" Marcellus looked, then hailed an attendant. "First aid over here!"

My arm was oozing blood from the cut. With all of the excitement of the open door, I just didn't notice it.

"Quick, come this way," the attendant said after she retrieved some gauze from a small white pouch and placed it over my arm. She escorted me to the front of the craft, catching the attention of onlookers.

"Ouch!" I yelled. I couldn't believe that I was hurting.

The attendant was about five-seven with smooth caramel skin. She wore her long micro-braided hair in a neatly coiffed bun.

Medical Aid in bright red letters were on the white door that led to the first aid room. It was white and looked sterile. To the right rear was a glass cabinet with shelves of pills and needles. To the left was an examining table, complete with stirrups and lined with tissue paper. *Stirrups?* I thought. *Strange dream I'm having.*

The attendant led me to a chair behind the door. Next to it was a table complete with blood pressure monitoring cuffs, thermometer, cotton swabs, alcohol, and other first aid supplies. *I sure do dream thoroughly*, I thought. *I'll just enjoy it.*

"You've been cut pretty bad," the attendant said.

"She'll be all right … right?" Marcellus asked as he stood beside me.

"Yep," the attendant said. "I see this all the time," she said as she washed her hands in the tiny silver sink next to the table. She dried her hands and donned white gloves from a disposable glove box that looked like a tissue box.

The attendant placed a white plastic basin under my arm as she rinsed it with a brown solution that smelled like vinegar. I didn't see it coming, but next thing I knew, she stuck me with a needle. She seemed oddly familiar somehow. But it was all a dream, so I figured that I probably saw someone like her on TV or something.

"Ouch!" I yelled. "What's that for?"

"It's an antibacterial," she said.

Antibacterial? I asked myself. *In a dream?*

Then, she started to stitch me. The shadowy figure that appeared a few moments earlier was standing behind her—laughing.

"Who are you?" I asked the figure. It just laughed and faded away.

"I'm nurse Dewey," the attendant said as she continued to stitch.

"No," I said. "I was talking to the person behind you."

Marcellus and the nurse looked behind her, then at each other.

"No one's behind me," she said. "You must keep your arm still." She looked at Marcellus and said, "Fever … must be badly infected."

"But there was someone behind you," I insisted.

Marcellus and the nurse again looked at each other.

I looked at my arm as it continued to bleed. The attendant gave me another shot in my arm near the wound, then continued to stitch. I began to feel woozy. Tiny red-and-purple spots appeared before me, grew to the size of grapefruits, then popped before my eyes, over and over again.

I looked at Marcellus and his face looked distorted; his eyes and mouth drooped down to his neck. I blinked for a moment, and the whole room appeared warped, like I was looking through a special effects mirror at an amusement park.

"Are you OK?" Marcellus asked, then rubbed my good hand, the one closer to him. The once passionate pulses that he sent through my body suddenly turned into painful electric shocks. It felt if though I had stuck my finger in a power outlet.

The nurse's skin faded into a deep purple hue and began to form deep creases. When she looked at me again, her eyes had popped out of their sockets and dropped to her chin.

The room began to darken to a deep shade of midnight blue, and the air thickened to the point that I couldn't breathe. I felt myself fade in and out of consciousness, as the attendant continued to stitch and Marcellus continued to hold my hand. *I've died and gone to hell,* I thought. *But I don't care. It can't be worse than my life is already.*

***

Is that you way you felt at the time, Demeter?

Uhh, yes.

Is that how you feel right now?

Yes.

Why? A thriving career, two handsome sons, beautiful home and new car aren't enough to make you happy?

Well, Dr. Iverson, everything is crashing in on me. Sure, to everyone around me, I am pretty well put together. But behind the scenes, I am really falling apart. All I do is work all the time. No one, and I mean no one, appreciates anything I do. Not the damned boss, not the damned coworkers, especially Trevor and D'Angela, no one. I am taken for granted. I get no support from anyone. Not the boss, not the coworkers, no one. Then, when I get home, I get no support or respect. Keston and Kevin are always about me-me-me. Always, "Mom, I want this," or "Mom, I need that." How about what I need for change, huh? How about my needs? If I were to fall off of the face of the Earth, no one would even miss me.

Don't say that, Demeter. That's not true.

Nnnnn!

Well, back to the dream. What happened next?

***

The annoying whistling returned, that time more shrill than ever.

I tried to speak, but couldn't. My whole body became numb. It began at the soles of my feet, then gradually crept up my legs, arms, neck and face. The whistling became louder and louder. I felt myself falling from great heights into a bottomless pit, the great unknown below. I kept falling and falling, faster and faster until I hit the soft, cushiony bottom. My lungs filled with air as I bounced up in bed. I looked to the right, and there it was again. That darned alarm clock, doing its job. With one click of a button, the annoying whistling sound had been silenced.

Five more minutes, I said. Just five more minutes. No, ten more minutes. Then, I set the snooze for exactly ten minutes.

***

"Turn the A/C off, Keston!" I tried to yell, but was too overpowered by slumber. "Turn that water off! Who's running the dishwasher this time of morning? You should've cleaned the kitchen last night, Keston!"

I was freezing. The goose down comforter was of little value. It was fall, but Keston liked to have the house really cool and turned the thermostat down to sixty degrees.

"Mom, it's hot in here," he would always complain. I guess being a jock with head-to-toe muscles can do that to a young stud.

Birds sang melodious tunes just outside the window. My eyes were opened to a slit and I saw the gentle light of daybreak. I began to panic. *Can't be! I hope that I didn't oversleep! It can't be past six o'clock! Can't be!*

I felt a warm, furry body burrow under the comforter. I knew for sure that it was that dog, Sampson. He was a mixed breed of St. Bernard and something or the other, and ate like nobody's business. I don't know why I let Keston and Kevin talk me into getting that dog. It was probably because we were passing the pet store in the mall when the Humane Society was offering puppies for adoption. Sampson looked like a brown-and-white powder puff back then. The boys caught a glimpse of him and well …

"We'll feed him and walk him and bathe him and take care of him," they assured me. They named him Sampson because of his long, fluffy fur. That was five years ago when he was a puppy. But now ...

Keston and that mutt! I told him not to have that dog in my room! I thought. What I felt was no Sampson. A gentle kiss caressed my left ear, as a big strong, warm hand tickled my hips. "Good morning, Mrs. Angellel," a voice said.

I rubbed my eyes and turned in that direction, it was Marcellus smiling at me. His head was saddled on his right hand while his elbow sank deep into a huge white pillow, exposing his black underarm hairs. His long, hard muscle and two big brown nuts stood at attention. That big red head—the one below—was preying on me almost.

He looked ever so masculine. I couldn't resist running my fingers through the hair that covered his strong, masculine body. His chest, stomach, legs, every inch of his body, it seemed, was covered with soft, black hair.

He pulled me closer and warmed my freezing body. He attempted to kiss my lips, but my mouth felt pasty, in need of a good brushing. I covered my mouth and tried to get out of bed. I don't know why, since I didn't know where the bathroom was.

"It's all right, Demeter," he said then pulled me in closer again. "I want to experience you in the raw."

His big, hairy hands pulled me into his soft, hairy chest as his lips covered mine. Our tongues engaged in a quiet interlude, twirling around and around in unison, stopping occasionally for a brief whiff of air.

His hands caressed my back down to my rear, as he ran his hands in and out of my crack, squeezing my tender cheeks with each stroke.

He broke our kiss long enough to nibble my earlobe and lick every nook and cranny of my ear, my neck, all the way down to my breasts.

My nipples were so hard awaiting his electric touches that sped straight to my clit. He sucked down to my bellybutton, leaving a trail of passion marks along the way.

He spread my legs, eased his face closer to my loins, then blew several soft, arousing streams of air on my womanhood, over and over again. I welcomed his tongue against my swollen clit, as he twirled it around and around as though he were balancing a jellybean on the tip of his tongue. Amazing, but he covered my entire womanhood with his mouth, its warmth sent me into a tizzy, as his lips collapsed on my clit. I ran my fingers through his thick, black, wavy mane, all the while drawing him into my midst.

My clit became riper and plumper as he sucked harder and harder, and gently nibbled his way around my feminine paradise. He licked my inner lips up and down, side to side and inside to outside until they were sore with spine-tingling pleasure, a sinful delight that I had never experienced until that time.

All nerve endings, it seemed, were rerouted to my clit and inner lips. My inner walls cringed with each skillful stroke of his tongue. I strained to hold back, but when he pointed his tongue and squeezed it inside my cunt, good God almighty, I couldn't restrain myself.

Marcellus stopped shy of me reaching the peak of ecstasy. He released his lips, and a long sticky film attached itself to his chin, pure evidence of the passion we shared.

"Don't stop," I pleaded, then pulled his head closer, he resisted.

He looked up at me and smiled. "Why?"

"Please don't stop," I pleaded. "Please!" The room was freezing cold, but all I craved was complete satisfaction.

He looked at me one more time and laughed. Then, he buried his nose, lips then his entire face in my moisture. Mercy!

I moaned soft and low from the pleasure he had given me. My loins were exploding in excitement with each of his wicked touches. Balls of passion ran rampant through my body as he again nibbled my clit ever so softly. I moaned louder and louder ...

***

"Wake up, mom," Keston said as he shook me back to reality. "Wake up! You're having a bad dream!"

"What! What!" I said.

I was still groggy, but Keston quickly shook me out of it.

"We heard you down the hall screaming," Kevin said as he stood by the bedroom door looking in. "You must've been having a really bad nightmare."

I sat up on my elbows. "What time is it?" I asked.

"It's five-thirty," Keston said.

"You boys go and get dressed for your trip," I told them. "We still have time. Give me a minute, and I'll cook some grits and eggs."

"You're not about to go to sleep again, are you?" Keston asked.

"No."

"Are you sure?" Keston insisted.

"Yes. I'm sure," I reassured. "Now, go and get dressed."

They both went down the hall to their rooms to get dressed. To the extreme left of my room, through the arched doorway that led to the large walk-in closet, was the master bathroom. The golden highlights in the burgundy paisley striped wallpaper seemed to sparkle when I turned on the light. The room was aglow, different somehow. Strange, but the garden tub seemed more round. The golden faucets sparkled more than usual.

I turned to my left to look into the mirror over the sink. Somehow, the glass seemed so clear, almost as if I could have climbed through to the other side and started a new life. The wallpaper and fixtures looked so much more beautiful on the other side of the mirror.

I turned on the water in the shower stall, walked in, then closed the double-mirrored, sliding doors behind. As I lathered Zest soap on the washcloth, the scent was ten times more fragrant than I had remembered it to be. *I did just open this bar. Maybe Procter & Gamble changed formulas or something.* The soothing warmth of the pulsating water stimulated my skin more than ever. *The Water Department must have increased the water pressure to this area. That's right, the water restrictions for the summer have been lifted.*

When I began to wash, I noticed that my loins were still tingling and moist. My breasts were softer and more tender than usual, like they had been stimulated by a gentle lover. *I must have really fingered myself last night while I was dreaming,* I reasoned.

I stepped out the shower more relaxed than ever. As I patted myself dry, Sunlight began to peek through the mini-blind over the garden tub. *It can't be that late. Maybe it's the neighbor's headlights or something.*

I noticed a long, thin scratch on my arm. *That mutt, Sampson, must have scratched me in bed again,* I thought.

I went into the walk-in closet to get dressed. Hints of sunlight peeked through my bedroom window, pure evidence that dawn was upon us. The alarm clock read *6:45.*

No way, I told myself. *I couldn't have been in the shower that long.*

I went into the kitchen and noticed a dirty frying pan and pot that were used to cook grits and eggs, proof that the boys had eaten. I checked around upstairs, but they were nowhere in sight. When I went into the basement, there they were, watching TV and waiting for me.

If it weren't for the fact that the principal didn't want any cars left on school property over the weekend, I would've let Keston drive the other car to school that morning. Then, I could have slept in late.

"We were just coming up to get you," Keston said sarcastically. "We thought you went back to sleep or fell asleep in the bathroom or something or all that different stuff like that."

Kevin sat on the black velour sectional fastening his spats in a hurry. His maroon-and-gold hat, with its tall golden plume, was on the coffee table in the middle of the room.

***

We barely made it to school in time. Keston grabbed his duffel bag from the trunk and ran toward the bus for football players. Kevin got his hat and black saxophone case and joined his fellow band members.

A tap on the window startled me, as I began to back out of the lot. I looked, and there was Coach, so I opened the window.

"Hello, Ms. Pickens," he said with a smirk.

"Oh, you startled me, Coach," I said as I caught my breath. "How are you?"

He leaned into the open window. "I thought you promised to chaperone?"

"Keston said that you had enough chaperones," I said.

He looked behind him and smiled, "Oh, he did, huh?"

I looked behind Coach and noticed Keston rolling his eyes at us near the bus. He looked mad, probably because he knew that Coach had a crush on me.

"Maybe the next game. Enjoy the rest of your day, Ms. Pickens," he said then headed for the bus.

I think Keston anticipated Coach's move. He quickly boarded the bus before Coach turned around.

Keston couldn't stand to see any man look at me. That's probably why I never dated much, because he would do something to run them off.

***

Like what?

Well, I'm not sure what, but I suspect that he would tell them something or the other if they happened to call when I wasn't at home. I can't prove it, but I strongly suspect that he was the reason why they would never call again.

Is that what he did to Coach too?

Oh nooo! He wouldn't dare do that with Coach because he is assured of getting a football scholarship. Coach has the right connections to make it happen.

Tell me about Coach.

Well, three years ago, Coach retired from the Atlanta Falcons football team. The school approached him at that time to help out with the team. He agreed because he claimed he wanted to give back to the community. The team has won all State Championship games since that time.

Besides, I never would even think of dating any of their teachers or anyone else at the school for that matter.

Why not?

Because, I would never do anything to embarrass Keston and Kevin. Children like to feel proud of their parents, you know. Besides, that's why these so-called men don't know how to treat or relate to women.

Why?

Because they grew up seeing their grandmothers, mothers, aunts and other female relatives act like whores. So, they don't know what a respectable lady is supposed to act like.

Chapter 6.
Away Mundane

I arranged to meet Percy and Letitia for lunch at Lenox Mall later that day. We also planned to catch a movie and do a little shop ... well, no shopping. I hate to shop till this day. It's a complete waste of time. I don't understand how people can go to the mall when it opens and leave when it closes. That's just plain dumb!

Well anyway, we always ended our days with coffee and dessert at one of the coffee shops in Buckhead on Peachtree Road. I still don't like the restaurants because the service is so poor. Hell, they act as if they're doing you a favor when you come in.

Anyway, that Saturday I stopped by the office to finish a project about eight. I planned to meet them around two-ish, plenty of time.

A large black gate blocked the entrance to the parking deck on weekends. So, I drove up and was prepared to punch in the magic code to enter the garage. *Open Sesame! Open!* Lo and behold, the gate opened by itself.

I walked off the elevator leading from the parking deck. The sound that my shoes made when the heels tapped against the beige marble floor echoed through the hallway. It sounded as though the building were collapsing. I guess it was because no one else was around.

As I continued down the hallway, I noticed that Chap's was opened. *Good.* It seemed that he always knew what I wanted and had it ready by the time I walked in the door. Amazing. Those other restaurants could learn a thing or two from Mr. Chap.

***

He was opened on a Saturday morning?

Yes. He opened until about four in the afternoon on Saturdays. People from surrounding buildings worked on weekends, and Lenox Square is right down the road, so there were plenty of customers on weekends. Besides, his shop had an entrance on Peachtree Road, so he could stay open when the rest of the building was closed.

***

Well, that morning, unlike the other times when I worked on the weekend, I decided to go to my cube first instead of to Chap's. A few minutes later, I heard voices near the elevator.

"Hello, Demeter!"

"Dan!" I was surprised. "I didn't know you were working today."

"The testing team and I are going to be *experimenting* again today," Dan informed me. "See you later."

I watched as he walked down the aisle between the cubicles. He glanced backward, and I could have sworn that he winked at me as if he knew I weren't looking.

"I figured you was gone be here."

It was good old Trevor. He snared at me then threw his briefcase on his desk. I hated that Trevor sat directly across from me. *Damn!*

"It sho' is hot up in here," Trevor said. "If y'all want people to be workin' on Sat'days, then y'all need to be havin' it cool up in here!"

Trevor started complaining and cussing about something else or the other. I just tuned him out as usual. The more he tried to capture my attention with his antics the more I ignored him. The more I ignored him, the angrier he became.

"Stop all that fussing and cussing, boy!" It was Mr. Chap carrying an aromatic cardboard tray of my favorite breakfast—a freshly baked blueberry muffin and a hot cup of café' au lait. "Can't you see there's a lady present?" Mr. Chap told Trevor. "Show some respect, boy!"

"How ya doin', Mr. Chap?" Trevor asked. "That sho' smell good. You got some fo' me?"

Mr. Chap always seemed to command Trevor's respect.

"Don't be disrespecting my woman," Mr. Chap said. "That's my wife, you know."

Trevor laughed and said, "You the man, Mr. Chap. Still a playa."

Mr. Chap turned to me and smiled as he gently placed the goodies on my desk.

"For you, my sweet," Mr. Chap said. In one snap, he unfolded a large white paper napkin and placed it in my lap, smiling and maintaining eye contact the whole time. Well, it was hard to see his eyes through those thick glasses. But that's a whole other issue.

Anyway, then he carefully placed another white napkin on my desk along with a white plastic knife and fork. "I saw you walking down the hall coming from the parking deck. I thought you were going to stop. But since you were in such a hurry and didn't stop, I thought I'd come to you. You're a hardworking young lady, and a hardworking young lady needs her nourishment to get her work done."

"You're too kind, Mr. Chap. Thank you so much," I said.

"A fine, talented, young lady like yourself shouldn't be working so hard. You shouldn't be working late nights or on the weekends like you do," Mr. Chap said.

"Unn, hnn," Trevor moaned. "Tell 'er, Mr. Chap. Preach on! She need to get a life!"

Mr. Chap turned to Trevor. "No, no, Trevor! If somebody would've taught you young men out here how to really be men, then ladies like Demeter wouldn't be working so hard. Back in my day, a man knew how to be a man and provided for his family." He turned to me, took my hands in his and rubbed them gently as he gazed into my eyes. His hands were masculine and warm. "Ladies like Demeter are delicate flowers and need to be taken care of."

Trevor laughed. "You somethin' else Mr. Chap. You the man," he said, staggered over to my cube, and gave Mr. Chap what my sons called "dap." They balled their right hands into a fist, then bumped the tops, bottoms and knuckles together. Trevor then returned to his cube.

Dan and a few others gathered around Trevor's cube for a meeting of sorts. Whew! That kept Trevor quiet!

Mr. Chap eased his hip against the far edge of my desk while I savored my muffin and café au lait.

"I told you that I was going to marry you, didn't I, Demeter?" Mr. Chap asked.

"Oh, Mr. Chap," I said. "You're always teasing."

He looked me straight in the eyes and said, "It's true, you know. It's true." He slowly eased his hip up from the desk. "You just think about what I said, about working all the time. You ... you just ponder that one." On that note, he smiled at me, retrieved the empty cardboard tray, then waved good-bye, smiling all the way.

As Mr. Chap started for the elevator with the empty cardboard tray in hand, Trevor and the others who had gathered around his cube, all said good-bye to Mr. Chap.

"What's up with that?" D'Angela asked as she pointed to the muffin and café au lait.

"What?" I asked.

"Mr. Chap always be bringin' you a li'l somethin'-somethin'. He don't never bring the rest of us nothin'," she said. "Oooo, I feel sooo neglected."

"That's not true," I said. "He always brings people who are working late or on the weekends a little something, something."

Somehow I managed to catch everyone's attention. They all became quiet and looked at me as though I were a visitor from Mars.

"No, it's just you, Demeter," Dan said. "I think he likes you."

Everyone started to laugh.

"Chil', what you gone do wit' a old man anyhow?" D'Angela laughed. "Look, he prob'bly can't even get it up!"

Everyone laughed.

"Well, he is old," Trevor said. "Marry him, he probably ain't got too much longer for this world anyhow. Then ... you know ... kaboom ... just get his 'surance money ..."

They all laughed.

"Stop it!" Dan yelled. Everyone probably stopped laughing because he seemed so serious—as usual. And because he was the *big boss* over the project. "I think he's really in love with Demeter. Love has no boundary of age. It's not funny!"

Trevor arched his eyebrow and pretended to dust himself off. "Well!" he said in a mocked insulted type of way, then turned his nose up.

Everyone soon got back to work. A few minutes later, they gathered their things and left the area. They probably went to the QA lab. Heck, I didn't care where they went, as long as they were away from me so I could get some work done.

***

You know, Dr. Iverson, it was so strange.

What was so strange, Demeter?

That every time Mr. Chap was around, he put off this strange energy, almost like a static charge. It would start right before I saw him and would last for hours.

What did you make of it?

Well, I guess it was because he was such a cheerful person. He was always smiling, always a gentleman. Everyone liked and respected him. I really think he was the last genuinely beautiful human being. There'll never be another Mr. Chap. He was truly one of a kind. I still miss him. I can't believe he's gone. But he was old, and it was just his time. But I just think there's something about him that still lingers. I can't put my finger on it, maybe it's my imagination, but I sense something more.

***

Percy, Letitia and I went shopping at Lenox Mall. I don't know why I let Percy talk me into shopping. I-hate-shopping ... with a passion! Anyway, we decided to skip the movie and went straight for coffee and dessert and took it back to Percy's highrise condo.

It was such a nice fall day—that's my favorite time of year, you know—so we sat on the balcony, sipping endless cups of café au lait, chatting the time away, as we watched the redness of the setting sun cast its shadow on the floors. The vast Atlanta skyline served as a backdrop. A crisp breeze caressed our skin, taking with it the stress and strain of the past week, as we sank deeper and deeper into the cushiony melon and pale-green floral print patio chairs.

I sat there, with my feet propped up on the balcony's edge; I eased my fork into the fudge brownie cheesecake. It looked so good with the chocolate raspberry swirl drizzled across the top and puff of whipped cream with two ripe raspberries sunk in the middle. That used to be my favorite dessert. That rich, creamy New York-style cheesecake topped with summer berries and moist chocolate brownie bottom, layered on a thin, moist chocolate crumble crust. Ummm!

"Uhhh!" I yelled then jumped out of my lounge chair. My facial expression must have frightened Percy and Letitia because they immediately ran to my aid. I began to gag and dropped the remaining cheesecake on the floor, breaking one of Percy's good pink floral porcelain saucers.

"What's wrong, Demeter?" Letitia asked.

Percy ran inside and quickly returned with a glass of water. "Here, drink this," Percy said. She didn't seem a bit concerned about her saucer, which was surprising, especially since she bragged about how expensive her china was.

I tried to speak, but could not get the words out. The cheesecake had a strange tart taste, as though it was well past the rancid stage, if there were such a thing. It had a pasty feel, as though I had been chewing a large piece of chalk, you know, the kind your second grade teacher used to scribble on the blackboard. My stomach began to contract as I struggled in vain to retain my lunch.

The scene dimmed to a pale shade of gray; all sounds were muted. I noticed the same shadowy figure that I saw in Antoine's the night of the party and in my dream. It leered at me behind Letitia as she stood in front of me—with her arms around me—patting me on the back.

In an instant, the scene brightened to normal and all sounds returned. The figure vanished into the brilliance of the setting sun. The scene faded to a pale shade of gray, then back to light again, back and forth, back and forth. Gray to bright, and bright to gray. Over and over again until I realized that Percy had taken me into the bathroom and splashed cold water on my face. Then, I snapped out of the stupor that had held me captive for what seemed like an eternity. I looked down and realized that I was wearing one of Percy's *Atlanta Braves* T-shirts and an old pair of black spandex biking shorts. It felt as though tiny baby hands were massaging and tickling the insides of my stomach. What a strange sensation, almost like being on a roller coaster or something. Interesting.

"I'll wash your clothes. You can get them on your way from work during the week," Percy said. Her words were slurred and garbled. As she walked away holding the clothes, her movements resembled fleeting droplets of paint whisking in the wind.

"Are you all right, Demeter?" Letitia asked as she escorted me to the living room. Each step we took walking down the hallway was like traveling through a long, dark tunnel on some type of locomotive moving very fast.

I looked toward Letitia and I saw her lips move, but the words didn't come out. It looked as though she were looking at me through a trick mirror in a carnival; her face changed shapes as she spoke.

The room swayed back and forth, making it hard for me to keep my balance. Back and forth, back and forth the room continued to sway. I closed my eyes and counted to three, thinking that everything would be back to normal. I could still feel the room swaying back and forth, back and forth. I heard garbled voices, probably those of Percy and Letitia, echo through the room; they sounded like an old 45 record with the speed slowed down to 16.

I managed to make it to the sofa a few steps away. When I sat down, the soft back and cushions and gentle leather smell welcomed my body. They felt so plush, warm and very comfortable indeed. Still a bit dazed, I didn't care about the world around me.

***

It's hard to explain, Dr. Iverson, but I was overcome by a cool void.

A cool void?

Yes. It was like being inside an air-conditioned bubble. It started at the crown of my head and moved through my body, engulfing me in its midst. The thick cushions swallowed all the stress and strain of the week from my body. It was so cool ... so soothing ... so comforting—like coming into an air-conditioned room after being outside on a ninety-five degree day of a New Orleans summer. I wanted that feeling to last forever.

***

Percy removed my shoes and covered me with a soft white comforter that smelled like fresh jasmines. She uttered something that I couldn't understand, but I tuned her out. I enjoyed the feeling of the comforter over my body and the softness of the sofa. I was so relaxed that I thought I had spent the day in a spa getting a full body massage; no stress, no strain, only relaxation and comfort.

The sun began to set and the room darkened. Percy closed the vertical blinds straight ahead, making the room dark. She popped in a tape of Kool and the Gang's "Summer Madness," my all time favorite song.

I gently closed my eyes, as I sank deeper and deeper into the sofa. The music reverberated louder and louder as I began to relax. Slumber was upon me.

I felt the room sway back and forth, back and forth. I opened my eyes, and the room swayed to the rhythm of the music. I didn't have a care in the world. I didn't know where Percy and Letitia were. Did they desert me? I didn't know. I didn't care.

I continued to listen to the music, completely captivated by its vibrating rhythm. I became more and more relaxed, sinking deeper and deeper into the softness of the sofa. Back and forth, back and forth the room swayed.

***

In an instant, my walls pulsed violently around his tongue as I came to a delightful climax. I felt the warmth of my wetness ooze from deep within and flow onto the tip of Marcellus' tongue. He squeezed my cheeks—in and out—as he eagerly partook each drop of my feminine juices, moaning with pleasure, welcoming each drop. Mercy!

My femininity was raw from the pleasure that Marcellus had given me. I eased away from him and sat up in bed.

He reached for me.

I pulled away.

"What's wrong?" he asked.

I didn't answer.

He reached for my right calf, but I tucked it closer to my body. "What's wrong?" he asked again.

My body began to quiver. A strange, warm energy engulfed my being as I stared deeper into his dark, dreamy eyes. It began as a tingling sensation at the crown of my head that radiated through every cell of my body. I lay there on my back in the softness of the lavender-fresh, white, cottony sheets.

From the corner of my eye, I noticed that a bright, white sunbeam had eased its way through a crack in the large white French doors to the right of the bed. The walls—well, what I could see of them—were all antique-white. The cathedral ceiling was also antique-white … it was freezing cold, but the gold-trimmed, white ceiling fan directly overhead spun ever so quietly, cooling the blistery passion that filled the air. The scene was serene, peaceful and safe.

I let my back fall deep into the many large soft, white, lavender-scented pillows that lined the tall mahogany headboard. I curled my knees into my chest, crossing my legs in front of me. The temperature in the room began to rise, as the sun showed more of its brilliance.

Marcellus was lost in the plush white comforter that covered most of the bed. Only his head, arms and chest peeked through. With one stroke of the arm, he threw the comforter to the floor. A smirk crossed his face as he crawled closer and closer, not once taking his eyes off of me. His manhood stood at attention as he neared—closer and closer—until his body completely blocked the sunbeam from view.

He put his arms on either side of me, his fists plunged into the pillow where I rested. The warmth of his body radiated an indescribable sensation: a strange cool sensation, yet at the same time tepid and soothing. His hardness tickled my leg, up and down, up and down.

Marcellus reclined on one elbow next to me and let out a loud, teasing moan, letting me know that he craved complete satisfaction from me. He looked up at me as he stroked my crossed legs with his free arm, which sent balls of fire through my very being.

I uncrossed my arms and slid down to be near Marcellus. I combed his thick, black hair—beginning at his navel and up to his nipples—one hair at a time, untangling each strand with my fingers; my nails caressed his bare skin. Yumm!

I turned him on his back, then twirled my tongue around each of his nipples, making them harder and harder, while reaching for his hot, throbbing cock and squeezing it gently in my hand.

Marcellus reeled me in with his arms and looked deep into my eyes before engaging in a long, hot passionate kiss. His mouth completely covered mine, as his tongue reached the depth of my throat.

I continued to squeeze and tease his cock, making it ever so hard.

He ran his hands all over my back, as though I were dipped in oil. He parted my legs and thrust his finger deep inside. "Ooo," he moaned between kisses. "You're so wet!"

In that moment, I so desired to have Marcellus deep inside me. "I'm sooo wet because you make me sooo hot, Marcellus," I moaned in his ear as he kissed my neck. I moved my hips to the rhythm of his finger—in and out, and around and around—while continuing to stare deeply into his eyes. Mercy!

Still on top, I reached for his cock, desperate for penetration. I don't know what I did that for, but he made me pay for it! Marcellus cradled me in his strong, masculine arms. In a single move, he turned me on my back. By the look in his lust filled eyes, he was even hungrier for me than I was for him.

I opened my legs.

By the expression on his face, he beheld all my feminine glory. "Ummm," he moaned as he rubbed my clit between his fingers. Not once did he take his eyes off me. Mercy!

It seemed like every nerve ending in my body was rerouted to my clit.

As he neared closer and closer, I combed his chest hairs with my fingers.

With one hand, he tried to enter me.

I was too tight to penetrate.

He tried again and again, each time with a bit more force.

I had begun to feel sore, so I pushed him away. It actually hurt! "Ouch," I yelled. "That hurts, Marcellus." I couldn't believe that it actually hurt ... in a dream!

He paused for a moment. Was he too afraid of hurting me again? By the look in his eyes, he so desperately wanted the experience to be pleasurable for both of us.

"I'll be right back," he said. He backed away from me then got out of bed. He disappeared through an archway to the left that led into darkness. A soft white light flashed on, followed by the sound of running tap water.

I plopped back on a pile of lavender-scented pillows and covered myself with the comforter. Just then, a violent gust of wind blew the French doors open, filling the room with the scent of wild jasmines. A faint symphony of birds sang melodiously in the distance.

The wind whistled through the air, banging the French doors against the walls.

The glass panels on the doors will break. I rushed out of bed toward the doors, the gentle breeze tousled my hair as the sun's warmth caressed my bare skin.

Beautiful! The French doors led to a cream colored marble veranda lined with tall white marble columns that overlooked a plush landscape of rolling hills below.

I need a robe. Where is a robe? I asked myself, realizing that I couldn't go out on the veranda in my nakedness. I started for the bed to take one of the sheets for cover. *No, wait.* I reasoned. *This is a dream. No one is out there looking at me! This is my world!*

I headed back to the veranda with all its splendor. The coolness of the floor beneath my feet sent a chill through my body. The vast beauty of that strange, new place was unlike anything I had experienced before: the vibrant colors of exotic flowers; singing birds that mimicked lilting melodies of flutes, oboes and saxophones; mellow yellow sunlight against a periwinkle sky abundant with bright, white clouds.

I realized that I was looking into the valley where I had first entered the dreamland … when I saw Marcellus for the first time as fleeting images of paint.

A gust of wind blew through the trees, screeching far away. It started as a faint whistle, but grew stronger and shriller with each gust. Stronger and louder the noise grew, echoing louder and louder as it came closer and closer …

***

The phone rang and suddenly I sprang out of the sofa into the air. "Hello," Percy said in the next room. Shame on Percy for decorating her condo in such dreary, awful colors. Goodness! That's what made me drift off to sleep like I did. She had a sofa, love seat and reclining chair all done in genuine black, imported Italian leather. Straight ahead, soft melon draperies adorned the sliding white French doors leading to the patio. Soft melon wallpaper with dark melon borders lined the antique-white walls. The white tiled ceiling brightened the room a little, but not enough.

I looked at the mahogany Grandfather clock in the corner as it began to chime. *Eleven o'clock! It can't be eleven o'clock*, I thought. But it was.

I walked to the bedroom and gathered my things. As I passed Percy's room, I heard her telling someone that I was all right. It must have been Letitia.

Percy had placed my belongings in a large Bed & Bath shopping bag. They were freshly laundered and neatly folded.

I retrieved my shoes and put them on. I figured that I would just keep Percy's things on, especially since she had taken the time to wash mine. I headed for the door. As I reached for the knob, Percy came up behind me.

"Where do you think you're going?" she demanded.

I slowly turned to face her. She made me feel like a teenager who was sneaking out of the house at midnight.

"You could stay the night until you're feeling better," she said. "Letitia just called to check on you. She's been worried about you and has been calling every hour to check on you."

"I'm fine," I told her. "I've just been putting in a lot of hours at work. It's just starting to catch up with me. That's all. I'll be fine."

I smelled coffee brewing, not just any coffee, Mr. Chap's coffee. I know his coffee anywhere. I turned around and went straight to the kitchen.

"What's that?" I asked. "Is that the coffee I bought from Chap's yesterday?"

"Yes," she said as she poured some in a *Chap's* plastic thermal cup with reclosable lid. "I thought that you would need some coffee to wake you up, so I brewed some. That coffee brewer you gave me for Christmas last year came in handy after all," she said. "Something just popped into my head that you would want some of Chap's coffee, so I brewed some." She repeated herself; that was Percy's way of making sure she had her way. In this case, that was her way of saying, "I went through all this trouble to fix a pot of coffee and you're going to drink it—even if I have to make you."

I was a bit annoyed that she had gone into my bag, but at the same time I was glad she did. Percy lived two blocks away from Lenox Mall and my office building. Since Chap's was still open when I left work on the way to meet Percy and Tish, I just couldn't resist stopping by and getting some grounds. Mr. Chap threw in two thermal cups for free. What a sweet man! The bag was small enough to put into my purse. Well, I carry a large purse, so I just kept it in there the whole time.

I decided to finish two cups of coffee before heading out. Percy didn't get any.

"Have a cup, Percy," I insisted.

"No," she said. "I don't like caffeine. It irritates my stomach."

I finished the last drop of coffee, rinsed my cup, then headed for the door again.

"Well," Percy said as I opened the door. "Drive safely."

As I walked down the hall toward the elevator, the paisley-print wallpaper seemed more brilliant than before. The pattern almost seemed to have jumped out at me. The sconce fixtures shined a soft orange glow, which brought out deep sienna hues in the walls. The gold elevator doors were shinier than usual, almost like mirrors. My feet sank deeper and deeper with each step I took in the plush, royal blue carpet.

I stood there admiring the hallway. The elevator bell startled me because it sounded so loud, almost like a gong, knocking me out of my fascination with my surroundings.

As I got on the elevator, the music was so soft and uplifting. I had never noticed it before. I listened so intently that I almost forgot to press *P3* to go to the parking deck. The gold railings that lined the elevator car contrasted nicely with the mahogany wall paneling. I nestled in the corner, looking straight ahead as the red digital light beeped each time it passed a floor on its journey down to the parking deck.

Another giant ding sounded as the indicator light read *P3*. A gust of air flooded the elevator car as the door opened. It felt so refreshing, almost as if its intent was to wipe away the stress from the past few months.

"Good evening, ma'am," a security guard said, startling me. He wore a gray uniform with a black security stick attached at the waist.

I gasped for a bit before catching my breath. *This building has security on every floor. Thank goodness!* I thought.

He was young, maybe twenty-one, twenty-two. He looked like real good security too. He had coarse blond hair; thick, busy, blond eyebrows; and he was clean-shaven except for that long, bushy, blond beard. He wore a white T-shirt under his uniform, but about three inches of busy, blond hairs peeked over the top button. His eyes were medium brown; the pupils were almost fully dilated.

"I didn't mean to startle you, ma'am," he said. "I'm just doing my rounds."

"That's all right," I told him as I continued to my car.

As I passed the glass-enclosed station straight ahead to the right, I noticed textbooks scattered about the white countertop. Another guard, also young, tilted his hat as I passed by. He was doing what looked like homework. He had deep ebony skin, a large Afro and his hands were covered with long, thick, black strands of hair. They were both probably college students who wanted a job that allowed them to study. *Hairy bodies must be in with young college folk today*, I thought.

As I neared my car a few yards away, I noticed all those station monitors that changed to different scenes of the building every few seconds.

I got in my car, fastened my seatbelt, started the engine and immediately inserted your *Sounds of Sea* tape, Dr. Iverson. My head was pounding as I drove out of the parking lot. I decided to go to one of the nearby twenty-four-hour pharmacies to get some aspirin and Pepto Bismo for my stomach. *That cheesecake must have really been rancid,* I thought.

What a combination, huh? Aspirin and stomach medicine. Meanwhile, the *Sounds of Sea* tape, with its crying seagulls and ocean waves, soothed my spirit for the time being.

Peachtree Road in Buckhead was deserted! After midnight on a Saturday night in September! As I waited for the traffic light to change, several small white pieces of paper were blown through the air. Around and around they swirled until they landed on my windshield. The giant waning gibbous moon filled the night sky. The stars looked larger than usual and were the size that the moon usually was. They sparkled brightly; each twinkle of light beamed against the glass skyscrapers as I drove by, almost blinding me.

The moon and stars almost seemed to have been following me. Every turn I took, they were on my tail, flashing in the rearview mirror. When I changed lanes, they inched along behind me, glaring in the distant sky. As they got closer and closer, the glare became brighter and more intense. I felt the smoldering heat radiate against my neck …

Chapter 7.
Say Good-Bye

I was blinded by the sun's rays peeking through the bright, white clouds above the veranda. I stood alone, admiring the deep green rolling hills of the valley below. Millions of flowers were everywhere—swaying to the wind's rhythm—blowing hither and tither. Just then, a giant black bird with a yellow beak flew just overhead. It had crimson-red feathers and a long black tail painted with thin royal blue stripes. Tiny yellow dots covered the underside of its wings and belly.

As I turned to go inside, I bumped into Marcellus.

"Are you playing hide and go seek?" he asked.

He was completely nude. I stood there, admiring him with all his splendor. He had a body of a man who visited the gym and lifted weights. His slender frame, with all those hard, toned muscles from head to toe, made my body quiver. The soft black hairs that covered his chest, arms and legs contrasted nicely with his soft caramel skin. I couldn't resist running my fingers through every strand. His long, hard muscle stood at attention as though it were longing for my gentle touch.

I watched with anticipation as Marcellus emptied a small vile of clear jelly in his cupped hands and began to rub it all over his hot, throbbing cock. He began at those big brown balls, then worked his way up to the shaft, then to that big red, swollen head.

A smirk ran across his face, as a ray of sun shined on his magnificent body. Marcellus was the star performer, and the spotlight was on him. From what I could tell, he was ready, willing and able to please his audience. And his audience longed for pleasure.

He came closer and ran his sticky fingers through my hair. We gazed into each other's eyes as he stroked my lips with his tongue, then nibbled my cheeks down to my neck and back again. Next thing I knew, we were engaged in a hot, passionate kiss unlike any I had ever experienced before that time. Our tongues twirled endlessly around the other, pausing for quick breaths of air. I was so hot and so wet as he held me close with those strong, masculine arms. The warmth of his body and his hairiness sent me into a tizzy. Mercy!

Marcellus kissed every inch of my face, down my neck and breasts. My nipples stood at attention as Marcellus twirled his tongue around one, while pinching the other with his thumb and index finger. Balls of passion shot to every cell of my body. I craved him more than ever.

In one quick move, Marcellus swooped me into his arms and placed me on the edge of the thick stone guardrail that surrounded the veranda. With one arm still wrapped securely around my lower back, he spread my legs with the other arm. His oiled hardness slowly penetrated the depths of my womanhood. He slowly moved in and out, in and out, inch by inch until my walls completely devoured him.

He thrust all the way in, then slowly pulled out. All the way in he inched, then slowly withdrew all the way out in strong, calculated bursts. The ride became more slippery as his cock stroked and pulled my inner lips all about with each entry. He rotated his hips around and around—all the way in and all the way out—until he was completely in. Then, he withdrew his hardness. Mercy! By the look on his face, he looked as if he'd longed an eternity for my wetness.

It felt so good to be with a man at long last, even if it was a dream. I felt loved and protected in Marcellus' arms, feelings that I had never experienced before. He was so warm, so tender and so loving. I felt a profound sense of love emanate from his body as he held me close to his heart.

My womanhood was so tight after being celibate so many years that it was as if I were gripping Marcellus' manhood with a strong vise.

His lips hung loose; his face was tight. I knew that Marcellus struggled to contain his raging fire and fought desperately to stay in control.

I closed my eyes and wrapped my arms around his neck and legs around his waist, holding on for dear life. His rhythm ignited unbridled passions that dwelled deep within me. I felt myself tighten and release continuously from within, as I moaned deep and hard from the gut. I was completely lost in Marcellus' strong arms.

I released my legs from around his waist and placed my feet against his hips, which sent Marcellus plunging deeper into my murky waters. The cool breeze that caressed our bodies brought with it the scent of sweet wildflowers. Melodies of birds played continuously in the distance. I felt as one with nature making love to Marcellus in the great green forest of no man's land. At that moment, my inner walls pulsed violently and uncontrollably against his cock, as I felt two warm streams gush from deep within me.

Marcellus' gait hastened. His heart pounded faster and faster, and so did he; in and out, around-and-around, deeper and deeper. He began to moan like a wild animal on the prowl to satisfy its ferocious appetite. He took my bottom in his hands and rotated me to his beat—in and out, around and around—over and over again. The sea of life that dwelled deep within him erupted. "I love you so, much," he moaned in my ear as he held me close. He continued to hold me tighter than ever until his hardness was no more, repeating "I love you so much. I love you so much."

Judging by the look on his face and the quick hardness of his manhood, Marcellus became instantly aroused when I jumped down from the guardrail, and a giant stream of come oozed down my leg. He began to rub it on my legs—up and down, up and down. He gazed into my eyes, then stroked his fingers against my lips.

I sucked each of his fingers and licked every bit of our juices from each one. It was salty and slimy, but all so stimulating.

He began to rub my legs again, that time taking a big clump of come and rubbed it on my lips. He licked it off as we engaged in a deep, passionate kiss.

A gentle breeze blew against our bodies, as the sun's brilliance shined on us from the morning sky.

In one swoop, he brushed me off my feet and into his arms. He carried me through the open French doors and into the bedroom. He cradled me in the middle of the bed and hovered over me with a sinful look on his face.

He walked to the front of the bed and began to crawl slowly toward me.

"Are you ticklish?" he asked as he ran his fingers on the soles of my feet.

I jerked away and sat up giggling. "Yes." I laughed. I tried to tuck my feet under the covers, but he uncovered me and threw the covers to the floor.

He began to tickle my feet again. "You can't hide from me, Didi."

I pulled away giggling again. "Stop, Marc!" I laughed. I laughed harder and harder as he tickled me more and more. I think he got a kick out of it.

"Why should I stop?" he asked.

"Because," I started between laughs, "it tickles."

"You know how the tale goes, don't you?" he asked as he stopped. He continued to hold my right foot in his hands, and started playing with my toes.

I looked him straight in the eyes. "What tale might that be, Marc?"

"The one that says that the key to finding your erogenous zones is to find where you are the most ticklish," he said then licked the sole of my right foot.

It sent chills through me. "Oh, yeah," I moaned as I gazed deep into his dark, dreamy eyes.

"Yeah," he said as he caressed my calves. "You have pretty toes."

"Why, thank you," I teased then touched his nose with my big toe, then slid my foot close to his lips. .

"Such soft, pretty toes," he said. He took my foot in his hands and sucked each of my toes, then ran his tongues between each one. He gently kissed every nook and cranny of my foot. The warm moisture of his mouth made me wetter than ever.

I ran my fingers through his thick black, wavy hair, as he moaned with pleasure.

He stopped for a moment, looked at me and said, "Playing with my hair turns me on, Didi. You keep doing that, you'll get yourself in some serious trouble."

I just smiled at him.

He kissed my ankles, calves, knees and worked his way up to my inner thighs.

I slid down on my back.

Marcellus combed his fingers through my moist pubic hair. He parted my lips, then ran his tongue up and down and around my clit. Over and over again, he tantalized my womanhood until I cringed with delight.

He caressed my clit with his fingers with one hand, while he stroked my breasts—one by one—with the other. He eased his middle finger into my twirling vortex, while I quivered in delight.

"You're sooo, wet," Marcellus moaned as he looked into my eyes.

"That's because you make me so hot, Marcellus," I said in a crackling voice, then reclined on the bed. I spread my legs far apart, giving Marcellus clear view of my red swollen clit. "Forget making love to me," I said. "Just fuck me. Fuck me *real* good!"

***

Oh my!

What's wrong? Dr. Iverson? Why are you so shocked? It was *my* dream, *my* fantasy. If *I* want to talk nasty and want to be talked nasty to, then … oh well!

***

Anyway … Marcellus grinned for a moment, then spread my legs even farther apart. He took my left foot and ran his tongue between each of my toes and carefully sucked each one. I never knew that my toes could give me such pleasure. He kissed every inch of my sole ever so gently, then proceeded to my ankle, calf, around my knee, and up to my inner thighs, where he nibbled and sucked, and nibbled and sucked. Mercy!

"Oooo," I moaned. I tried in vain to pull his head to my clit, but Marcellus just chuckled. I yearned for him to satisfy all my womanly desires—real or imagined.

I went into a frenzy when he licked my outer lips and delicate, black pubic hairs. He slid his lips around my inner lips, then nibbled my clit.

Marcellus moaned as he twirled his tongue around my red, swollen clit. He paused for a moment and looked me deep into my lust-filled eyes.

"Don't stop!" I pleaded as I pulled his head closer. My womanhood became hard and erect in anticipation of the next kiss.

"You want me to fuck you?" Marc asked. He raised to his knees and balanced on his fists, one on either side of me.

Those words sent shock waves through my body. I felt myself getting wetter. I just looked at him without saying a word.

He asked again, only more demanding, "Do you want me to fuck you, Didi?"

Again, those words sent shock wave through my body. I didn't answer. I lay there helpless, looking into his lust-filled eyes, wanting him more and more.

He put all of his weight on his knees and sat back on the bed. He began to rub his cock, up and down, as the veins popped up more and more.

"Until you answer me," he said as he rubbed his cock more fiercely, "you won't get any of this dick."

"Yes," I said then reached for his cock, but he pulled away.

"Yes, what?" he moaned as he continued to stroke his hot, juicy cock.

"Yes, I want you to fuck me, Marcellus," I said then spread my legs and reached for his cock once more.

"I didn't hear you, Didi," he said. That time he bit his lower lip and swung his head back while he continued to stroke his hot, juicy cock.

I was afraid that he was about to come so I blurted out, "Yes, Marcellus, Yes! I want you fuck me!"

He looked at me with his cock in his hand. "I'm a freak, baby," he said as he looked deep into my eyes, "and I love to fuck!"

He got down on his hand and knees and rammed his tongue in my soaking-wet cunt with one long, calculated stroke, as my entire body trembled to ecstasy's tune. Then, he straddled me, looking down at me with a smirk on his face.

I lay there, shaking like a leaf in the autumn breeze, waiting for his gentle touch. In a flash, Marcellus eased his long hard cock inside of me. Even though we had made love only moments before, my womanhood was still so tight from being dormant so many years. Marcellus took his time.

"I love you sooo much, Demeter," he moaned soft and low in my ear as he glided deeper and deeper within me.

Those words opened a floodgate that dwelled deep within me that welcomed him into my loins. That's what I had been missing all those years. I had been in lust, but not in love. I just had sex. I had never made love until that time. I submitted myself completely to Marcellus—mind, body and soul.

His stride was deep and slow, as I wrapped my legs around his waist. "Umm, ummm!" he panted, almost like a wild animal. "Uuhh, uhh!" His stride increased as the life force deep within him could be contained no more. He collapsed by my side, then held me close in him arms. He gently kissed my hair and my forehead, then held me even closer.

Birds were chirping in the background as the sun's rays became brighter and brighter. The chirping became louder and louder to point that I could stand no more.

"Marc," I said as I tugged on him. "Close the door. The birds are singing too loud."

Marcellus had fallen fast asleep and wouldn't budge. I tried to shake him again but he wasn't there. I looked all about the room, but he was nowhere in sight. I even checked under the sheets and bed, yeah, like he could have hidden there, but no sign of Marcellus. I almost panicked, but realized that he was only a dream, a figment of my imagination.

How do I wake myself up? The chirping is just too loud, I thought.

As I neared the French doors, I was blinded by the sun's rays. It had instantly become so bright that I had to close my eyes and feel for the doors to close them. The chirping had become unbearable. I wished it to go away; it was so loud. The sun had become so bright that I turned away from that direction and closed my eyes. That didn't work because the sun was becoming more intense with each passing second. I felt its heat baking on my skin. With my eyes still closed, I fumbled around the comforter that Marcellus had thrown to the floor. I stumbled back into bed and covered my head, but to no avail. Even with my eyes closed and the comforter over my head, the sun was still too bright to bear. I covered my ears with my hands and closed my eyes tighter than ever, but the birds got even louder and the sun became more intense.

It was becoming brighter and more intense, and the birds chirped louder...

* * *

In an instant, I was sucked into a black void, falling from great heights. A tapping noise jolted me back to reality. The tapping became louder and louder. The sounds of birds dissipated, but the sun was brighter than ever.

I lay flat on my back. "Turn the lights off, Kevin," I said. "Turn that TV down! I'm trying to sleep!" I was annoyed that he didn't comply, so I decided to do it myself.

My heart began to race as I opened my eyes and sat up. I panicked because I was flat on my back, stretched across the front seat of my car, with my legs bent. I looked straight ahead when I sat up and was startled to see two police officers standing next to my car.

One was average height with a thick, dark moustache and dark hair. It was so dark outside that I didn't notice much else about him. I couldn't make out the other man. His back was facing me, and he was twirling his hat around his finger.

My heart had begun to race faster and faster until I could actually hear each beat. *Oh, oh,* I thought. *I must have been in an accident.* The last thing I remembered was that I was headed toward an all-night Drug Emporium or CVS to get some medicine ... *I think.*

I turned on the ignition, then pressed the automatic window to open it. With cars nowadays, the ignition must be on the do anything.

"Are you feeling all right?" a female voice asked.

As I looked around, bright lights were everywhere. I heard the echos of two-way radios nearby, probably from one of the police cars. Just then, an ambulance pulled up just ahead of my car. The scene started to sway as everyone and everything faded into a giant sea of color, then back to normal; to a sea of color, then back again. I batted my eyes a few times, still disoriented, then everything became clear.

The officer started speaking to me again, but her words were slurred and garbled, as if she were speaking in slow motion. My heart raced faster and faster. An eerie nervousness crept along my spine, then radiated out to my arms and legs. I began to tremble something terrible.

In a flash, the back door of an ambulance flung open and two EMT's pulled a stretcher of sorts onto the ground. I was blinded by the lights from the interior of the ambulance, so I closed my eyes.

Someone opened my car door and took me by the arm. I couldn't see who it was because my eyes were still closed.

"We're taking you to North Carolina Baptist Hospital," a female voice said.

"Is there anyone you want us to call?"

"What ..." I tried to speak, but the words couldn't quite get out.

I noticed bright lights everywhere. It was if the area were closed off.

"Hospital?" I was puzzled and my heart started racing faster and faster. "What ..."

"We were passing by," the male officer said, "and saw you parked on the side of the road, hurched over your wheel. We tried to get your attention, but you wouldn't answer."

"Didn't seem like you were breathing," the woman said in her Southern drawl. "We called for the paramedics. We didn't know what was going on."

I saw another car pass to the right as the two officers who were attending to me waved them on. I panicked even more when I saw *North Carolina State Patrol* written in blue letters across the car.

"It's right down the road there," she said and pointed straight ahead. "They're really good."

"What happened?" I finally squeezed out.

"We got word of a car parked on the side of I-26 near Asheville. You wouldn't budge and didn't seem to be breathing, so they called us," she said in that southern drawl.

I-26? How did I get to I-26? What is I-26? Is that a real road? Asheville? I must be lucid dreaming again. How do I wake up? I thought.

"Was I in an accident?" I asked as I got out of the car. I noticed the male officer on the passenger side. Apparently he got my registration and insurance card out of the glove compartment, and my license from my purse compartment because he was calling it in over his two-way radio.

"No," the woman said. "You were just sitting there. That's why we think you should let the paramedics take you to the hospital to make sure you're all right."

The scene started to sway and I began to feel light-headed. The two paramedics brought the stretcher nearer and tried to put me on it. I pulled away.

"No!" I said. "I'm all right."

"We have the paramedics here and they can take you to the hospital," the female officer insisted in that whining, squeaky drawl. "I wouldn't feel right leaving you alone out here. It may be a good idea if you go to the hospital."

I was still confused and didn't know what to think. *Was I working too hard?*

"Well, if you won't go in the ambulance, at least let me take you in our car," the female officer insisted. She probably noticed that I was trembling something awful because she had a concerned look on her face. "You don't look like you're in any condition to drive."

"OK, OK!" I agreed.

I remembered getting into the front seat of the police car. I blinked for a second, then all of a sudden I was in a bed covered with a white, heated blanket. An IV was in my arm with two bags attached to an IV pole: one bag was filled with a clear solution that read *Dextrose*, and a smaller bag contained a white, cloudy solution. A nurse entered and injected a syringe filled with a clear, white substance into the IV joint nearest my wrist. It hit my bloodstream instantly because in a matter of seconds, a warm, tingly sensation quickly circulated through my body; it went from my arms, legs to all over. I actually smelled and tasted its minty tinge as it circulated to my nose and mouth.

"Phenobarbitol," I think the nurse said, then she left.

There were some gadgets attached to me to monitor my vital signs. I realized that I was in a hospital room wearing a blue-and-white gown tied at the back. The heart monitor to my right sounded like those chirping birds. The light overhead was so bright, but I was so groggy that I didn't care.

I was feeling queasy as the room twisted around and around, then returned back to normal. I must have been administered a tranquilizer because nothing fazed me.

It was a small, private room. To my right, I noticed an opened door that led to a small bathroom. The walls and floors were tiled in white. A white basin was next to the door, and a mirror lined in silver was directly above it. To the rear was the white commode. Next to that, white shower curtains revealed the shower/bathtub combination, which was partially hidden by the wooden door. Fred Price preached from the TV overhead in the left corner of the room.

I heard people talking outside of my room. Then, Percy walked in with a concerned look on her face. The doctor was by her side. *What is Percy doing here?* I asked myself.

"Hi, I'm Dr. Dewey," the woman said.

Something seemed familiar about her. She was tall with a soft olive complexion and low-cut hair. She flipped through my chart without looking up and said, "You gave us quite a scare."

Where do I know her from? I asked myself. Then it dawned on me. I remembered her from one of my first lucid dreaming experiences. Yes! That's it! She was Nurse Dewey on the aircraft when I cut my arm. Her hair was different as Dr. Dewey though.

***

Thinking back, she looked like a woman I saw in your office one day, Dr. Iverson.

***

I started to panic, but whatever medicine they pumped into me quickly quenched my fear. *She's a colleague of Dr. Iverson,* I tried to reason. *Maybe I met her before. That's why I dreamed about her.*

***

Did I meet her in your office before, Dr. Iverson?

What happened next, Demeter?

Did I meet her before?

Maybe …

When?

Anyway, Demeter. Try to stay focused. What happened next?

But …

Stay focused, Demeter. You can't solve your problem by focusing your attention on the irrelevant.

***

Percy sat in the lime-green leather chair next to me. She carried a tartan-print flask and put it on the table beside her, then began rubbing my hands. She had a concerned look on her face. "I got a call early this morning from the Police Department. I had panicked, especially after getting a call earlier from …" She stopped and a concerned look crossed her face. I didn't think much of it, but looking back, I should have pressed her for more information. But then again, I didn't know that there was any other information to press for.

"I'm glad you gave the police officers my number, sweetie," she said. "Everybody always calls me when there's trouble," she grumbled under her breath, then sighed.

I didn't recall telling anyone to call Percy. But I was so out of it, I very well could have. At that time, I had a hard time remembering my own name and phone number, let alone anyone else's.

Percy said in a concerned granny voice with a New York accent, "Victor is downstairs in the coffee shop."

Percy moved away to New York after college and just picked up an accent. How about that?

"Victor?" I asked. "Isn't he supposed …"

"He'll drive your car home, while you ride with me, sweetie," she said and stroked my hair away from my face. "Victor would be here, too, but you know how he hates hospitals. That's why he's downstairs in the coffee shop and not here. Don't take it personal, Didi."

"Yeah, yeah," I said.

Just then, I noticed a large digital clock in the right-most corner of the room above the door. In big, bold, red letters against a black background was the time—*12:15. It's afternoon?* I couldn't believe it.

"What time is it?" I asked Percy.

The doctor froze in her tracks when I asked the question. She and Percy stared at each other for a bit, then at me.

"It's a little past noon, sweetie," Percy said.

I just stared at her without a word, without any expression. It was noon, but it was still dark when the officers took me to the hospital. My world was slowly falling apart and out of control. There wasn't anything I could do about it.

"I'm referring you to a colleague of mine in Atlanta," the doctor said as she clicked her retractable pen and began writing on a white pad. "Have you ever had panic attacks before?" she asked while continuing to write.

"No," I said. But I should have told her about the recent episodes that I had experienced. I was hesitant to say anything because she and Percy probably would have thought I was crazy and would have sent me away to the funny farm for sure.

She handed me the paper. Then I noticed your name and number, Dr. Iverson, before Percy took it away from me. *I knew it! I must have seen her in Dr. Iverson's office,* I thought, *or maybe at one of her seminars.*

"I want you to see Dr. Iverson," she said. "From what your sister has been telling me ..."

I looked at Percy and she looked back at me like the cat that had just eaten the canary. *I wonder what she told the doctor?*

"... you've been working too hard and you're probably stressed," the doctor continued. "I suggest that you rest for a few weeks and take it easy. Please see Dr. Iverson when you get back to Atlanta.

"You were dehydrated," the doctor said. "You rest here for another hour or so. Finish your breakfast," she smiled then pointed toward the IV, "then, your sister here can take you home." She walked to me and smiled. Percy looked up at her. "Just take it easy. I've seen plenty of cases like yours where women will just work and work and stress themselves out. It's just stress. Just relax, take a few weeks off," she said and patted my arm, "and you'll be fine," then smiled. She gave me two more prescription sheets, but Percy took them away from me. "Take these sedatives in the meantime until you can get an appointment with Dr. Iverson," she said then left.

"You really need to take better care of yourself," Percy said in that *caring grandma* manner. "I'll look in on the boys this week, okay, sweetie? When do they come home from their trip?"

"Tomorrow afternoon at about three o'clock," I said.

"I'll take off tomorrow and sit with you. I'll be waiting at the school at three. I'll keep you company and cook or clean or whatever."

"Fine," I said. I agreed because I didn't feel up to arguing with her. She was quite stubborn at times.

"By the way, Didi," Percy said, "what were you doing in North Carolina? I thought you were going home? Were you going to see a new boyfriend or something? Are you holding back on me?" she teased.

I was still groggy, because I didn't get excited when I tried to remember how I got to North Carolina. I didn't answer.

"Well?" Percy tried to probe.

I gave her a blank stare because I honestly didn't know. She waited in anticipation for an answer.

"Well?" she asked in excitement.

"Well, what?" I asked back.

"Well, who is he? In fact, where is he now?"

Why does she think that everything a woman does, especially if it's drastic or irrational, relates to a man? I thought. *If I weren't so groggy, I would be very annoyed with her right now.*

"Well," I said, "that's for me to know, and for you," I pointed my finger deep in her arm, "to find out."

She laughed then took the gray remote control with all its little square, black buttons on the table next to her and changed the TV station. "I wonder what else in on? Oh," she said with excitement. "I almost forgot." She reached over to the table for the tartan flask, unscrewed the black top cup and black inner cap, then poured something into the cup. As she handed the steaming cup to me, the aroma was unmistakable. It was Mr. Chap's coffee. I took a sip ... then another ... and another.

"Ummm," I said, then drank the rest. Percy poured more into the cup.

Am I supposed to be drinking this in the hospital? I thought. But I didn't care. I couldn't go one day without Mr. Chap's coffee. That's why when he started to grind and package the beans and sell them, I bought two packs a week. I bought two more that Saturday when I went in to work.

"I thought that you would want some," Percy said. "So, when I received the call, I realized that you hadn't taken the pack of coffee that I brewed last night. So I just brewed a little more this morning, put it in this flask, and came on out. I didn't make it as strong as I did last night, though, since it's morning and all."

Doesn't Percy know that that she's supposed to make coffee stronger in the morning? I thought. Then I realized that Percy wasn't a coffee drinker and probably didn't know any better.

The doctor left the door halfway open when she left. It must have been visiting hours. I saw doctors and nurses dressed in scrubs walking to and fro; visitors carrying flowers, plants, teddy bears and other goodies for their loved ones; then, I saw a shadowy figure coming down the hallway toward my room, slowly putting one foot in front of the other. The corridor was dark and dim; it was almost indistinguishable from the shadows that lined the walls, as it went against the flow of traffic.

It paused for a few seconds outside of my door, staring at me almost. I saw that it was an old man carrying a tattered, brown bag; wearing a tattered, brown suit; wing-tip shoes and an old brown hat with a black rim. *The old man from Underground Atlanta,* I thought. *It can't be. Maybe it's just someone who looks like him.*

"What's wrong?" Percy asked. She looked at me, then a worried look crossed her face. She looked toward the door. "What are you looking at, sweetie?" she asked.

"That old man," I said. "Tish and I saw him at Underground Atlanta. That's the strange old man I told you about."

Percy looked to the door again. "What old man?"

I looked to the door, but the old man was not there. *I've been working too hard,* I thought. *I probably do need to rest.* That was just another old man.

The room began to sway. Percy was laughing at a cartoon or something on TV. Her laughs became as echoes, like the ones you hear in horror movies, as I felt myself fading away. The room swirled into a giant sea of color, one blending into the other. Back and forth it swayed. I closed my eyes, but still saw the colors moving before me ...

***

I was resting on a soft white throw rug near a raging fireplace, securely wrapped in the warmth of Marcellus' arms as we looked deep into each other's eyes.

"I've waited so long to take you into my arms," he said then licked my lips, "and make hot," he kissed my lips, "hot," followed by another kiss, "passionate love to you."

I was lost in his arms as our tongues intertwined in a quiet interlude for what seemed like forever. I ran my fingers through his chest hairs as he held me near and dear to his heart.

It was the room near the patio where he had proposed marriage to me only days ago, a fixed point in time and space of all that's eternal. It was dark, but a hint of the setting sun peeked through a tiny crack in the French door to the rear. All was still and calm as the raging, orange and white fire crackled through the eve, radiating its heat to every corner of our glorious abode. It was our world. I was queen, and Marcellus—with all his valor—reined as king.

Marcellus turned me over on my stomach, then lifted me onto my hands and knees. The next thing I knew, he had slid his big, juicy cock inside of me. Mercy!

In and out he slid, bringing balls of fire to every cell of my body. I followed his stride and rotated my hips to the rhythm of passion's beat. The ride became more and more slippery for Marcellus as I arrived at ecstasy's door time and time again.

He teased and tantalized my rear, squeezing it in and out as if he were kneading bread dough, giving it an occasional slap. I welcomed his index finger into my back door as he continued his stride.

Marcellus began to moan hard and long from the gut, as he pounded me deeper and faster.

"Uhhh!!" he moaned. "Uhh."

I felt the sea of life flood my loins once again, but that time it was different. It felt warmer than before, almost like steaming water. My insides felt tingly, as if I had douched with mentholated oil. We lay there in each other's arms, admiring the fireplace. The tingling sensation increased until it felt like menthol bubbles were festering in my lower gut.

We spent the night talking and laughing about everything and anything right there in front of the fireplace, admiring the nudity of the other. Marcellus poured us glasses of tikti as soft jazz played in the background— piano, saxophone, and trumpets. The tingling still didn't go away. I must have looked worried, because Marcellus had a concerned look on his face.

"What's wrong?" he asked.

"You must have really socked it to me, Marc," I moaned, "because I feel so tingly down there," I said then rubbed my pubic hairs.

He smiled and looked to see my *down there*. He took a sip of tikti and reached for me. I thought that he was going to stroke my public hairs, but instead, he rubbed my belly, looked at me, then smiled. He rubbed my belly again, that time not just with his fingers, but his entire hand.

"What's wrong?" I asked. "Does it inflate your masculine ego to know that you satisfied me to the nth degree?" I laughed as I rubbed his chest hairs.

"That too." He smiled, then finished his glass of tikti.

"What?" I asked.

Marcellus became more playful.

"Oh nothing, nothing," he said with a laugh.

I poked him just below his rib cage.

He cringed.

"That tickles," he said.

I poked him again and again. Each time he laughed and tried in vain to stop me. Then, he grabbed me, reclined on the rug, and rolled me on top of him. We looked deep into each other's eyes, as he gently removed my hair out of my face.

The golden flames from the fireplace brought out delicate hues of brown in his eyes.

"I love you so much, Demeter," he said then pulled me even closer.

Those words pierced the depths of my soul as I gazed hypnotically into his dark, dreamy eyes. I felt the warmth of his hands against my ...

***

I fell from great heights and was jolted in my seat as a nurse rolled me toward a set of glass, automatic doors straight ahead. It was getting dark outside. *Probably no more than two hours of sunlight left,* I thought. I was right because the big, black digital clock on the *Information* desk to the left read *4:30*. I saw Percy standing beside her car. She opened the door as the nurse pushed me through the second set of glass doors—the ones that led outside.

I was still a bit groggy, but I noticed that I was dressed in the same Braves T-shirt and biking shorts of Percy's. *Whatever,* I thought. I just wanted to get home and get some sleep.

Percy and the nurse helped me out of the wheelchair and into the car. It was a long drop down getting into that teeny-weeny, two-seater sports car. I had become so accustomed to the high seats of my sedan.

Percy thanked the nurse. They talked for a few minutes, about what I didn't know. The nurse handed her a few white pieces of paper—*prescriptions I guess*—then she got in on her side.

"How are you feeling, sweetie?" Percy asked.

"Fine," I said.

"I'm going to take real, real good care of you," she said while she ran her hand up and down my thigh, trying to calm me. That's what she did after Great-Gran and Great-Aunt Ruby disappeared, and when my mother left us. She also did it after I had given birth to Keston and Kevin and I was aching after the surgery; and when what's-his-name and I divorced. It always soothed my nerves. "Don't worry about a thing," she said.

***

I was still groggy when we began our three-hour drive back to Atlanta from Asheville. All was still and quiet except the revving of the engine. Percy's wild driving didn't bother me. Even when I looked out the window and discovered that a good portion of I-26 was on the side of a cliff, separated by thousands of feet from the ground below, I remained calm.

It was dusk on a cool, breezy fall eve. We were high in the Appalachian Mountains. The sky looked so crisp and clear from that altitude. The sun appeared as a large, glowing, orange ball sitting over the western horizon, struggling in vain to fight back the darkness of night. What a beautiful scene, but I was too medicated to enjoy it.

Percy stopped for gas right after we merged onto I-85 South headed to Atlanta.

"I'm going to pump some gas, sweetie," Percy said as we pulled up to the BP station.

The bright, green and yellow sign was a welcome sight to see. Especially since the low fuel indicator had been blinking for the past fifteen minutes or so.

"Di ..." Percy started.

I was deep in thought, very relaxed. So, she startled me when she tapped on the window.

"I'm sorry to startle you, sweetie," she said. "I'm going in to the store to pay for the gas now," she said almost in slow motion, as if speaking to a small child. "Are you going to be all right, sweetie?"

I just stared at her and shook my head yes.

"I'll be right back ... okay?" she said. Again, she spoke slowly and deliberately as if she were speaking to a toddler.

"Do you want me to bring you anything back, sweetie?"

I stared at her again, then shook my head no.

"Do you need to use the restroom?"

I stared at her, then shook my head no.

"Are you sure, sweetie?" she asked again.

I just stared at her without as much as a blink. I was too tired and groggy to argue with her.

Percy finally started for the store. She took a few steps, then glanced back; took a few more steps, then glanced back. Once, she almost turned back around, but decided to keep going.

The convenience store was about twenty feet from the pumps. Glass windows lined the front, giving clear view of aisles of shelves stocked with snacks and such. To the extreme right was the cooler section with sodas, milk, and beer, and to the rear was a large, bright blue sign with white stick figures. I believe that was the restroom. Bright lights were everywhere—outside, inside, in the cooler—and gleamed against the white floor.

I heard two more cars pull up to the pumps. I had always paid close attention to my surroundings—every sight, sound and smell. But that night, I just didn't care, so, I didn't bother to look around.

What's taking Percy so long? I wondered.

I heard footsteps behind the car. Soon, a young man wearing a blue T-shirt and baggy blue jeans appeared. He retrieved money from his wallet and headed for the store. Then, I heard another set of footsteps. That time, it was an older gentleman wearing a dark colored suit. As he got closer to the store, he looked like the same strange old man from the hospital and Underground Atlanta. He wore the same brown, tattered suit, wing-tip shoes and brown hat with a black rim.

"Are you ready, sweetie?" Percy asked.

I was so engrossed with the old man that I didn't notice Percy leave the store.

"I don't believe it!" she exclaimed.

"Yeah, that's him, isn't it?" I asked. I thought that she was excited because she remembered the old man from the hospital too.

"That's who, sweetie?" she asked.

"The man from the hospital. It's him!" I told her.

"What man?" she asked.

"The one going into the store," I said.

Percy looked in the direction of the store. "There's no one in the store that I can see," she said.

The old man had vanished. Again.

"Let's get you buckled up, sweetie," she said. "I can't believe that I let you ride all this way without wearing your seatbelt!"

She reached over and pulled the strap across my shoulder. After she secured it in place, she gently and slowly rubbed my thigh, looked me in the eyes and said, "Everything will be all right, sweetie. Percy is here to take real good care of you now." She smiled, gently kissed me on the cheek, started the ignition, then sped off. "When we get back, sweetie, I'm going to get you settled in," she said. "Then, I'm going to go to the all-night pharmacy in Kroger to get your prescriptions filled."

I shook my head in agreement.

The rest of the ride home was pretty much uneventful. I must have slept the whole way. I remembered being at the gas station one second, blinked my eyes, then all of a sudden Percy had pulled up into my driveway at home.

"While you were sleeping," Percy said, "Victor called me on my cell phone. He'll keep your car overnight and bring it back tomorrow before I go get the boys from school tomorrow. Then, I'll take him home."

I shook my head in agreement.

We went in through the front door. I immediately kicked my shoes off, then turned on the outside light.

"I'm going to Kroger's to get your prescription filled, sweetie," Percy said. "Why don't you go upstairs and get some rest. Are you going to be okay until I get back?"

"Unnn," I grumbled as I started up the stairs. I waved her on.

"I'll be right back," she said. "Just rest yourself."

The front door slammed. A few seconds later, I heard the sound of screeching tires and a revving engine. Percy was gone.

I was still slowly making my way upstairs, one step at a time. An intense feeling of fatigue overtook me as I struggled to put one foot above the other. I finally reached my bedroom then flicked on the light. My digital alarm clock flashed *8:45*. *Good to be home*. I went into the bathroom and started the shower...

***

"You're still tired," Letitia said.

Tish? Where did she come from? If I weren't so groggy, she would have startled me. I assumed that Percy must have called her over. I was too tired to care. *The more the merrier.*

Everything was blurry. *Either I need glasses or that sedative is affecting my vision,* I thought.

"You need help with your clothes," she said.

Somehow, I was wearing a clingy, knee-length, sky-blue V-neck T-shirt dress.

Letitia began at the knees and inched my dress all the way off over my head. She did the same for my black, lacy slip.

I started to unclasp my black, lacy bra.

"No," Letitia insisted. "Let me."

Letitia unclasped my bra, then turned me around to face her. She slid both hands inside of my black, lacy panties and slid them all the way to the floor. For some reason, she looked more youthful. She looked a few pounds lighter too.

I twisted my hair in a bun, then put on my shower cap and entered the shower. The warm cascading water felt so relaxing.

"I need a shower too," Letitia said.

I looked behind me and Letitia was standing in the shower with me—completely nude.

"Besides," she said. "You need help."

She took my washcloth from me and lathered some liquid body wash. Letitia began at my ears, down my neck, back and arms. She turned me around the face her, then proceeded to wash my breasts, stomach and belly button. For some reason, she kept going back to wash my breasts over and over again.

She washed my private parts with much care, down to my legs and feet. She took the shower nozzle and rinsed me off.

"My turn," she said.

I lathered more body wash into the same towel. Beginning at her ears, I washed down to her neck, back, arms, front, private parts, legs and feet—all very quickly. I had never noticed her body before, but her breasts were like big, water-filled balloons. I wanted to play with them so badly and rub soap all over them, teasing and tantalizing. But I didn't. I wanted her to tease and tantalize my tits too. But she didn't. Her skin was so soft and supple, and her body was ever so sensual. I didn't know what to expect or what to do, so, I took the shower nozzle and quickly rinsed her off. I turned off the water, opened the shower stall door, and grabbed a towel from the rack. *Enough naughty thoughts! Shame on me!*

"Let me dry you off," Letitia said. She patted my ears, neck, back and stomach. I thought that it was my imagination, but when she reached up to my breasts she gently squeezed each one, focusing the most attention to the nipples. She dried my legs and feet. Then she ran the towel between my cheeks, back and forth, squeezing gently until my loins started to crackle. Next, she dried my pubic hairs and tried to go further.

"No." I stopped her. I didn't want her to feel my wetness. I was sooo naïve. *What would she think?*

I followed suit and dried her off. Quickly.

Letitia led the way to the bedroom. Watching her sensual stride—that large, shapely, firm rear switching left and right and around—made me want to grab her from behind and knead her bottom like fresh bread dough.

She jumped into the middle of the bed.

I followed suit.

She retrieved a small bottle of spearmint and eucalyptus lotion from her purse, which was on the nightstand next to the bed.

"Lie on your stomach," she instructed then took a heaping handful of lotion.

She began massaging my neck, down to both arms, and every inch of my back.

I noticed a pause.

"Lie back down," she said as I looked around to see why she stopped.

She took another large handful of lotion. That time, she rubbed it all over my rear and began to knead. She took one cheek in her hands—one near the hip and the other in my crack—massage me up and down and around and around until I thought that I was on fire.

Chills ran up and down my spine with each touch. I became wetter when she massaged the other cheek. The moisture that oozed from deep within me began to crackle. My rear tingled with satisfaction.

She paused again and took another handful of lotion and began to massage my legs and feet and then she stopped.

I looked up, anxious to see her reach for the lotion again. She didn't. I turned around on my back to face her.

"You have such pretty titties, Didi," she said as she ran her hands across my breasts. "Can I suck them? I'm just a stickler for big, juicy titties and can't resist wanting to suck yours. I've always wanted to suck your titties, Didi. May I? Please."

"OK," I said. *Shocking*!

She twirled her tongue endlessly around one nipple, as she fondled the other.

I felt my heart race faster and faster, as the scene became very heated. I didn't know what to make of it and was completely surprised by Letitia's actions. *She couldn't resist breasts? Since when?* I never knew that side of her until that night.

She slid her hand down my belly and began to rub my clit. Thrilling!

I was becoming quite excited, to say the least. Confused, yet excited nonetheless.

"You're sooo wet, Didi," she said while sucking my breast. "I've always wanted to suck your pussy. I want to make you come. May I? Please."

The next thing I knew, she had spread my legs and started to lick my clit. I had never been with a woman before. *Are you going to let this woman have you?* I asked myself. When she twirled her tongue up and down, and around and around, I told myself *Yes!* It was so thrilling, being nude in the midst of sinful desire with Letitia. We had taken our friendship to another level, which made the experience that much more pleasurable.

Letitia nibbled my inner lips up and down, and licked up, down, and side to side, faster and faster. The hardness of her tongue made my womanhood cringe with pleasure. The goodness was unbearable; I trembled uncontrollably as I violently reached the peak of ecstasy.

She spread her lower lips, spread my lower lips and got on top.

The feeling of her hot, juicy clit rolling around and around on mine was unlike anything that I had ever experienced before. I squeezed her big, firm rear, running my fingers up and down the crack, as I danced to the beat of passion. We engaged in a long, lusty kiss. Our tongues twirled around and around each other. Fireballs began in my clit and pulsed all through my body. I had always heard that a woman's clit has the same sensation as the head of a man's cock. *This must be the way a man feels when he's with a woman,* I thought. *No wonder men crave women sooo much.*

Letitia rolled faster and faster, and she kissed me deeper and hungrier, almost like what a man would do when he's about to come. I was right.

"Uhh, uhh, Didi," she moaned. "Your pussy is so good. I'm about to come, Didi. I'm about to … Uhh! Uhh!"

The thought of giving another woman pleasure unlocked a secret passageway to my body that I never knew existed. The passion that dwelled so deep within me exploded. I began to jerk and tremble, as my inner walls contracted strong and hard, releasing a stream of liquid from deep within me. *This must be the way a man feels when he comes.* I thought. *What a hot, sexy feeling!*

Letitia collapsed beside me. We cuddled in each other's warmth. I wrapped my arms around Letitia's soft, supple body. I couldn't resist resting my head against one of her tender, cushiony breasts. The nipple was so firm and erect that it tickled my ear. I was at peace—satisfied. Slumber was upon me, so I gently closed my eyes.

I heard the front door slam downstairs followed by keys being slung onto the table in the foyer. I quickly fell from great heights, hitting rock bottom as my lungs quickly filled air.

***

Heavy footsteps started up the stairs. *Oh no!* I was alarmed. I assumed that

Keston and Kevin had arrived earlier than expected from their trip and that they got a ride home with Coach. *What would the boys think if they caught me in bed with Letitia? They probably saw her car parked in the driveway.* I was panic-stricken to say the least. *Maybe they'll go to their rooms and go to bed right away and never see us.*

The footsteps were at the top of the stairs headed toward my room. The door was open. I always left it open. There was no time to escape or think of some clever lie. *I'm busted!*

"Hey, sweetie!" a voice said. It sounded if though it were muffled and in slow motion. "I got your prescriptions filled."

The sound of rustling paper bags echoed through the room and made the loudest, most annoying sound, almost like clapping symbols.

"Sorry it took so long," the voice apologized. "The pharmacy in the Peachtree City Kroger was closed. I had to go to the one in Union City."

I was still groggy. Whoever was in the room didn't seem bothered by Letitia and me being in bed together and just ignored us. *Who busted me? Percy?*

I opened my eyes. The room was blurry for a few seconds. I sat up, careful to cover myself with the blanket. I blinked a few times and things were still fuzzy. I looked at the clock and strained to see the big, bold numbers—*9:45. Thank goodness for bright digital clocks with red, large numbers.*

"Here's some water to take your medicine, sweetie," the voice said. "The label says that you should take this one twice a day. The other one you should take three times a day with food."

Whoever was in the room still didn't seem to care that I was in bed with Letitia. Is this person trying not to embarrass us? Why didn't Letitia say or do anything? Wasn't she embarrassed?

The phantom put the water on the nightstand next to the clock. It took all the strength I had, but I reached for the water. *Oh no!* Reaching for the water meant that I could no longer cover myself with the blanket. So it fell.

"Those are the cutest pajamas," the voice said. "Tartan is my favorite print."

Pajamas? I thought that the phantom was looking in my closet. Then, I looked down. In my blurriness I saw that I was wearing my flannel tartan pajamas. *How did I get pajamas on? When did I put pajamas on? Wait a minute ... something's strange here,* I thought. *I have to reach over Letitia to get to the water, so ...*

I looked down. Things were still blurry. I blinked a few more times, and all was clear.

I had been hugging my pillows, not Letitia. What I thought was a nipple was the pointed edge of one of the pillowcases. *I must have been dreaming,* I thought.

I looked up. *Percy?*

"Are you feeling all right, sweetie?"

I snatched the white paper bag from her.

"What's wrong, sweetie?" she asked.

I looked at the prescription label and receipt on the bag —

Kroger Pharmacy, Jonesboro Road, Union City, 17:30.

So, that meant that the prescription was filled at about nine-thirty. It was about nine-forty-five, and it took about twenty minutes to get from my house to the Union City Kroger. The receipt said nine-thirty, which meant that she paid for it at about nine-thirty. She probably had to wait a few minutes for the prescription, so that put it at about nine-fifteen. If she went to the Kroger in Peachtree City before that, it would have taken about twenty minutes. I got home at eight-forty-five. So, that meant that she left at about maybe eight-forty-five. That couldn't be because Letitia and I spent about ten minutes in the shower, then maybe another thirty or forty minutes embodied in passion.

"Here," Percy said then opened one of the bottles. "Take your medicine, sweetie."

I swallowed that bitter, pale-blue pill. That was unlike me to take medicine without knowing what it was for. But I didn't care. I did it anyway.

Something else was strange. Percy wore a baseball cap earlier, which meant that her hair wasn't curled. But as I looked at her, it didn't seem like she had been wearing a cap at all. Her hair was bouncy and curly the same as it was after a visit to the beauty parlor. In order for her 'do to look that nice, she would have had to blow-dry it then curl it. She lied to me! She didn't really go to Kroger in Peachtree City. She spent that extra time washing her hair in the downstairs bathroom, blew it dry, then curled it with my curling iron. She probably used my shampoo and conditioner too.

A strong sense of rage engulfed me when I thought of her using my blow dryer and curling iron without my permission. I darted out of bed and straight for the bathroom. Percy was right behind.

She had the gall to use my blow dryer and curling iron without telling me!

"What's wrong, sweetie?" she asked in that concerned voice of hers. "Perhaps you should get some rest."

I searched under the sink frantically.

"Can I help you find something, sweetie?" she asked. "Just tell me what you're looking for."

"My blow dryer!" I said. "Where is it?"

"Your blow dryer?" she repeated.

"I know that you used it Percy," I said. "Where is it?"

"Wha …" she started to say something.

"My curling iron," I said as I searched. "Where is it, Percy? I know you used it. Where the fuck is it?"

I went into the bathroom, but it was clean. It didn't smell of burning hair, but I thought that she must have used it downstairs or in the boys' bathroom down the hall. The bathroom was cool and dry, as if I hadn't taken a shower all day.

I reached for the towel bar. The towels that I used were folded, fluffy and dry—the same as they were before I had taken the boys to school that Saturday. I always put the used towels in the towel basket in the laundry room after using them. I've always hated dirty towels around the bathroom. *Maybe Percy or Tish put fresh towels on the rack,* I thought.

"I didn't use your blow dryer, sweetie," Percy said. "But I'll help you find it."

"What!" I was still trying to figure out why fresh towels were on the rack. Percy's comment quickly jolted me back to reality. "You fuckin' bitch," I got in her face and screamed. "I know you used my moth' fuckin' curling iron! Where the fuck did you put it, bitch! Did you put them in your moth' fuckin' purse, you moth' fuckin' 'ho'?"

My anger exploded to the point where I slapped her a few times. "Where the fuck is my fuckin' curling iron." I slapped her again, that time she hit the wall. I grabbed her by the hair, and she struggled to get away.

"Stop it, Didi," she pleaded. "You're not well! You're not well! Just take it easy, go sit down, and take your …"

"I'm sick and tired of you telling me what the fuck to do, bitch! Who the fuck put yo' tired, fuckin' ass in charge any fuckin' way?"

I pushed her away.

By the expression on her face, I had frightened her; she started to breathe heavily as fear crossed her face.

I threw everything out of the cabinet and onto the floor. Buried in the back corner was my curling iron. It was cold and the cord was wrapped neatly around the wand. Dust had started to settle on it, as it hadn't been used in months.

"See Didi," Percy said as she tiptoed toward the door, almost as if to escape from some sort of hostage situation. "It was there all along," she said with a nervous laugh.

I looked away for a second, and Percy was gone. I looked around the bedroom, hallway, but still no Percy. I ran back into the bathroom. Letitia was standing directly behind me. She startled me because I almost ran into her.

"Where did Percy go?" I demanded of Letitia.

She didn't answer.

"Where were you when Percy came back?" I asked Letitia. "Do you think she caught us?"

"Caught us?" she asked. "I stepped into the bathroom for a second," she said. "I better let you get some rest now," she said, then tried to leave the room. "I came to say good-bye. It's time for me to leave now."

Her hair was curly and bouncy like she had just stepped out of the beauty parlor. She didn't wear a shower cap into the shower, so her hair shouldn't have looked that nice … not so soon anyway. *She used my blow dryer and curling iron too!*

"Your hair is nice and bouncy," I said as I pulled one of the curls.

She brushed my hand away.

I was livid. How dare she have her way with me then leave! Wham, bam, thank you ma'am! *Ain't it bad enough when a man does it, but not one of your long-time friends,* I thought. My heart was hurting. "Where the fuck do you think you're going?" I demanded as she tried to head out of the bedroom door. I grabbed her by the arm and pulled her back. "Do you think that you can bring yo' ass up in here and fuck me, then go 'bout yo' business? Who the fuck do you think I am any fuckin' way?" I pushed her a bit as she inched to the door. She looked frightened. "You think I'm some moth' fuckin' 'ho' or something'? Huh, bitch?"

"Didi," she said nervously. "You're not well. Just take your ..."

Letitia tried to get away. I pulled her by the hair.

"You're hurting me, Didi," she said. She was beginning to get mad. "Let go!"

I pulled harder and tighter.

"Who the fuck you think you fuckin' talkin' to, bitch?" I asked her.

"You're hurting me," she said.

"Now you know what it feels like to be hurt. Comin' all up in here, fuckin' wit' me, then leave. What the fuck you take me fo', huh bitch?"

She elbowed me in the stomach. That hurt, so I released her. I was really pissed. She grabbed her purse off of the nightstand, then began to run downstairs.

I ran after her, madder than ever. Before she could get all the way down the stairs, I pushed her to the hardwood floor below. There were only two steps left any, so it probably didn't hurt her ... right, Dr. Iverson?

Her keys fell out of her purse, so I grabbed them before she could pick them up.

I pulled her off the floor by the back and tore the red suit that she was wearing.

When she tried to get to her knees and run away, I punched her in the back of the head. My knuckles hurt. I was so angry at her; the rage burned deep inside of me. The thought of Percy or Letitia using my blow dryer and curling iron ran through my head. I had had them since college, and no one else ever used them except me. How dare they touch them! Then, to top it off, Letitia was trying to take advantage of me. I was so angry that I punched her again, and again. The thought of Percy using my things and Letitia using my body really irked me.

She tried to fight me off, but I had overpowered her. "Don't you ever," I said as I punched her in the face, "ever," followed by a right to the left cheek, "touch my moth' fuckin'," a left to the right cheek, "stuff again," followed by a right to the left eye, "do you hear me, bitch!"

She kicked me off with her knees, as I hunched over in pain.

That really ticked me off.

She tried to head for the front door.

I picked up my favorite lamp in the foyer on the table next to the door and banged it over the back of her head. She fell to the floor before reaching for the knob. The room went pitch black. All became quiet and still; it was almost like being in a black void.

I felt myself spinning faster and faster; my heart began to race.

"Percy!" I yelled. "Letitia!"

No answer.

"Percy! Letitia!" I yelled frantically. Still no answer. My words echoed over and over, *Percy, Percy, Percy, Percy, Letitia, Letitia, Letitia,* like being in a cave. The sound of my voice echoed louder and louder in my head. I tried to feel my way around the room, but it rotated faster and faster and faster ...

***

"Wake up, sweetie, wake up," a voice said. "You're having a nightmare."

I again found myself in the midst of a big, black void falling from great heights to the great bottomless pit below. Air quickly filled my lungs as I took one long breath. My heart raced with lightening speed as I came to.

I blinked and rubbed my eyes a few times until my surroundings were crystal clear. Percy was standing over me wearing the same baseball cap that she wore to the hospital. I looked at the clock on my nightstand and *9:50* blinked in big, bold numbers. *Was I dreaming about fighting with Tish?*

Percy sat down next to me and looked away. Tears welled in her eyes. A concerned look crossed her face like something terrible had happened. I knew for sure that I had hurt Tish by hitting her with a lamp and that I wasn't dreaming.

"Where's Tish?" I asked Percy. "Is she going to be all right? Is she going to be all right?"

"Wha ..." Percy tried to get out, but I interrupted her.

"I didn't mean to hurt Tish, Percy," I said as I sat up in bed. "I didn't. Is she going to be all right?" I was still heavily sedated, so feelings of remorse or sorrow didn't enter my bones ... not exactly.

A look of shock overcame Percy, and she looked even more concerned. She put her head down. It was if she wanted to tell me something but couldn't quite get the words out. Then, I knew for sure that I must have hurt her really badly with the lamp. I had hoped that that didn't mean the end of our friendship. *Perhaps I'll take her on a shopping spree,* I thought. *That should do the trick.*

Percy started to get up, but sat down beside me on the bed again.

I sat up to face her. I noticed that I was wearing my tartan print flannel pajamas. I looked to the nightstand. An empty glass and a bottle filled with pale-blue pills were behind my clock, pure evidence that I had taken my medicine.

"Is Trish hurt?" I asked.

"But how d ..." Percy asked, a bit surprised.

"I hit her in the head with the lamp in the foyer," I said. "I'm so sorry," I cried.

Percy stumbled a bit through her words until a coherent sentence finally came out. "Lamp?" she asked. "Wha ..." She laughed as the surprised look melted from her face.

"The one in the foyer," I said. "I accidentally hit her in the back of the head with the lamp. I smashed the lamp and the room went dark. The pieces crumbled in my hands. I really liked that lamp, now it's broken. I got it last year when I went to Ghana. It can't be replaced."

"Sweetie," Percy said in that granny voice again, "your lamp is still downstairs. You must have been dreaming. Tish wasn't here tonight."

I just stared at her without as much as a blink. "She wasn't?" I asked. "How do you know. You were at …" She cut me off. I hated it when she did that!

I tore away the comforter, jumped out of bed and ran straight into the hallway. I could see the lamp shining through the banister so I knew that I didn't hit Tish with the lamp. I was so relieved that I had not hit Tish. But I was troubled that my dream seemed just as real as being awake. *Must be the medicine*, I reasoned, but I knew that those little blue pills couldn't have kicked in so soon. *Could they?* I stood there at the top of the stairs staring at the lamp.

"What's wrong, sweetie?" Percy asked as she tugged my shoulders in the direction of the bedroom.

"Nothing," I said, then walked back to the bedroom and eased into the comfort of my bed. My loins were still moist from my time with Tish. I reasoned that that too, was a dream. But I never, ever imagined being with Tish or any other woman. Where did those desires come from? Were they buried deep in my subconscious waiting to be unleashed?

"Sweetie," Percy said as she stroked my hair, "Tish wasn't here tonight."

"But …" I tried to get out, but she interrupted me again.

"Tish wasn't here tonight," she said as she stroked my hair and looked me straight in the eyes like a mother does when she's tucking a child in at bedtime. "Okay, sweetie?"

Percy covered me with the comforter and gently kissed my forehead. By the look in her eyes, something was troubling her. I thought that she was worried about me. Well, yes, she was indeed worried about me, but something else was troubling her. She carried a heavy burden; it was a secret that she fought hard to conceal from me, and a truth that cut into my sanity sharper than a hunting knife. Both our worlds were falling apart. Percy the Great was helpless and out of control for the first time in her life. That was scary since she was my pillar of comfort in time of need. Maybe if she would have told me what had happened, her burden wouldn't have been so heavy. I still resent her for protecting me like she did. Didn't Percy know that secrets like that come to light sooner than later?

Chapter 8.
Dare to Wish Upon a Star

I slept like a log that night and dreamed the most fascinating dream. All was hazy, like a foggy, overcast day, but only indoors. Mellow sounds of piano echoed softly in a background of garbled voices. The air was thick like sudsy bubbles, and staticky. Specks of tiny, white lights filled the air as the scene became clearer.

"Marc, Didi!" a voice echoed from behind. "I'm glad you could make it. Come!"

I felt myself floating across a room, but I couldn't feel my body. Other faceless phantoms continued to speak, but each appeared as a blurry blob of paint.

Slowly, I began to feel my body as the room became clearer. The tingly sensation in my loins that I felt during my last lucid experience was still with me.

"Let's dance," a voice said.

I looked to my left, and it was Marcellus. He was ever so handsome in a black tuxedo. The matching black cummerbund and black bow tie gave him an air of distinction.

I followed Marcellus' lead to the black-and-white, diagonal tiled dance floor. As we waltzed, I admired the scene around me. We were in a ballroom. Straight ahead toward the front of the room was a stage with red-velvet curtains lined in metallic gold. In front were several large, round tables with formal table settings. A busy red, black and navy print Berber carpet adorned the floors—well, except for the floor to the rear, which was diagonal, black-and-white tile. To the right were buffet lines, each attended to by a helpful server. To the right of that was the bar. A large crystal chandelier hung from the center of the room. What seemed like hundreds of people all clad in formal attire were everywhere. Several couples danced beside us, while others chatted or walked around.

"Oh," I yelled and caught the attention of nearby giggling couples. I was startled because something moved inside of me. It was in the same spot where I felt the bubbles. *They're laughing at me,* I thought. *Wait. This is a dream. It doesn't matter if they're laughing or not.*

Marcellus smiled then reached down to touch my belly. When he did, I realized that I looked as if I were about five months pregnant. I was so busy admiring the scene, that I didn't even notice myself. I was wearing a short, black evening gown. I reached up to touch my hair, and it was done in a French twist. I looked down, and I was wearing low-heeled pumps. I never wore shoes without heels, except when I was pregnant with Keston and Kevin.

I felt it move again. That time, Marcellus felt it too.

"That's our little bundle of joy!" he said then smiled at me.

The look in his eyes emanated a deep sense of love for me as a wife and the pride of being a new father. That's something I never experience being pregnant before, but longed for.

He took my hand and we walked among the myriad of people to what was our table. A small white sign read—

President and CEO - Mr. and Mrs. Marcellus Angellel

A waiter dressed in a black-and-white checkered uniform approached our table as we sat down. He looked a bit odd, but it was a dream, so it didn't matter. *Did it?*

He was tall and slim. His facial features were normal, you know, ordinary lips, nose and ears. Nothing special. But his eyes were round like circles, not oval like almonds. Something else was strange too. Large, crinkly circles surrounded his eyes. They reminded me of an elephant's eyes. I looked into them, and was almost hypnotized. The irises were medium brown with what looked like a glass film over the top, kind of like the eyes of a dog. He had no pupils either.

Though he appeared young, his skin had a grayish-brown hue like that of Mississippi River mud. It was thick with deep creases all about his hands, arms and neck. I took a second look and smaller lines criss-crossed his face.

"Two glasses of tikti ..." Marcellus stopped, then looked at me. "No, one glass of tikti and a glass of water for my wife."

"Yes, Mr. Angellel," the waiter said.

Far into the corner, I saw what looked like Trevor. He was scrubbing the floors on his hands and knees. His head hung low, almost as if he were ashamed of something. A few other people, probably his bosses, yelled degrading remarks at him.

"You bumbling idiot!" one of the men yelled. "Can't you do anything right?" His voice was rather loud to the point where one of the headwaiters went to him and whispered in his ear, probably for him to be quiet. The boss grabbed the Trevor figure by the arm, dragged him to his feet, then kicked him in the butt as they left the general area.

I looked on in horror as my heart went out to him.

"Can't find good help these days," Marcellus said with a laugh.

"I know that's right," another voice laughed behind us.

"Adonis," Marcellus exclaimed as he jumped to his feet to greet his friend.

"Adonis, meet my wife, Didi, and our new baby," he said, then patted my belly. "Adonis is my brother."

I turned to greet him and was shocked. It was … well it looked like a younger version of the old man from Underground Atlanta and the hospital.

"Good to meet you, Didi," he said as we shook hands. His shake was firm and strong, and he looked me in the eyes—a sign of leadership, supposedly. "And you too, baby Angellel," he said as he looked at my protruding belly.

Adonis sat to our right.

"Echo won't be joining us tonight, Marc," Adonis said.

"Echo?" I asked. I immediately thought of Percy. *Her middle name is Echo.*

"My wife," he informed me.

"Oh," I said.

"Well, hello, Marc!" a voice said from behind me. "Good to see you!"

"Hey there, Cynthia," Marcellus said. "This is my wife, Didi. Didi, this is my assistant, Cynthia Dewey."

"Hello, you must be Didi," Cynthia said in a flat tone. "Good seeing you."

Now where have I heard that name before? Then, I realized that Cynthia Dewey was the doctor's name who treated me in Asheville. But, she looked a bit different—a few years younger and a few pounds lighter. She wore her hair different than *real* life. There in the dream, her hair was low-cut, almost like a man's. And she wore no makeup, not even lipstick. Her nails were cut short with no hint of polish, not even clear polish. She wore a tuxedo, complete with pants and cummerbund.

We shook hands. I was surprised that she knew who I was. Well, it was a dream after all. And she looked at me so intently, so much so that the other guests had odd looks on their faces.

"Cynthia takes good care of us," Marcellus informed me. "She's tough as nails too."

"I'll probably see you guys later," Cynthia said. She blew a kiss at me before going to her table.

The lights began to dim, and the announcer came on stage. Everyone listened attentively. I was too awed by the scene to really pay attention to what was going on. Next thing I knew, the applause went to a roar as people stood to their feet. Something about man of the year, then Marcellus tugged my shoulder—my hint to join him on stage.

It was wonderful. All the people were applauding us, smiling at us as we approached the stage. Our table was so close to the stage that we didn't have to walk far. I looked out to the audience as the applause quieted down. All the smiling faces, all the attention made me feel like a queen. Little did I know how true that statement was—and still is.

***

To feel like a queen is every woman's fantasy, right Dr. Iverson? What happens when a fantasy comes to life?

***

Marcellus took the podium, and I stood in the background. He cracked a few clever jokes, and the audience laughed each time. *What a brilliant speaker*, I thought because he had captured the attention of all. For each word and action Marcellus took, the audience gave an equal and pleasant reaction. But I didn't hear a word he was saying. *What a perfect man,* I thought. *Good speaker, CEO, wealthy, smart, talented, handsome and an excellent lover. What more could I ever want?*

He motioned for me to join him at his side. The audience went into an uproar and stood once more. The lights began to dim—softer and softer—gradually fading to absolute darkness. All became quiet and still. What started as a faint buzz grew louder and louder, shaking the background into a thunderous roar. The air thickened. I was overtaken by an eerie staticky sensation that penetrated the very depth of my soul. I tried to call out to Marcellus, but the words were trapped deep inside, unable to form. I reached for him in the midst of darkness, but my body was weightless, as I drifted aimlessly through the night sky. The buzzing got louder and louder, piercing every cell of my being. Louder and louder it became, unbearable almost. Louder and louder ...

***

A warm, thick substance surrounded my feet. I sank deeper and deeper, struggling in vain to escape. My heart raced faster and faster as I was being pulled deeper and deeper.

Someone grabbed me from behind, trying desperately to rescue me. It was pitch black, so I couldn't see who it was. The harder my savior tugged to free me, the harder I was being sucked away until in an instant, the floor collapsed beneath me. I fell from great heights, taking that mysterious savior along for the ride. Its body clung to mine as we spiraled into the great deep, dark void below.

Air quickly filled my lungs as I hit rock. My body bounced in bed as though I had been dropped from the ceiling. But there were two thumps. Something else was hurled down beside me. My eyes were closed tight. I was flat on my back. That was strange because I never slept on my back.

A strange buzz ranged over and over in my head. I wanted to stop it, but I couldn't move. I tried and tried, but still, I couldn't move. My body was paralyzed. Something pressed firmly against my chest, pinning me down in bed. I couldn't move. I couldn't breathe. My breath was being siphoned away—whiff by whiff—by some mysterious force.

The buzzing became a little quieter, then I realized that it was my doorbell. Someone was adamant about waking me from slumber.

The room smelled of hickory-smoked bacon. It was that morning that I started to hate bacon. The smell made me sick to my stomach. If I didn't know any better, I would say that I was pregnant because that's just what it felt like—morning sickness. I wanted to cover my nose to kill the hickory-smoked aroma, but my limbs were numb.

A hint of light peeked through the curtains. Though my eyes were closed, I knew that it was the break of dawn. I wondered who was cooking that early in the morning—Monday morning at that. I heard cabinet doors open and close, and pots and pans rattling about. Between the sunlight and racket in the kitchen, my head was pounding hot and heavy. I wanted it to stop.

I mustered up all the energy I had and wiggled a pinky toe. A tingly sensation ran through my foot, pure evidence that circulation had started again. So I wiggled the other pinky toe. In a rush, some strange energy peeled away from inside my body, beginning at my feet, then gradually moving up my legs, thighs and loins. When it reached the center of my chest, it floated away gracefully, leaving behind a profound sense of peace and tranquility.

I slowly opened my eyes. What looked like transparent images of people were all about the room. Far in the distance were figments of trees surrounding some large structure of sorts. *Must be a mirage from sleeping in the dark, then having my eyes exposed to the sun,* I reasoned. Ghosts of pale-blue images moved to and fro. It was like looking at double-exposed negatives—only in real-time. I rubbed my eyes a few times and the room became clearer. The pale-blue images gradually faded with the break of sunlight. I dismissed the whole scene to just one more episode of sleep paralysis. Perhaps, I shouldn't have.

I heard voices downstairs followed by footsteps climbing the stairs. My head pounded harder with each passing thump, and my stomach churned tighter and tighter as the smell of hickory-smoke flavoring grew stronger. I tried to get up, but my stomach quickly reminded me that it—and not me—was in charge.

"Hey, sweetie."

I looked toward the door and it was Percy carrying a tray. She wore a pink-and-blue, plaid cotton nightshirt with white buttons down the front, white cotton socks, and pink bunny slippers. As she neared me, I noticed that her hair was pushed back into a ponytail decorated with a large pink ribbon. She looked so funny dressed like a high school girl in that get up. When I started to laugh, a tight knot suddenly shot through my stomach.

"I made you some breakfast, sweetie," she said in that whiny New York granny voice that was really starting to irritate me, especially early on a Monday morning. "Why don't you get up and go rinse your mouth out so you can eat."

How dare she tell me what to do! I thought.

She moved my alarm clock, which read *6:45*, placed the tray on the nightstand. *How dare she rearrange my things!* I thought. I really became sick when I looked at the platter of food—four strips of bacon; a stack of blueberry pancakes covered in thick, gooey maple syrup; grits with melting butter; ham, cheese and mushroom omelet; half of a toasted cinnamon-raisin bagel with a smear of cream cheese; home-made country potatoes and a tall glass of orange juice. Was she cooking for an army? Did she really expect me to eat all that?

The sight of pink and yellow really did me in: the rich, fluffy eggs; the melted cheddar cheese on top of the eggs; the butter that dripped from the grits with a remaining sliver in the middle. Yuck! And the pink! Percy's pink getup, the bacon strips and chunks of ham that poked through the eggs really did me in. Oh, it was just an awful sight! I could take no more. I dashed to the bathroom and straight for the commode. My stomach cramped really hard and strong.

Then, I realized that except for the IV in the hospital and medicine from the night before, I hadn't eaten anything since Saturday afternoon. I felt really sick, especially since the hickory-smoke smell just filled the air. I just sat against the wall next to the commode curled up in a little knot, too afraid to move.

"What's wrong, sweetie?" Percy asked. "Is everything okay?"

Does it look like I'm OK? I started to ask, but I just sat there on the floor and looked up at her without saying a word.

"We better get you to bed," she said as she lifted me by the arm. "You don't look too good, sweetie."

I got up and followed her back to bed. I was too sick and too tired to argue with her.

"No food," I mumbled.

"What?" she asked. "I didn't hear you, sweetie. Talk up."

"No food. Please, just move the food," I said.

"You need something in your belly," she said.

"No!" I insisted.

I sat on the side of the bed, trying hard to compose myself.

She cut a piece of omelet with the fork and tried to feed me like a baby.

I moved my head over and over again, but she still insisted on feeding me. The smell of ham and eggs so close to my face made my stomach cramp even more.

"I said no, damn it!" I finally yelled. I eased back into bed and pulled the comforter over my head.

"Well, all right," Percy said.

I heard a long sigh, followed by mumbling, so I uncovered my head and turned in Percy's direction. At that moment, I heard what sounded like thumps up the stairs.

"Did you say something?" I asked.

"No," she said with a sigh. "You really need to eat something, sweetie."

She left the room carrying the tray in hand. As she entered the hall, I heard her talking to someone. It sounded like a man's voice. I couldn't make out what they were saying, but I did hear Percy say *Didi.* Nothing else was coherent. The voices went downstairs and I could still hear them in the kitchen. Suddenly, two sets of footsteps neared my room. Percy came in holding those blue pills and a glass of water.

"I'm going to take Victor home," she said. "He came to drop the car off, now I have to drive him home. I won't be gone long, sweetie. There are bacon and pancakes downstairs in the kitchen. I covered them with aluminum, so they should keep warm."

My stomach started to feel better. But when she mentioned the bacon, it started to cramp again. Not as much though.

She opened the pill bottle and guided me to sit up. "Here," she said as he shook a pill out of the bottle and into my hand. "It's time for your medicine, sweetie."

Silly me! I was hoping that the medicine would have made my stomach feel better. So, I was a good little girl and swallowed the pill and full glass of water.

Percy stood there until I finished every drop, took the bottle of pills and empty glass with her, then headed for the door. "Oh," she said from the hallway, "I'm going to call your job to make arrangements for you to stay off for a few weeks. You've been working really hard. The doctor and I both agree that you need to take it easy, sweetie."

The doctor and I? I asked myself. *What doctor? The one from the hospital? The gall of Percy talking to the doctor about me without my permission! Isn't there some law against that?* I was too groggy to argue with her. Then it hit me... Victor! I just had to see who that Victor was. I mustered up all of my strength, forgot about my stomachache, and rushed to the hallway to see him. I caught a glimpse of him from the upstairs banister as he was leaving with Percy. He was tall, with dark hair and a soft olive complexion. He turned slightly to close the door, that's when I noticed that he wore black wire rim glasses. If I didn't know any better, I would have sworn that he was Dr. Daniel Batchelor, the scientist from work. But it was just a coincidence that they looked the same from above, behind, and slightly from the side. I ran back to my bedroom and peeked from the window, hoping to get a good look at him in the driveway. I caught a glimpse of him in the car as he and Percy backed out of the driveway.

He didn't seem like Percy's type. She liked tall, deep-dark chocolate men. Victor wasn't much taller than Percy, and she was five-nine. He definitely wasn't deep-dark chocolate, either. Come to think of it, Marcellus wasn't my type. I like my men, well ... the few that come my way ... the blacker the better. I still don't know why I even conjured him up. He was ... is ... was ... whatever, tall and athletic like I like, but he had ... has ... had ... whatever ... Mediterranean ... maybe pale Egyptian features. He had a soft olive complexion with a long, straight nose; full, pale lips; jet-black, wavy hair; and deep, dark ebony eyes. I never would have considered dating anyone with Mediterranean features, but he was a dream. Perhaps buried deep in my subconscious I desired someone like him. Maybe it stemmed from my trip to Italy in '92, or maybe he was what I imagined one of the gods would be like when my great-grandmother used to read Greek mythology stories to my sister and me. Marcellus seemed to be a mixture of Egyptian and either Greek or Italian—an image from a Michelangelo sculpture. Well, except that Marcellus was much better endowed than any statute that I'd ever seen. That's for sure!

***

I began to feel light-headed, so I went back to bed. Before I could pull the comforter over my head, I felt a hand on my shoulder. Someone sat beside me. *What does Percy want?* I turned to face what I thought was Percy. I was surprised because it was Letitia. She was wearing the same red outfit that she wore the day before. I looked her up and down. There wasn't a scratch on her. *Maybe I really did dream about hitting her.* I was relieved. *But did we really make love?* I asked myself. I was too afraid and ashamed to even hint such a thing to Tish. *She would be appalled if I were to ask her something like that,* I figured.

"Where did you come fro ..." I tried to ask.

"Shhh." She put her finger over my lips to hush me and stared straight in my eyes.

I assumed that she was with Percy and decided to remain behind.

"I'll be right back," she said then went into the bathroom.

I assumed that she wanted me to save my strength, and that she was there to take care of me. I was right. She wanted me to save my strength, and yes, she was there to take care of me. Kind of.

I looked up and Tish was standing before me completely nude.

She caressed her nipples, then eased her fingers down to her clit, rubbing it ever so gently. She pulled the comforter away from me.

I looked again, and I was completely nude.

Tish crawled into bed from the middle, slowly moving toward me. She placed her fists on either side of my shoulders, looking down at me with a devilish smirk.

We engaged in a long hungry kiss, our tongues danced around and around for what seemed like an eternity.

Tish paused, then kissed my lips, my face, my ears and my neck. She licked my hard, erect nipples one at a time, while she slid her fingers into my soaking-wet cunt. Yum!

She licked down to my belly button, down to my clit, where she rolled her tongue up and down and around and around, even better than Marcellus. Tish pinched my nipples with one hand, sending balls of fire rampant throughout my body, while she licked every nook and cranny of my femininity—my inner lips, outer lips—as she blew short bursts of air into my cunt before lashing her tongue deep inside of me. Mercy!

My womanhood was ablaze. I was a helpless victim of wanton lustful desires. I ran my fingers through Tish's hair, begging for more. My inner walls began to tighten, as the pleasure became unbearable. I began to tremble uncontrollably and came to a graceful climax.

Tish looked up at me with a smirk on her face, as a long stream of come dripped from her lips.

She looked so feminine, so ripe. I wanted her more than ever. That time, I was the aggressor.

I ran my fingers through her long, luxurious hair. It was so soft and silky to the touch."You're sooo beautiful, Tish," I whispered in her ears.

She just smiled. Tish looked several years younger and a few pounds lighter, just like the day before. Again, I reasoned that I probably I had never seen all her feminine splendor before. In that moment, I wanted to take care of Tish, give her the world and make her my lover and partner for life. She was the one for me.

I kissed her long and soft, holding her gently in my arms, feeling her very essence. I nibbled her ear lobes, her neck, then down to her firm, erect nipples.

She was so soft, so delicate. For the second time in my life, I knew what it was like to finally make love.

I blew into her belly button, making strange noises.

She giggled and giggled, just like a schoolgirl.

"That tickles." She laughed.

I kept blowing and blowing, and she just laughed and laughed. I enjoyed making her happy.

I paused as we stared deep into each other's eyes. Then I did it. I kissed, licked, and sucked every inch of her thighs, down her legs, her knees and her calves.

Tish moaned with pleasure. Her body was at my command.

I sucked each of her toes, and ran my tongue between each one.

She moaned in delight, yearning for my touch.

I ran my tongue up and down her calves, around her knees, then back up to her thighs. I parted her lower lips and ran my tongue around and around her swollen, red clit. That was my first time, but oh, what an experience! She felt so soft and wet, as I nibbled her clit and inner lips. They were soft and firm like the texture of rubber bands, only slicker and warmer. Her clit swelled more and more with each stroke of my tongue, up and down, around and around. I slid one hand up her silky, smooth body, as she shivered in delight, up to her firm nipples, my other hand penetrated the depths of her soaking-wet cunt. Her walls pulsed around my finger as I slid it in and out, around and around. She felt warm and wet, like being inside of warm, firm gelatin. I felt her walls tighten, as she rolled her hips to the rhythm of my tongue licking her clit and finger piercing her womanhood.

She began to moan long and hard. I paused for a moment and removed my finger. It was wet and sticky and I licked every drop. Her juices were soft and salty, but all so sweet. I beheld her femininity as it pulsed in and out, in and out, as a long stream of come oozed from deep within her loins—the fountain of youth discovered.

I heard a car drive into the driveway. Then, several swift footsteps led to the front door.

"I'm back, sweetie!" the voice said while opening the door. Footsteps hurried up the stairs.

Oh no! I thought. *What will Percy think finding me in bed with Tish!* I panicked. There was no time to hide or come up with some clever excuse. We were stone cold busted ... again.

***

"Do you need anything, sweetie?" Percy asked as she entered the room.

Oh, oh! Busted! But she didn't even do or say anything to let me know that anything was out of the ordinary. She just plopped herself on the side of the bed. *Wait a minute!* I thought. *She can't sit there unless she's sitting on Tish.*

Air quickly filled my lungs as I was jolted in bed. I turned to face Percy and what I thought was Tish's soft body was again my pillow. What I thought was her nipple, was again the edge of a pillowcase. I looked down and noticed that I was still wearing those tartan-plaid pajamas from the night before. *Maybe I fell asleep and been out longer than I realize*, I reasoned. *Maybe Tish is downstairs or something.*

"Where's Tish?" I asked Percy.

She looked as if I had asked her some unreasonable question.

"What?" she asked.

"Tish. Wasn't she with you this morning?" I asked.

She looked at me like I was from another planet or something.

"No, sweetie," she said. "Tish wasn't here this morning."

"Yes, she was," I insisted. "She came right after you left."

"Sweetie, no she didn't," Percy said then got up to open the curtain to let in sunlight. A look of concerned crossed her face as she came back my way.

"Yes, she was," I said. "She was here after you left."

She raised her hands over her face. It seemed like she was either trying to hide something from me or she was extremely frustrated with me.

"Sweetie, no she didn't," she said.

"Yes, she was," I insisted. "Let's call her." I reached for the phone on the nightstand and started to press speed dial. Letitia's number was programmed into the *F2* button, right on the dialing pad. *Maybe she's concerned for me and just wants me to get well*, I thought.

Percy took the phone away, pressed the *End* button to hang it up, then placed it back on the nightstand. *The nerve of her!* I thought. *How dare she take the phone away!*

"Why don't you get some rest, sweetie," she insisted. "By the way, I called your boss and told her that you would be out for a few days. I called when I got to Victor's."

"But, Tish…" I tried to get out, but Percy changed the subject again. I was frustrated that she wouldn't hear me. It was if I didn't matter. Percy had always been bossy, but she was never quite as overbearing as she was since we left the hospital that Sunday. She was different somehow, but I couldn't quite place my finger on it.

"I'm going to get the boys today. What time are they scheduled back?"

"At thr…"

"That's right, at three o'clock. I'll get them then," she said on her way out of the bedroom door.

"Percy," I called. "Victor…"

"What about Victor?" she asked as she stopped dead in her tracks, not looking once back at me.

"He looks familiar," I said.

She paused for a second or two and put her head down. "I'm going to be in the kitchen, sweetie. Yell, if you need me."

Percy walked into the hall and completely ignored my comment about Victor looking familiar. I wondered if the reason why she ignored me was because she thought I was sick or tired or something. *That's it!* I thought. *Maybe*

I'm sicker than I realize, she knows it, and is hiding it from me. At that time, I didn't want to find out if Percy knew something about me that she wasn't revealing. My stomach had started to ache again just thinking about something being wrong. I just wanted to rest and make the pain go away. For that fact, I wanted Percy and her whiny New York granny voice to go away too. She was beginning to sound like one of the old lady characters on the Seinfeld TV show. I just wanted her and that whiny voice to keep on marching down the hallway and straight out the front door, then head for her car never to return. Well, perhaps to return later, but just to go away at that time.

Percy's footsteps stopped halfway to the stairs, then she turned back around. *What now, Percy?* I asked myself. *Is it time to take my medicine again?*

"Oops," she said when she ran into the bedroom, then removed the cordless phone that sat next to the clock on the nightstand. "You need to rest, sweetie. You don't need that silly phone disturbing you. I'll put it back on its base in the kitchen."

"But the base is in Ke ..." I tried to let her know that Keston kept the base in his room, but she just ran right back on out of the door. I was too confused, weary, groggy, sick and everything else to argue with Percy. I let her take the phone away. "Whatever," I mumbled then rolled over on my side again. I pulled the comforter over my head to shield the sunlight that had begun to beat through the window.

It must have been a little after noon because the sun seemed brighter than usual. *I guess I'm never home at this hour to notice how bright the sun can get,* I reasoned. I buried my head deep between two pillows and tried hard to fall fast asleep.

Chapter 9.
By Faith or Chance, There You Are

My stomach cramped more and more with each passing moment. I couldn't sleep and couldn't stay in bed all day, that was for sure. Everything was so quiet. Percy usually had the radio playing, but there wasn't a noise in the house except the sound of the refrigerator motor from the kitchen downstairs.

I glanced at the clock. It read *2:10*.

***

It's unlike me to stay in bed all day, Dr. Iverson. I feel as if I should be doing something, even if it's ironing for the week. I need to account for every second of every day, just like I account for every single penny I spend. That's how I keep my life in order—by being super organized. My father, the great Dr. Pickens, used to say, "The way you spend your time is the way you spend your money. Show me a poor planner, and I'll show you a poor man." I live by those rules.

***

Anyway. I quickly sat up on the side of the bed. Why did I do that? The room began to sway back and forth, and back and forth, and my stomach cramped and churned even more. It was like being on a bad roller coaster ride with no escape in sight. A gray mist suddenly appeared before my eyes with tiny sparkles of light flashing intermittently. It grew darker and dimmer until I was engulfed inside. I blinked my eyes a few times, but it wouldn't go away. I thought that the mist had appeared because I had arisen too quickly after being in bed so long. My stomach was cramping so hard.

Muffled voices echoed in the distance and the mist had begun to gradually fade. I thought that Percy had forgotten to turn off one of the TV's or radios. My stomach, in all the confusion, cramped harder and stronger until ...

***

"Push Didi, push!" I heard someone say.

The fog hadn't completely cleared, but the voices were distinct.

"Push Didi, push!" the voice said again. "I can see the head!"

I felt a gentle kiss on my left check and a set of arms around my mid-section. All became clear. I was nude and seated in a birthing chair of sorts. The thing was made of wood with no back and an extra seat in the rear, probably for the father to help with the birthing process. Marcellus was seated behind me. My arms were over my head and wrapped securely around his neck. I felt my bare back against his bare, hairy chest. His strong, masculine arms held me near and dear to his heart, balancing me upright over the birthing chair. My legs were curled tightly on either side in wooden stirrups, as my bottom squatted over an opening the size of a bowling ball. I looked down to my right, then my left, and noticed Marcellus' bare feet on either side of me. He wore white cotton pants that resembled doctor's scrubs.

I was in what looked like a nursery. The birthing chair was against a back wall. The sun poured through white Venetian blinds covering large French window straight ahead. The walls were painted in a soft pink with ABC block wallpaper borders around the top of the room. To the left of the window was a large white crib with dangling toys overhead. To the right of the window was a sink with pink faucets and basin. An array of pink shelves lined the walls. What looked like pink diapers, large pink baby pins, pink towels, and sundries of other pink baby items were stacked neatly on the pink countertop next to the sink.

"That's right, push some more, Didi," Marcellus said then kissed my cheek once more. That deep voice being whispered in my ear and his gentle touch sent shock waves through my body. I almost forgot about the pain.

I felt tired and worn and couldn't push anymore. Oddly enough, I had never been in labor before. Kevin and Keston were both born by scheduled C-section because they were well over ten pounds each.

I felt more and more tired, as my body contracted stronger and stronger.

"Almost, Didi, almost," the raspy voice said again.

I looked, and it was Great-Aunt Ruby. Her voice sounded kind of like the way you sound today, Dr. Iverson. She was dressed in what looked like a white scrub suit, complete with headwear and white, plastic gloves.

It was like my body worked without me. I felt one giant contraction followed by an intense pressure in my loins to push. Something squirted from deep inside of me and into the hole of the birthing chair. I collapsed into Marcellus' arms. The next thing I heard was the sound of a baby crying.

Great-Aunt Ruby took the baby across the room to the basin. She ran water, removed her bloodstained gloves, gently cleaned the baby with a damp cloth, then wrapped her in a soft, cottony, pink blanket.

"Congratulations," she said as she neared me. "Here's your new baby girl."

My Great-Aunt Ruby placed the baby in my arms. She looked so sweet and innocent.

It was strange seeing Great-Aunt Ruby. Maybe deep in my subconscious, I had always wanted her to be there for me when Kevin and Keston were born. Maybe that's why she appeared in that dream—if you can call it a dream. She looked just as young and beautiful as she did when I last saw her in the late '70s.

"We'll name her Hera—after my grandmother," Marcellus said. "Every first born girl is named Hera."

The baby looked so much like Marcellus with that full head of jet-black hair set against her soft olive skin and pale, pink lips. Her little fingers curled in and out uncontrollably, and Marcellus caressed her tiny, little hands. She actually turned in his direction, opened her beady, dark eyes slightly, and smiled at him.

"Thank you," Marcellus said.

"Thank you?" I asked. I tilted my head up and to the left to face him. We looked deep into each other's eyes.

"Yes. Thank you for giving me such a beautiful baby girl."

My loins began to cramp a little. I looked down and Great-Aunt Ruby had inserted her hands inside of me.

"What ..." I tried to ask.

Marcellus hopped from behind me and proudly took baby Hera into his arms, completely ignoring what was happening with me—just like a typical man.

"I need to make sure that all of the placenta was expelled," Great-Aunt Ruby said. "I don't think it was."

I never cramped so bad before as I felt Great-Aunt Ruby's hands inside of me. The pain was so great that the room began to spin around and around and upside down. All the voices were muffled into one sea of confusion as ...

***

I fell from great heights as air quickly filled my lungs. I looked around my bedroom and all was normal. I was still sitting on the side of the bed. *I must have fallen asleep on the side of the bed*, I tried to reason. My stomach was cramping so much until it was unbearable. I had to do something. It took all the strength I had, but I managed to drag myself out of bed. The stomachache was too much to stand—just too, too much.

I dragged myself downstairs—one slow, long step at a time—to the kitchen and fixed one of my Great-Gran's concoctions. She used to say, "This'll knock an'thing out yo' system, from a belly ache to som'ing the root man done poisoned you wit'."

I retrieved a pot from the cabinets below, filled it with filtered tap water, then placed it on the stove.

***

I like that stove, Dr. Iverson, but I'm glad I didn't have one like it when the boys were younger. The entire surface is smooth with no burners. So, you just place a pot down, push the corresponding button on the front panel, and it's on. It is really easy to clean up because all I have to do is spray some cleaner on the surface, then wipe it clean.

Stay on track, Demeter.

***

Anyway, I scrimmaged through the cabinets for the ingredients. I always kept the ingredients because I never bought the over-the-counter remedies for the boys. I only used Great-Gran's magic potion. Perhaps if more people were to get back to kitchen medicine, like using natural herbs and spices, then more people would be healthier.

I put two tablespoons of baking soda, two tablespoons of mint oil, a pinch of thyme, two bay leaves, a dash of ginger, a dash of cinnamon, a teaspoon of Cayenne pepper and a teaspoon of sugar in a big coffee mug, then poured the boiling hot water from the stove right in as I stirred it with a spoon. It steamed and fizzled as the scent of mint filled the air. I hated it when Great-Gran made me drink that stuff when I was sick, but it sure did make me feel better. I drank every drop, trying hard not to breathe as the liquid slid down my throat. That stuff'll clear your nose, that's for sure!

By the time I rinsed the mug in the sink and sat down at the breakfast bar, my stomach was feeling a whole lot better. I had a sudden urge to run to the commode, but I wasn't cramping. I barely made it upstairs. I glanced at the digital clock on my nightstand as I ran by—*2:45*. It seemed like I had emptied the contents of a cow, just one long stream of slush flowed endlessly from my insides, bringing a strong feeling of relief along with it. The bowl filled a few times, but the slush within me kept flowing and flowing like a lava stream. That was strange because I hadn't eaten in a few days. *Granny's cleanser,* I thought. I thought that my deep cleansing was the result of fasting, so I didn't think anything of it. Well, I didn't really fast, I just didn't eat anything. Same thing, right?

The stream finally stopped. I got up and took a peek, and was horrified by what I saw—my skin began to crawl in disgust. A big dark brown pile with small patches of white foam floated about. What looked like large white worms swam around the bowl. I looked a little closer and noticed two tan worms. Their heads resembled that of snails and they were speckled with green spots. They were about two inches long and one inch in diameter, too large to be worms I thought. They swam around, wiggling their little bodies in and out of the slug, opening and closing the tiny slits of mouths, blinking their big black eyes. *The parasites must have been inside me for a while,* I thought.

Not once did I think about going for a medical check up. I thought that it had come from eating too much meat over the years. My system was clean thanks to Great-Gran's potion. From that point on, I pledged to be a vegan. No more meat!

Strange, but the room smelled of fresh mint as I flushed the commode one final time. I felt so much better that my system was clear and free of toxins. *What a relief,* I thought.

My nose started itching something awful—like the time I had stepped into an anthill and was bitten by hundreds of ants. I touched my mole and it was covered with soft strands of hair. Looking down cross-eyed, I swear the thing wiggled. *Maybe it's filled with pus,* I thought. My nose itched more and more like a bad insect bite, so I looked in the mirror to check it out.

"Oh, Lord!" I screamed. *My mind must be playing tricks on me.* What looked like a big spider rolled up in a ball wiggled on my nose. I grabbed twisters from the vanity drawer to squeeze the mole, but one by one, it unfolded its hairy black legs and crawled across my nose toward my eyes. It felt like velvet covered sticks brushing against my face with each of its movements; the thing was about four-inches long. My skin began to crawl as I looked into the creature's beady, black eyes as its feelers wiggled in the air. Before I could do anything, it jumped into the sink and vanished into thin air. I got closer to the mirror to examine my face, but the mole wasn't there.

***

You know, Dr. Iverson, though I had that mole forever, there's not as much as a pimple or any other evidence that the mole was even on my nose. No one seemed to notice that my mole was gone—not even Percy.

***

I remembered what ol' Great-Gran used to say, "The stuff all up in ya sho' can scare ya when it come all out ya. That's why it be best to keep yo' system clean! Watch what you put in yo' system!" Great-Gran's potion did it every time.

Chapter 10.
In The Mind's Eye to Behold

I was feeling so much better that I decided to go down two flights of stairs to the basement and watch TV. The boys were gone, and it was so quiet and still in the family room.

***

When we first moved back in the early '90's, Dr. Iverson, I hired a contractor to convert the daylight basement into a family room. It was one big unfinished area, but he added an enclosed laundry room and office. That room sits off to the right leading from the garage. The teal carpet and teal wallpaper with tiny golden specks is a nice contrast to the black velour sectional. To the rear, the contractor added a nice wet bar enclosure complete with bar, stools, mini refrigerator and wine rack.

***

Anyway, I reclined on the floor in front of the sectional, covered myself with the green-and-white, plaid comforter that I brought from upstairs, and flicked on the big-screen TV with the satellite system remote control. Ahhhh! That was sooo relaxing.

All these channels and nothing good to watch, I thought as I continued to flick through what seemed like thousands of channels on the satellite system. *Enough!* I thought. I reached in the tape cabinet in the entertainment unit and pulled out my all-time favorite movie—*Harlem Nights*—starring Eddie Murphy.

My stomach had a tingly sensation, and I felt refreshed all over. Good ol' Great-Gran and that potion. She had a potion for anything—from an upset stomach to headaches and toothaches—and it worked like a charm. They must have worked because people came from miles around to get her potions.

Speaking of charm, she used to tell Percy and me stories about spirits and witches that had us scared to sleep at night. Her stories were so real, and she told them like they really happened. But that's how I grew up with such a fascination for the paranormal. Anything about special powers and abilities has always piqued my curiosity. Everybody else in high school had hobbies like swimming or playing the clarinet. I did those things too, but I also read books on palmistry, Tarot or about people like Edgar Cayce.

When I went off to Spelman, many of the young ladies were from the Midwest or North and turned their noses up at Southern rumors. I tried hard to fit in, so I just let my pastimes fall to wayside. But I learned fast that we can only be who we were born to be.

I was accepted, somewhat, because of who my father was—the great Dr. George Pickens. He donated tons of money to both Morehouse and Spelman through the years.

***

That's right, Dr. Iverson, my maiden name is Pickens. I have children and still went back to using my maiden name after the divorce. Besides, what's-his-name wasn't my father, so why should I keep his name?

***

Anyway, my father was a Morehouse graduate, so naturally he wanted Percy and me to attend Spelman, the sister school. My father went on to Meharry Medical School.

My father assumed that Percy and I would meet our mates while at Spelman. It was different with the guys at Morehouse or Morris Brown when I went there. As you know, Dr. Iverson, Spelman, Morehouse, Morris Brown and what's known now as Clark-Atlanta University, all make up what's called the University Center because the schools are across the street from each other. For that reason, my father thought that Percy and I should have caught nice, young men from Morehouse, Morris Brown or Clark-Atlanta.

Anyway, when the guys learned that I was from Louisiana, I heard them tell their friends things like, "Don't eat no red gravy from her, man," or "Be careful not to leave your hair or drawers around her," or "Don't mess with her. She might work some roots on you."

Percy, on the other hand, had plenty of dates, despite being from Louisiana. She was always the pretty one. She was five-nine, with long, flowing lustrous black hair like our mother. Her deep ebony skin and dark eyes were so beautiful. Me, well ... I'm only five-four with long, thick, frizzy hair. I tried relaxing my hair through the years, but the chemicals were either too mild or too harsh. Most of the girls said that I had *good hair*. If you'd ask me, I thought I looked like a wild woman at times because it would just frizz up. One time, Spelman had a celebrity impersonation contest on campus. I won the Dianna Ross look-alike contest because the judges said that my hair was styled like hers, and that I looked a lot like her too. You know, Dr. Iverson, people still say that I look like Dianna Ross.

Anyway, needless to say, unlike my dear sister, Percy, I never dated while at Spelman. Like I said before, Percy was always the pretty one, like our mother. I took after my father's side of the family.

The guys said that I looked like a witch because I was of Creole background with long, thick, jet-black hair; copper-tone skin; a long, pointed nose with a large black mole the size of a raisin over the left nostril; thick, black eyebrows; and dark brown eyes. It didn't help that I wore my nails long with deep plum polish. Being from Louisiana, some people automatically assumed that I was into Voodoo. The boys, rather young men, said that I looked like the wicked witch from the South.

You know, Dr. Iverson, I could never get that mole removed. It seemed to have grown larger and larger each year. I had it for as long as I could remember. When I was a teenager, I wanted to have it removed, but my father and grandfather looked at me as though I were from another planet each time I had asked. Once I was grown, I went to doctor after doctor through the years, but no luck. Something odd would happen to postpone the surgery, like a rare ice storm or blizzard, for example. Or, the doctors would try to cut it off, but something would happen to their instruments, or the local anesthesia wouldn't work. One time, the outpatient clinic section of the hospital experienced a power outage right when the doctor started the surgery. Out of the entire hospital, only that section was affected. Amazing! I took that as an omen that it was my beauty mark, and I should be proud of it. Well, as you know, Dr. Iverson, the mole finally came off by itself back in October. I knew that no one would have believed me if I'd told them how I got rid of the mole, so I said that I went to the doctor's office. But it really happened like I said it did, Dr. Iverson. Really!

Anyway, after graduation, I moved back to New Orleans to start graduate school at Tulane University. That's when I met what's-his-name. He was an internal medicine resident at Tulane School of Medicine.

***

I'm telling you, Dr. Iverson, the next time that I want to see what's-his-name is on the last day of eternity.

He's already gone, and eternity doesn't have a last day. You won't ever see him again, Demeter. Trust me.

I wish him well, wherever he is. Bless your soul, Dr. Mark Breaux. Bless your soul.

***

Anyway, a few months later, we got married and had children. I still managed to finish graduate school in three years, then I entered the corporate world soon after. That's when Juanita decided to move in on my territory. I was so busy advancing my education; while she was busy making advances on my ex.

I just didn't have time to dabble into my hobbies anymore. After the slack I got from the guys back at Spelman, I just lost interest in the paranormal.

***

How did you get back into your hobbies, Demeter?

***

About two years ago, the boys started getting involved in school activities, and I had more free time. One day I cleaned out the all the closets in the house and ran across one of the first books that Great-Gran ever read to Percy and me. I started reading it again. I thought that my mother had thrown it away long ago.

I was pleasantly surprised when I found the book. I didn't even realize that I had it. It was big and red like a reference book from the library. It had a strange inscription written on the front cover. I flipped through a few pages, and some of it was in Old English and some was in some other language. I remembered Great-Gran saying that part of the text was written in ancient Greek. She said that she studied ancient Greek in school so that's why she was able to read those parts to us in Old English. Percy and I asked her to teach the language to us. "Wait 'til y'all get grown," she always told us. Percy and I never questioned Great-Gran even though we knew that she probably never made it past sixth grade. Everyone from miles around knew that Great-Gran was smarter than the most educated doctor and had what they called *mother wit*.

***

Tell me about the book, Demeter. What was it about?

The book was sort of an anthology of epic tales about Greek Mythology. I always loved those old legends about Zeus, Hera, Hercules and other gods, goddesses, nymphs and divines. They were all so fascinating. I took Greek Mythology classes in high school and college, but they didn't compare to the stories Great-Gran told us. My parents must have been fascinated by Greek mythology too, because they named my sister and me Persephone and Demeter. It seems that Percy's name should have been Demeter.

Why so?

Because in Greek mythology, Demeter was Persephone's mother. Since Percy is older, she should have been named after the mother, not the daughter. Persephone, as you probably know, spent a part of the year in the underworld with the god Hades. Demeter was one of Zeus' mortal lovers, so Persephone was his daughter. What a tangled web Demeter tangled for her daughter, Persephone. Ironic, but it's kind of like the web my father tangled for Percy and me. Well, supposedly, according to Fern. But you think that was only my imagination. Right? Fern is my friend and wouldn't lie to me.

We'll discuss Fern later.

So, Demeter, is that how you rekindled your fascination with the paranormal? By finding the book that reminded you of your great-grandmother?

***

Well, no. The former café owner in our building at work suddenly decided to retire. It all happened so quickly that everyone was surprised. He still had just renewed his lease for another two years, so rumor had it that the building manager was quite upset and was threatening to sue. The manager was concerned that there wouldn't be a café in the building.

A few weeks before the café was to close its doors, Mr. Chap took over without skipping a beat. He redecorated the place over one long weekend and completely livened the look.

***

So, what do you think Mr. Chap taking over the café have to do with anything?

***

Because, I ran across a magazine in Mr. Chap's. Well, actually, Mr. Chap started stuffing his customers' bags with this magazine from this New Age shop called The Space. I guess because The Space paid for the advertising, and Mr. Chap was new to the building, so he was obligated to put them in the people's bags.

I was fascinated by the gargoyle on the front cover. It was strange, but just when I though I had lost it, thrown that thing away, or given it to someone else, I found it mysteriously buried with papers at home, in my brief case or in my desk at work. That magazine just kind of showed up at odd times. I knew for sure that that must have been a sign to peruse it and perhaps enroll in some of the classes. So I did. That's how I met you, Dr. Iverson, because you ran an ad for the lucid dreaming class in the magazine. After calling your office, I was pleased to learn that some of your classes and services were covered under the mental health portion of our insurance plan at work. Then, I knew there was no excuse not to enroll in some classes or attend a lecture or two.

***

Get back to your great-grandmother and how you developed your fascination with the paranormal.

***

For as long as I can remember, we used to visit her across the river in Algiers when I was little. I remember that my father drove us over there the last Saturday of the month and we stayed overnight to the first Sunday of each month. In December and June—for winter solstice and summer solstice—our mother used to spend the weekend with us. I thought it was strange for our mother to stay with us because Great-Gran was my father's grandmother, not our mother's.

Well, anyway, we left at about six in the morning on Saturday and returned a little before midnight on Sunday. Come to think of it, my two brothers never came along. They always went to play with our cousins at our grandpa's house when we went over. It was always my father, my mother, Percy and me.

We lived in the Seventh Ward—in the Gentilly area—off of Elysian Fields Boulevard near Dillard University. Where Great-Gran lived was called across the river because we had to cross the Mississippi River Bridge to get to her house. I remember that people used to come from miles around to get to her and my Great-Aunt Ruby next door. People used to say that my Great-Aunt Ruby was one of The Three Sisters and called her Mother Ruby. I never paid it any mind back then. Perhaps I should have. I thought they meant that she had two other sisters. I never met her two sisters. She looked really young, too young to be a great-aunt. For that fact, Great-Gran looked far too young to be a great-grand mother. She looked younger than my father! She had waist-length, thick black hair. Five white streaks—each made up of ten strands of hair—adorned her head. The texture seemed more like that of an animal's hair, not human hair. It was more like that of a Tibetan yak's hair, only thicker. She had large, full, dark eyes; a long, straight nose; and a soft pecan-tan complexion. Her skin was baby soft with not as much as a wrinkle in sight.

One day, we stopped going to see Great-Gran. Rumor had it that she just disappeared off the face of the Earth. As I grew up, I thought that was what the elders in the community said to keep us children from getting sad when in fact Great-Gran was gone. But each time I asked my father, my mother or one of the other family elders what happened to Great-Gran, they got really quiet, changed the subject and sent me to do some crazy chore like straighten the napkins in the China cabinet or wash the baseboards.

One time when I was fifteen, two years after seeing Great-Gran for the last time, Percy and I took the bus across the river to see Great-Gran for ourselves. She didn't have a phone, so we couldn't call. When we got to where we remembered Great-Gran's house to be, it was gone. All that was there was the levee. It was as if no house had ever existed. We wanted to go to Great-Aunt Ruby's house, but we couldn't find her house either.

Friends of our father's, an older couple by the name of Mr. and Mrs. Marshall, owned the store on the corner of Newton Street and Teche Street. The husband was a semi-retired shipyard foreman who needed something to do, so he and his wife bought the store. He was tall and dark with cottony strands of gray hair everywhere—his head, hands, arms, chest and whiskers. His wife was the sweetest, nicest old lady you'd ever want to meet. She was about my height with a slight build and long gray hair that she pulled back into a bun. Her deep, dark skin was as smooth as silk with not as much as a wrinkle.

The outside of the store was white with hunter-green trim. Two cement steps led up to the double-glass doors. Shiny speckled, brown-and-white tile adorned the floors, and the place smelled of fresh pine. Three cash registers were a few feet ahead of the entrance. When they weren't busy with customers, the three sassy cashiers usually gossiped about the latest neighborhood news. Behind the registers were six grocery aisles, each with a white descriptive sign with bold black letters. To the far left was the dairy center. Gallon milk jugs and eggs were visible from the front of the store.

That day, as usual, the cashiers were gossiping when Percy and I walked in. We didn't pay attention to what they were saying, but I noticed one of them signal the other to stop talking when she saw us enter the store. They all seemed shocked to see us and just stood there motionless.

"Hello," Percy and I said.

"Hello," the women answered in unison while continuing to stare at us.

"We're wondering if you can help us," Percy said.

They were staring awfully hard at us. I thought that it was because they knew that Great-Gran had passed and were part of the big conspiracy to hide that fact from us like all the other elders.

"Y'all wait right there," one of the ladies said then ran between one of the aisles. She was tall and dark and chewed gum like there was no tomorrow. "Mr. Marshall," she called without taking her eyes off of us as she smacked that gum. "Mr. Marshall!"

A few customers went up to the registers. They seemed annoyed that the cashiers were preoccupied. But they stared right along with the cashiers when they noticed us. I felt a bit uneasy, but was hopeful that someone would finally tell us something about Great-Gran. Percy and I stood there, huddled together, anxiously awaiting Mr. Marshall to come forth. We ran our fingers across the silver grocery buggies in the front of the store to occupy ourselves.

Mr. Marshall strolled out from the back of the store. For an old man, he looked mighty fine. He wore a white, short-sleeve T-shirt that highlighted his strong arms and chest. He was mighty fine indeed! It was quite evident by his body that he was a hard-working man in his younger years. Mercy!

"What ya need?" he asked the lady who had called him.

She didn't say anything, but pointed to Percy and me. He jumped back a few steps and his eyes popped wide open when he saw us. He walked to us and asked, "How can I he'p you?"

"We're lost," Percy said. "We're trying to find our great-grandmother's house. We thought that it was on Teche Street near the ferry, but all that's there is the levee."

"Yeah," I said. "We tried to find our Great-Aunt Ruby's house..."

"Ruby?" one of the customers asked. She was a woman in her thirties with a young son of about six with her "You mean Mother Ruby?"

"Yeah," the same cashier who called Mr. Marshall whispered. "They supposed to be her kin."

"Lord have mercy, Jesus!" the woman yelled then marked her chest with the symbol of a cross. She grabbed her child and ran from the store, leaving her groceries in the checkout line.

What's going on? I asked myself. *What really happened to Great-Gran and Great-Aunt Ruby?* I assumed that she ran because she knew something that she didn't want to tell us. Well, that was partly true.

"Let's go in my office," Mr. Marshall said. Percy and I followed him through the bread aisle, the smell of fresh yeast was everywhere as we passed by. There were shelves upon shelves of wheat, pumpernickel, rye and Louisiana's own—the famous Bunny Bread in that familiar yellow and blue bag. To the rear was the Meat Department. The people stopped their conversations when they saw us approach. Behind the Meat Department was a set of swinging, silver doors. It was dark and cold when we entered the back area. To the right, the green metal time clock and beige time cards with red letters sat on a wooden table. Straight ahead was a set of doors that led outside, probably for deliveries and such. To the left was the office, and we followed Mr. Marshall right on in.

It was a small neat room with blue Berber carpeting. The walls were bare, but a nice off-white color. The large wooden desk that sat in the middle and large black chair behind the desk, seemed to occupy the whole room. Percy and I sat in the two wooden chairs facing Mr. Marshall. He closed the door behind us and walked around to his big chair and sat down.

"Mother Esther and Mother Ruby … they gone," Mr. Marshall told us.

"Gone?" Percy asked. "You mean they've passed away?"

"What happened, Mr. Marshall?" I asked.

He looked us straight in the eyes. "Nobody knows. One day they were here, the next day they were gone. They just up and moved."

"Moved?" I asked. "Do you know where they moved to?"

He gave me a strange look as if to say, *You ain't too bright, is ya, gal?* "I… don't … I … I …" Mr. Marshall said as he rubbed his hands together. I knew he was stomped for words. When he stood up, we took that as our cue to leave.

"Thank you, Mr. Marshall," we both said.

Mr. Marshall walked around us, opened the door to his office, then escorted us back outside. We passed through those large, silver doors, back down the bread aisle and back to the front of the store. I thought sure that I heard someone say," Shhh, here they come, here they come!" as we walked down the bread aisle—mmmm, that fresh baked aroma—and neared the checkout lines. The cashiers and a set of new customers stopped their conversations when they saw us approach. Then, we knew for sure that the grown-ups hid the fact that Great-Gran had passed on and they were keeping it from us. We never understood why they did that. We didn't get a chance to say good-bye to Great-Gran. We never forgave them even till this day.

Then, a few weeks later while Percy and I were coming from the corner store near our house in Gentilly, we thought that we had seen our Great-Aunt Ruby walking a few blocks ahead of us with our mother and two brothers. That wasn't out of the ordinary because they always used to take walks before Great-Gran and Great-Aunt Ruby supposedly disappeared. They turned the corner and disappeared behind some bushes. We thought nothing of it until later that night.

"Isn't that Great-Aunt Ruby with Mother?" Percy asked.

"It looks like her," I said.

"I bet that Great-Aunt Ruby isn't gone at all. She probably moved and the people in Algiers just don't know where."

"Yeah," I said. "You're probably right, Percy. She's probably been so busy moving and unpacking, that she just hasn't had time to let Daddy know where she moved to."

Mother used to have hot cookies, muffins, beignets or something waiting for us after school to munch on before dinner. That day, nothing had been cooked, and she didn't come home for supper.

"Mother and Great-Aunt Ruby are probably going to bring us something back," I said.

"Probably so," Percy agreed. "I wonder where they went."

Percy and I were watching TV and studying when Daddy came home from the hospital. He was head surgeon at Touro Infirmary.

"Connie! Connie!" he yelled. He went all through the house yelling, "Connie, Connie!"

Finally, he approached Percy and me. "Have either of you seen your mother?" he asked us.

"We saw her after school walking down the street with Great-Aunt Ruby," Percy told him. A solemn look crossed his face and his skin turned pale. He backed up slowly away from us.

"What's wrong?" Percy asked.

He said nothing, turned around and quickly ran upstairs to his room, closing the door behind him.

Percy and I were confused and didn't know what to think. We became worried because later that week, Mother and our brothers still hadn't come home. When we got home from school and our father was at the hospital, Percy and I sneaked into our parents' and brothers' room. We checked the closets, the master bathroom, everything. There was nothing of theirs—not even a single strand of hair. We concluded that our mother had walked out on us and took our brothers.

A deep void sank deep in our hearts. We didn't know what to think, and we sure didn't know what to do. Daddy refused to discuss it. We kept ourselves occupied to avoid facing the reality that our mother loved our brothers more than us.

Percy joined every club and team possible at school. She joined the chess club, debate team, yearbook club and tennis team. She even became senior class president.

I was always the quiet one, but decided to join the marching band anyway. I practiced day and night. My hard work paid off because I became first chair flute. When it wasn't football season or concert season—and we didn't have band practice—I studied long, hard hours. That, too, paid off because I was able to skip a grade and graduate a year early. Not only that, I was part of the Honor Society and was Valedictorian of my class—1978.

One day, Grandpa—my father's father—came over. Percy was gone, so they must have thought that I was gone, too, but I was studying for a calculus exam. I heard my father and grandfather arguing from my room upstairs.

"Boy," Grandpa said, "those children are working themselves really hard. They're hurting. It's all your fault. They miss their mother and brothers."

"We don't need to get into this!" Daddy said.

"If you wouldn't have been messing with Bot and Mother Esther and Mother Ruby in the first place, and let some things be, then ..."

"Look! I said ..." Daddy started, but Grandpa interrupted.

Messing with Mother Esther and Mother Ruby? I asked myself. *Did Daddy do something to offend them? And who is Bot? And why is Grandpa calling them Mother Esther and Mother Ruby? Isn't he Esther's son and Ruby's brother?*

Then I realized that Grandpa never really talked about his mother or sister through the years. He always insisted that both his parents were deceased and so were all of his brothers and sisters. "Boy!" Grandpa would say to Daddy. "Why are you telling those girls that Mother Esther and Mother Ruby are kin to them? Don't tell them those lies!" When we visited our other cousins, the children of our father's sister and brother, they always laughed at us when we said that Esther was our great-grandmother and Ruby was our great-aunt. They thought that we were making up the tales. We thought that it was strange that our own cousins didn't know about Esther and Ruby. So, we chucked it up to our grandfather's *axe to grind* with the two women. We assumed that because our father was the youngest of the three children, that Esther and Ruby took to him because he was the baby of the family. You know that old saying about assuming too much—you make an ass out of you and me.

"You don't even know what kind of children they are anyway," Grandpa said. "That ol' dark shadow woman and dark shadow children ..."

They continued to argue. Grandpa was old, he was over ninety, so I thought that he was *talking out of his head* when he said that he didn't know what kind of children we were. I thought that he meant that what kind of children work so much and are gone from home all the time. I just dismissed it as just an argument. Perhaps I should have listened more carefully.

Then it hit me that he called us dark shadow children. All our cousins had very fair skin and either straight or wavy hair like Grandpa. My brothers and I, on the other hand, had copper-tone skin and thick, wavy hair. But Percy had deep ebony skin and straight, wavy hair like our mother; they looked so much alike. Despite our skin tone or hair texture, Grandpa should have loved us just as much as the other grandchildren.

Grandpa always looked at us curiously through the years. He bought us presents for Christmas and on our birthdays, but he never wanted to get too close. We always thought that it was because he was from *the old school* when men didn't get too touchy-feely with children. Again, I should have paid attention to his motions because he always hugged and kissed our cousins through the years. Later, I realized that it was probably because we were the *dark shadow* children—you know, too dark in complexion.

"Don't know what kind of woman that was anyway. Look like a zombie or..." I heard my grandfather say later. I was still mad at my mother for deserting us, and agreed in my mind, with the harsh things Grandpa said about her. He really didn't like my mother's style and mannerism. In addition, he did not like Mother's deep, dark skin or the fact that she was part Choctaw Indian.

Our mother never seemed quite happy for as long as I could remember. With a father-in-law like Grandpa, I understood why. She went through the motions of the day—cooking, cleaning, laundry, PTA meetings, Daddy's parties—but she never seemed to have enjoyed any of it. Come to think of it, I don't ever recall being touched by my mother—not a hug, a pat on the back, a kiss—nothing. It was as if she were going through the motions because that's what was expected of her. She never smiled, never laughed, come to think of it, she never really talked unless it was absolutely necessary, like when she called us for dinner or needed us to do a chore. Her demeanor was more like a robot than a mother. Percy and I envied the relationship that the other girls at school had with their mothers. They went shopping, had long conversations together, or got plain old advice.

Percy reached puberty when she was twelve. At that time, our father, and not our mother, explained to both of us about the monthly cycle and how to use feminine products. It's a good thing Daddy was a doctor and was probably used to explaining such things to young girls.

When I started my cycle, I was too ashamed to ask Daddy more questions, so Percy explained what I needed to know as best she could. We assumed, again, that our mother was too lazy and too sorry of an excuse for a parent to be bothered. When Percy and I needed bras, again, it was our father and not our mother who helped us get our first one.

Percy and I concluded that she wasn't happy being a wife and mother. Add a troublesome father-in-law to the picture, and it's no wonder that she decided to run away from home.

Mother was probably just burned-out, we tried to tell ourselves. The optimal word was burned-out in the '70's. Now, in the '90's, it's *stressed-out*.

***

Right Dr. Iverson? You said that I'm just stressed out, right?

***

Anyway, after all, my mother had four step-ladder children; Percy was born in '59, George III in '60, I was born in '61 and Craig was born in '62. We accepted that fact, but we couldn't understand why she left with Great-Aunt Ruby because she was our father's aunt, not hers. Why would an aunt betray her nephew and his children like that? Or, did we really see our mother leave with Great-Aunt Ruby, or did the two women look like Great-Aunt Ruby and our mother from a distance? We'll never get answers to those questions.

Even when my mother was around, we spent most of our time with our father anyway. He took us places like to Pontchartrain Beach Amusement Park, to the movies or to Bonanza Steakhouse—our favorite restaurant. Mother just stayed at home. All she did was stare off into space for hours at a time with not as much as blinking an eye. We children often wondered if she were mentally ill and if my father had her secretly committed to an institution without telling us.

Percy and I had a theory. We thought that Great-Aunt Ruby took Mother to a mental hospital, like the one in Mandeville, and just left her there. She probably did it because she knew that Mother was a horrible wife and mother and wanted to spare us any more heartache and pain.

***

That was only speculation, Dr. Iverson, because till this day, I still don't know what happened to our brothers. There are just so many questions and too few answers. Just too many.

***

Anyway, when we visited relatives, it was always my father's side of the family. Our father said that our mother was the only living member of her family. We assumed that something terrible had happened, which lead to her cool demeanor. Each time we asked, our mother ignored us or our father sent us to do some ridiculous chore like straighten the spice rack. Our other kinfolk didn't want to talk about it either. Through the years, we just stopped asking. They were hiding something from us. We just knew it.

The people in the community, the children at school, even the teachers and principal all seemed extra nice to us. They all walked on eggs shells after the news about our mother. We always assumed that they felt sorry for us and wanted to make us feel better. People just seemed uncomfortable around our family, like we would bite or something. All Percy and I had were each other.

People looked at us curiously and stopped their conversations whenever a member of the family approached. Again, I should not have assumed so much and asked questions. Come to think of it, everybody was so *hush-hush* about my mother and our family. Asking questions probably would have proven futile.

***

On this day, Dr. Iverson, with you as my witness, I finally find it in my heart to forgive all those people who hid the truth from us.

***

Anyway, ever since two months ago in October until … well … you know… Percy was hiding something from me. I could accept a stranger withholding information from me, but not my own sister.

Percy should have prepared me for what was coming—about what had happened to Tish and our father's marriage to that woman. She had known about Tish for the past year and didn't bother to tell me! I never quite forgave her for that … until … well, you know …

***

Percy shouldn't take all the blame.

***

Well, perhaps I shouldn't blame Percy for what took place over the past year. But she knew about what went on back in October. For that, I can't forgive her. Perhaps I should.

And Percy knew about our father's new wife too. I blame her for not telling me about that. That woman, what's-her-name, had a past with our father. Not just any old past, noooo, they were engaged. But what's-her-name ran off with someone else, then he married my mother a few months later. Not only that, what's-her-name looks exactly like my mother. It seems like they could be identical twins.

***

Are what's-her-name and my mother related, Dr. Iverson? Is my father the reason why my mother's family cut all ties from her? And, according to Fern, and I know that you don't believe what I say about Fern, Dr. Iverson… Anyway, according to Fern, that woman, what's-her-name, is the reason why Percy pulled that stunt last month. And, what's-her-name is the reason for my condition today, this so-called dementia. I don't know why, but if Fern says it, then it must be true.

***

Do you believe everything that Fern tells you? Do you know if you can trust Fern?

I still trust Fern. Why shouldn't I? You don't think that Fern was trying to gain my confidence to betray me do you, Dr. Iverson? Fern was right on target about D'Angela. So, Fern is probably right about what's-her-name, too, even though the story is a tad farfetched.

Chapter 11.
The Heart's Desire to Unfold

A sound from the garage jolted me in place. I looked around the room for a second and realized that I was still in the family room. The TV screen was royal blue and *6:45* blinked in bold, white letters in the lower-right corner. Apparently, the *Harlem Nights* tape had finished its course. It seemed as if I had fallen asleep on the floor in front of the TV. I woke up refreshed and rejuvenated. Come to think of it, I didn't dream during that time. Interesting.

I heard echoes of voices in the garage, then the door opened. Percy, Keston and Kevin walked in.

"The bus was late getting back to the school. Then, we stopped at Ruby Tuesday's for dinner, sweetie," Percy said. "I brought you something back." She lifted one of those white take-out bags with the silver aluminum lining.

"Maybe later," I said. "How was your trip?" I asked the boys as I sat up.

"It was a'ight," Kevin said.

"Yeah," Keston agreed. "What are you doing in your pajamas for?"

"Your mom wasn't feeling well, like I told you guys at dinner," Percy said as she glanced back at me. "She just needs to rest up. Now you boys go upstairs and unpack."

I saw that the boys were exhausted from their trip as they headed upstairs.

"I'll be upstairs," Percy said. "Just yell if you need anything."

Amazing, they listened to Percy more than they listened to me. Keston usually argued with me, but did everything that *Aunt Percy* told him to do. If I had asked them to jump, their response would probably be something like, "Why?" If Percy had asked them to jump, they would ask, "How high?"

With Percy in charge of the boys, I climbed on the sectional, covered myself with the comforter, then went back to sleep.

Ever since we were kids, Percy always took really good care of me. I sure do miss her. I wish she were here now. Why did she leave me, Dr. Iverson? Why?

***

I woke up to the smell of fresh homemade apple-cinnamon and raisin oatmeal. I knew that smell anywhere. Then, I heard thumps down the stairs. I peeked my head from under the comforter and saw a glimpse of Keston and Kevin as they raced out the garage entrance door.

"Have a good day," I yelled.

"You too," they both said while they retrieved their book bags from the office. They studied and did their homework there, so it made sense for them to leave everything in *grabbing distance* for school.

"Hope you feel better," Keston said as he darted out the door.

"Yeah," Kevin agreed as he followed his brother.

I heard the engine of the Ford Explorer rev up, followed by the outside garage door opening and closing.

"Go and rinse your mouth, sweetie," Percy yelled from the kitchen. "I made some oatmeal and biscuits. You really need to eat something."

I sat up and rubbed my eyes. Percy was carrying a tray of food down the stairs; she never looked so beautiful. My stomach started to growl as I smelled the fresh cinnamon and saw the steam rise from the big bowl of oatmeal. I was actually hungry. I hadn't eaten since the previous Friday, and it was Tuesday.

"Yes, ma'am," I said then jumped up and ran into the half-bath straight ahead under the stairs. I didn't feel like going to my bathroom to get my personal items. Percy could have got them for me, but it would have taken too long, and I was just too hungry. So, I picked up a toothbrush and toothpaste from the laundry room. I bought non-perishable items, you know, detergent, soap, toothpaste and such, in bulk for the whole year and stored them on shelves in the laundry room. I saved time by not having to buy the same things over and over again. I did the math, and I saved over three hundred dollars a year by buying in bulk. Amazing.

Anyway, I brushed my teeth and washed my face in less than a minute. Then, I rushed into the family room to the feast that awaited me on the coffee table. I sat on the floor next to the tray of food and dug right in.

"Slow down, sweetie," Percy said.

I ignored her, then gobbled the oatmeal, dripping a few spots on my pajamas. When the oatmeal was gone, I broke big pieces of biscuits and ran them across the bowl to get every drop. Then I gulped down every drop of the freshly squeezed orange juice that she prepared.

I ate so quickly that I didn't even notice the taste of the oatmeal or biscuits. That was a pity because Percy and I prepared oatmeal just as good as our mother used to. We never used the quick oats. Nooo, we always used the old fashioned oats, you know, the ones that have to be cooked for about a half-hour. We would cut up some fresh apples, grate a fresh cinnamon stick and whole nutmeg, then add them to the pot, along with some fresh raisins and brown sugar, while the pot simmered. We also made biscuits from scratch, you know, with freshly sifted flour, baking powder and butter. They came out really flaky, too, just like our mother's.

"Are you going to be all right today, sweetie?" Percy asked.

"Yes," I said.

"You're looking much better today, sweetie."

I didn't answer her because I just didn't feel like being bothered. Instead, I flicked on the satellite system and turned to "The Early Show" with Bryant Gumbel. In a way, I wished that I could have flicked Percy away that morning; I just felt like being alone that day. If I had known then what I know now, I would have heeded old-time advice: *Be careful what you wish or it just might come true.* I never realized how true that statement was until November—when Percy pulled that stunt.

Percy wore her pink pajamas and fuzzy, pink slippers. She sat beside me on the floor. It felt like we were kids again. When we were growing up, Percy and I used to sit in the family room—in our pajamas of course—and watched cartoons for a good part of the morning. Sometimes, we ate our breakfast in the family room too. We used to talk about school, boys or whatever. When Percy went off to college, we never spent quality time together like that again, even when she came home on break. I guess she thought that she was too grown for such antics. But until that morning in my basement, I didn't realize how much I had missed our morning quality time together. It really meant a lot to me. You know what they say—you never realize how important something is to you until it's gone.

"I've arranged for a reflexologist to come over this afternoon," Percy said.

"Reflexologist?" I repeated. That sounded good, so I wanted more details. I hadn't been to a spa to pamper myself since … well … two years ago …1997 … when all that Year 2000 hype first started at our company.

"Well, she'll massage your feet. Her assistant will give you a pedicure… Lord knows you need one. Looks like crust has been building up on your feet, sweetie. You never used to go around with crusty feet before! You haven't been taking care of yourself. You're letting yourself go."

I was surprised by Percy's comments and couldn't believe what she had said. I didn't know how to respond. I just sat there and watched "The Early Show."

"Besides, it should help to relax you. She comes to my house all the time. I don't like going to those crowded, old nail places. They're nasty. They use the same nail utensils on everybody," she said then turned her nose up. "You'll never see me with crusty feet! All her equipment is portable. She fits it nicely into a Pullman's tote. So, she could come here, to your office or just about anywhere. It's just no excuse for you to go around with crusty feet! There's just no excuse. That's why you don't have a man, because you don't take care of yourself. You just pull your hair back into a ponytail." She grabbed one of my hands and said, "You don't take care of your nails. You should at least put some clear polish on them or something."

I snapped my hand away from her. She was lucky that I didn't slap her right upside the head. The more Percy spoke the more shocked I was. I was too taken away to say a thing.

***

Have you ever been in a situation, Dr. Iverson, when someone says or does something so bizarre that you don't know how to respond?

***

Where did she get off lecturing me like that? Maybe she was concerned about me. Maybe. Perhaps.

Anyway, I looked forward to my reflexology session. Percy knew how to pick me up and dust off the dirt, so to say. I suddenly changed my mind about flicking her away with the remote control. *You're all right, Percy,* I thought. *Maybe.*

"It's good to see you eating again, Didi," Percy said as she rubbed my back. "The way you gobbled down your breakfast with oatmeal and crumbs all over your face and pajamas, it was as if you haven't eaten in months. You already look anorexic, sweetie, like a good wind can come along and blow you away. You look like a stick with a big marshmallow of a butt poking out from behind," she said then laughed. "Remember how we used to make smores over the stove when we were coming up?" She laughed some more, that time, falling to the floor. "You look..." she laughed and held her stomach, "like that marshmallow." She couldn't control her laughter. Percy actually rolled over on her back and laughed and laughed until tears rolled down her face and her voice was weak. "You're butt looks like a marshmallow on a stick."

Oh no she didn't, I thought. What was she up to? She knew that I was sensitive about my butt. Was she on drugs or something? She made me wonder. I just ignored her and turned up the volume on the TV with the remote control to tune her out.

She then took a napkin and wiped my mouth, but I knocked her hand away and continued to watch TV.

"What are you doing?" I asked, annoyed.

"Do you know what you reminded me of?"

"What?" I asked in annoyance as I continued to stare at the TV.

"You remind me of Keston and Kevin when they were babies and used to get food all over the place. Their bibs ate more food than they did." She began to laugh long and hard, as I continued to ignore her.

She started to rub my back when she finally saw that I wasn't amused by her sick humor. I hated her rubbing my back like she did because it reminded me of that incident with our grandfather, but I let her do it anyway. She probably would have caused a big fuss if I had told her to stop. Flicking her away with the remote control started to appeal to me again.

Anyway, it sure felt like I hadn't eaten in months. But good old-fashioned, homemade oatmeal and biscuits can satisfy the greatest of appetites.

"Let me fix your hair, sweetie," Percy said as she started to comb my hair. "It's all nappy and knotted up."

I didn't notice that she had come downstairs with my comb and brush tucked inside her oversized pajama pockets.

"You really need to cut some of this hair off," Percy said as she struggled to get the comb through my hair, one handful at a time, starting from the ends and moving up to my scalp. She tugged and tugged.

"Ouch!" I yelled. She pulled harder and harder. If I didn't know any better, I'd say that she was trying to pull my hair out from the roots!

"I cut my hair ten years ago and just love it. All I do is wash it, blow it dry and go. Simple," she said.

"I have good, straight hair like Daddy," she reminded me for the millionth time. "I don't know where you got this thick, wavy, kinky stuff from. Still," she said as she started to massage that coconut-smelling, pink hair lotion into my scalp, then brushed my hair. It actually felt good. The gentle strokes stimulated my scalp, especially when she reached the nape. "You need to cut this stuff off. This is just too much hair. You don't need to have all this hair, Didi. You're almost forty years old ... too old to have long hair."

How dare she tell me to cut my hair off, I thought. "I like it long," I protested, then pulled away from her in disgust. She really got on my last good nerve, especially with that squeaky New York granny voice. Where did she get that voice from anyway? She went to live in New York for a few years, then came back sounding like a TV character. Amazing!

Anyway, Percy knew why I never cut my hair, and I felt her remarks to be very insensitive. She made me so angry that I wanted to grab that brush right out of her hand and beat her to a pulp, but... I didn't, probably because I was emotionally weakened by the long-lost memories of our grandfather and cousins that she stirred in me.

I then realized that I had a fear of cutting my hair that stemmed from my junior high school days. Back in the '70s, everybody wore Afros. That was the style and I wanted to follow the trend. So, I cut my hair really low and tried to wear one, too, especially for the new school year. But the texture of my hair just wouldn't do. I had kind of a curly-wavy 'Fro.

That Labor Day, we all met at my grandfather's for a mini-family reunion. His backyard was about an acre with the greenest, plushest grass. My uncle was barbequing some chicken, ribs and corn-on-the cob on the grill. To the right by the chain-link fence, my father stirred a giant, steaming, black kettle of crabs and crawfish. The wind blew the aroma of seafood and other spices into the air. Boy, I was sure hungry. It sure smelled good. I probably gained ten pounds smelling the herbs and spices.

My younger cousins were playing on the white swing set that my grandfather built for them in the middle of the yard. The other cousins who were near my age, stood around talking and listening to music and such. None of them interacted with our family. It was as if we weren't there, until our grandfather noticed my new 'do.

"George," he said to my father between laughs at the top of his lungs. His loud voice captured the attention of the entire clan. Everybody stopped all other activities and focused on him. "What you want to go and let that gal cut all her hair off for. She looks just like a little old pickaninny! At least when she had some hair, it hid that big old square head of hers and those big old eyes of hers and those funny-looking Dumbo ears."

All my cousins laughed really loud and hard. The grown-ups like my aunt, uncle and invited neighbors laughed like nobody's business.

My father tried to laugh to go along with my grandfather, but I knew that he was upset deep down inside and didn't want to show it. I never forgave him for that until now. He never stood up to my grandfather and let him treat us like dirt through the years, putting us down in front of both family and strangers.

I was so embarrassed that every muscle in my body froze. It was as if the Earth would have swallowed me whole if I had moved. Then, I saw my cousin, Juanita, directly in front of me. She was my uncle's daughter and our grandfather's favorite granddaughter. We were the same age. That winch was a scrawny thing with pale, yellowish skin; dark, beady eyes; and long, wavy, jet-black hair. Our grandfather often bragged of how pretty she was and often gave her all sorts of gifts in front of Percy and me without as much as giving us a piece of bubble gum. That 'ho' looked like a fuckin' witch if you ask me. I never liked the bitch myself … well … until … well … you know when.

My life turned out all right even though good old Grandpa and my cousins didn't expect it to. When I bought my house in Peachtree City—one that I worked for myself, my second house thank you very much—Juanita was living back in New Orleans with about four children, which we later discovered had different daddies, on Section 8. I earned a B.S. from Spelman in 1982—before I had turned twenty-one—and an M.S. in Computer Engineering from Tulane University, while dear, sweet Juanita got pregnant in her senior year and barely finished high school. Sure, she married a much older man who was well-to-do and lived on the lakefront for a quick minute. I guess the old buzzard got too old for her, so she decided to steal my ex—what's his name

***

Does what's-his-name have a name? You said his name before.

I don't want to say his name again. It's too painful.

It's been a long time. You need to release him. Now, what's his name?

Dr. Mark Breaux. Are you satisfied, Dr. Iverson? Keston and Kevin are Breaux's.

***

But—and I mean but—Juanita didn't appreciate what's-his-name and fooled around with everybody in town. They deserved each other, if you ask me. That served his ass right. He refused to pay child support, thinking that would hurt me, but I had my own. I didn't care. I hate to admit it, but I secretly gloated when one of her millions of boyfriends told what's-his-name everything. Juanita thought she was hot stuff and that that man would put up with her foolishness because she was pretty. For that, I blame our grandfather. "Good looking girls don't need all that education," my granpa always told Daddy. "They know they'll always have a good man to provide for them. But girls like Didi and Percy…"

Well, from what I was told, five years later, what's-his-name finally got tired of her whoring around and put her out. "You came to this marriage with nothing, and you're leaving with nothing," he told her. What probably really hurt him was finding out that none of the children he'd raised were his.

That man had serious legal connections. If I couldn't get child support, then I knew she couldn't even get alimony. Check this out, the two children who were supposedly his, weren't. So, Juanita couldn't get child support either. She tried to go after the first husband for child support, but the courts couldn't find him. All the children were spoiled rotten and thought they were hot stuff too. I bet it was shocking for them to go from living on Lakeshore Drive and attending private schools, to living in the projects with rats and roaches. How sad.

What's-his-name later apologized to me, but it was too late. Last year, he was only forty-two years old and had a stroke. Daddy told us that he was asking to see Keston and Kevin, but the boys refused to see him. What's-his-name, excuse me, Dr. Breaux, accused me of poisoning the boys against him. Did he expect the boys to smother him with affection when he never wanted anything to do with them? I actually felt sorry for what's-his-name. Daddy said he looked really bad. He had lost a lot of weight and was nothing but skin and bones. He got to the point where he couldn't even feed or go to the toilet by himself. Over the past twelve years, he went through three marriages and three divorces. None of his ex-wives went to see him in the hospital. Last year, he passed away and, according to Daddy, no one even attended the services. Pitiful.

***

It's good that you're releasing age-old feelings, but stay focused on the matter at hand. What else happened at the party? You may get clues as to what's happening now.

***

Anyway, back to the mini-family reunion. That heifer Juanita looked me straight in the eyes, opened that big mouth with those big, bubbly, pink lips of hers, and just laughed and laughed. The look on her face and sound of her laugh put a bad taste in my mouth, so to say, and I completely lost my appetite. I felt so low ... so worthless ... undignified. Somehow, I managed to run and sit under the big oak tree that sat at the rear of the back yard and cried my eyes out. Percy missed the barbeque and music just to sit under the tree and comfort me all afternoon. Neither of us had a bite to eat all day. No one even noticed or cared that we were gone—not even our father or brothers. They were too busy eating and dancing.

"Don't mind him," Percy said as she rubbed the center of my back in a circular motion. Sounds of "Do It Baby" by the Miracles played in the background. The song's soulful beat and my sister being near chased away the hurt of my grandfather's word. "He's just a silly, senile, old man. Your hair makes you look very pretty."

I felt so ugly and so self-conscious of my looks since that day. When my hair finally grew back, I never cut it again ... well, except an occasional trim.

Then, that morning, Percy stirred up all those buried emotions. I had

completely forgotten about that incident until then. Sometimes I wasn't sure
what her intentions really were. Was she out to get me in some way?

***

It was two o'clock in the afternoon when I heard the doorbell ring. I peeked
out the front window in the foyer and noticed a tall, slender woman wearing
leopard-print spandex pants; black, high-heeled sandals and a black halter-top
rolling a large, black Pullman's tote from a black Mercedes Benz. The
reflexologist and her assistant had arrived. Her hair was slicked back high in the
middle of her head into an elegant, long, bouncy ponytail. She wore small black
oval rim glasses and too much makeup for her honey-brown complexion.

Percy opened the door as she and another woman, mind you, who I didn't
see standing near the bushes, hugged and air kissed. "Hey there, Dewey! Thanks
for coming all this way from Alpharetta."

Dewey? I wondered. *Now where have I heard that name before?* That name
sounded so familiar. Then, when she walked in pulling a large Pullman's tote
close behind, she seemed so familiar. *But from where?* I wondered.

Dewey appeared to be around my age and dressed more conservatively than
her younger counterpart. She and the other woman looked so much alike that I
assumed that they were either mother and daughter or sisters. Dewey was about
my height, only a few pounds heavier. Her hair was pulled back into a bun,
bringing full attention to that smooth heart-shaped face and full, brown eyes.

"Dewey and Cynthia, this is my sister, Didi," Percy said.

We exchanged handshakes and hellos.

Dewey and Cynthia, I wondered. *Where have I heard their names before?
Where have we met?* They just seemed so familiar, but I couldn't quite place my
finger on it.

"This is a lovely home you have here, Didi," Dewey said as she looked
around. Her voice was deep and raspy, as if she'd been a heavy smoker most of
her life.

"It sure is," Cynthia said. Her voice was so shrill and squeaky that it sent
shock waves through my body.

Dewey's and Cynthia's eyes were almost hypnotizing. Really, Dr. Iverson.
Their eyes looked … different. They were large and wide. Not large as in poppy,
bulging-large, but … their eyes appeared to be … well … about three inches
wide … really. Don't get me wrong. Their eyes were pretty. In fact they
reminded me of the eyes you see on ancient Egyptian sculptures.

I must have been staring at them for awhile because Percy shook me from
an almost trance-like state. "Let's get your things set up," Percy said then
escorted them to the sunroom straight ahead and through the kitchen.

It was a good thing that I put that red-and-black Persian runner between the
front door and the kitchen or the wheels from the Pullmans could have scratched
the hardwood floors something awful.

"Are you all right?" Percy asked, startling me. She had returned from the
sunroom, and I was still standing in the foyer in a daze of sorts.

"I'm all right," I tried to reassure Percy, but a concerned look crossed her face.

I managed to make it through the kitchen and into the sunroom. That's where I kept my four plants because it was so bright and airy.

French windows lined most of the walls, giving a clear view of my backyard garden. The boys kept the fescue grass fertilized, so it was plush and green like that of a golf course. I bought the house because it was on a wooded lot with two big magnolia trees mixed between the pines and oaks. I planted different varieties of shrubs that changed colors with the seasons, and caladiums near the stairs leading from the sunroom to the backyard in the spring and summer.

Well, Dr. Iverson, the sunroom was always my space and Percy had the audacity to invite other folk into my space! The nerve of her!

Usually, the sunroof directly above makes the room look bigger than it actually is, especially with the sun shining and all. But, that day, the room looked too small to fit all of us. I had just bought a tan leather love seat and sofa with those big cushions, so I didn't want any nail polish or anything accidentally spilling on the furniture. I had just put a tan-and-black Persian rug in the center of the room along with a large square marble coffee table on top, and I didn't want them ruined either. That was for sure.

Anyway, the ladies unpacked their Pullman's totes in lightning speed. I didn't realize so much ... stuff ... could fit into those things. First, Dewey pulled out a large, clear zippered bag that was large enough to fit a foot basin, polish, emery boards and other things. A big white label with Percy's name on it was attached to the zipper.

I didn't realize that Percy brought in two metal folding chairs with the cushioned backs from the garage. Dewey lined the floor with large plastic covering that she had retrieved from a smaller black case, while Cynthia had unfolded two small white, plastic tables with round stools attached. Next, they both disappeared with the electric footbath and other gadgets. A few minutes later they returned with each one filled with sudsy water. They pulled a new footbath out of a box, then proceeded to open new packs of emery boards and other things. Next, they disappeared and returned with the foot basin and other things filled with sudsy water.

"Here," Dewey instructed. "Put your feet in." She started to tend to Percy.

I obeyed. The pulsating water felt sooo good against my feet. Dewey pulled one of the portable tables nearby, sprayed some lemon-scented oil on my hands, then put them in the hand massager. The warm water against my hands felt really good too.

Meanwhile, Cynthia cut open a clear plastic bag that contained two small blue brushes. With my feet still submerged, she massaged my feet—one by one—with the larger brush. She started at the ankles, moving in small circular motions, across each foot, down to and between each toe, then finally up and down the soles, sending chills up my spine. Her firm strokes were so relaxing, so heavenly.

Then, she took one foot out and placed it on the stool in front of her. She took a pair of tweezers and carefully removed old, dried skin that had formed around my toenails, then she did the other foot. She took my hands and a smaller brush and carefully massaged the back of my hands, down to my fingers and palms. The tiny back and forth motions were so relaxing.

Out of nowhere, Dewey entered the room with a square, blue container of hot wax. When Cynthia dried my feet and dipped them in the wax and covered them with two clear, plastic foot covers, I thought I was in heaven. The warmth traveled up my legs and up and down my spine, especially since it seemed like Percy had turned the air conditioning down to sixty degrees. Next thing I knew, Cynthia had dried my hands, dipped them in a hot wax bowl, then wrapped them in clear plastic. The warmth traveled up my arms, sending a tingly sensation along with it. The thought of nail polish ruining my new furniture completely vanished from my mind. All I thought about in that moment in time was the soothing, hot wax covering my hands and feet. I was in my own little world and didn't even notice or care what was going on with Percy.

Dewey and Cynthia sat down on the couch and flicked on the TV. One of those drama talk shows was on. The guest ranted and raved about this, that and the other. Percy and the ladies commented about the show, while I was lost to the hot wax treatment and didn't care about anything else. About fifteen minutes later, Cynthia removed the plastic wrap from my hands and feet, while Percy continued to stew, so to say. The wax just peeled right off, taking with it old dried skin and pent up stress of working long hours for the past two years.

Then, Cynthia took a callous remover and peeled even more skin from the soles my feet, then worked on the two corns on my pinky toes. That felt so good and relaxing. My feet look brand new and I felt like a brand-new woman.

Then, she rubbed some hot oil on my calves and feet and began to massage long, strong strokes up and down and around my calves. She moved down to my feet with strong gliding strokes up and down, then massaged each of my toes and between each one. Heavenly. Then, out of nowhere, Dewey started to rub hot oil on my arms and hands. My mind became clearer and more focused with each of her deep, penetrating strokes. She tugged and twisted my flesh up and down and side to side, over and over again, gliding on the rose-scented hot oil that covered my skin.

"Be sure to drink plenty of pure water tonight and tomorrow," Dewey said.

Huh? I thought. "Why?" I asked.

"Reflexology loosens the toxins in your body," Dewey explained as she rolled and kneaded the palms of my right hand. "They need to be flushed out with water or they'll just stay in your body. Toxin buildup is what causes different kinds of diseases."

***

Well, her therapy must have cleaned the toxins from my mind, too, Dr. Iverson, because things that bothered me only a few days earlier, didn't seem to matter anymore—not even my unexpected trip to North Carolina. It was like she had cleared away all my concerns and fears.

***

"Choose a color," Cynthia said. I was so engrossed in the hand massage that it took a moment to comprehend Cynthia's presence.

Then Cynthia opened a case of over one hundred unopened bottles of nail polish and asked me to choose one. I decided on a nice color called "Pussy Red." She even had matching lipstick. Cynthia polished my toes—one by one—until the color came to life. Then she started on my fingernails. I'm telling you Dr. Iverson, they've never looked more beautiful. And that deep red color brought out the red undertone in my skin. *Percy is right*, I thought. *I should take better care of myself.*

Chapter 12.
A Point in Time When Dreams Come True

It was four-thirty on Friday morning. The house was mostly dark and quiet... well, almost quiet. Percy snored like nobody's business. I heard her loud and clear from down the hall. The boys slept right through it, but they'd sleep through a fire.

Anyway, I couldn't get back to sleep, especially with choo-choo train Percy snoring down the hall. So, I decided to get up, go to the bathroom and try one of the meditation CDs that you gave me, Dr. Iverson. Until that morning, meditation never worked for me.

I started for the bathroom, the one place in the house that tuned out background noises. The only way that I made my way around in the dark was with that eerie, yellow bug light from the porch that beamed through my bedroom window. Certain times of the year, the moon and stars would shine through my window too. But that morning, the sky was pitch black without as much as the twinkling of a far away galaxy.

I found my portable FM radio and CD player in the walk-in closet to the right. It was sitting way in the back on the floor. That was where I had left it some time ago. I bought it back in '91 to use for emergencies, you know, tornadoes, ice storms and such. But, since the blizzard of '93, I never really had to use it. Even so, I made sure that the batteries were always fresh, because you just never know.

Anyway, being up that early in the morning without having to go to work brought back many fond memories. My Great-Aunt Ruby used to tell her visitors, "Universal elements are always the most powerful during the predawn hours. If you truly want the desires of your heart to come true, then say what I told you to say."

Great-Aunt Ruby had hundreds or even thousands of three-by-five laminated index cards that had Bible verses, chants, prayers or affirmations printed on them. She told her clients—if you can call them clients—to memorize and repeat the words during the wee hours of the morning. The likelihood of the wish coming true was multiplied by the power of a full moon. The brighter the moon—like the September harvest moon—the stronger its power to shape universal elements. Great-Aunt Ruby was something else. She was eccentric, but definitely something else.

Anyway, I finally made it to the bathroom. The bright floodlights from the garage gave the room a soft glow, enough for me to find the big white candle and matches buried in the drawers under the vanity. I kept the little brass gargoyle holder in the same white bag that you gave it to me in. I got that thing from you over two years ago, but never thought about burning it until that morning. So, it just sat under the sink all that time. Shame on me!

The candle was still wrapped in clear cellophane. It crackled so loud when I removed it that it echoed through the room. I sat on the floor near the shower, then placed the candle into the large round cup. When I lit the match, the flame flickered behind the open slots of the gargoyle's eyes and mouth, making them more true to life.

I sat with my back straight against the wall, directly in front of the candle. I positioned the CD player to my left, then carefully placed the "Winter's Wind" meditation CD right in. A bit of the flood light from above the garage and the candle brought out the deep sienna tones in the wallpaper …

***

A tall, slender figure in a dark, hooded robe guided me down a long, dark, steep stairway. The figure held a torch in its hand, but the dark garments concealed its fingers. I was close enough to feel the fiery heat against my skin. Bright, white flames cast our shadows on the walls as we descended farther and farther down the passageway. It was cool and dim, like being inside of a cave.

I, too, wore a long, dark, hooded robe. Each stair step was a deep golden yellow and resembled that of old, eroded limestone. A powdery residue covered my bare feet with each step, protecting my soles from the long descent into the great dark unknown that waited below.

A few feet below, I noticed that the stairway curved to the right, completely blocking the view of what was below. It appeared brighter as we neared the bend. One step at a time we descended until we circled about the bend. At the bottom, I noticed that two large torches protruded from the walls on both sides of us. Straight ahead was a large stone door that was slightly ajar. Looking inside, I saw nothing but the purest of black, as though it were a void of some type. The figure chanted in a strange, yet familiar language.

***

Well, come to think of it, the words reminded me of those my great-grandmother spoke as she read passages from that book I told you about. You, know Dr. Iverson, the one with the strange, old Greek letters on it. I hadn't heard anyone speak like that in years. Probably finding the book two years ago stirred up memories that were buried in my subconscious. The meditation probably brought up thoughts of my great-grandmother that I had forgotten.

***

Anyway, we entered the room, as the torch lit our path. The floor was made of limestone; hieroglyphics covered the walls and ceiling. We continued to walk straight ahead into a large triangular opening that seemed to lead into another pitch-black room. As we entered the second room, a ray of light entered through a tiny square opening toward the top of the ceiling. Just like the first room, the floor was made of stone and hieroglyphics covered the walls. It was completely barren, with not as much as a bench.

That was the end of the journey. The only way out was either back through the doorway that we entered or through the opening in the ceiling, which looked to be fifty feet above ground. I felt at peace.

The figure stuck the torch into a hole in the wall to put out the fire, then sat on the floor, still with the smokey torch in hand. The smell of sulfur filled the air.

I realized that I was having a lucid experience; only the figure seemed to be controlling the chain of events.

"Who are you?" I asked.

It didn't answer and remained motionless against the wall with its back toward me. I walked closer, trying to discover who the mysterious stranger was. *Do you really want to know?* I asked myself. *What if it's a hideous monster or something?* Then, I realized that it was a mirage brought on by meditation. *This is my world,* I thought. *I'm in control.*

"What is this place?" I asked.

It began to remove its hood, and I saw the back of a woman's head. Her hair was long, jet-black and wavy. She turned to face me, but hesitated at a forty-five degree angle. That was enough for me to catch a glimpse of the facial features that her hair didn't hide.

Her skin glistened in the sunlight, making it appear as smooth and creamy as dark chocolate. The bridge of her nose was long and straight, almost sinking into those high, pronounced cheekbones. And I'd never seen long, curly lashes like that before except... For a split second, long lost images of my mother returned. Then ... then ...

***

I snapped back to present time and present place. I was sitting against my bathroom wall staring into the gargoyle's blank eyes. I moved closer. Strange, but the candle had been extinguished though it had not burned much at all. Birds sang outside the window as I noticed that it was daylight. The CD player was still going, and the "Crackling Campfire" track was playing. I looked closer and noticed that the *Repeat* indicator was set to *Track 8,* which was "Crackling Campfire."

Why did it start with "Winter's Wind" and end with "Crackling Campfire?" I asked myself. I reasoned that probably the player was set to track 8 some time ago. It probably had to play through all tracks until it reached track 8, then repeated itself.

The mental exercise refreshed me so much. I wondered why I hadn't made an effort sooner to master meditation.

I looked at the time displayed on the CD player—*7:00* displayed in flashing green numbers.

It's still early, I reasoned. *Think I'll do it again.* I flicked through the CD to Track 1, "Winter's Wind" and set *Repeat.* I reached over and lit the candle again, then reclined against the wall.

"Take one long breath in," the voice instructed from the CD as I inhaled long and hard. The sultry female voice was soft and mellow and sounded amazingly like the night announcer on that classical radio station that Percy used to listen to. I always hated that station. *I didn't recall the voice before,* I said to myself.

"Exhale," the voice said, and it was like being transported inside a world created by the CD. Gentle tones of a wind chime clang amidst the whistle—of what I imagined to be—a winter's wind on a cold December night. "Take one long breath in … "

I crossed my legs in the Yoga position, concentrating on the voice that bellowed from the CD. With my hands—palm side up—on top of my knees, I began to gaze into the gargoyle's flaming eyes. The creature almost seemed to come alive the longer I studied its amber eyes. Deeper and deeper I stared, concentrating on the golden flame with not as much as a blink. The clanging chimes grew louder, and the wind blew harder, as the bellowing voice dimmed to a quiet whisper. Deeper and deeper…

***

I was engulfed by some strange energy that tingled at the crown of my head and quickly covered my entire body. The sensation was better than any orgasm that I had ever had, that's for sure, as it tingled and massaged every cell of my body. It brought me to what I can best describe as a spiritual climax, forcing me to take one long inhale, longer than any I had ever taken until that time. In an instant, I exhaled longer and harder than I ever had done. I felt breath rush through my nostrils with lightning speed, vaporizing into gargoyle's flaming eyes.

My entire being fizzled into oblivion, as I became one with the universe. I was transported to a room by a large bay window looking out on the darkness of night. It was like a blizzard. Mounds of snow covered the grounds. Moonlight reflected off of the bright, white flakes. What looked like a pine forest sat in the distance. The sound of the whistling wind blowing through the snow-covered trees was so peaceful and serene. I was at peace.

The room was mostly dark and still. I sensed a fireplace far behind me that ignited the room with a soothing warmth that radiated to the depths of my soul. Its golden flames crackled in the distance and provided a hint of light to the dim setting.

I was alone in my sanctuary, a private place to be shared with no other. The physical part of me was back in the bathroom, but my consciousness remained in the night of the winter's wind. I had taken a vacation from life or … or … stepped into another room of this thing we call existence. I was overcome by a strong sense of knowingness that welcomed me into its midst; it offered me the chance to visit whenever I wanted a sterile harbor that was free of the world's ills. It was a resting place along life's journey—one that always was and always will be. I had discovered a secret compartment of humanity that I never knew existed until that time.

I was nestled in the warmth and comfort of that strange new world, as I continued to stare out into the coolness of night.

The intensity of the fireplace behind me grew stronger with each fleeting moment. Its fiery flames were as brilliant as the rising sun. A magnetic force emanated from its core, slowly pulling me into the brightness. I felt myself being drawn backward into its midst. The snow outside looked so beautiful that I decided to drift toward the window. Again, I felt myself being drawn into the light. I struggled to flee the stronghold, but the more I struggled to be free, the harder it pulled.

I remained in the room, yet everything got smaller. It was like looking inside from a far distance. The surroundings became dim and hazy. All that remained before me was a gray mist that expanded rapidly as it neared.

The only time that I had ever seen anything like that was a few years ago. Early one Saturday morning, our team was trying to make a deadline, so we worked that whole weekend. We learned that two buildings were scheduled to be destroyed at nine o'clock that morning, so we had to get in around six o'clock because all the streets leading to the area were closed. The developers scheduled the demolition for Saturday morning, probably because they didn't expect anyone to be in the immediate vicinity.

As the time neared, a crowd of fifteen of us gathered around the break room window. We watched as the buildings were being imploded a few blocks down Peachtree Road. It all happened so quickly, in a matter of seconds. The buildings crumbled to the ground in lightening speed. All of a sudden, the floor vibrated beneath our feet, and it turned pitch-black outside the window. "Whoa," a few people yelled. We were all taken by surprise when those big, twirling gray dust clouds surrounded the building. I knew for sure that a tornado had struck. Some people backed away from the windows and went back to work. A look of concern crossed the faces of many as if to say, "Perhaps this wasn't a good idea coming to work today." Amazing ... we experienced all that ... but we were on the twentieth floor ... and a few blocks away! We were later told to remain inside for most of the day until the dust had settled.

But that's just what it looked like during the morning meditation session: dust from a fallen building, as a foggy, gray mist clouded the room.

Anyway, the haziness expanded more as it neared me; silvery dots sparkled through the clouds like tiny specks of diamonds. The light pulled faster and harder, it felt like being on a roller coaster, only in reverse. I welcomed the mist as it came closer and closer, completely surrounding my being. The air thickened to the consistency of hot, sudsy bubbles. The force continued to pull me. Shimmering silver and gold bubbles floated all about, appearing as graceful fireflies on a hot summer's night.

"Didi," a familiar voiced echoed in the distance. "Didi."

I was overcome by a feeling of bliss. The fog quickly dissipated as the energy began to reel me in; each silver and gold bubble exploded as firecrackers on New Year's Eve as it entered the light.

The most brilliant, brightest of pure, white light surrounded me. It was like nothing I had ever seen. Tiny light waves vibrated all around...

Chapter 13.
And Reality Fades Before the Eyes

"Didi," a voice called.

The sound of my name rippled through my being causing air to quickly fill my lungs. I was jolted back to what I knew as reality.

"Didi," the voice said again. That time, I recognized the voice as Percy.

I slowly opened my eyes and the room appeared to be composed of millions of tiny vibrating waves—like the ones that I saw in the light.

"Didi," Percy called again. "Are you all right? Why are you on the floor?"

"Yes," I managed to get out. "I'm all right."

"Were you sleeping on the bathroom floor?" she asked. "That doesn't make any sense."

I didn't feel the need to explain anything to Percy.

"What were you sleeping on the floor for, Didi?"

I uncrossed my legs and tucked them against my chest. The room was still vibrating fiercely and I needed to regain my composure. I tuned Percy out.

"What were you sleeping on the floor for?" Percy demanded. One thing about my sister, she sure was persistent and wouldn't budge until you spilled your guts.

"What?" I asked in annoyance.

"That doesn't make any sense," Percy said. "I don't know why you would want to sleep on the floor for anyway. And why were you sleeping sitting up?"

"I was ..." I tried to tell her that I was meditating, but she cut me off. I rubbed my eyes a few times, then the room stopped vibrating.

She gathered up the candleholder and CD player. She looked down on the floor and saw the CD case. "You're not supposed to fall asleep when you meditate," she informed me. "That's cheating," she said then walked away. Percy knew that I was meditating all along, but she probably wanted to rub it in that I had fallen asleep.

***

But I don't think that I had fallen asleep, Dr. Iverson. Those scenes were so real, so vivid. They couldn't have been dreams—well, maybe lucid dreams. They were just so bizarre.

***

I managed to stand up and stretch long and hard.

"It's almost nine o'clock," she yelled from the bedroom. "You need to eat something. You can't just sleep all day!"

I neared the bedroom and saw a tray of food on my nightstand. My stomach immediately reacted to the sight of pancakes piled high on a plate, a large bottle of maple syrup and a tall glass of orange juice. Umm, I suddenly became just too hungry!

"Go brush your teeth," Percy instructed as she poured the syrup over the pancakes.

I hated her telling me what to do. She was just too bossy.

I went to brush my teeth like a good girl. The sweet smell of Mr. Chap's coffee traveled from the kitchen and through the door of my bathroom, tickling my nose.

I sat on the side of the bed, eager to please my appetite. Percy had stacked more on the tray than I realized. Hidden behind the mound of pancakes were two of the white porcelin espresso cups that Keston and Kevin gave me for Christmas last year. One cup was filled with homemade strawberry syrup still hot and bubbly from simmering on the stove; and the other was filled with pecan-maple syrup. The steam that rose from its bubbling center filled the air with the smell of butter, fresh pecans and vanilla extract. Boy was I hungry, so I sliced the pancakes with my fork and dove right on in.

"Umm, banana pancakes," I moaned. The pancakes were so light and fluffy with just the right amounts of freshly creamed bananas, vanilla and honey. Percy made the best pancakes in the whole world. She sifted the flour just so, sprinkled in the perfect amount of baking powder and added four eggs with a teaspoon of cream beat in.

***

The eggs are what made them so fluffy. But that's our family secret, Dr. Iverson, so promise not tell anyone … please.

***

Anyway, Tish and I called her pancakes "Man Catcher's Cakes" because each of her five fiancès proposed to her after eating her homemade buckwheat pancakes—from scratch of course.

"What are you putting in those things?" Tish teased. "You're not working roots on 'em, are you?"

Percy walked in the bedroom carrying another tray. Her moves were slow and easy, as she was careful not to spill what she was carrying—my sterling silver coffee server set with serving pot, cream and sugar containers. *How dare she use my sterling silver server set!* I thought.

***

Don't say it, Dr. Iverson. You were about to say something about me not being grateful and how she went out of her way to fix breakfast for me and I was worried about her touching my silver server set, right? You probably think that I should be more grateful. After all, Percy took a whole month off from work just to take care of Keston, Kevin and me. You're going to say that my dear, sweet sister, Percy, toiled all morning over a hot stove just so that I could have a nutritious meal to eat, right? Even though I did pay over five hundred dollars for the set and wanted it purely for show in my china cabinet. I bought it brand new and had never touched it. You're going to say that I was being selfish, weren't you Dr. Iverson?

***

No, Demeter, I wasn't.

Oh.

***

Anyway, back to breakfast. Under that long pink floral robe and matching pink slippers, I noticed sheer, black hose. She wore a hint of makeup and her hair was curled. *She must be going to work,* I reasoned. *But she never wears that much makeup to work, ever! Maybe she has a mid-week or mid-day date or something.*

My stomach was satisfied, which put me in good spirits. So I just wanted to relax and read for a spell. "Where's the newspaper?" I asked Percy.

She froze in place as she poured coffee, spilling a few drops on the nightstand. *I sure hope that coffee doesn't ruin the nightstand,* I thought.

"Well ... uh ... uh ... " she stammered then wiped the spilled coffee with one of the napkins from the tray. Percy poured in plenty of cream and three tablespoons of sugar. She knew just how I liked my coffee. *I wish that she would wipe up the rest of that spill!* I thought.

"I've been working so much that I haven't read the paper in a long time. I don't even know why I still have the subscription." She looked a bit concerned, but I pushed on. "Well," I said then sipped some coffee. "Umm, ummm," I moaned. Mr. Chap's coffee hit the spot, especially since I hadn't had any in a few days. But the coffee was richer than usual, and had a nutty taste. "This coffee is good."

"I opened the red canister of coffee in the cupboard," Percy said.

That was the *Java Lava* that I bought from Chap's the Friday before. He said that it was a special new blend, one that he didn't serve in the café.

She glanced at the clock on the nightstand. "Ten-thirty!" she exclaimed. That's when I noticed that she was wearing her *good* pearl earrings—the ones she wore for special occasions only. Percy headed for the hallway as though she were in a hurry to get someplace. She removed her pink robe and carelessly slung it over her shoulders. Just as I had suspected: she was fully dressed in what I call a "double-breasted suit-dress." It was black and looked like a knee-length double-breasted jacket with black-and-gold buttons along the front. Apparently, she had placed a pair of black pumps with metallic gold heels outside my bedroom door. She literally jumped into the shoes.

"Where's today's paper, Percy?" I asked hoping that she would get it for me before she left. Ever since I left the hospital, I noticed her reading the paper. When I approached, she always put it away. I never thought about it before.

She froze in her tracks. "I don't know," she said, but her tone of voice indicated that she did in fact know where it was.

Maybe she threw it away, I reasoned. "Don't you usually read it in the morning?" I asked, hoping that she would have admitted to throwing it away.

"Uhhh … uhhh …" she stammered. "Not every morning, Didi." She began to straighten her clothes and proceeded down the hallway toward the stairs, not even looking back once at me. "Listen, Didi," Percy shouted while hurrying down the stairs. "I'm running late for an appointment." Her voice faded with each step she took. "I cut up some red-leaf lettuce and tomatoes and put them in that blue Tupperware thingy in the fridge and I bought some lemon-pepper turkey, honey-roasted ham, baby swiss cheese, gouda cheese and oatmeal-wheat rolls from the Kroger deli early this morning, so make yourself a sandwich for lunch. Okay, sweetie?" I couldn't help but chuckle because she spoke so fast, and sounded just like the "fast talk" that you hear in those car commercials. Then I heard the clank of her pump against the marble foyer floor. "Oh. Don't forget to take your medicine," she yelled one final time. A few short steps later, the front door slammed so hard that it shook the walls. Before I had taken another sip of coffee, I heard a car door slam, quickly followed by screeching tires out of the driveway.

She must be running seriously late for a really important meeting, a really hot date or both, I thought. I didn't care one bit. I sat with my back against the headboard, sank into the big, fluffy pillows, and enjoyed my cup of coffee. It was so good. One sip of Mr. Chap's coffee and all my cares quickly vanished. The more I drank, the more my problems disappeared. His coffee had that affect on folks. Though I didn't feel like it, I was a good girl and decided to take my medicine anyway.

I started to feel a bit light-headed, so I blinked three three times. When I opened my eyes the first time, the room looked dim and hazy. Only seconds before, the sun lit up the whole house, it seemed. *Maybe a cloud is covering the sun,* I thought.

I closed my eyes the second time, then opened them slowly. A buzz started low and gradually grew to the point that I couldn't stand it anymore. *Maybe it's the electrical circuits outside,* I thought, so I slid out of bed and headed toward the window, believing that I would see electric workers outside. The room began to vibrate to the tune of the buzz, knocking me off balance. Like many times before in previous weeks, the air thickened to the consistency of hot foam, making it hard for me to breathe. Hair stood up on my arms as a strange static charge filled the place. I began to panic and wondered if taking my medication was such a good idea after all. My heart pounded hard and fast to the rhythmic buzz. An unseen force weighed on my chest, tackling me to the floor in a matter of seconds. No screams of help; I couldn't muster up enough strength to utter a word. The buzz became unbearable, rippling through my body, tearing it apart cell by cell. Not a muscle in my body stirred. I lay helpless on the carpet as the sensation of stinging ants covered my skin.

I blinked a third time…

***

Bright, white clouds with silvery-blue, sparkling dust were before me. Laughter and garbled conversations echoed in the distance, almost surrounding me. A faint buzz, like that of a doorbell, went off and on every few seconds.

I felt my shapeless form drifting aimlessly through yet another unfamiliar world. Feelings of excitement stirred within me as I continued my journey to no man's land, in anticipation of the unexpected.

That time was different. Something else was in the fog—a presence that I couldn't see or explain. But I sensed its core essence slightly behind me to the left. A portion of me was joined with it on a spiritual level. The silvery mist was cool and dry, but the presence exuded a hot, tingly sensation like being submerged in a hot bubble bath on a cold winter's night.

My physical body materialized—bit by bit—as the fog slowly began to dissipate. I was a bit surprised by what I saw all around me.

***

Never did my wildest fantasies stir in the direction of what I witnessed. Where the images originated—till this day—is still a mystery to me. I know that you probably don't believe me, Dr. Iverson, but I never, ever imagined such a scene before. Perhaps, maybe, I read about such things or saw them on some movie, but I never imagined being involved. Really.

***

All about were large French windows that revealed the lush landscape of exotic trees in the distance. The walls were antique-white. Shiny, black-and-white, diagonal tiles seemed to rush across the floors, as Roman columns stood in the middle of the room. To the right was a shiny, black grand piano where two couples shamelessly engaged in acts of passion—one on the top and one below.

Hundreds of people gathered in the room, it was a party of sorts. Sultry sounds of jazz—cello, trumpet, saxophone and raspy drums—led me to a grand archway revealed another ballroom straight ahead. I looked all about. Laughter of a small crowd caught my attention as I passed by. Two women drank a clear, pink liquid from a single fluted goblet, while their male counterparts nibbled from a tray one of the many servers carried. Directly behind them were three more couples who laughed, drank and just enjoyed each other's company. The shining, white sun eased its brilliant silvery beams, highlighting the back wall. Abundant merriment and laughter filled the air, as I was overcome by a strong feeling of contentment. Then, I realized that, except for the band members who wore black tuxedos, everyone else was completely nude. No one seemed to care.

I suddenly felt the presence upon me. After quickly glancing back, I saw that nothing was there. Yet, the feeling persisted.

A warm, tingly sensation started on my left. At that point, I decided to walk toward the French windows. I noticed couples seated at wrought iron tables on the balcony as I neared.

The presence grew stronger and hotter with each step. I searched desperately for an exit, hoping to escape that menacing feeling, whether real or imagined. Somehow, I reasoned that I would escape imminent danger by going outside. I looked to the right, then to the left—nothing. Then, I noticed a door in the far corner of the room near the band that was hidden behind a small tree. I weaved in and out of couples, desperately trying to reach the door.

I finally reached the door, but the golden handle wouldn't turn. I felt the presence get closer and closer, but the door still wouldn't budge. Apparently, I caught the attention of someone on the patio who noticed my struggle.

"It opens out," the woman said as she pulled the door toward her.

"Thank you," I said.

The presence was upon me, as a fiery heat etched away at my left, leaving an invisible void into nothingness at my side. My ears started to ring … no … the ringing came from the void … from the depths of infinity.

"Join us," the woman said. "I'm Cynthia Dewey, but everyone calls me Dewey. I just shed my skin," she said, looking at me with those deep, dark, hypnotizing eyes. I knew that I was at her mercy.

"All right," I said as I followed her along the patio. She said, "join us," so I expected us to join a party of others. But we were alone in a secluded corner. It had to be a dream, because who would say something like, "Shed my skin," in real life, right?

I felt my loins moisten with every seductive step she took. Something seemed familiar about her. She was tall and slim with low-cut, jet-black, wavy hair. I couldn't help but notice her smooth, caramel nude body. Her hips were round and full, a perfect complement to her full breasts and protruding, brown nipples. She sat in a white chaise near the rail, with her legs propped against a column, giving full view of her silky, black pubic hairs and swollen, red clit. Her inner lips stood at attention, almost begging for me to stroke them and the hollow treat between them. Mercy!

"I know you want it," a voice said from nowhere, startling me from behind.

I turned. Marcellus was standing directly behind me with a smirk on his face.

"What?" I replied, almost instinctively.

"I know you want to have her don't you, Didi?" Marcellus asked. "Don't you?"

Shocked, I didn't know how to respond. He was right, I desired for our bodies to collide.

Marcellus took my hand. Together, we walked toward the chaise where I sat beside Dewey.

"She just shed her skin," Marcellus said.

I knew for sure that I was in a lucid dream because that was the second or so time hearing something about shedding skin.

They looked at each other with big grins, then at me.

"Everyone is here for the sake of enjoyment. I know you crave a woman's touch, so enjoy it," Marcellus said as Dewey eased my hands over my husband's cock. "Take her," he told Dewey. "Lick her tits. Didi likes having her tits played with and licked."

She smiled at him, next thing I knew she had begun to fondle my nipples with one hand, while she tickled my clit with the other. That was so delicious. Even though it was a dream, I felt guilty about being with someone else, especially in Marcellus' presence.

Marcellus leaned toward me, as I looked up at him. A big grin painted his face as if he were up to something. All the while, Dewey licked both my nipples, moving one to the other. She brought me so much pleasure that I didn't want her to stop—not even for Marcellus. I lay there motionless, hoping that Dewey would have me in any way imaginable.

Marcellus took my hand.

"What are you doing?" I started to ask, but the words couldn't quite get out. Dewey put me in such a tizzy; I didn't know what to do.

Marcellus eased my hand over Dewey's clit, it was wet, firm and swollen. Then, he eased my hand into her soaking-wet cunt. Mercy! He moved my finger in and out and around and around. I felt her hot walls pulse, squeezing my finger.

"That's it," Marcellus moaned and eased away as I continued to finger Dewey.

We engaged in a long, hot, passionate kiss. Her was tongue almost down my throat, as I continued to finger her hot, soaking-wet cunt. She opened her legs wider, allowing my finger to slip deeper and deeper into her paradise.

She hungrily rubbed my clit, as we continued to kiss long and deep. My femininity was on fire. I could take it no more. I rolled her on her back and got on top. We rolled clits like nobody's business, up and down and around and around. Shock waves rolled through my body, as every nerve ending was rerouted to my clit. She squeezed my rear in and out, in and out and ran her fingers down my crack just shy of stroking my backdoor, bringing me to a delightful climax. Goose bumps covered every inch of my quivering body as I began to jerk uncontrollably, collapsing on Dewey's soft, supple breasts. Only one other person knew my "spot" like that ... Tish. But that wasn't real. Was it?

"I'm coming! I'm coming!" Dewey yelled, then she purred like a helpless kitten, her body fell limp. "Whew!" she said, looking at me.

"Uhh," Marcellus moaned, long enough to break my concentration.

I was so engrossed in Dewey that I had completely forgotten about Marcellus. *He must be heartbroken,* I thought. *But this is a dream. Do dream images have feelings?* I felt so guilty, until I saw the look of pure lust cover his face as he moved over to us. He was moving his cock up and down and around and around in his hand—masturbating.

Tired and weary, Dewey and I looked up at Marcellus.

"Go back to what you were doing," he moaned as he continued to stroke his hot, throbbing cock. He squeezed and stroked his cock faster and faster, closing his eyes. "Uhh," he moaned long and hard from the gut, pure evidence that he was about to come.

Dewey reached up for his cock, but he pulled away.

"This is for my wife's body only," he managed to say between moans and biting his lower lip.

I crawled away from Dewey. In a flash, Marcellus let go of his cock long enough to grab my waist and place me on a glass top table near the balcony's edge. "Come here woman," he said as he slapped my rear, then plummeted deep inside of me.

"Oooh," he moaned. "You're so wet."

Still bent over, Dewey squeezed beneath me and began to lick my nipples.

"Suck her titties, baby," Marcellus moaned.

Having my breasts licked with such skills ... ooooh! Dewey twirled her tongue up and down and around and around one nipple while playfully pinching the other. She sent fireballs straight to my already swollen clit. Her motions were timed just right with each of Marcellus' long, hard, deep thrusts. I had never been so excited before that moment.

"Get from under there," a man said.

"We got something for you," another one said while he grabbed Dewey by the waist, pulling her to him.

He bent her over and entered her from the rear. She began to lick and tantalize the big, brown balls of the second man, while playing with his big, juicy head.

"Uhhh," Marcellus moaned again, as his moves slowed. I knew that he was holding back on me and wanted to regain his composure.

I looked up and back at him; he watched as the two men gained pleasure from Dewey's body. She licked the second man's cock up and down and around and around like an ice cream cone. Finally reaching the head, she licked and sucked and licked and sucked him so hard that he exploded in her mouth. I watched as she swallowed every frothy drop of come, as the other man continued to pump her from the rear. That must have been too much for Marcellus to stand because he, too, exploded, but inside of me.

"Uhh, baby," Marcellus yelled at the top of his lungs, rivaling the mating ritual of any wild bull.

I felt his big balls against my loins, as his river flowed for what seemed like a blissful eternity. Yum!

I returned to a standing position, as long streams of come oozed from inside of me. Strange, but it didn't ooze down my legs. I placed my hand "down there," and discovered that it had hardened into a gel-like substance and remained at the opening of my womanhood, sealing it closed.

Marcellus buried me with those big, strong, masculine arms, and held me near and dear. I pulled away for a second. A strange bubbly sensation stirred deep within me. It felt as if I had been covered with mentholated jelly on the inside. The last time I felt that way was in another lucid dream, the one when Marcellus and I were on our honeymoon. That was something, Dr. Iverson, having recollections in a dream. Amazing.

Other couples joined us on the balcony, but my loins burned so much, that I didn't pay attention to what they were doing.

"What's wrong?" Marcellus asked, as I looked deep into his dark, dreamy eyes.

"I'm burning inside, Marc," I said. "You really got me good."

He rubbed my belly and smiled for a moment without as much as taking his eyes off of me.

A bell sounded in the distance and rang louder and louder.

"What's that noise?" I asked.

No one else cared, they were kind of busy, you know, Dr. Iverson?

"What's that noise?" I asked Marcellus, but he continued to stare into my eyes as if the noise weren't there.

The bell got louder and louder ...

***

The air quickly filled my lungs as I bounced to a sitting position in bed. *How did I get in bed?* I asked myself. *It must have been the medicine.* I welcomed the thought of not having passed out on the floor. Whew!

My loins were still moist and tingling from the pleasure Dewey and Marcellus had given me. The loud bell turned out to be the phone ringing from my nightstand.

"You have reached 770-842-4792. Please leave a message after the tone. Thanks. Bye-bye."

It was my answering machine, followed by one long beep.

"Demeter," the voice started, "this is Trevor. When is you gone come back to work?"

I'm not answering, I thought. Percy must have forgotten the cordless phone in my room because it was next to the clock. I took a double glance at the clock and was a bit surprised when *10:40* appeared. *10:40!*

Trevor's message went on and on, and on and on. I thought that the machine would have cut him off.

"My team had found some defects in the software. Somebody had said that you had worked on that part of the program a couple years back and ..."

"What?" I asked after pressing the *Call* button on the phone.

"'Bout time you answereded 'yo phone," Trevor said. "I had called you yesterday and some lady had answereded the phone. She said she was yo' sustah."

"How can I help you, Trevor?" I asked. What I really meant to say was, "Why the fuck are you fuckin' bothering me, moth' fucker?"

"Is you comin' back to work, Demeter?" Trevor asked.

"In two weeks," I said in annoyance. "Daniel Batchelor is my back-up and you should be contacting him while I'm out."

"Two weeks?" Trevor exclaimed. "You ain't sick is you? You ain't got nothin' 'tagious or nothin' like that, heh? 'Cause I don't want to be comin' down wit' nothin'"

"Look, Trevor," I said. "Just get in touch with Daniel, all right." I sighed in annoyance and was tempted, and I mean very tempted, to hang up the phone on him.

"Well," Trevor said. "What's wrong wit' you anyhow? You had got some female problems or somethin'?" he asked.

The nerve of him. Some people are way too nosy. "No, Trevor," I said. *Everybody at the office probably put him up to calling me to find out what's going on*, I thought.

"Then what then?" he asked.

There was a bit of silence as he waited for an answer. Unbelievable.

"Nothing, Trevor." I was getting even more annoyed and started to hang up on him. I decided not to because he only would have called back. Worse yet, he would have had dear, sweet D'Angela to call. I needed to get rid of him in a way that no one else would even think to call or bother me either.

"Okay, Trevor," I said. "I'll tell you, but you have to promise not to tell anybody."

"Okay, promise," he said in a hushed whisper. "What? What?"

"I don't know, Trevor," I teased.

"Don't know what?" he asked, curiosity flowed through his voice. "What?"

"Well …"

"What, Demeter, what?" he begged. "Don't do me like this. Come on!"

"Oh all right," I said. "But you can't tell anybody. I mean nobody."

"Come on. I won't tell nobody!" he said, almost whimpering.

"I was pregnant and …"

"What!" he exclaimed. "You was pregnant?" he asked.

"Yes, Trevor," I agreed.

"You lyin'!"

"Nope."

"What happened? You lost the baby?"

"Yes, Trevor," I said, because it sounded good to me. "That's …"

I expected Trevor to feel really guilty for disturbing me in my time of sorrow. I knew for sure that he was going to apologize for calling and quickly find a reason to end our conversation.

"Who the daddy is?" he asked.

"Uhhh …" Trevor caught me off guard.

I was speechless. Then, I thought of the many times when our father warned Percy and me about what he called, "fabricating tales." He told us, "It's better to tell the truth. When you tell one fib, you have to tell another and another. After a while, you have too many tales to keep straight."

"Well …" I started.

"I ain't even know you was goin' wit' nobody."

"Well …"

"You be workin' all the time. What time you got to be goin' with somebody?" he asked.

"Well ..."

"It's somebody I know?" he asked.

"Uhh ... no," I said.

"Then who?" he pried further.

"You don't know him." I said.

"How you know I don't know 'im?" he said further. "You don't know who I know, and who I don't know!"

"I just know," I said. I thought of my first born to Marcellus, the figment of my imagination. So, there was no way for him to know my imaginary playmate.

"His name is Marc," I said, playing with him.

"Marc?" Trevor asked.

"Yes, Marc." I said.

"Where he work at?" Trevor asked.

"Uhh ..." I was stomped for words.

"He don't work in our buildin', do he?" Trevor asked. "You don't mean Marcus Williams at work do you?"

"No, Trevor," I said, then decided to have some fun. "He doesn't. In fact, he doesn't even live in Atlanta. He just visits on weekends."

"He don't live in Atlanta? He ain't married is he?"

"No, Trevor."

"How you know that?"

"I just know, Trevor."

"Umph," he said, followed by a long pause.

I twirled locks of hair around my finger, giggling as I waited for Trevor's next remark.

"He make good money?" Trevor asked.

"You ... you can say that."

"What type o' work he do?"

"He's in business."

"In business?"

"Yep."

"What dat 'posed to mean, in business?"

"Well ... "

"Dat don't even sound right. In business."

"He's in business, Trevor. What can I say?" I almost broke out laughing to the point where it was hard for me to keep calm. I couldn't believe that he fell for it. He was so gullible.

***

If I'd known then what I found out later, Dr. Iverson, I would have ended the conversation from the get-go. Sure, it eased my nerves from the side-effects of the medicine, but now I think that I should have done something else to divert my attention.

***

"What he look like?" Trevor continued.

"Well, he's tall with dark, wavy hair."

"Wavy hair? Is he a brotha? Tall wit' dark wavy hair don't sound like no brotha to me. Or one o' them light skinneded brothas."

He was huffed, which urged me to go on.

"He's Greek," I said.

Trevor yelled to the top of his lungs so loud, that I couldn't hold the receiver to my ear. I got a kick out of his reaction though.

"Lord, have mercy, Jesus!" he said. "Hold on, Demeter."

Trevor placed his hand over the receiver. If I were him, I would have used the *Hold* button so I wouldn't hear what he was saying. "Demeter got pregnant by a white man and lost the baby," I heard him say. That person's voice wasn't clear because Trevor's voice muffled the background noise, so I couldn't make out who he was talking to. "You heard me," he continued. "Demeter got pregnant by some white dude and lost the baby," he repeated. A muffled conversation went on for a few seconds before he came back on the phone. I started to hang up. But if I would have hung up, Trevor would have just called back.

"I'm back," Trevor said. "Sorry 'bout that, Demeter. D'Angela had needed some o' my files, so I tol' her where to find 'em. Oh, D'Angela said, 'hello.' Now back to you Miss Missy."

"Well ..."

"What you want go get some ol' Greek man fo' anyhow?"

"Well ..."

"Where you meet him at?"

"Just around and about."

"'Round and 'bout, heh?"

"Yep," I said.

"What's dat 'posed to mean? 'Round and 'bout?"

"Well, just being out with friends."

"Where y'all be hangin' 'round and 'bout at anyhow?"

"I don't know ... Buckhead ... "

"Buckhead?" he shouted.

"Yep," I said, then eased my back into the row of pillows that lined my headboard. I was enjoying Trevor ... for once.

"Why can't y'all hang out up in the 'hood ... like 'round South Dekalb or Greenbriar? They got some pretty nice 'tablishments in South Dekalb like 'round Stone Mou'ain. They got some real nice, I mean real nice 'tablishments 'round off o' Greenbriar Parkway over 'ere by the mall."

"Yes, Trevor," I said.

"For real. And they got some nice places o'er there off o' Cascade Road too."

"Umm, uhmm," I said.

"Y'all just don't like hangin' 'round us folk no mo'."

"We just like Buckhead," I said, knowing that statement would rile him.

"That's why y'all can't find no brothas 'cause y'all be hangin' 'round in Buckhead."

"That's not true, Trevor," I said. "We see *brothas* in Buckhead."

"Not no *real* brothas," he said.

"No," I said, knowing that that would provoke Trevor even further. "We don't look for *real* brothas."

"What?"

"You heard me."

"Lord, what is this world comin' to?"

"You tell me, Trevor,"

"The black man ain't good 'nough fo' ya? Heh?"

"Trevor ..." I was trying to tell him that I made the whole thing up, but he wouldn't let me get a word in edgewise. Sometimes—well actually all the time—Trevor didn't think before words jumped out of his mouth. You wouldn't believe the things he said to people, Dr. Iverson. He would make some outrageous comment, you know—say something really outrageous—it wouldn't dawn on the person what he actually meant until days later.

"Y'all strong, in'pen'nt, ed'cated, black women think y'all too good fo' the black man, don't you?"

"Trevor ..."

"Y'all be lettin' them otha folk just be messin' ova' y'all."

"Look ..."

"They get they li'l choc'late dip and just a keep a steppin'."

"Now, Trevor ..."

"I bet he ain't even been by to see you since you lost the baby, heh?" Trevor asked.

I said nothing.

"Heh?"

"That's not true, Trevor."

"Yeah it is. He ain't dere now or he woulda answereded the phone. Tell me I'm lyin' " Trevor was really worked up.

"He just left a few minutes ago," I said. In a way, I was telling the truth because I left Marcellus' company a few minutes ago. He was my imaginary playmate, but I was still in his company.

"Ya lyin'," Trevor said. Boy was he huffed. "I bet he ain't even been by there since you been out. I bet he made you get a abortion."

"That's not true."

"Sho' it's true," he said after a long pause. "He prob'ly ain't won't no black babies runnin' 'round nowhere."

"Trevor ..." I had started getting pissed because he was taking the joke too far ... just too far.

"Chil'," he said after a long pause. I could tell that he was upset and trying to regain his composure. "I bet' let you go and get you some rest. Let me get off this here phone."

Before I could utter another word, he had hung up the phone.

Should I have done that? I asked myself. *Now, he's going to go back and tell the world that I was pregnant and had an abortion ... and no telling who he'll say the father was.* Telling something to Trevor was like sending a mass e-mail over the Internet, broadcasting something on the evening news, and plastering it all over every magazine and newspaper in the world.

***

Well, Dr. Iverson, Trevor was my entertainment that day. Talk about a stress reliever ... that was the first time that Trevor took away my stress; he usually causes me to be stressed. He always, and I mean always, riles my nerves ... and really, really bad too.

I wished that he had called on the following Saturday. That's when my mind needed clearing the most. So much happened so quickly that afternoon. I couldn't digest it all at once. Have you had days when it was better to just stay in bed all day? Well, that was one of those days. If only Percy had been honest with me, I wouldn't have been so shocked, so overwhelmed. How could she have hidden such a thing from me and not expect me to find out?

One thing is for sure, Dr. Iverson. Never in a million years would have I imagined myself actually looking forward to holding a conversation with Trevor. Ever! Trevor Mason, Dr. Iverson ... of all people! Did you hear me, Dr. Iverson? I said Trevor Mason!

Yes, Demeter. I heard you.

***

By Sunday, I found myself waiting by the phone, desperately wanting Trevor to call me.

Chapter 14.
In a Trap the Seeker's Caught

The lucid dream I had that morning reminded me so much of Tish. I knew for sure that Percy didn't tell her that I was sick, because Tish would have been there with me for sure. When Keston was born, she flew from Atlanta to New Orleans to tend to me. Her twins were just two years old and she brought them along for the trip. Eighteen months later, she flew back to Atlanta with the twins to take care of me when Kevin was born. I hadn't heard from Tish since the Saturday before the drive to North Carolina. *Tish wouldn't desert me,* I thought. Boy, was I ever wrong!

I picked up the phone and pressed the *F2* button, Tish's speed dial number. Percy's number was set to *F1*.

"We're sorry, but the number you've reached is either disconnected or is no longer in service. Please check ..." the prerecorded voice said. *Keston has been screwing with the phone again,* I thought. So, I dialed her number the *old fashioned way*, by pressing one number at a time, slowly and carefully to make sure that I got it right. Again, the computerized operator came on again.

Tish's number can't be disconnected, I thought. *Maybe the lines are down.* What do you think I did, Dr. Iverson? I called Tish's cell phone. Some strange music played and a computerized voice said something or the other that I couldn't understand. I redialed, and the same message came on.

Never in a million years could I have imagined Tish's phone or cell phone being cut off. I started to go downstairs and send her an e-mail, but I didn't feel like turning on the computer.

I looked at the clock and was surprised that it was after eleven-thirty.

"I can't stay in bed all day," I said to myself.

"We're going to visit Tish," a voice echoed in my head. "We are aren't we?" myself asked. I couldn't believe that I got an answer from myself.

"Yes, we are," I said.

I took a shower so fast that I didn't smell the soap. I threw on a pair of black jeans and white T-shirt, pulled my hair back into a ponytail, grabbed my keys and headed for the garage.

"Percy would have a fit if she knew that we're going out of the house," myself said right before we reached the door.

"Is Percy here?" I asked myself, then headed for the car.

"No," myself said.

"Then, what Percy doesn't know can't hurt her, right?" I asked myself as I activated the remote controlled garage door opener.

"Well ..." myself said.

I ignored myself as I backed out of the garage and headed down the driveway for the street.

"Besides, Percy can't hold us hostage in our own house, can she?" I asked myself.

"No," myself said back. "No she can't."

Myself and I popped in a Norman Brown CD and began our one-hour drive to good ol' Alpharetta.

***

Myself and I finally reached the Winward Parkway exit off of Georgia 400! Whew! It seemed like it took forever to get there. And all that traffic ... it was lunchtime and people were going to the mall for lunch. It took another fifteen minutes to drive three miles from the exit to Tish's house. Amazing, metro-Atlanta traffic is heavy all over just because some crazy folk don't want MARTA to ruin their community. "We don't want inner-city perils near our homes," people would say over and over again. Yeah, like someone'll rob a bank, then wait for the MARTA train to get away. Right!

Myself and I finally turned into Tish's subdivision minding our own business. Then, I had to jam on my brakes because some crazy woman drove her golf cart right in front of me. She had the audacity to curse and give me the finger. I started to run her down. I'm telling you Dr. Iverson, some people shouldn't be behind the wheel of anything ... not a car ... and certainly not a golf cart.

Then, I realized that traffic was heavy in the neighborhood. Cars lined both sides of the street. Well, if that were some other neighbor I would think nothing of it, but people just don't park their cars on the side of the street in Alpharetta. They just don't.

The closer I got to Tish's house, I noticed cars parked in the neighbors' driveways as well as Tish's driveway.

"What's going on?" I asked myself.

"I don't know," myself said.

"Maybe it's some country club meeting or something like that." I said.

"Naw," myself said. "Wouldn't they be at the country club?"

"Yeah, you're right 'self," I said.

"Look!" myself said.

"What?" I asked.

"Isn't that Percy's car in Tish's driveway?" myself asked.

"Yeah," I said. I noticed her *BadGrl* license plate as I drove by the house. "And it's the first one next to the garage door back there."

"Yeah," myself said. "That means that she got here before everyone else."

"Self," I said. "You sure are smart."

"Why thank you," myself said. "Wait, wait!"

"What?" I asked.

"Where are you going? Don't pass the house. Park behind the cars in the driveway," myself said.

"But that's illegal," I said.

"We're going in. So, if someone needs to get out, all we need to do is move our car," myself said.

"Self, you're so right," I said.

At least ten cars lined the red-brick driveway in double formation. I got out the car and looked around at all the cars parked in the of the neighbors' houses.

"Isn't that blue BMW 525 Tish's boy's car?" I asked myself.

"Yeah, it is," myself said. "And isn't that red Corvette Tish's girl's car?" myself asked.

"Why yes," I said. "Yes it is. But who do the other cars belong to?" I asked myself.

"Don't know. Let's go and find out," I said.

"Maybe it's a family reunion or something," myself said. "But the only way to find out is to go and ring the doorbell."

"I'm a bit nervous. What if something bad has happened," I said.

"Don't chicken out on us now," myself told me. "We've driven all the way to Alpharetta, over sixty miles, mind you, and you're just going to turn back around? I don't think so. Now, let's march up the stairs and find out what's going on."

"You're right self," I said. "Let's find out. Besides, it's probably just a family get together."

Tish's lawn was always well-manicured with that plush, green grass. The house sat far off the street on a steep hill, just like a castle. It was a three-story red-brick house with what looked like two round steeples and black roof tops on each side. Running ivy and other exotic plants lined the steps leading to the mahogany front door. A tall security gate opened on the side, leading to the triple car garage and parking lot behind the house.

As I headed up the steps, I heard a car pull up to the house followed by a slamming door.

"Excuse me, miss," a man's voice yelled.

I turned around as a limousine chauffeur dressed in a black suit ran toward me.

"Is this the Hollinger residence?" he asked.

"Yes," I said. "It is."

"Thank you," as he ran down the stairs and signaled for two other black limousines to pull up. Then, he headed back up the stairs toward me; I didn't take my eyes off of him for a second.

"Go on," myself said. "Ask him what's going on."

"How can I do that without him knowing that I don't know what's going on?" I asked myself.

"Make a joke or something, that's how," myself said.

"Quite an event," I told the man as we both approached the door. "With three limousines and all."

He rang the doorbell, then turned to face me. I couldn't tell if the expression on his face was one of sorrow or indifference; he looked straight at me, but I couldn't see his eyes because he wore such dark sunglasses. That black, wide-rim cap hid his face even more.

"Did you know ..." he started, but someone had answered the door.

"Robert!" I said. It was Tish's ex. I was so surprised to see him. He wore a black pin-striped suite and a black bow tie. He was a bit huskier and his hair sparser than the last time I saw him five years ago.

"I didn't think you were coming," Robert said to me as I entered the foyer. "Percy said you were sick and couldn't make it."

"Well," I said. "I'm here."

I noticed that Robert looked at me strangely; he scanned me from head to toe as if to disapproved of my wardrobe.

"Wait right here," Robert told the chauffeur. "We'll be right out."

The house was definitely cleaner than the last time I had visited. Tish said that the maid was off that day. Come to think of it, I hadn't been by to visit in over six months. Papers were scattered all over and the floors were dingy. But that day, the white marble floor looked like it had just been waxed, and the banister looked shiny too. But something was strange. The artwork was missing out of the foyer. Before, three oil paintings lined the stairwell, and three tall African wooden carvings stood next to the door. All of them were gone that day.

I followed Robert to the living room. Everyone was dressed in black. In the far corner near the French window were Tish's children, cradling each other, rocking back and forth. Next to them were Tish's parents. Her mother looked as if she had been crying all night; her eyes were red and swollen. Tish's two brothers and their families were scattered throughout the room.

"What's going on here?" I asked myself.

"You don't want to know," myself said.

"The limousines are here," Robert announced, catching everyone's attention.

Percy noticed me. A look of surprise—like the cat who ate the canary—crossed her face.

Everyone gathered personal belongings and slowly followed Robert to the door.

"Thank you for coming," Tish's father said. "Percy told us you took Tish's transition pretty hard. But I'm glad you came out today," he said, then hugged me.

Tish's mother hugged me too. She held me so tight and cried so hard. Her husband had to pull her away.

My heart sank. Every nerve in my body shut down. *Tish's transition? What happened?* I had so many questions. *No,* I thought. *This can't be what I think a transition is.*

"Thanks for coming today, Didi," Tish's daughter said as tears flowed endlessly from her eyes. "Thanks for letting Keston and Kevin come to the viewing last night." She hugged me so long and hard until I felt a tear roll down my cheek. *Oh God!* She looked so much like her mother with that deep caramel skin, only she was a few inches taller. I remember when she was just a teeny-weeny baby.

"What are you doing here?" Percy asked from behind, startling me. Everyone else had gone to the limousines, leaving an empty parlor.

"What viewing?" I asked Percy. "Keston and Kevin ..."

"I took Keston and Kevin to the viewing last night," Percy informed me. "You were resting from your medicine, and we didn't want to disturb you."

"I just had a thought to visit Tish. I hadn't seen or heard from ... "

"Why don't you go home, sweetie," Percy said. "You've had enough excitement for one day dear."

"No," I said. "I'm staying. What happened anyway? What's going on?"

"You really should be home," Percy said.

"What happened, Percy? What happened?"

"Well ..." Percy started, then looked away. "

Robert must have heard our conversation and decided to come over. "You can ride in our car, Didi," he told me.

I noticed Robert and Percy look at each other as if to say, "She'll find out eventually. Why not sooner than later?"

Robert took me by the shoulders and led me down the brick steps, one by one. It kind of reminded me of the meditation session I had earlier that morning when that strange woman led me down the limestone steps of the pyramid.

The chauffeur opened the door for us, as Tish's parents and children waited inside. I sat on the right wall, sandwiched between Robert and Percy. What looked like a black leather sectional lined most of the back wall. In front, near the chauffeur's section was a bar fully stocked with mixed nuts, canned sodas and spirits. Wine goblets rested neatly on rack that hung over a small sink next to a mini-refrigerator.

"Would you like a drink?" Robert asked.

"No thanks," I said, but realized that I shouldn't have declined.

Robert fixed drinks for everyone else: filtered water and lemon; Gin on the rocks, and soda with crushed ice. Amazing how a limousine can offer running, filtered water and crushed ice.

Robert flicked the remote control and on came a flat-screen, twenty-seven inch TV that I didn't notice before. It was hiding right in front of me near the door and wet bar.

We drove for what seemed like hours in complete silence. Everyone slowly sipped drinks and stared at the TV. No one uttered a word.

The sun was bright. The sky was so blue and clear. Days like that are for walking in the park and enjoying a gentle breeze. The leaves had turned the most beautiful shades of goldenrod and burnt sienna. That was definitely a day for just sitting outside and enjoying life. I watched as trees blew in the wind, but couldn't find any joy in that day. I sat there as every emotion slowly leaked from my body.

An hour later and we had finally reached Bethany Christian Center where Tish attended church in Lithonia. Hundreds of cars filled the parking lot as the limousine pulled up to the curve.

"She shed her skin," a voice whispered in my ear as I got out of the car. No one was close enough to me, as everyone had exited the limousine. I didn't know where it came from. But, from the corner of my eye, I noticed a strange figure. I turned to face it, but nothing was there.

It's my imagination, I thought. Then I realized that I had heard those words in a dream earlier that day. *I'm thinking too hard.*

A strong presence followed me into the church. *It's just Robert,* I reasoned, then I realized that he had joined a conversation far in the back of the church. The presence stayed with me. *It's my nerves.*

So this is Bethany Christian Center, I thought. Tish had always invited me to service, but I never got around to attending. "A church with twenty thousand members is just too big for me," I always told Tish.

The church was white and square like an office building. Several narrow rectangular, stained-glass windows lined the front. Straight ahead through the doors was a hallway.

"This way please," an usher said, steering me away as from the main auditorium where church services were held. She gave everyone a booklet. On the cover was a black-and-white picture of Tish. The caption read, "Letitia Cynthia Dewey Hollinger—1957- 1999." *Cynthia Dewey!* I thought. Then, I remembered hearing that name in several lucid dreams. I had almost completely forgotten that Tish's middle name was Cynthia and her maiden name was Dewey.

My heart began to race, and I was overtaken by a strange hot energy.

"Didi, Didi," a familiar voice said. "Good to see you," Tish's father said as I turned.

It was my father shaking his hand. What a surprise. A strange, yet familiar woman was with him. I couldn't see her face, but she was tall and dark and wore her salt-and-pepper hair in a French twist. She wore a navy-blue suit that stopped at the knee, showing off her strong calf muscles. My father looked like a young buck with that smooth, soft caramel skin; thick, salt-and-pepper moustache; and slicked-back salt-and-pepper hair. He looked so handsome in that navy-blue, pin-striped suit and spit-shiny wing-tip shoes.

***

I must give it to my father, Dr. Iverson, he always likes to look *good.*

My father and Tish's father are both graduates of Meharry Medical School. Tish's father moved back to Atlanta, and my father moved back to New Orleans.

They both belong to the same fraternity too and have remained in close contact all these years. In fact, Percy and my father had dinner at Tish's parents' house the first day of registration at Spelman. Percy and Tish have been friends ever since. Then, when I attended Spelman, I met Tish and fell in love with her too, but not the way you're probably thinking, Dr. Iverson.

***

"How are you girls holding up?" my father asked Percy and me. "I know that you and Tish were really close."

"We're holding up," Percy said calmly.

"Fine," I said. "I'm holding up fine." Percy took time to call our father way in New Orleans, but couldn't tell me what was going on? *Well, maybe I'm being too hard on her. Perhaps, father's friend told him,* I thought.

"Are you sure?" he asked again, almost bringing me to tears. *How do you think I'm doing? I just lost my best friend,* I thought, but didn't say it.

"When did you get in town?" I asked. "Where are you staying?"

"I flew into town early this morning. Charles told me the news yesterday."

"Char ..." I started to ask. Then, I realized that's Tish's father's name—Dr. Charles Dewey.

"I'm staying with Pearl-Elizabeth. She lives here in town," he said. He must have noticed the baffled look on my face because he decided to tell me more. "I know that this is not a good time," my father said, then turned to face Percy. "Did you tell her, Percy?"

"Tell me what?" I asked, but I felt so low then that I couldn't care less of what other secrets they were keeping from me. It couldn't have been as bad as that, so I pushed on. "Tell me."

"Daddy is getting married," Percy said.

Just then, my future step-mother walked up next to Percy. I couldn't believe it! They looked like mother and daughter! In fact, they looked more like mother and daughter than my own mother, wherever she might be. They were the same height, had the same 38DD bustline, same ebony skin and straight-wavy hair.

"Didi," my father said. "I want you to meet Pearl-Elizabeth, my fiancee'."

"I've heard a lot about you," Pearl-Elizabeth said as we shook hands. Boy, that woman had a powerful handshake. "I feel as though I know you already."

When I touched Pearl-Elizabeth, an electric shock ran rampant through my body. It began in the tips of my fingers, to my shoulders, then quickly traveled to my chest and legs. I looked into her dark, dreamy eyes, hypnotized almost ...

***

For a split second, I was knocked into another time and place. I was transported to that strange, dark room that I visited in my morning meditation session. As I ran my fingers across the soft, powdery limestone walls, a hand touched my shoulders from behind. I turned to face the stranger, not at all afraid. Behind me was the same strange woman who led me down the dark stairway in the meditation. Only she looked like a younger version of Pearl-Elizabeth. I stared deep into her dark eyes and was brought back into present time, present place.

***

The room started to spin and sway back and forth at the same time.

"Are you all right?" Pearl-Elizabeth asked, jolting me even faster into reality.

"When did ..." I tried to ask Percy when she found out, but she cut me off.

"I found out early this morning," Percy said. "You were still sleeping when Daddy called this morning. I didn't want to wake you."

Percy's words were slurred and garbled, as if she spoke in slow motion.

"Are you all right?" Pearl-Elizabeth asked. "We better get you some water."

Daddy, Pearl-Elizabeth and Percy went to find the kitchen to get me some water.

A tingling sensation ran through me as I gained enough courage to read the brochure that the usher had given me a few minutes before. Reading the announcement was like sticking my wet finger in a light socket. My mouth went dry as I continued to walk down the long, winding hallway, hundreds of mourners moving in the same direction. The walls were white, a nice contrast to the pale blue carpet. I blinked my eyes a few times and was able to steady myself long enough to take a few steps. *Probably nerves,* I reasoned, hoping I was right. Then, my inner self started talking again.

"Percy was right," myself said.

"About what?" I asked myself.

"About Tish visiting the Sunday that you came home from North Carolina," myself said.

"She had already ..." I tried to finish, but was too overwhelmed.

"Who's she talking to?" I heard a woman ask her male companion, as I caught the attention of other passersby.

Robert and Percy joined me just before I entered the Special Events center. I saw father and Pearl-Elizabeth head my way with a glass of water.

"Who were you talking to?" Robert asked me.

"What?" I asked.

"He means our private conversation," myself said.

"Oh that," I said to myself.

"Oh what?" Robert asked me.

Then, I realized that other people overheard my conversation between myself and I.

"Be more careful," myself said.

"Be careful of what?" I asked myself.

"Be careful of what?" Percy asked as she and Robert looked at me curiously.

"That's what I mean," myself said. "Be careful that other people don't hear what you say during our private conversations. Okay? If I say something to you just cough to let me know that you acknowledge it. Understood?"

"Nnnn," I moaned to let myself know that I understood, but I caught Percy's and Robert's attention in the process.

"What's wrong?" Percy asked.

"Nothing," I said.

"Here's some water." Pearl-Elizabeth handed me a glass of ice water right as we entered the room.

"No, thanks," I told her as I gave the glass back. "I'm feeling better now."

"I think you better drink it," Daddy insisted.

I drank a few sips. That water sure was icy-cold. It was so cold that I felt the coolness of each swallow travel from my mouth down to my stomach.

I held on tight to Percy as we walked into the Special Events room. Two ushers dressed in white held the swinging doors for us. I blinked a few times and took a long sigh before entering. It was standing room only; the place was jam-packed with people. The walls were antique-white, and the carpet was blue like in the hallway outside. To the far right, three large blue-and-red stained glass windows lined the walls. A golden rail lined the pulpit, behind which was the organist. Elevated to the rear was the choir dressed in blue robes lined in white.

An usher escorted Percy and me to our seats. The royal blue cushions that covered the pine pews were soft and comfortable indeed, but nothing could bring comfort to my spirit. Three wooden "pockets" lined the pew in front with six Bibles. The books had red leather covers and the outer pages were lined in gold. I should have taken one of them and turned to Psalms 91 for comfort, but I didn't. My Great-Aunt Ruby used to tell her clients to read Psalms 91. Somewhere along the way in my pursuit of education and career, I forgot about the wisdom of the Bible that Great-Aunt Ruby taught me. The elders sure knew what they were talking about back then. I guess we're all too educated and sophisticated to go back to the teachings of the elders. Well, that's not completely true; we still go to church and read the Bible, but only in superficial ways.

Robert sat in front of us with the twins and Tish's parents. Mrs. Dewey rocked back and forth, crying uncontrollably. Three ushers tried in vain to console her. All I heard were sounds of sorrow from the family that drowned out the organ and choir.

I fought hard to control my tears, especially hearing Mrs. Dewey carry on like that. So, I looked away from the family. What a mistake. Glancing away forced me to look front and center—unbelievably it was Tish in the same red outfit she wore the night Percy brought me home from North Carolina. That's when it hit me: the time I spent with Tish that night must have been in a lucid dream. Did she visit me from the great beyond? Or did I visit her in my dreams? Or, did I hear about what happened to her on some subconscious level, which caused me to dream about her? Too many questions and too few answers. The possibility of being in contact with a spirit being was mind boggling to say the least. I became light-headed as the room began to dim more and more ...

***

Till this day, I don't recall how I got in Charter Peachford Hospital. Everyone said that I fainted during the service. Percy said my skin was ice cold and took on a grayish hue. Applying smelling salts and splashing cold water on my face didn't revive me, so Robert called the paramedics. That explained why I was taken to a hospital, but till this day, no one ever told me—truthfully—how and why I was admitted into a psychiatric hospital.

I came to in a dark room covered with a white sheet and thin white wool blanket. The digital clock that hung over the door flashed *9:30* in big, bold, red numbers. It was about three o'clock the last time I remembered anything. What happened to over four hours of my life, I couldn't tell you. I was in the church one second, and in the blink of an eye I was in the hospital.

Percy was by my side holding my hand. To the right behind her, a rising moon and twinkling stars shined through the window—which was the only light in the room. Shadows of the mini-blinds appeared as diagonal, black lines against the wall.

"Where am I?" I asked.

"You're in the hospital, sweetie," Percy said in that New York granny voice, stroking my hand.

"What happened?" I asked.

"You fainted, sweetie," Percy said. "Pearl-Elizabeth and Dr. Dewey tried everything to bring you around, but nothing worked."

"Pearl-Elizabeth?" I asked.

"She's a retired RN, so she helped Dr. Dewey tend to you."

The thought of that woman touching me ... oooo ... gave me the willies. And how about my father? Why didn't he help me? He's the great Dr. Pickens, surgeon extraordinaire.

"What hospital am I in?" I asked.

Percy looked away and paused before answering. "Sweetie," she said, then took a long sigh. "You're in Charter Peachford."

"Charter Peachford?" I asked. "What! Why am I here?"

"You had a mild breakdown," Percy said.

"What?" I asked in disbelief, but deep down I knew that my sanity was being held together by a thread—a thin thread at that. I was losing it. "Says who?"

"The paramedics took you to the hospital down the road from the church. You were out cold until you reached the hospital. Daddy, Pearl-Elizabeth and I stayed with you the whole time. Dr. and Mrs. Dewey stayed for a while too, but they're still distraught over Tish."

Chills went up and down my spine just hearing Pearl-Elizabeth's name. Something about that woman didn't set well with me. I didn't trust her somehow. Did she poison me at the church?

"Where are Daddy and Pearl-Elizabeth now?" I asked, even though I was hoping they weren't around.

"They stayed for about an hour then went home," Percy said.

Thank goodness! I thought. I was so relieved that they weren't around.

"Did you notice that Pearl-Elizabeth looked like Mother?" I asked Percy.

"Since you mention it, there's a slight resemblance."

"Do you think that Pearl-Elizabeth and Mother are related?" I asked.

"I'm not sure," Percy said, then rubbed my hand. "Sweetie, you shouldn't be concerned about that right now, okay? You need to concentrate on getting well."

I knew for sure that Percy was hiding something from me about Pearl-Elizabeth. Was that woman related to us? Like I mentioned before, Dr. Iverson, we never met any of our mother's people. So, I wondered if she could have been one of my mother's sisters. And how about the meditation session with the strange woman that morning? Was that a precognitive dream about Pearl-Elizabeth and my mother? But so much was going on that I wasn't sure if I was ready to find out anything else about that woman. So, I just shoved thoughts of her deep in my mind.

"You still didn't tell me why I was taken to this hospital, Percy."

"The doctors said that you started shaking and speaking out of your head. One of the nurses said that it sounded like you were speaking in tongues. They told the paramedics to transfer you to Charter Peachford because you were suffering from a breakdown."

"Shaking?" I asked. "I don't recall shaking. And I don't recall speaking in tongues. Isn't that what Great-Aunt Ruby used to do?"

"Yes, Great-Aunt Ruby sure did," Percy said with a smile. "Great-Aunt Ruby was something else." Percy continued to smile as she sighed. "They wouldn't let me in the room with you so I don't know if that's what it sounded like or not."

The door gradually opened straight ahead, letting in hints of lights from the hallway into the room. I started to panic because I didn't see anyone pushing the door. I thought it was opening by itself. I gasped for breath and quickly sat up in bed. *Am I dreaming again? Maybe I'll wake up.*

"What's wrong?" Percy asked. She must have noticed me looking toward the door because she turned quickly around to see what was going on. "It's just the nurse, sweetie," she said as she faced me, rubbing my hand.

I looked around and noticed an IV plugged into my right arm. A shrill beep echoed through my ears, sending my nerves in a tizzy. I looked again, and noticed teal lights flashing my vital signs on a small square black contraption next to the bed.

"Just relax," the nurse said. The door had begun to close behind her and she wasn't standing in the lighted path from the hallway. She was tall with shoulder length brown hair, but I couldn't make out the details of her face. "Dr. Iverson said that she can go home tonight," she told Percy.

"All right," Percy said.

They were talking about me as if I weren't there. I resented that.

"Dr. Iverson said to make sure that she takes her medicine three times a day. It's a bit stronger than the last prescription, but will help with the episodes," the nurse said then handed Percy the prescription.

Episodes? I thought "What episodes?" I asked the nurse. Both she and Percy looked at me as though they were surprised that I spoke.

"You've been having panic attacks, dear," the nurse said in a slow, loud voice as if I had difficulty hearing.

"Was Dr. Iverson here?" I asked. "When? Where is she? Can I see her?"

"She was here about fifteen minutes ago. Now she's gone," the nurse said as she checked my vital signs.

"Did you speak with Dr. Iverson?" I asked Percy.

"No," she said. "The doctor must have stopped in when I went to the coffee shop downstairs."

"Could you turn the lights on please?" I asked the nurse.

Percy and the nurse looked curiously at each other.

"The doctor thinks it's best if you rest with the lights off for awhile, okay?" The nurse spoke to me as if I were an infant. Then, she injected medication into the IV. "This'll make you relax," she said, then patted my arm.

A warm feeling started at the crown of my head and quickly moved through my body. The next thing I remembered was waking up in my bed the next morning.

Chapter 15.
In a Spider's Web

I went through most of Saturday in a stupor. Keston and Kevin were at a football game, leaving me alone most of the day. Percy tended to me.

I took a quick shower, threw on some jeans and a wrinkled, white T-shirt, pushed my hair back into a ponytail, then went outside to get the morning paper. It was such a pretty day with the bright, orange sunrise and cool, fall breeze rustling the colorful leaves. But the sunshine didn't seem as bright and the trees looked just plain old ordinary. Percy prepared breakfast, but her banana pancakes weren't as fluffy and the pecan-maple syrup was too sweet. Percy offered to brew some of Mr. Chap's coffee, but I didn't want that either. All I wanted was to have my Tish back.

"Sorry about Tish," Keston said from behind startling me as I came back inside. He held his football attire on a hanger.

"Me too," Kevin said. He wore his spats and shoes, but his band uniform was still in the drycleaner's plastic. The hat and plume were over the hanger.

"Thanks, guys," I told them.

"We have a game today at one," Keston said. "We'll be leaving in a few minutes."

"We'll be back about six o'clock," Kevin said.

"Good luck," I told them as they ran out the door.

I usually went to all their in-town games. But that day, I just wasn't up to it. The burden of losing my best friend was just too heavy. Nothing seemed to matter anymore.

I went to the sunroom to relax, not realizing that Percy was sitting on the love seat. It seemed as if she were surprised to see me standing there.

"Let me call you back," Percy said, then pressed the *End* button to end her call. She still held the cordless phone in her lap.

"Percy," I said. "I need to ask you a question."

"Sure, sweetie," she said, as I sat beside her. "If you're wondering about your car, Daddy drove it back last night from Tish's when you were sleeping."

"Good," I said, even though that wasn't my question. It was good to know that my car was safely back home.

That's when I realized that she had curled her hair and made her face. She wore a black, silk blouse with two buttons undone—showing her ample cleavage—black pants and black snakeskin shoes. *Mourn attire?*

"Are you going somewhere?" I asked.

"I'm going to Kroger to get a few things ... you know," she said.

She looked awfully dressy to be going to Kroger, but I didn't want to push the issue.

"What happened to Tish?" I asked. A look of shock crossed her face as though my question made her uncomfortable in some way.

"Let's talk about that later, sweetie, okay?" she said, then stood up.

"Why?" I asked. "Why won't you tell me what happened to Tish?"

No one told me how it happened, and I didn't bother to ask until then. Was she ill? Did she suffer? Was she in an accident or in pain? Perhaps I was too afraid to ask. Percy should not have hidden the truth from me.

Percy dropped her head and sighed long and hard. "All right," she said, then sat back next to me. "Sweetie," she said, rubbing my hands and looking me straight in the eyes, "sweetie, Tish overdosed on sleeping pills last Sunday morning."

"Sleeping pills?" I was kind of shocked. Thinking back, for about two weeks before then, Tish seemed somewhat distant like something was on her mind.

"Yes, Didi, sleeping pills."

"Why?" I asked. "Did she leave a note?"

"Yes," she said.

"Well?" I asked.

"Well what, sweetie?" Percy asked, but she probably knew that I wanted her to tell me the details.

"What did the note say?"

Percy put her head down and took another long, hard sigh before facing me again.

"I'm running late," she said. "Why don't we discuss this when I get back? Okay, sweetie?" Percy got up once more and tried to rush for the door.

"Who found the note?" I asked.

Percy froze in her tracks. "What?" she asked, not once looking back at me.

I got up from my comfortable seat and confronted her. "I said who found her?"

She was at a loss for words. "What?" she repeated.

"Who found her?" I asked.

"Dr. Dewey, her father found her," Percy told me.

"Dr. Dewey?" I asked.

"Yes," she said. "Sit down." Percy escorted me back to the love seat.

Oh my, I thought. *Do I really want to know?*

"I got a call from Dr. Dewey about five o'clock on Sunday morning. He said that Tish was in the intensive care unit and I should get to Northside Hospital right away. I asked him what happened, because I saw Tish only a few hours ago. He wouldn't say, but just urged me to get to the hospital right away. So I did. He said that he tried to call you at home and on your cell phone, but he couldn't reach you."

"Did he try leaving a message?" I asked.

"I don't think so. Anyway, when I got to the hospital, he was waiting for me in the lobby.

'What happened?' I asked.

'Let's go up,' he said, then, he took me up to Tish's room.

"He looked cool as a cucumber, like nothing was wrong."

"What do you mean?" I asked.

"Well, Dr. Dewey didn't look like he was excited or worried or anything. He had a nonchalant, cavalier attitude the whole time. First of all, he was dressed to the T with a white, silky shirt. His hair was slicked back and he had on some cologne."

"Well, you know that Daddy and his pack always believed in looking sharp, regardless of the occasion," I said. "They like to smell fresh too."

"Yeah, but cologne doesn't last that long. Dr. Dewey smelled like he just stepped out of the shower," Percy said.

"Well, maybe he took Tish to the hospital, then went back home to change," I said. "Or, maybe he freshened up at the hospital. Wasn't he on staff at Northside before he retired a few years ago?"

"Perhaps," Percy said. "Anyway, when I got upstairs, Tish was sleeping. Looking back, she was probably unconscious. She was hooked up to some monitors and I think a breathing machine, I'm not sure. A blue tube was stuck down her throat and this gadget went up and down like a pump. The gadget sounded like a steam machine when it went down, and I saw Tish's chest fill with air. Looked like it was helping her breathe ... I didn't know what to think. From what I could see, she was in a fetal position. Most of her body was covered with a white sheet. But her hands ... her arms were kind of distorted; twisted. The best way I can describe it is that her hands and fingers were curled inside each other, like they were shriveling up. And that look on her face ..."

"What about the look on her face?" I asked.

"She looked like a corpse. She just didn't look real. Her skin looked greenish-brown. I knew something was wrong when I looked at her face. It looked all crooked and distorted.

'What happened, Dr. Dewey?' I asked him.

'I found her on the kitchen floor around two o'clock,' he said. 'She had a bottle of pills next to her, so I called 911.'

"He showed me the bottle of pills. He flashed a piece of paper in front of me. I saw that it was Tish's writing, but I didn't get a chance to read the note. He just stuffed it back in his pocket."

"Did he say what was on the note?" I asked.

"He said that it was personal, so he didn't care to share it with anyone outside the family, not even Tish's mother."

"But why did she do it?" I asked Percy. "Why?"

"From what I can gather, she just wasn't happy. Nothing worked out the way she wanted. I guess she had a lot of issues. I don't know. At this point, we can only speculate."

"I wish she would have reached out and confided in us," I said. Then, I wondered if she did in fact confide in Percy. I had to know. "Did she confide in you, Percy?" I asked.

"All she said was that her alimony was running out in a year and she didn't know what to do," Percy said. By the tone of her voice and lack of body language, I believed that she was telling me the truth.

Tish was a bit depressed by the fact that her alimony would be cut in the next eighteen months. But she wasn't the first woman to make it on her own. "You have a degree from Spelman and a Master's from Emory University, Tish," Percy and I tried to stress to her time and time again.

"But I haven't used my skills in years," she told us.

"You just recently completed your English dissertation at Georgia State two years ago," I told her. "You have a Ph.D, why don't you consider teaching at a college level?"

"I don't even know how to begin," she said.

"But your house is paid for; you don't have a mortgage. Your car is paid for, so you don't have a car note," I often reminded her. "All you have to do is pay for utilities and car insurance."

She just didn't realize how blessed she really was. What a pity.

Percy looked at her watch. "Look, Didi," she said as she stood. "I'll be back in a few minutes."

Before I could say another word, Percy grabbed her purse off the coffee table and darted toward the front door.

"Oh," she said, returning from the kitchen with a large white gift basket in gold cellophane. It was filled with a few mangoes, one large pinapple, a big bunch of black grapes, bananas, red apples, kiwi, smoked gouda cheese and crackers. A giant card the size of a box of cereal enclosed in a lavender envelope was attached.

"This was delivered yesterday morning. I forgot to give it to you," Percy said.

Inside the card were several cartoon animals. Everyone at work signed his name next to one of the characters, how cute, except for Patricia. I looked and looked, turning the card over and inside out, but her name was nowhere to be found. *She must have been busy or something.*

I sure do miss being at work, I thought. Some of the people were challenging to work with at times, but those are the ones who made going to the office interesting. Besides, who wants to work in a boring office?

"I'm going down the road to Kroger. Be back in a few," Percy said before running out the door.

***

The thought of Tish facing the unthinkable was just too, too much.

That day, emotional pain pierced my heart like a silver bullet, penetrating deeper with each passing moment. I moped upstairs to my bedroom and took two of those blue pills you prescribed, Dr. Iverson. Like a fool, I thought the pills would soothe my bleeding soul, but it didn't. I needed a diversion—anything—to ease my aching heart.

I waited for phone to ring, hoping desperately for someone to call, even Trevor. But Percy took the liberty of hiding all three phones in the house. I checked my purse, and she had taken my cell phone too. What if there was an emergency? I wished she wouldn't have done that, but I didn't have the strength to argue with her. She probably did it for my well being, so I really shouldn't have been upset with her. Somehow, I think there was more to her doing it than just my well being, but I was too weak to ponder the notion any further.

It was two o'clock and still no Percy. What was to be a few minutes at Kroger turned into hours. Three o'clock—no Percy. Four o'clock—no Keston, no Kevin, no Percy.

"Hello, Didi! We hungry up in here!" I heard a voice say. I didn't exactly hear it with my physical ears, but it was kind of like a feeling and hearing combined into one.

"She been eatin' real good with them waffles and shit, and ain't even feed us. Ain't that some shit?" another voice said.

I must be stressed out, I reasoned and didn't give the voices a second thought.

***

I felt heavier and heavier. My heart sank lower and lower just thinking of how I'd never see Tish again. I cried until my face was swollen with grief. It was just too unbearable, so I took another one of those blue pills. The heaviness was still with me an hour later despite repeated attempts to go downstairs to the basement and watch TV. Another hour had gone by and the pain was still with me. So, I dragged myself back upstairs and took another blue pill ... then another ... then another. Deep down inside, I wanted the same fate as Tish. My eyelids became heavier and heavier as slumber was upon me. I blinked my drooping eyes for a second and boom ... the next thing I recall was being awakened on Sunday morning by Percy.

***

It was Sunday morning and I was still tucked in bed with pillows over my head when Percy woke me. All I saw was Percy's long, boney hand extending from the sleeve of that ugly, pink floral house robe.

"You really need to eat something, sweetie," Percy said as she shook the daylights out of me. "Wake up, Didi."

I peeked up and a tray of homemade blueberry waffles and bacon was on the nightstand next to the clock. *Nine o'clock!* I was surprised because it was seven o'clock on Saturday evening the last thing I remembered. I felt heavy inside knowing that Tish was gone.

"You're not staying in bed all day like you did yesterday," she said as she poured orange juice from a clear glass pitcher into a tall glass. "Now go and rinse your mouth out so you can eat."

"Uhhh," I moaned. "I don't wanna."

"Go on," Percy said as she nudged me some more to get out of bed. "Stop acting like a big baby."

"I'm not hungry." I plopped my head right back into the pillows, but I perked right on up when the aroma of Mr. Chap's coffee tickled my nose. "Is that coffee I smell?" I asked Percy.

"Yes," she said, heading for the bedroom door. "I put some on to brew right before I came up here. It should be ready. Would you like some?"

She got my attention, so I sat up in bed. "You know it," I told her.

"Give me five minutes," Percy said then proceeded down the hallway to the stairs.

Offering to make coffee—like she did the day before—didn't faze me. But actually smelling Mr. Chap's coffee brewing was a different story. It was as if the coffee contained some extra special stimulant of sorts.

***

I'm telling you, Dr. Iverson, Mr. Chap put some special ingredient in his coffee. I just know he did.

Like what?

I don't know. Probably some extra strong doses of caffeine or something.

***

Anyway, I jumped out of bed and ran to the bathroom. In a flash, I flossed then brushed my teeth and washed my face. The smell of Mr. Chap's coffee was so stimulating that I decided to take a quick wash-off. I filled the basin with water and lathered soap in the face towel on the rack. I threw off my tartan pajamas and started rubbing the warm soap all over my body. Dipping the towel into the warm water again and again was so relaxing. I finally rinsed the soap off and felt like a new person. In lightening speed, I brushed my hair back into a ponytail, threw on a fresh pair of jeans and T-shirt. I didn't even put on any underwear.

Percy was headed upstairs, carefully carrying a tray. It's amazing how she fit the coffee server, cream, sugar and cup all on the same tray.

"I think I'll have my coffee in the sunroom," I told her.

"It's good to see you up and about," Percy said, then carefully followed me downstairs.

The light from the sunroof and French windows filled the room. The brightness, combined with the aroma of Mr. Chap's coffee, started to bring me out of my emotional slump.

"Where are you guys going this time of morning all dressed up?" Percy asked. "You two sure look handsome." She was right outside the sunroom, still holding the tray of coffee.

"We're going to church, Aunt Percy," Keston told her.

"To church?" Percy sounded surprised.

"We go most Sundays," Kevin told her.

"Well, don't you want to eat?" Percy asked. "I made some more waffles."

"Naw," Keston told her. "We always hook up with some friends for lunch after church."

"We'll be back around three o'clock," Kevin said.

Now, Kevin and Keston never told me when they would be back from anything. That told me that they were concerned for my well-being. Then it dawned on me: did they know about Tish since the previous Sunday and think that I was out from work for that reason? That was a good thing, because I wouldn't want them to think that anything else was wrong with me.

I heard Keston and Kevin run down the stairs leading to the basement, while Percy sashayed in with the tray.

"I didn't know that the boys went to church," Percy said as she sat the tray on the end table. "I thought you didn't believe in going to church?"

"They've been going since they were little," I told her.

"Going to church is a waste of time. It's a business, and all they want is your money. You shouldn't let those boys get caught up in all that."

I dug right into my waffles. "If they want to go, then I don't see any harm in that."

"We didn't grow up in church and turned out okay."

"Yeah Percy," I said, trying to finish my breakfast.

"That was enough for me," Percy said. "I didn't like being around all those people yelling and screaming. If you ask me, it was just a party."

"Yeah Percy."

"And those folk were just hypocrites," Percy said as she poured me some coffee.

"Yeah Percy."

"They were," she said while adding cream and sugar to the mug.

"Yeah Percy."

"Couldn't wait to get out of church to start gossiping about somebody, or stabbing somebody in the back, or trying to steal somebody else's husband," she said.

"Yeah, Percy."

"What's all this 'yeah Percy' shit?" She was huffed. "You know I'm right."

"I'm just listening to you," I said, keeping my eyes fixed on the coffee.

"Look at how they used to talk about Great-Aunt Ruby and Great-Gran. They used to talk about Momma and us too."

I took a few sips of coffee and the warmth instantly filled my soul. "That's the past, Percy," I said, then gulped most of the coffee. "Who cares what those tired, old biddies used to say anyway? They're not even worth talking about."

"Well, did you know that Aunt Gertrude used to be right there with them talking about Momma?" Percy asked.

"Who?" I asked. I'd lost touch with my relatives and didn't give them the time of day. Then I realized that Aunt Gertrude was Juanita's mother. She was married to my father's brother.

"Aunt Gertrude, Didi," Percy said as she kneeled before me. "Juanita's mother. That yellow bitch with the big black mole on her face. The one who looked like a witch. The one who was married to…"

"All of Daddy's people are yellow, Percy," I said. All I cared about was enjoying my coffee, not digging up old memories of those people.

"That's right," Percy said. "All of them are yellow and couldn't stand us either."

"Who gives a shit, Percy?" I said.

"We turned out better than their children, that's for sure." Percy sat back on the love seat and stared at the ceiling for a few seconds. "Maybe you're right, Didi."

"Right about what?"

"Those people aren't worth a damn," she said.

"Do you ever call any of them?" I asked. "To see how they're doing?"

"Hell no!" she exclaimed. "How about you?"

"No," I said then reached for the coffee pot. "I don't have their phone numbers to call or their addresses to write."

"Sometimes, I'll get a Christmas card from some of them. That pisses me off too," she said, staring at me.

"Why?" I asked as I stirred some cream and sugar into the coffee delight.

"Because only Daddy could have given them my address. I strictly forbade him to give any of the moth' fuckers my damn address or damn phone number. I forbade him! All he says is, 'Those are your relatives, and kin should know each other. That's wrong to write kin off.' "

"You forbade him?" I asked.

"Damn right!" Percy said. She stood up and starting pounding her fist into her hand with each word. "I said, 'Daddy. I forbid you to give any of them my phone number or address. I don't want those folk calling me. And I sure in hell don't want them writing me or God forbid, coming to Atlanta to visit me.' "

"What did Daddy say?" I asked.

"I told you what he said before, Didi," she said. "You need to pay attention."

"Whatever," I said under my breath.

"What did you say, Didi?" Percy asked.

"Nothing," I said, knowing that she would start something.

"Sounded like you said something else," Percy huffed.

"I didn't, Percy," I said.

"Honey, you better recognize," she said, rolling her eyes.

"How about your cousin, Juanita?" I asked Percy.

"My cousin?" Percy asked. "That bitch is your cousin too. I don't consider that bitch my cousin. I can't stand her sorry ass."

"Whatever happened to her?" I asked, not that I even cared.

"She has a bunch of kids, all with different daddies."

"No!" I said. "Did she ever get married again?"

"Nope," Percy said. "And your Grandpa used to always say how we would never amount to anything and how we would get pregnant and drop out of school. And that 'ho' Juanita got pregnant and dropped out of school, his little precious got pregnant ..."

"Well, it's true what I've heard, she doesn't even know who the father of a few of her children are?" I asked.

"That's what I heard. And Grandpa had the audacity to ask for us when he lay in the hospital bed about to keel over," Percy said with a frown.

"Did you go see him?" I asked.

"Hell no!" Percy exclaimed. "I was in New York then. I wasn't going to waste my fuckin' time or money on a moth' fuckin' plane ticket to go to no fuckin' New Orleans to see that moth' fucker in the moth' fuckin' hospital! Shit, I had other more important things to fuckin' do. And before you ask, I didn't attend the moth' fuckin' services either. Besides, I didn't want to see the moth' fucker when he was alive, so why the fuck would I want to see his fuckin' ass when the moth' fucker was dead?"

"Well, I saw him in the hospital before he passed," I told Percy.

"You did?" Percy asked. "You never told me."

"That was in April, right before I moved to Atlanta," I said.

"Did you go to the services?" Percy asked.

"No. The services were in late-June. I was getting settled in a new apartment here in Atlanta and had just started a new job. I was just too busy. Besides, Keston and Kevin were five and seven at the time. And you know they say you're not supposed to take children under twelve years old around sick people, to wakes, funerals or graveyards. I'm not superstitious, but you never know."

"Honey, I don't blame you for not going," Percy said. "If you barely spoke to a person when they were alive, why bother to see them when they're dead? That won't change anything. It's a waste of time."

"The old man was talking out of his head in the hospital," I said. "I mean really talking weird, crazy stuff."

"Did he recognize you?" Percy asked.

"Yes," I said. "He recognized me."

"Did he apologize for the way he treated us?" Percy asked. "You know folk try to get straight before they go."

"Kind of," I said.

"Kind of," she asked with a puzzled looked on her face. "What the fuck is that supposed to mean? Kind of?"

"He kept saying that something was all Daddy's fault."

"What?" Percy looked surprised. "What the fuck does Daddy have to do with the mean shit Grandpa did? Did he mean that Daddy shouldn't have allowed him to treat his children that fuckin' way or what?"

"These were his exact words from what I can remember:

'Y'all children scared me,' he said.

"Scared him," Percy exclaimed. "What the fuck ..."

"Let me finish," I said.

'How did we scare you Grandpa?' I asked. 'We didn't mean to scare you, Grandpa.'

'Your daddy went down to Morgan City to see a medicine man named Bot. He was desperate.'

'Desperate?' I asked. I tried to humor Grandpa since he was old and senile. I didn't know how else to respond.

'Yeah,' he went on, 'your daddy made a promise to Bot before you were born, but he didn't think that Bot was serious. I warned him not to be fooling around with Bot, but he wouldn't listen. He got what he wanted from Bot, but there was a cost. I guess your daddy didn't care because his children will have to pay the price, not him. You go and ask your daddy.'

"He became quiet when Daddy walked in."

A blank stare crossed Percy's face, as if she'd seen a ghost. I assumed that it was because she didn't believe what I said about Grandpa. Perhaps I should have paid more attention to her body language back then.

"Don't forget to take your medicine," is all Percy said. "I put it on the tray next to the water." Percy started toward the kitchen without saying a word.

I took my medicine like a good girl and gulped that big, nasty, horsey pink pill down with Mr. Chap's coffee. The blue pills were smaller, but still nasty.

The dull, overcast sun that peeked through the sunroof only minutes earlier suddenly changed into the brightest most brilliant light that I had ever seen. Melodies of birds outside the windows were ever so sweet. The fog of depression that clouded my mood quickly faded. I felt like myself again— bouncy and full of energy. But then, all of sudden I felt tired. *Perhaps it's the medicine*, I thought. So, I rested my head on the arm of the love seat. A dull pain pulsed through my head and stomach. A white mist with sparkling white light appeared before my eyes. I blinked a few times, but the mist only grew thicker and more pronounced. Still, I assumed it was the medicine kicking in as the ...

Chapter 16.
Of Diamonds, Rubies and Cotton Cloth

"Please come back," a man's voice echoed through the thick, gray mist. Something was familiar about the voice, but I still couldn't quite place it.

"I missed you Mommy," a little girl's voice echoed. "I want you to get better, Mommy. Please come back."

"Mommy is sick, sweetie," the man said.

"Why does Mommy have to be sick, Daddy?" the little girl asked. My heart went out to the little girl because she missed her mother. What a sad thought.

"Mommy needs to shed her skin to be with us," the man said.

"Why don't we have to shed our skin, Daddy?" the little girl asked.

I felt my essence floating in a void. Strange, garbled voices continued to echo all around me, as tiny, white lights flashed all about. A strong feeling of peace fizzed through me, as my physical body slowly materialized. The fog soon dissipated

"We don't have skin to shed like Mommy, sweetie," the man said.

"But why does Mommy have skin to shed Daddy?" the little girl asked. She couldn't have been more than four years old.

"Because everybody where your Mommy comes from has skin to shed," the man explained.

Images of a man with a little girl wearing a green-and-white plaid jumper on his knee slowly appeared. Though I couldn't see her face, the little girl had two long black pigtails. They were sitting at a portal, as if waiting for someone to arrive from a trip.

"You were born here, so you don't have skin to shed. Those who come here from your mommy's land have thick skin. The smarter and wiser they become, the more they shed their skin. They can't stay in our land with skin."

"Then why is Mommy here? She has skin, Daddy."

"Hera, sweetie," he said.

"Hera!" I exclaimed. They both turned my way. Strange, but in a matter of seconds, knowledge of four years suddenly flooded my being. I felt myself singing to Hera as an infant, as she looked up to me with those soft, dark eyes. I remembered stroking her curly locks as she suckled from my breasts. I remembered watching her grow before my eyes, as she, Marcellus and I were one happy family.

"Mommy!" Hera yelled. "You're back, Mommy! You're back! We missed you, Mommy!" She hugged me so hard and long.

I looked into her dark eyes. Hera looked like a miniature, female version of Marcellus. She had a soft olive complexion and long, dark hair. Her big, bright smile with those little baby teeth touched my very soul.

"Oh, I missed you too, Hera!" I said as I hugged my little girl long and hard. Her body was so warm and cuddly; her hair was so soft and silky to touch. The warmth of her breath against my earlobe was unmistakably real.

"I didn't think you were coming back," Marcellus said sarcastically.

We locked glances for a few seconds and communicated telepathically. It was the same way I sensed the voices earlier telling me that they were hungry. Anyway, I certainly didn't expected at-ti-tude from a dream image. How dare he get upset with me!

I immediately recognized the large fireplace and French doors leading to the patio. That was my home ... well, my dream home anyway. How about that? A new meaning for the term *dream home.* Interesting.

But somehow, I felt that this was my home, like I belonged there somehow. With each passing moment, the *real* world seemed more like a nightmare that I didn't want to visit anymore until ... well ... you know, Dr. Iverson ... until they wouldn't stop anymore ... until they took over.

Something moved inside of me. I flinched, loosening my hold on Hera.

"What's wrong, Mommy?" Hera asked as she looked up at me with those beautiful, dark eyes. I had met the purest form of love embracing my daughter and stroking her hair. My heart beat with a profound sense of joy like nothing else I had ever experienced before that time.

Looking down, I noticed my protruding belly.

"Look, Daddy!" Hera exclaimed. "Mommy's belly moved!"

"That's the baby kicking, sweetie," Marcellus told Hera.

A big, bright smile lit Hera's face. She pulled my white cotton blouse up, then hugged and kissed my belly over and over again.

"I love you baby brother," she said with a smile. The sparkle of excitement was definitely in her eyes.

A doorbell rang and Hera ran toward the door.

"Uh-uh-uh! Slow down, Hera," Marcellus said as he picked Hera up and threw her over his head. Hera looked so delicate and fragile in her father's big, strong hands, but Marcellus was so gentle and loving to his daughter. Hera just laughed and laughed as he tickled her. He finally put Hera back on the floor and held her delicate, little hand.

"Is that the lady who's going to help Mommy shed her skin, Daddy?" Hera asked.

Marcellus looked back at me, then at Hera. "Yes, sweetie," he told her gently. "It is."

"Yeah!" Hera yelled.

They were dream images, so I didn't pay any attention to that shedding skin theme that kept recurring. I assumed that it was some phase of something that I was going through in *real* life.

***

It probably relates to my illness, right Dr. Iverson?

***

Right Dr. Iverson?

***

Well, Dr. Iverson?

Before long, you'll figure that one out for yourself, Demeter. Keep talking.

***

Okay ... anyway. I heard voices coming from the foyer.

"Where is she?" a woman asked. Her voiced sounded familiar, but I couldn't quite place it.

"She needs to get out of the house more," Marcellus told the woman. "I'll stay here with Hera so the two of you can spend some time together. You have a lot of catching up to do."

"Are you going to help my mommy shed her skin?" Hera asked in that sweet, innocent little girl's voice. Marcellus and the woman giggled for a second.

"Yes, sweetie," the woman said. "I'm here to help your mommy shed her skin."

"Yeah!" Hera yelled excitedly. "You have skin too. Your skin is thicker than my mommy's. Will my mommy help you shed your skin too?"

"I sure hope so, sweetie," the woman said. "I'm counting on it."

While they were talking, I strolled out on the patio and enjoyed the beautiful landscape. Colorful, exotic flowers and trees filled the air with delightful fragrances with each breeze. A big, bright rainbow arched over the raging waterfall. Three large, black pterodactyls—like the one that almost crashed into my car—flew in formation overhead. Those birds sang melodies even Verde Aria would envy.

Loud footsteps broke my fascination with the landscape.

"There's someone you need to see," Marcellus said.

I turned to face him and was outraged by what I saw. *How dare she defile my dreams!* I wondered what that woman was doing in my sacred place. Then, I assumed that it was my fault because I talked about her with Percy earlier that day. You know what they say about assuming.

"Hello, Didi," she said, then hugged me. "Good seeing you again. I see you've done quite well for yourself. You have a lovely family and home."

It was my cousin, Juanita, but she was remarkably different, more polite and humble. She looked different somehow, but I couldn't quite place it. *She is not going to steal my dream husband.*

"Why don't the two of you go to the mall," Marcellus said.

I started to tell him that I didn't know how to get to the mall, but he interrupted me in mid-thought.

"The driver will take you," he said.

Then, I thought about money when he interrupted my thoughts again.

"All you need are your two index fingers," he said. "Look in the zippered compartment of your purse."

"What purse ..." I looked again and a soft black lambskin purse—well what I thought was lambskin—adorned my shoulder. It had a long golden strap and golden zipper. The inside looked like black velvet and was silky soft. What looked like a golden designer tag dangled from the small flap on the front. It was so soft and smooth to touch.

I unzipped the top and dug down into another zippered compartment. There I found a small black wallet with what appeared to be plastic cards—green with silver letters, red with yellow letters, gold with black letters, and a white one with silver letters.

"Each card is for shopping centers on different..." Marcellus paused. "Anyway, just touch the label of the card and it'll show you what's going on at that shopping center."

I took one of the cards and pressed the label, which activated a mini TV screen. "Welcome to..." the voice said, followed by scenes of the shopping center. A map of the shopping center stores and parking lot appeared.

"Well, I guess I'm set," I said. I pressed the label again to close the card's program, then put it back in my purse.

"Are you ready, Didi?" Juanita asked.

"Ready?" I had to be sure what she meant. Even though it was a dream, I didn't want any more surprises.

"Ready to go to the mall?" Juanita asked.

"Oh yes, I'm ready."

Interesting, but that was my first venture outside the dream house. I was so anxious to see what the dream world had in store for me. At that point, lucid dreaming was the best thing that had ever happened to me. Well, of course, until... well you know when, Dr. Iverson.

Anyway, a long, bright hallway lead to the front door. The floors were a solid chocolate marble slab with piercing gold and mauve specks. Deep, rich, decorative mahogany panels adorned the walls, as four massive solid gold columns extended to the cathedral ceiling. The front door—with its shiny golden knob—was wide and tall with a crescent-shaped window carved into the woodwork above its frame.

"Have a good time," Marcellus said, then gave me a quick peck on the lips as he opened the door.

Oh right, a good time, I thought. I never, ever liked going to the mall. I just never thought of shopping as being entertainment. Never.

Wow! I thought as I stepped onto the cobblestone path that led to the driveway. *The sky is so beautiful.*

The sun shined directly overhead, creating a clear, blue tinge across the sky. The light was so intense, yet subtle at the same time. Several pterodactyls flew directly overhead in formation, as their wings flapped to the beat of their happy melodies. A gentle breeze rustled through my hair, as the sweet scent of exotic flowers aroused my senses.

A shiny, black vehicle sat at the end of the path. It resembled the largest of SUV's, but the body was a bit wider and sat low to the ground. Two long silver axlerods protruded from the sides holding large, wide tires. A chauffeur dressed in all black—wide rim cap, suit, gloves and shoes—stood near the car with his back facing us. He opened the door as we approached. I sensed something familiar about him, but I couldn't place it. *He's just a dream image,* I thought. *He probably reminds me of someone in real life.*

I tried to get a peek at his face as he closed the door, but the windows were tinted black, so all I saw of him were his cap and dark glasses. He walked around to the driver's seat, not once did he turn to face us. A thick, black glass panel separated the passengers from the driver.

"This is nice," Juanita said as she ran her hand across the soft seats and looked all about the car.

I was so busy trying to find out why the chauffeur looked so familiar, that I didn't even realize that we had to walk up four black steps to get inside of the car. Two long, black seats faced each other with a small, black marble table in the center. The floors were a deep, plush, black carpet. I sat facing Juanita; she faced forward, while I chose to look out of the back window. A tickle ran up my spine as the driver cruised along taking me backwards. That reminded me of the times my father used to take us to Ponchartrain Beach and we rode the backwards roller coaster.

"Yes," I said. "It is nice."

Black, tinted windows shielded the bright sun, giving a clear view of the landscape. Trees as tall and wide as skyscrapers lined the white concrete road. High above, golden sunbeams darted through thick, winding branches barely touching the thick blades of grass below. Cars of different colors and tinted windows passed us on occasion—going in the opposite direction.

"You are blessed," Juanita said, breaking our silence and my fascination with the new world. "Truly blessed." She shook her head as if to say yes, all the while smiling at me with those big, pink lips. "You have your very own world," she said. "Your father sure knew what he was doing. You chose the right father. I wish I would have chosen the right father this time. I wish my father would have done the same. Now I have to go and put on some more skin. I'll have to keep putting on new skin until it peels right on off. I hate putting on new skin. This is my fifth time in two hundred Earth years putting on skin, you think I would get it right." She laughed. "Funny thing, once you put your skin on, you forget about the other times you put it on until you take it off."

I remained silent and listened to Juanita babble on and on. *Lucid dreams are just as weird as regular dreams,* I thought as I listened to the bizarre words that Juanita spoke. *The characters say the strangest things.* I couldn't help but notice the recurring theme of skin.

"It's not so bad wearing skin," she started up again. "It's just so delicate and you have to be careful how you treat your skin. You have to wash it, clean it, feed it ... whoa." She started laughing. "Skin is just high maintenance. It's a game you know. The people who take the best care of their skin win the game."

Why won't this dream shut up? We rode down that road for what seemed like hours. Finally, the trees started to thin; we neared civilization at last. Buildings of all sizes, shapes and colors were on either side of the highway. *This looks familiar,* I thought.

We were suddenly on what appeared to be a freeway with traffic speeding by in all directions. All sorts of green signs with white lettering were posted along the guardrail: Speed Limit—7 LL, exit ramps, highway numbers and directions. *I know why it looks familiar,* I thought. *This is the same skyline I saw when Marc and I had dinner overlooking the city.*

***

Amazing, seeing the same place in a dream, but from a different angle. I've heard of people having recurring dreams, but never heard of visiting a dream and looking at something from a different angle. Have you heard of such, Dr. Iverson?

Just go on, Demeter.

***

I looked again and noticed that we were on an incline. The golden sun glistened on the clear, blue river below—an artery leading from a vast ocean in the distance. Ahead and below were large ships, ocean liners perhaps. A long, white dock was piled high with large, wooden crates and white sacks, as three large yellow forklifts unloaded cargo from the ships.

"What!" I exclaimed. "The water is so beautiful." I looked out the window and saw straight to the bottom. It's a good thing that was a dream because I'm afraid of heights to this day. The water must have been over one hundred feet deep. We descended, but were still on the bridge, so I took a closer look into the water. Bright, royal-blue and yellow coral reefs covered the bottom. Exotic sea creatures swam downstream—schools of fish with yellow and black stripes, blue with purple polka dots, and black with blue stripes. Several lavender dolphins danced in and out of the water near the shore.

Juanita continued to babble on and on about wearing her skin, and I continued to ignore her. The scene was just too beautiful to let the likes of Juanita ruin it for me. Besides, I never liked my cousin, Juanita, in real life, and I didn't want her in my dream. I hoped that she would have disappeared if I had ignored her, but she was still there.

The sign read—Deneb Mall—next two exits.

"See what you can have without skin holding you back?" Juanita asked.

I ignored her. Besides, she was just a babbling dream image after all, and couldn't possibly have feelings. If it were real life, she wouldn't have cared about my feelings.

"Wow!" Juanita exclaimed. "Look at that! It looks just like a crystal palace. That must be the mall!"

Go away, Juanita, I thought. I tried to will her away to no avail. *Why won't she go away? This is my world, why can't I make her go away?*

The driver exited the ramp, which was almost a full three hundred sixty degrees. It seemed like he drove around that ramp forever before we reached the main street. I became a bit dizzy from the ride and had to blink a few times to regain my composure.

"Look, look!" Juanita exclaimed. She sounded like a child about to go into a toy store.

And exactly why is this person in my dream? I asked myself. *And why am I going shopping with her? I hate to shop in real life ... and in real life, Juanita is the last person... theeeee last person... I would do anything with ... especially go shopping.*

I tried pinching myself, but I wouldn't wake up. *Wake up, Didi, Wake up, Didi,* I told myself, but I was still in the dream and about to go shopping with my cousin Juanita. What a nightmare.

"Look, Didi," Juanita exclaimed again. "Look," she said then shook my leg with one hand while pointing out the window with the other, "look, look!"

"What?" I was annoyed until I saw the Deneb Shopping Center.

The building was made of crystal that reflected the sun's rays. It overlooked the pinnacle of a mountain with a tall, cascading waterfall as a backdrop. A steep, winding stone road twisted and turned between a breath-taking landscape of plush, green grass, exotic flowers of all colors, and shrubs.

As we approached the entrance, crowds of people crossed an enclosed bridge overhead that led from the parking deck into the main building. Others crossed haphazardly between passing cars—weaving their way between traffic—as if they were made of rubber.

The chauffeur pulled up into the passenger drop-off zone and came around to open the door. I tried to get a look at him, but he had positioned himself between the car and the door in a way that hid his face. I was determined to see his face, but the car was waxed as bright as glass. The chauffeur closed the door, and a sudden glare of light bounced off the building in our direction. Juanita stepped up on the curb, and I noticed a long, dangling, transparent, silver cord behind her. It lined down her back, extended out like a prehensile tail, gradually disappearing a few feet behind her.

For a moment, a chill ran through me as goose bumps covered my body. *This is a dream,* I told myself. *She's a mirage.* When I managed to calm myself, the chauffeur had disappeared to the other side of the car.

"You have to be back here when the sun crosses over zenith, three degrees past the high point," the chauffeur said as he got in the car.

"What time is it now?" Juanita asked.

"The sun is one degree before the high point," the chauffeur said, not once facing us. "You have six Earth hours."

Six hours? I thought. *He can't count.* I looked at the large round watch on my arm. Sixteen numbers circled the face instead of the twelve that I was used to seeing in real life. The numbers were divided into four strange segments: *1-2-3-4; 5-6-7-8; 9-10-11-12; and 13-14-15-16.*

"Six hours?" I said out loud, trying to get around to the front of the car to see his face.

He repositioned himself with each step I took. His back faced me, so I still couldn't get a look at him. "Be back on time. Is that clear?" There was a sense of urgency in his tone.

"Don't worry," Juanita shouted back as her silver cord dangled in the wind. "We'll be back on time."

"Start back at about half-passed fifteen," he said. "That'll give you about forty minutes to get back here."

I looked at my watch. Let's see, I thought. Half-passed fifteen means that the little hand would be on 16 and the big hand would be on 8. What an interesting thought—eighty minutes to an hour; thirty-two hours to a day. Only in a dream.

"Be back on time," the chauffeur said. "Don't have me come looking for you." He got in the car and closed the door. I still couldn't see his face.

"Understood," Juanita said.

How dare he tell me what to do, I thought. *This is my dream, my world. And how dare Juanita answer for me.*

When I looked up from my watch, he had driven away.

We went through the automatic, revolving doors straight ahead. The mall was more spectacular than anything I had ever seen before. It was even more incredible than Lenox Mall in Buckhead in Atlanta. The floors were a brick-colored marble with tiny, silver and gold specks. Mahogany benches trimmed in gold were placed between each shop. Exotic flowers and shrubs surrounded a giant fountain at the intersection of two corridors. Gentle sunlight sparkled through the crystal ceiling far above.

"Let's go upstairs," Juanita said.

Two mirrored sets of spiral mahogany stairs lined in gold were on either side of the corridor. As I looked up, each of the ten levels had identical sets of spiral staircases.

"No," I said as I noticed an elevator far ahead around the corner. "Let's take the elevator."

"All right," Juanita said.

Several other people waited for the elevator: two teenage girls who were giggling in response to antics of three teenage boys; a pregnant woman with a baby carriage holding a conversation with what must have been her mother; and a frisky couple who were holding hands and kissing.

"Looks like you're due any time now," the older woman said. She wore a pair of navy-blue shorts with a matching blue-and-white, short-sleeve, checkered shirt. Her arms and legs were very muscular like that of an athlete's. "Your belly has dropped."

"Yeah," the pregnant woman said. "Looks like you're having a boy. Your stomach is low and round." She was of average height, but looked like a teenager—too young to have two children, and too young to tell me anything about my stomach. She wore blue pants and a matching blue-and-white, checkered blouse. In fact, the baby stroller was blue-and-white checks, so were the baby bag and baby blanket. The baby even wore a blue-and-white checkered outfit. But that was a dream, and anything and everything can happen in a dream.

A ding sounded, followed by a crowd of people exiting the elevator. We strolled right on in.

"Let's go to *10*," Juanita said.

"Okay," I agreed and pushed the round *10* button, which was the highest number.

I always hated glass elevators, but that was a dream, so I enjoyed the ride.

"You know," the older woman said. "Girls sit high and your stomach would be pointed. I know. I have four of my own, six grandchildren, and ten great-grandchildren. That's my first great-great grandchild," she said then pointed to the pregnant woman's belly.

The elevator doors opened on *2*, bringing in bright sunlight reflected from the crystal footbridge that led to the parking deck straight ahead. A little girl around five or six got on with her mother.

"Wow," the little girl said while pointing to Juanita's silvery cord, which sparkled in the sunlight. "Look Mommy! That lady has a silver cord hanging down her back."

"That's her leash that pulls her back to that bad place so she can't get loose," the woman whispered to the little girl while pulling her close.

"What bad place? You mean Earth?" the little girl asked.

"Yes," the woman whispered.

Everyone turned to look at Juanita's cord, becoming very still and quiet. A look of embarrassment crossed Juanita's face as most of the crowd eased away from her and huddled together against the back wall, as if she would harm them in some way.

Now she knows what it feels like to be embarrassed in front of a crowd of people, I thought, *even if this is a dream.* I remembered the many times when Juanita and my grandfather embarrassed me in front of the family, neighbors and even complete strangers.

The frisky couple and the teenage girls got off on *5*. More people got off on *6 and 7,* leaving Juanita and me alone with the pregnant woman, her mother and the baby. They were the only ones who didn't seem bothered by Juanita's dangling silvery cord.

"Whose baby?" Juanita asked as she looked at the baby stroller, probably in an attempt to ease her embarrassment and divert attention away from herself.

"Oh, I'm watching my neighbor's child," the pregnant woman said. "She and her husband went to the Honey Moon for the weekend."

"Oh," Juanita said. "That's nice."

I thought of the time on the craft when Marcellus and I were headed for the Honey Moon. It was interesting to hear of the Honey Moon again.

More people got on at *8*. *What a relief!*

We rode in silence for the short distance up to *10*.

I looked at the woman, but she didn't appear to be much older than forty years old. How could she have a great-great-grandchild? But, that was a dream, and anything was possible. Then, I thought of Great-Aunt Ruby and how young she looked.

***

Ooh, now I think I got it, Dr. Iverson. Great-Aunt Ruby was my father's aunt, which made her my grandfather's sister. But my grandfather denied that Great-Gran, Ruby's mother, was any kin to him. If she was my grandfather's sister, then she was … my great-grandmother was married to my great-grandfather … no, wait … they weren't married. Great-Gran was not too much older than my father. Ooohh … Ruby was an outside child, so that would explain why she was so much younger than my grandfather. She was even younger than my father. That's why he hated Great-Gran and Great-Aunt Ruby so much. Yeah, that's it. But that still doesn't explain why my father was so fond of Great-Gran and Great-Aunt Ruby. I don't know, maybe it's because Great-Aunt Ruby was near the age of my father and my great-grandfather probably made them play together. I don't know.

***

Anyway, the bell dinged, our signal to vacate the elevator. The idle conversation prevented me from enjoying the view from the elevator. *Maybe I'll enjoy the view on the way down,* I thought.

It took forever for the pregnant woman to maneuver the stroller off the elevator. Her mother … well, great-grandmother and a couple who were trying to get on, held the doors open.

***

Just listen to me, Dr. Iverson, calling her "the pregnant woman" and I was pregnant too. Well, in the dream anyway.

***

"Let's go in the lingerie shop over there," Juanita said. "I like that red number with the frills the mannequin is wearing."

A dull pain started in my lower back, followed by a sudden sharp spasm. "Ooo!" I said. I paused for a moment.

"What's wrong?" Juanita asked.

"Nothing," I said. I spotted a bench nearby. "Why don't you go ahead. I'm going to sit on the bench."

"Are you sure, Didi?" Juanita asked.

"Yes. Go ahead. I'll be waiting here on the bench."

"Well, all right," she said, then strutted herself right on in the store, that transparent, silvery vestige trailed behind her.

I settled on the mahogany bench, and the pain soon subsided. Like the first level of the mall, the floors were a brick-colored marble with tiny, silver and gold specks. I looked behind and each of the ten shopping levels were identical. The atrium extended high above, as tiny prisms danced off the crystal dome. Golden guardrails surrounded the corridors and three catwalks cut across each one—shortcuts to the stores on the other side.

This mall would be a paradise for Tish and Percy, I thought. A heavy emptiness filled me as I realized that Tish was gone forever. *Maybe I could will her to my dream world,* I thought. Excitement of being able to create anything I wanted at will erased the emptiness of not seeing my Tish again. That was my world, and I was queen. Pain, heartache and stress were strictly forbidden.

Hundreds of shoppers walked through the mall without a care. Mothers with strollers, couples holding hands, teenagers, grown folk and ... but there were no old folk; no one appeared to be over about forty years old.

Several hours must have passed and Juanita's hands were filled with shopping bags; pink with white stripes, green with yellow lettering, and glossy red with gold trim. I spent my time sitting on benches watching the passersby as Juanita shopped and shopped. It was kind of fun watching her try on outfit after outfit and shoe after shoe. "How does this look, Didi?" she asked each time.

"That's you, Juanita," I said. "That's definitely you."

We visited all ten levels of the mall, weaving in and out of boutiques, department stores and shoe barns. Juanita and I had started to bond as family. I felt almost as close to her as I did Percy. I had tasted the sweetness of kinship and family that were stolen from us by our grandfather.

Juanita and I laughed and giggled like a couple of schoolgirls, not caring what others thought of us as we savored each moment together. That was the type of relationship that I could have had or should have had with Juanita. Over thirty years of love and closeness were restored in a matter of one afternoon.

I had always felt a void in my life, like something was always missing. That day, I had discovered what I had been missing all those years: a sense of belonging to an extended family. I had finally forgiven Juanita for the way she treated me years ago. I released those feelings forever. In that moment, I had finally pardoned Juanita at a spiritual level of all the mean and callous things she had ever done to me. It wasn't her fault after all. Our grandfather, in his ignorance, encouraged our cousins to mistreat me. I had forgiven him too, realizing that he was being the best person that he knew how to be. How could I hate him for just being himself?

Did I desire a close relationship with Juanita through the years on a subconscious level? Perhaps. What made those feelings surface after so many years? Is that why each hour was elongated to allow us more time together? I didn't know or care. I just wanted to enjoy Juanita's company that day and perhaps other days too.

Our time together was so magical and profound. We talked mostly about clothes or shoes—things I never found to be stimulating—but I had a good, fun time with her. Was there still time for us to have such a relationship at that point in our lives? I thought it was worth a try and decided to initiate contact with her when I returned to real life. I never really got to know Juanita. Was she as funny and down-to-earth in real life? What made her tick? What were her hopes and dreams?

"Let's get something to eat," Juanita suggested as we passed the food court on the first level.

The black-and-white, diagonal floors reminded me of the first date Marcellus and I had. I looked around again, and that was the site of my first lucid experience with Marcellus.

We both got large cups of frozen doce and decided to relax at one of the window tables. The ice was so creamy, and the syrup was so sweet and tangy.

"So, how've you been?" Juanita asked enthusiastically. She took a long sip of frozen doce. "You have two children, right?"

"Yes," I said. "Hera and this one in my belly."

"No," she said. "I mean Keston and Kevin."

I was a bit taken. Until then, I thought that my real life and dream life were separate.

"Keston and Kevin?" I asked.

"Yes," she said. "How old are they now? When you left New Orleans, they were little boys."

"Well … ahh …" I didn't know how to respond. "Well, Keston is seventeen. Kevin is almost sixteen."

"They look just like their father," Juanita said.

"Yes they do," I said. I hadn't thought of their father in a long time. The last thing I wanted or needed was for my ex to violate my dream too.

"It's a shame he missed out on the boys growing up," Juanita said between sips. "But, he got what was coming to him. Men like that always do. Karma got him really good."

"Hnnn," I moaned. That was my paradise and I sure didn't want to defile my heaven talking about my ex. Sure, I had forgiven him, but that didn't mean that I wanted to see him again—especially in my sacred place.

"Life is but a game," Juanita said, staring into space. "It's like a game of Sorry. Someone else can make a move to make you go back to square one."

Memories of childhood rushed back. At Christmas, we used to go to our grandfather's house. Percy, Juanita, one of our other cousins and I used to play Sorry. As always, Juanita used to cheat. When the rest of us complained, Grandpa always took her side. In his eyes, Juanita could do no wrong.

"That keeps happening to me."

"What keeps happening to you?" I asked. I don't know why I asked because she was just a dream image talking dream talk. Gibberish.

"So I have to keep taking on skin. If only we could remember everything in our skin. But it's just a riddle," she took a sip of her drink, "a riddle that you only figure out outside your skin. It's just a game."

The skin theme repeated again. I knew for sure that my subconscious was trying to tell me something. I just didn't know what at the time.

We sat in silence for a few minutes, sipping our frozen drinks and enjoying the sites around us.

"You were always special, haven't you noticed?" Juanita asked.

"Special?" I asked.

"Yes," she said. "You're of the world, but not in the world."

More dream gibberish, I thought. "Interesting," I said.

"Have you ever noticed how you didn't quite fit in anywhere?" Juanita asked.

"What do you mean?" I asked.

***

She was just a dream talking foolishness. But I remembered how you always said, Dr. Iverson, that we can all benefit from what our dreams are telling us. So, I decided to play along.

***

"You were always different," she said.

I thought that I was different because no one liked my mother or our family because of the way we looked. Nothing more.

"Well?" I asked. I had started to feel a bit uneasy because I thought Juanita was referring to the way our family looked. Perhaps it was time to address those old demons head-on. It was time to put them rest once and for all. "People look at outward appearance. That can't be helped."

"No," Juanita said. "That's not what I mean. Just think about your times at Spelman and Tulane. You never quite fit in. And think about your times at work, you never quite fit in with any particular group either."

***

Come to think of it, Dr. Iverson, I was always on the outside. But again, my IQ is well above 155, so I've always had a difficult time making friends because I see the world differently than most. My interests are unusual, or so I am told. I've been accused of being eccentric. That's my father's fault. He kept books about dinosaurs, astronomy and Greek mythology around the house that I found fascinating. Percy wasn't that interested. My father took me to the Delgado Museum and Wax Museum in New Orleans. When I was sixteen, we went to Paris for the summer. When we visited the Louvre, my father fascinated me with the history of the sculptures like Michelangelo's David and paintings by greats such as Degas. He taught me about periods such as the Renaissance, Baroque and Rococo. We compared works of greats such as Salvador Dali, Pablo Picasso and Henri Matisse. Percy was bored to tears.

My father and I talked about dinosaurs, the possibilities that exist in our universe, ancient gods and such. Other children were interested in fairytales, so we never had much in common. At night, my father took me outside to study the constellations. He made me name each star in the night sky and the mythology behind each one. You know, constellations like Aquila the Eagle with Altair, its brightest star; Lyra the harp with Vega, its brightet star; Cygnus the swan with Deneb, its brightest star; Deneb … oh … Deneb was the name of the dream mall. What a coincidence. Then I realized that the dream was about family ties. Perhaps ties that I yearned for with Juanita and longing to be my father's little girl again. Why couldn't my father accept me unconditionally? I was still his little girl regardless of my lifestyle choices—of being a divorcee. He was ashamed of who I had become. I never forgave him for that until recently.

***

"Oh no!" Juanita exclaimed.

"What?" I asked.

"We only have a few minutes left to get back." She grabbed her bags and raced toward the front entrance. "I enjoyed our time together." She giggled. "Who knows, one day after I shed my skin, I'll be back for a visit."

I lost track of Juanita as she weaved in and out of the crowd at lightening speed. Straight ahead was the entrance. I moved as fast as I could to get there, especially considering my very pregnant condition. *What's the sense of urgency?* I asked myself. *This is just a dream. I shouldn't be rushing anywhere.* I slowed my pace until I reached the revolving doors.

I looked all around the drop-off point, and didn't see Juanita. People walked into and out of the mall, but still no Juanita.

Across the street, what looked like the old man from Underground Atlanta and the hospital started toward me. He wore the same old brown suit and tattered shoulder bag. I noticed his steps were slow and calculated as he struggled along the sidewalk.

I looked at my watch for a split second—*15:78* was the time—two more minutes to pickup time and Juanita was nowhere in sight. Eighty minutes to an hour—what an interesting concept.

"I see you made it," the man called out.

I looked up and the same old man walked toward me, except that he wasn't old anymore. He was tall and slim with smooth copper-tone skin and looked like he had just stepped out of the pages of GQ. The tattered tweed suit had transformed into a stylish tweed jacket and well-fitting brown pants with a sharp crease. He wore that classy brown-and-white hat cocked to the side—like something from an old gangster movie—showing his jet-black, curly locks. His matching brown-and-white tie and buffed, brown-and-white wing-tip shoes were a perfect complement to the ensemble. That worn brown bag was shiny and like new. His chestnut-brown eyes were as big and bright as his sparkling, white smile. That once slow stride had become a fast-paced strut. He looked straight into my eyes. "Yeah, I'm talking to you."

I pointed to my chest as if to say, "Me?"

"Yeah you," he said, then stopped right in front of me. "I see you made it. How ya like it here? Nice ain't it?"

"Yes," I said. "It is."

"When you get a chance, I'll take you on a tour." He winked at me then walked away. "Tell Marc I'll be by a li'l later." He winked again.

He knows Marc? I asked myself. *Of course he knows Marc. He's a dream too.* Then, I realized he was the young man in an earlier dream of a reception; only then, he wore a tuxedo. Marcellus introduced him as his brother, Adonis.

He went to the far end of the sidewalk and started talking to a woman who looked like Juanita. I wasn't sure if it was her because some shrubs hid most of her body. They laughed and talked for a spell.

Through the reflection of the revolving door, I saw the chauffeur approach from the same spot where the old-young man approached. I turned in that direction, but didn't see the car.

Perhaps he parked somewhere else, I reasoned. That didn't make sense, but I was in the illogical world of dreams.

I looked down the way to see if the woman was indeed Juanita. She had moved closer to the curb, and sure enough, it was Juanita. That silver cord was just dangling in the wind. I decided to let her know that the chauffeur had come for us, but I suddenly froze in position. I strained and strained to no avail. Crowds of people walked around me, becoming annoyed that I didn't move out of their way.

Juanita saw the chauffeur coming. By the look on her face, she wasn't happy to see him. It was as if she wanted to hang around a bit longer and didn't want to go with him.

The chauffeur was upon me. I tried to speak out that she wasn't ready to go yet, but the words were trapped in my throat.

He removed the chauffeur's cap and gloves, then stopped in front of me. His skin was a grayish brown like Louisiana mud, and thick and crackly like that of an elephant's. Large, round circles draped his dog-like, hazelnut-brown eyes. He peered at me long and hard, sending an eerie, tingling sensation through my body…

Chapter 17.
Snoop and Pry, Dabbling Bandit

"Wake up, Didi," Percy said, shaking the daylights out of me.

I fell from great heights and was jolted to an upright position.

"What? What?" I was still a bit disoriented.

"Why are you sleeping in the middle of the day?" Percy asked.

"I was tired," I said.

"Tired?" Percy asked. "Sweetie," she said then turned away. "Sweetie, you need to get out and get some fresh air. Here." She handed me my bottle of pills and a glass of cold water. "It's time for your medicine."

Percy opened the bottle and shook a blue pill into my hand. I gulped down the water so fast that I didn't notice the wetness.

"Daddy just called," Percy said.

"Oh," I said. "Did he want to come over?" If he did, I hoped that he wouldn't bring that woman with him.

"How can I put this?" she said, holding her head down. "He got a call from Aunt Gertrude. Juanita's gone."

"Gone?" I asked. I was shocked. "What happened?"

"One of her boyfriends dowsed her with gasoline and set her on fire." Percy put her head down. "I feel so bad because we were dogging her out a few hours ago."

"Oh, man," I said.

"Why don't we go to Duncan Park in Fairburn," I suggested. *Perhaps the cool fall air and pretty leaves would calm my nerves,* I thought. "We could walk around the lake."

"Now you're talking," Percy said. "Let me go and change." She jogged all the way through the kitchen, then I heard her run up the stairs in the living room.

"We hungry up in here," a raspy voice said.

"She ain't even feed us. She neglectin' us," a soft voice said.

I looked all around, but no one was in sight.

"That's right," the raspy voice said. "We talkin' 'bout you, Didi."

"Don't talk to her like that," a third, squeaky voice said.

"You need to shut yo' ass up," the raspy voice said. "She always be feedin' you first anyhow, wit' yo' brown self."

I got up and walked toward the window to find out where the voices were coming from. The TV wasn't on. The radio wasn't on either. But I noticed that my plants were in need of water. I hadn't tended to them in over two weeks. It didn't seem like anyone else had tended to them either. The two Chinese Ivy plants and running vine were fairing okay, but the leaves of the rubber tree had turned yellow and brown. I went into the kitchen and dug into the cabinet under the sink where I kept the watering can and Schultz Plant Food and prepared a concoction for my green friends.

"Here she come, here she come," the raspy voice said.

I watered the rubber tree first because it looked so sickly.

"Why you always feed him first?" the soft voice asked.

I must be tired, I reasoned. *Or maybe it's the medication. I really need to get out this house.*

Hearing the voices made me a bit nervous, so I tried to ignore them by watering the plants.

"It's 'bout time you feed us up in here," the raspy voice said.

Then, I realized that the plants were communicating with me. A chill ran up my spine. I dropped the watering can, spilling water on the floor, and had a sudden urge to leave the house.

"Look what you done did," the soft voice said. "You done scared her now we gone prob'bly starve up in here."

"Oh just shut the fuck up!" the raspy voice said.

I ran toward the living room as goose bumps covered every inch of my body.

"Percy," I yelled. "Percy, let's go. I need some fresh air."

I grabbed my purse and headed down to the basement, then to the garage. Percy was right behind me.

"What's the hurry, sweetie?" Percy asked.

"I need to get out this house," I said as I activated the garage door. "I've been cooped up too long."

I backed out of the garage and swung around the house, leaving tire tracks behind.

"Whoa, slow down, sweetie," Percy said.

A queasy feeling started at the crown of my head and slowly moved to my chest and stomach. It was a bright, sunny afternoon, but everything began to dim.

"Are you feeling all right, sweetie?" Percy asked. "Pull over, sweetie, and let me drive."

I pulled over to the side of the road near the stop sign. Sharp pains pinched my stomach, as the world grew darker and darker ...

***

"Push Didi, push," a woman's voice said. "Almost ... just a little more."

For the second time, I was nude in a birthing chair. My arms wrapped around Marcellus' neck as he hugged my waist.

All was black, but light soon eased into the scene.

"It's a boy!" the voice said.

It was so familiar. I looked again and it was my Great-Aunt Ruby dressed in white scrubs. She looked just as young and radiant as ever.

"It's a boy," Great-Aunt Ruby said, showing off his male member. She took him to the far side of the room to a basin to clean him. The baby screamed and kicked the whole time.

I felt something ooze from deep within me and fall below, catching Great-Aunt Ruby's attention.

"Good," she said. "The placenta just fell out."

"Thank you," Marcellus whispered in my ear. He kissed my neck, sending passion waves through me.

I looked up and back, as he stared deep into my eyes. "Thank you for giving me such a fine baby boy," he said, then kissed my eyelids.

He got up from behind me and joined Great-Aunt Ruby. He held his new son, quieting him in his arms.

"Can I see the baby?" Hera asked.

Great-Aunt Ruby, Hera and Marcellus crowded around the baby, leaving me to tend to myself. Something was still oozing from within me, but I wasn't sure if I wanted to know what it was.

Straight ahead were two large French windows. In the corner was a mahogany crib with light blue bedding. The entire room was powder blue— from the Berber carpet and basin to the shelves, towels, blankets and diapers against the back wall.

Great-Aunt Ruby came over and cleaned my bottom with a coconut-scented substance, then covered me with a sanitary pad as large as an undergarment. She closed the container below the birthing chair and took it out of the room.

Marcellus brought the baby over. "His name is Marcellus Angelell, Jr.," he informed me.

Except for the creamy caramel skin, the baby looked like Marcellus. His little hands curled in and out uncontrollably. He opened his little, beady, black eyes and looked all around.

Hera tickled her new brother. He looked up at his sister and he responded with a faint laugh.

"Feed that boy," Great-Aunt Ruby said as she returned.

She helped me out of the birthing chair, pulling one leg at a time from the stirrups. Marcellus draped me in a silky, white robe as I stood on my feet.

Great-Aunt Ruby led me by the arm to a powder-blue velour love seat near the crib. She exposed my left breast, which was swollen with milk, while Marcellus handed me the baby to cradle.

Instinctively, the baby grabbed hold of my nipple with his tiny hands and wiggled his opened mouth around until he started to suckle. Marcellus sat beside me with one arm extended around my shoulder. Hera looked on in amazement from the arm of the sofa. The baby looked so content and peaceful; we were one happy family.

I felt the milk pouring from deep within, sending a tickling sensation through my body. I wanted Marcellus near to behold the miracle that we had created. I held our baby close to my heart as I looked deep into the innocence of those dark, beady eyes and stroked his thick, black, curly hair.

Marcellus kissed and stroked my hair lovingly over and over again, as Hera smiled at her new brother. If there were such a thing as heaven, that was surely it.

I blinked …

***

I fell from great heights. In an instant, I was jolted to a seated position.

"What's wrong?" Percy asked.

I blinked a few times and realized that I was in the basement watching TV with Percy.

"What?" I asked.

"Looked like you got a chill there for a second," Percy said. "I told you not to walk around the lake today."

"The lake? I asked. "What lake?" I had no idea what Percy was talking about.

"You know … the lake at Duncan Park," Percy said as she changed the channel with the remote control. "It was a bit too chilly to be walking around the lake in the park."

"Who went to the park?" I asked. I honestly didn't know what she was talking about. I sure didn't remember going to the park.

"You're so funny," Percy said.

"I need to get out of this house," I told Percy. "I've been off work for about a month. I'm not used to being cooped up like this."

"It sure did you some good today," Percy said. "Walking the dog was a good idea. Playing catch with the dog really did you some good."

"Playing catch with the dog? You mean Sampson?" I asked. What on earth was she talking about. I didn't even like that mutt, so I knew for sure that I didn't play with him.

"Playing fetch, playing Frisbee, playing catch … it's all the same to me. Anyway, it did you good."

"I think it's best if I go back to work tomorrow. Staying cramped up in the house is driving me bonkers. It's not like me to stay at home." *That,* I reasoned, *is why I'm not myself anymore.*

"Do you think you're up to it?" Percy asked.

"I've never been more up to it than now. I'll try it for a few hours," I told her. "If I'm not feeling well, then I'll come home."

"That sounds good," she said then nibbled some pistachio nuts from the dish in the middle of the coffee table. "Why don't you use MARTA? You may not want to drive, especially since you're taking medication. You don't want what happened today to happen in the middle of the highway do you?"

I followed suit and grabbed a handful of nuts too. They tasted really sweet and were really crunchy. "What brand of nuts are these?" I asked, then opened the shells and popped a few more into my mouth. "These are really good."

"I got these from the Natural Food section of Kroger earlier today. I emptied them into the dish and threw the bag away. I'm not sure what brand they are."

"Percy," I said, trying not to let on that I didn't know what the heck she was talking about. What happened? I had to find a way to get Percy to tell me without letting on that the entire afternoon was a complete blur. "What would I do without you? Tell me why you were concerned for me today? Why don't you think I can drive tomorrow."

"You were driving all over the road, sweetie, that's why," Percy said. "It's a good thing we were still in the subdivision and there was nothing coming or no children in the way."

I certainly didn't remember driving all over the road. "Okay," I told her. "How about if you drive me to the MARTA Station at College Park in the morning. I'll call about an hour before I leave to let you know when I'm coming home so you can pick me up. How about that?"

"That'll work, sweetie," Percy said. "Just let me know when to come and get you."

"You know, Percy," I said. "Maybe I do need another day. I think I'll start back on Tuesday. That'll give me time to mentally prepare."

"That's a good idea, sweetie," Percy agreed.

November
In a trap the seeker's caught
In a spider's web of diamonds, rubies, and cotton cloth
Snoop and pry
Dabbling bandit
Scream and cry
Caught red-handed

Chapter 18.
Scream and Cry, Caught Red-Handed

"Come on, Percy!" I yelled from the bottom of the stairs. "What's taking you so long?"

"I'm coming, I'm coming, sweetie," Percy yelled back from the bathroom. "What's the hurry, sweetie?"

I was getting antsy, so I tiptoed quietly upstairs to find out what was taking her so long. The hallway was quiet and dark, so I was careful not to wake the boys. The bathroom door was ajar. Candlelight glowed from inside, so I peeked in. A small bottle of vanilla and cotton swabs were scattered across the vanity. Tiny, white crystals were piled high in a black thimble. Circles of steam rose from the back corner of the room.

Percy must be doing some type of meditating, I thought. *I'll give her a few minutes of quiet time. I felt so guilty for disturbing her privacy.*

I went into the kitchen, brewed a pot of Chap's coffee and toasted a blueberry bagel, then waited for Percy in the sunroom.

That coffee sure eased my nerves. I'd almost forgotten that Percy had been in the bathroom for over forty-five minutes.

"Psst," a voice said, scaring the daylights out of me.

It was pitch black, except for the counter light from the kitchen. I looked around to see if someone had left the TV or radio on, but everything was off.

"Psst," the same voice said again. "Didi, I need to talk to you," the voice whispered.

My eyes roamed the sunroom, but no one was in sight.

I looked out the back window. Everything was dark, but I heard loud snores in the direction of the backyard. It couldn't have been Percy, because she was in the bathroom, and the boys didn't snore. Who was it? Did the boys have a sleepover guest without telling me? That couldn't be because the snoring was so close, someone was definitely sleeping in the sunroom. But where?

"Psst, Didi," the voice whispered, barely audible for all the snoring. It was soft and raspy and all too familiar. But where ...

I knew for sure that someone was playing a trick on me. *I'll kick whoever's ass when I find them!* I thought. Who could do such a thing, especially knowing that I was ill. *I don't need this fuckin' bull-shit this fuckin' early in the fuckin' morning! Shit!*

"Can I come to work with you?" the voice asked. That time, it had communicated with me on some telepathic level. I heard and sensed it at the same time ... and it was one of my plants. I sensed that it was sad and lonely, which was the reason why its leaves had begun to turn brown and yellow. The hair stood up on my arms, sending an eeriness through my body. I high-tailed it into the living room.

"No, no!" the voice said. "Don't go, don't go! Please don't leave me. Oooh!"

"Percy!" I yelled. I didn't care what ritual she was in the middle of. I wanted her to hurry up and take me to the MARTA Station. Percy didn't answer, and I was quite annoyed.

I need my medicine. All I need ... is to take my medicine, I thought. I ran upstairs, my wobbly legs barely made it. I was shaking like a leaf in the autumn breeze all the way to my bathroom. I scrimmaged around the cabinet drawers. *Where is it? Where is it?* The bottle was on the vanity near the mirror. I couldn't steady my hands; it was a wonder that I managed to open the bottle. Still shaking, I poured two small blue pills into my palms and threw them to the back of my throat. A cup was nowhere in sight, so I let the tap water flow into my palms and gulped the pills down. I put the bottle of pills in the inner pocket of my jacket and retrieved my briefcase from the walk-in closet. After taking a few deep breaths, I returned downstairs to wait for Percy.

"Percy!" I yelled and caught a glimpse of the dark sunroom through the kitchen. Goose bumps popped on my arms just looking in that direction. I paced up and down, back and forth, waiting for Percy to hurry up. "Percy!"

Percy emerged from the bathroom. It took her a million years to step down each stair, probably because she was putting on her gold hoop earrings. She wore a low-cut, red silk blouse; black, pleated pants and black pants socks. Those pink house slippers were a bit out of place, to say the least.

"Come on, let's go, let's go," I told her.

"What's the hurry, sweetie?" She finally reached the bottom of the stairs. "Smells like you fixed some coffee. Have you eaten, sweetie, or do you want me to fix you something?"

"I had a bagel and some coffee," I said.

"Are you sure that's enough, sweetie?" Percy asked, then stared at me up and down, twitching her nose. Her clothes smelled of vanilla extract and some other sweet substance, but I couldn't place my finger on it. "Is that what you're wearing to work, sweetie?" My red-and-white turtleneck, gray-and-black tweed jacket and black denims probably didn't meet her approval.

"What's wrong with what I'm wearing, Percy?" I asked. It was five-thirty in the morning, way too early to start an argument. I let her talk me into taking MARTA to work, then she lagged around as if she didn't want to drop me off at the station. Unbelievable.

"Oh nothing, nothing," she said, fanning her hands through the air. "If that's what you want to wear ..." she said, hunching her shoulders. She mumbled something else under her breath as she neared the door leading to the basement.

"What?" I asked.

"Oh nothing, sweetie," she said with a smirk.

The boys were just getting up. I saw the lights from Keston's and Kevin's bedroom flick on.

I had forgotten my purse in the sunroom, but was too afraid to go back in to get it. Percy had already reached the bottom of the stairs in the basement; it didn't make sense calling her all the way back up just to get my purse. The boys were getting dressed, so that meant that I had to get my purse from the sunroom.

I looked past the dimly lit kitchen and into the sunroom. Nothing ever looked so gloomy. The soft white cabinet light combined with the white woodwork cast a dim, grayish shadow into the sunroom.

"Are you ready, sweetie?" Percy yelled from the basement in that annoying voice of hers. Argh! "You made me hurry up, sweetie, and you're not ready to go!"

After taking three long breaths, I finally had the courage to run back into the sunroom. It didn't look as dark and scary the closer I got. The kitchen light was bright enough after all.

It was just my imagination, I thought. *I just needed to take my medicine. That's all.*

I looked all about the room and couldn't find my purse. It wasn't on the coffee table like I had remembered. I looked under the table, between sofa cushions and everywhere—still no purse. Then, I glanced toward the window and there it was! One problem: it was on the windowsill next to my plants. Then, I started to panic all over again.

Slowly, I inched toward the window.

"Are you ready, sweetie?" Percy yelled from the living room. "Where are you, Didi?"

Anxiety flowed through my veins, as Percy's footsteps neared the sunroom. I knew for sure that I needed to just run over there and grab my purse. How could I explain to Percy that I was afraid of the plants? She would've had me committed for sure.

So, that's what I did. I ran over to the window to grab my purse.

"Take me to work with you," the voice said again, sending a cold chill across my skin. "Please."

"What are you doing?" Percy asked, frightening me. My heart never raced so fast.

"I'm looking for my purse," I said.

"Well, isn't that it over there by the window?" she asked sarcastically. "Get your purse and let's go." She turned toward the living room, but I remained frozen in position.

"Please," the voice begged. "Take me with you. Please don't leave me here with them." Its voice sounded so frail and helpless. Pain poured from it's very soul.

"Are you coming or what?" Percy snapped from the living room. "Are you sure you're ready to go back to work?"

I threw my purse around my right shoulder and grabbed the plant in my left hand, then started toward Percy.

"Thank you, Didi," it said. "You don't know how much I appreciate it. Thank you, thank you, thank you!"

My medicine hasn't kicked in yet, I thought. *It's just my subconscious making me feel guilty for neglecting my plants.*

***

After all, Dr. Iverson, the plants were birthday presents from Mr. Chap. He gave me the first Chinese Ivy in 1997 and the second in 1998. This year, he gave me the running vine and Fern. I'm not quite sure what type of plant Fern is. He has little thick, waxy round leaves, kind of like an umbrella plant, but the bark is like that of a miniature oak tree. I've never seen anything like him.

***

It was six-thirty when Percy dropped me off at the College Park MARTA Station. The large parking lot was almost empty, except for a few cabbies looking for the next fare. Percy gave me two little, golden coins when she pulled up to the curb.

"What are these?" I asked.

"Those are tokens for the train," she said, then pointed toward the station. "Do you see the silver slots that the people are going through?"

I looked around, but everything was dark. *What people?* Then, I looked slightly behind the car on the right, and sure enough, everyone was headed toward the train platform. The lights inside the station were almost as bright as daylight.

Percy flipped the switch under her seat that popped the trunk open, my cue to vacate her car. I grabbed my things from that tiny thing she called a trunk.

"Get off at the Buckhead Station," she said.

Buckhead? I thought. Then it hit me: Percy lived in Buckhead. "Wait," I said before Percy drove off. "You live right across the street from my office. Why don't you just drop me off at work, then stop home and get a few things. You haven't been home in a few weeks."

"What if you need me, sweetie," she said. "I'll be at the house if you call."

"But if you're at your condo—across the street—and I were to call, it'll be more convenient for you."

"But what if the boys need something, and I'm not there?" she asked.

"But... " She wouldn't let me finish.

"Are you afraid of catching MARTA?" she asked, catching me off guard.

"No, but... "

"But nothing, sweetie," she said. "You'll be fine. Just call me on my cell phone if you need anything." She activated the automatic window roll up button and drove off, leaving with the last word in edgewise.

With my purse over my right shoulder, briefcase in one hand, plant in the other hand, I boarded the train headed for Buckhead. *Buckhead,* I thought. *Percy lives in Buckhead across the street from my office. It was time for her to stop home for some fresh supplies and such. Why didn't she drop me off at work and run home? Maybe she wants me to get back into the swing of things.* I didn't think anything of it at the time, but I probably should have paid more attention to Percy's actions or inactions.

***

The train was bright and smelled of pine. All seats were goldenrod, the floors were a rust-colored Berber. Social service posters—AIDS awareness, domestic violence, teen pregnancy and whatnot—were between most of large double-glass windows. A strange, rotten smell filled the air. I looked a few seats behind me and two seats had become a bed to a sleeping homeless person.

"You ain't in Kansas anymore," the plant said.

"What?" I asked.

"You ain't used to bein' 'round common folk," the plant said. "Yo' sistah know she wrong fo' that."

A few of the plant's leaves had turned yellow and brown. I began to stroke its green leaves.

"Thank you fo' takin' me wit' you," the plant said. "When you be gone, I be made fun of."

"Made fun of," I asked.

"Yeah," the plant said.

"Who makes fun of you? How?" I asked.

"Them other two be making fun of me. They say I be talkin' funny."

"Nnnn," a woman across the aisle from me said to a friend. "That lady talkin' to her plant."

"That's what my stepmumma be doin'," the friend said. "She be always talkin' to her plants like they be people o' somethin'. She even got names fo' ever' last one o' 'em too."

I didn't even realize that I was talking to the plant. One woman in front of me rolled her eyes and moved to a seat in front of the train. Hot flashes rushed through me as other passengers gave me strange looks. *Maybe Percy was right,* I thought. *I'm not ready to go back to work.*

"Don't wurry 'bout them, Didi," the plant said.

But the young woman gave me an idea: perhaps I should name my plants. I decided to name the taller Chinese Ivy, China, and the other one, Ivory.

I asked the plant on a telepathic level about the name Fernando. "It vaguely reminds me of a cactus I had seen in San Fernando Beach a few years ago."

"I like the name Fernando, I think I'll keep it. But it's a bit long."

"How about Fern for short?"

"Hey," Fern said. "I like it. Anyway, like I was saying. Them other two be makin' fun o' me. They just be jealous o' me 'cause they is houseplants and I'm a tree. If you axsk me, they ain't good 'nough to be 'round me. Honey, I'm gone grow into a big tree some day, and they still gone be sittin' 'round in somebody house. I'm tryin' to tell you!"

"Tell me what?" I asked.

"I'm tryin' to tell you is just a expression, Didi," Fern said.

"Oh."

The train stopped at the Lakewood Station and more passengers started to board. To say the least, I caught the attention of a few passersby.

"I talk to my plants too," an older woman said as she sat next to me. "Plants need attention just like people. That's what makes them grow."

"Oh," I said.

She was at least ninety years old and wore a large gray Afro. A perpetual smile lit across her lips. Her face was heavily made up with large red circles of rouge on her cheeks. She looked oddly familiar, but I couldn't quite place where we'd met before. "Hello, Mr. Plant," she said, rubbing Fern's leaves and bringing quite a bit of attention to herself. "How are you today, Mr. Plant?"

"I'm fine," Fern answered back. "How 'bout yo'self?"

"Oh I'm just doin' wonderfully," the woman said. "What's your name?"

"Didi just named me Fernando," Fern said. "Just call me Fern."

"Hello, Mr. Fern," the woman said.

"Did you hear him?" I asked the woman in a hushed whisper.

"I sure did," she said. "I heard him loud and clear."

I looked all around the train and asked, "Did you hear the plant?"

The train was noisy and standing room only. But somehow, a few vacant seats remained in front and back of us. The crowd thinned near our seat, but people continued to stare our way. It became so quiet that you could hear a pin drop. I didn't realize that so many people would be on the train that time of morning.

"Didi needs to prune your leaves," she said, then tangled his leaves between her fingers, and spoke as if talking to a newborn, "so you can be a pretty-retty plant. Yes you are, yes you are ... a pretty-retty plant."

Fern laughed and laughed. "That tickle, that tickle!"

"My name is Dr. Dewey. Dr. Cynthia Dewey. Nice meeting you, Mr. Fern."

Cynthia Dewey? The pain of losing Tish immediately came crushing in on me. I missed her so much. What's the odds of meeting someone with that name on the MARTA train? Were the Cosmos playing a sick joke on me?

"Doctor?" Fern asked. "Is you a medical doctor?"

"I'm a retired educator," Dr. Dewey boosted. "I taught English at Spelman College for over forty years."

Ah, ha! I thought. *That's where I must have seen her.* But I didn't recall a Dr. Dewey when I was at Spelman. Maybe that was her married name. I didn't want to pry or seem nosy. "I received my undergrad from Spelman back in 1982."

The train approached the North Avenue Station when I noticed a woman of about seventy years old standing over Dr. Dewey. She must have been sitting to the rear of the train. She looked familiar, but I couldn't quite place her.

"Come on, Ma," the woman said. "Let's take you to the doctor."

Ma? I asked myself. *She must be really old if an old lady walking with a cane is calling her Ma.*

"Bye Fern," the woman said. "Tell Didi to take good care of you."

"Bye Dr. Cynthia Dewey," Fern said.

The woman took Dr. Cynthia Dewey by the arm and escorted her to the door. We made direct eye contact. "Oh God!" I said, again catching the attention of everybody on the train. When I looked into her eyes, she was an older version of Tish—of what she would have looked like at that age. The younger-older woman looked like what Tish's daughter would probably look like at that age.

My mind is playing tricks on me, I thought. *I miss Tish so much that I see her in everyone, even an eccentric, old lady.*

"What a sweet, old lady," Fern said.

"Yes," I said, not caring who overheard me. "Yes, she sure was."

***

Seven-fifteen and I had just arrived at my desk! *MARTA sure is fast,* I thought. Oh, I never thought it would be so nice to be back at work! I cleared a few papers and turned on the light under my credenza. That's where Fern called home.

"Ummm," Fern said. "This is nice. Very nice indeed. I can get used to this here!"

"I'm glad you like it, Fern," I said.

"At least you don't have one o' them li'l bitty cub'cles like them two o'er there," Fern said, referring to Marcus' and Trevor's cubicles. "You must be im'potant to have mo' space than ever'body else."

Important? *If I were so important, I would have an office.* "Well, Fern. I'm a Director. At this company, unlike other companies, Directors get cubicles," I said sarcastically while continuing to log on to the computer network and put my things away. "Now, if I were at some other company, I would have an office, not a little bitty, tiny cubicle." On that note, I threw my purse into one of the bottom drawers, slamming it forcefully.

"Oh," Fern said sarcastically, probably sensing my frustration.

"You could use a little water," I told Fern. We always kept party supplies in the tan metal cabinet against the back wall by the window. I got a Styrofoam cup and headed to the bathroom.

"Where you goin'?" Fern asked.

"To get you some water," I said. "I'll be right back."

"I'll be here," Fern said. "I ain't goin' nowhere."

***

The restrooms are in the middle of the building past the break room, Dr. Iverson. I switched on lights as I went along. Some of the corridors are far from windows and can get really dark. No telling who could be lurking in some nook waiting for his next victim of who knows what.

***

Anyway, I thought I heard something fall to the floor as I entered the restroom. The lights were on in the seating area, so someone was definitely inside. Sounded like metal or glass scraping against the marble vanity. Someone was in a hurry ... D'Angela. She threw a bottle of vanilla extract and cotton swabs into her large, black purse, applied a hint of pink lipstick and headed for the door.

She seemed shocked to see me standing near the mirrors. I assumed it was because no one had expected me back so soon.

"Demeter," she said. "I ain't know you was coming back today." She smelled of vanilla extract and the same strange scent that I noticed on Percy earlier.

"I just came to get some water for my plant," I said.

"Good to see you up and about," she said on her way out.

Again, I felt guilty. D'Angela was always high-strung. I had probably interrupted her morning meditation session, the one thing that she needed to calm her nerves. *What's with the vanilla?* I asked myself. *It must be some new homegrown type of aromatherapy treatment. I wonder why Dr. Iverson hadn't mentioned it to me before. It must be popular if Percy likes it; she only follows the crowd and never tries anything original.*

When I got back to my desk, I noticed a glare off of my computer monitor.

"Take me to the window, take me to the window!" Fern insisted.

I grabbed Fern and we went over to the window just behind the partition of my cubicle.

"So beauuuutiful!" Fern said.

Yes. The sunrise was very beautiful indeed. Brilliant sienna tones eased above the horizon, filling the sky with shades of burgundy that faded into goldenrod high above the Atlanta skyline. Some parts of the office were still dim—all was quiet—a perfect time for me to enjoy nature's splendor. What a welcome back to work.

"This is breathtaking, isn't it Fern?" I asked.

I sensed nothing from Fern. "Well, isn't it lovely, Fern?" I asked again. Still, no response. It was as if Fern were an inanimate object that was incapable of communicating. Was it all an illusion? *My medicine must have kicked in,* I reasoned.

I returned to my cubicle and put Fern in his new home under the light, then sorted through folders that were piled on my desk. Everything was the same as I left it the month before.

"Good to see you back," a voice said, almost from nowhere. The aroma of coffee and fresh blueberries tempted my nose. It had to be Mr. Chap. He greeted me with a smile and a cardboard tray piled high with coffee and a large blueberry muffin. "I saw you walking toward the elevator this morning. I thought you would stop and say hello."

"Oh, Mr. Chap," I said. "I planned to stop by a little later."

"Of course you were," he said. Carefully placing the tray on my desk, he unfolded a single white paper napkin across my lap.

"Thank you so much, Mr. Chap," I said. "You're so good to me."

I took a few sips of coffee; Mr. Chap stood over me staring into my eyes for a few seconds. "I missed you while you were gone, Didi," he said.

"Oh, Mr. Chap," I said. "I missed you too."

"You did?" He seemed surprised to hear me say that I'd missed him.

"Yes, of course," I told him. His eyes lit up hearing those words.

Was it a mistake to say I had missed him? I didn't want to lead that old man on.

"I see you decided to bring the plant in to work," he said, looking curiously at Fern. "It could use some plant food."

I felt guilty for not taking better care of Fern. Mr. Chap gave me the plant because he probably thought that I was responsible enough to care for it. "I promise to take better care of Fern," I said.

"Who?" Mr. Chap asked.

"Fern," I said. "All the plants you gave me have names. This one is Fern, short for Fernando."

"Oooh, that's nice," he said. "I'll be seeing you around, Didi." He walked toward the elevator in a pensive state. His stride wasn't as peppy; he struggled to put one foot in front of the other. Something was definitely on his mind. *Is Mr. Chap ill?* I wondered. *I hope not. He's such a nice old man.*

I wrapped the blueberry muffin in a napkin for later. The bagel I had earlier filled me pretty well. But, I couldn't get enough of Chap's coffee. I propped my feet on my desk, reclined back in my chair—thank goodness for ergonomically correct chairs—and savored each and every drop. Besides, no one was around—well in my area anyway—so who could see me? Charged with a tall cup of Chap's coffee, I was ready to face anything that came my way that day. Well, so I thought.

***

Have you ever had a day when it was better to stay in bed than venture out, Dr. Iverson? Well, that Tuesday was it.

***

I checked my e-mail. Whoa, over one thousand messages! A message flashed across my screen—

Warning, mailbox full. Please delete unnecessary messages.

My goodness. Go away for a month or so and things just pile up … and fast. *Maybe later for e-mails,* I thought. *But Fern could use a little work.*

Overwhelmed by the work ahead of me, I turned my attention to Fern for diversion. I carefully removed the brown and yellow leaves from Fern. Next, I took a tissue from the box on my desk and stroked his green leaves until they were shiny.

"I hope this doesn't hurt Fern," I said to myself. "I've always wondered if plants feel pain."

"Oh, honey," Fern said, alarming me enough to back off. "Don't stop. Work yo' magic honey. That feel too good."

"Does it hurt to prune your leaves?" I asked.

"No chil'," Fern said. "It feel real good."

"It does?" I asked.

"Yeah, chil'," Fern said. "It probably feel like when you had got yo' toes did the other day. Remember when that lady had came over to do yo' finger tips and toes and she had scraped away all that there dead skin?"

"Oh," I said, continuing to shine Fern's leaves. "You mean the two ladies, Cynthia and Dewey."

"What two ladies?" Fern asked.

"The ones who came over to do Percy's and my pedicures."

"Naw," Fern said. "They was only one lady who had came over. I was there, 'member? I think her name was Rose. I don't 'member no other lady. If you don't believe me, axsk yo' sustah Percy."

"I don't know, Fern," I said. "I remember two ladies. One was Cynthia and the other one was Dewey."

"Nnnn, talking to yo' plant? Just like my momma, always be talkin' to her plants like they people." It was Trevor who was just settling in. "Well how you feel? You doin' okay? We ain't 'pect to see you fo ' 'nother week or two. Honey, if I was you, I would take as much time as I could. If they say six weeks, I'd be pushin' fo' seven o' eight."

"Ahnnnn, hmmm," I groaned. "I only plan to be here for a few hours. It was driving me crazy being cooped up in the house like that."

"I heard that," he said. "I'm goin' downstairs to Chap's. You want me to bring you somethin'?"

"No," I told him. "Thanks anyway."

"I'm goin' to downstairs to Chaps," I heard Trevor tell someone. "You want to me to get you somethin'?"

"Naw," the other party said. It was Marcus Williams. He must have been surprised to see me because he almost jumped out of his skin seeing me sitting there. His cubicle was behind Trevor's, diagonally across from mine. "Demeter, I didn't expect you back so soon. Welcome back," he said.

"Good to be back," I told him. "I needed to get out of the house."

"Yeah," he said while he continued to settle in. His designer, black leather briefcase with gold trim looked a tad out of place sitting at the base of his tan metal desk. *You look fine. Not just any fine. Fancy—p-f-i-n-e—pfine*, I thought. But he stuck a pin in my bubble."My wife is the same way. She can't stand to just sit around the house all day. She's like you, can't stand to be idle. Just work-work-work."

It never amazed me. He always managed to squeeze something in about his wife, no matter the conversation. During product development meetings, somehow one of the system components related to his wife. It never failed that at the millions of training sessions we attended together—the room, which was usually freezing cold—reminded him of the way his wife turned down the thermostat in the summer.

"Marcus," I called.

"Yes," he answered, not looking up from his computer.

"Do you have a moment?" I asked.

"Sure," he said, looking at his computer monitor. "Give me one second while I finish logging on." He stared at his screen for a few seconds. "What you got?" he asked on his way to my cubicle.

"Could you sit in on meetings for me over the next few days. I need time to get caught up. Just fill me in on what happens."

"Not a problem," he said.

"Oh ... and another thing," I said. "Make sure someone on D'Angela's team takes minutes."

"Got it," Marcus said. "We have three meetings coming up tomorrow. Oh, the round table is today. It starts at nine o'clock in fact."

"Where is it?" I asked.

"In one of the ballrooms at the Ritz Carlton. I'm not sure which one."

Umph, a round-table. That could take all day. Maybe I can get some peace and quiet. See, that's what I'm talkin' 'bout. Comin' back to work and it's all peaceful and quiet, I thought.

***

Our company occupies seventeen out of thirty floors in the building, so I thought it would be quiet for sure, Dr. Iverson.

***

"How long is it planned for, noon?" I asked Marcus, hoping he would say that it was an all day session for all employees. "Is it just for managers this time, or everybody?"

"It's until about three. It's for everybody this time. "

Yes!

"They feedin' us breakfast and lunch chil'," Trevor butted in, toting a little brown bag and a cup of Chap's coffee, announcing his entrance.

Trevor must have noticed me watching him drink Chap's coffee. "Oh, I got me a li'l somethin' somethin' from Chap's downstairs. All they feed us is cantaloupes and bananas and that nasty coffee at them meetin's and call that breakfast. But, honey let me tell ya, they be throwin' down fo' lunch," he closed his eyes, "with some steaks," tossing his head in the air, "and some roast chicken," followed by raising his hands as if he were in prayer service, "mmm, mmm, mmm!"

Marcus and I just stared at Trevor. He was quite a performer, becoming rather dramatic at times.

"My wife bakes the best oven-roasted chicken," Marcus said. "She lets it marinate overnight in Sherry wine and lemon peels ... talk about good."

"You ought to bring some o' dat dere chicken to work fo' the rest o' us," Trevor said.

I cleared my throat, hoping to catch Marcus' attention. As an added bonus, I wouldn't have to hear any more about his wife. "Could you attend that one too?" I asked Marcus, breaking his fixation on Trevor and the discussion of food.

"Oh, I'm sorry," Marcus said, which indicated that he was paying more attention to Trevor than to me. "My wife's chicken is ... "

"Could you attend the round table for me and report back?" I repeated.

"Oh ... oh ... not a problem," he said. "You need time to catch up, I know how that can be. When my wife was on maternity leave with our first child ... no ... our second. Yeah, that's right. After our second child was born, she told me how much her work piled up at work. It took her a long time to catch up."

Whatever, I thought. *His wife really has him wrapped around her little finger.* Boy, was I ever wrong. But, that wasn't my problem, and I didn't intend to make it my problem; I had too many of my own to tackle. I always made it a rule not to get involved in other folk's business. Too bad other folk don't feel the same way about my business.

"Oh, thank you all for the fruit basket. I really appreciate it," I told them.

"Oh no problem," Trevor said as he sat down at his desk and began to unload his bag of goodies.

"Everybody liked the Thank You card you sent," Marcus said on the way back to his cubicle. "Dan pinned it on the corkboard in his office."

"Office?" I asked.

Marcus looked up from his computer and Trevor stopped chewing his bagel as though they were surprised by what I had said.

"Yeah," Marcus said, almost in slow motion. "He put it on the board in his office after he passed it around for everybody to see. Are you surprised?"

"Whoa," I said, then walked across the aisle to Trevor's cubicle. "When did Dan get an office? You mean Daniel Batchelor, right?"

"Yeah," Trevor said in a puzzled tone. "Honey, you been gone one month and you already forgot about us. Umph, umph, umph."

"Did Dan get a promotion while I was gone?" I asked Trevor.

"You really did forget about this job when you was gone," Trevor said. "Didn't you, Demeter?"

You can't blink your eyes in corporate America without someone trying to step on you on the climb up the ladder. I worked longer hours and harder than any other Director in the company. If anyone got the Vice President of Product Development position, it should have been me, not Daniel Batchelor. My stomach knotted up just knowing that he got the promotion ahead of me, especially while I was out sick.

Trevor was flip at the mouth, but I could rely on him to tell the truth. Marcus, I relied on to watch my back. Or could I? Was it wise to delegate duties to Marcus? Could I trust him? Well, I had no choice except to trust him. I was falling apart at the seams ... and fast.

Trevor was pulling my leg. He knew that I coveted the Vice President spot. So, I decided to check things out for myself. First, I went two aisles down to Dan's cubicle, but there were two laser printers and a fax machine in the space. Then it dawned on me, Patricia must have been promoted to Senior Vice President.

"When did we get these printers in the cubicle?" I asked one of the software engineers who sat across from Dan. She was eating her breakfast, so I think I surprised her.

"Hi, Demeter," she said, trying to swallow the mouthful of muffin, covering her lips with a napkin. "Welcome back. We didn't expect you back so soon. How are you feeling?"

"I'm fine, thanks," I said, trying not to seem to demanding. "When did these printers get here?" I asked again.

"Are we getting new printers already?" she asked, patting crumbs of a blueberry muffin from her mouth. "We just got them a few months ago. That's technology for you; it's changes right before your eyes. Are you going to move them? They can get a bit noisy, not to mention being interrupted by people getting their printouts and people stopping by the printer and holding conversations all day long."

"I'll see what I can do," I said. "Tell me, do you remember if we've kept printers in this spot?" I asked.

She perked up a bit. "They've been here since I came on board eighteen months ago, but I've gotten used to the interruptions. I can't say for sure about my neighbors though." She pointed to the cubicles that surrounded the printer station. "It would be nice if they could be moved some place else. With all this Year 2000 business going on, it would be nice not to be interrupted so often. I could sure get more work done."

"Thanks," I said. "I'll see what I can do about that."

"No problem," she said, then continued with her breakfast.

She said that the printers had been there for at least eighteen months. But eighteen months ago, Daniel Batchelor sat in that spot. Had I forgotten the layout of the office after being gone for a mere month? Determined to find out what had taken place in my absence, I set off for Patricia's office.

It was almost eight o'clock, and people were coming in by the droves.

"Hi, Demeter. Didn't know you were coming back so soon. Welcome back," was all I heard all morning. Stopping to talk to what seemed like hundreds of people and explaining my return took over thirty minutes. It's amazing how time flies while engaging in idle chatter.

"Sorry for your loss," someone said.

"Thank you," I told her, assuming that she was referring to Tish. *How did she know about Tish?* I wondered. *Word sure does travel fast.*

"I know how it is to have a miscarriage. I had one about two years ago. If you need to talk," she said, stroking my hand and looking me in the eyes. "I'm here for you," then walked away.

I was speechless. *That asshole!* I thought. Trevor probably told the whole world that I was pregnant. Well, if gossip started, I only had myself to blame. What was I thinking telling Trevor of all people something like that? *It'll blow over,* I thought. *We're all adults. No one probably cares.*

It was eight-thirty when I finally reached Patricia's office on the far end of the floor. *Daniel Batchelor—VP Product Development* was on the door. I peeked through his door and saw that he was talking on the phone and working on his black PC, notebook computer at the same time.

He looked up for a moment, then motioned for me to come in. "Let me get back to you," he said, then hung up. "Well, Demeter," he said, getting up to greet me. "What a surprise," he said, hugging the breath out of me, "I didn't know you were coming back so soon. Welcome back!"

That was the millionth time hearing those words that day—*welcome back, Demeter.*

"It's good to be back, Dan," I said looking around. Nothing was the same. The walls were antique-white, but they were almond before. That mahogany desk barely seemed large enough to fit into that space. To the right was a large mahogany bookcase; each shelf was filled with books of course. The large floor-to-ceiling window behind Dan gave a wonderful view of the Atlanta skyline.

"Have a seat," he said. "How've you been?"

Two beige Victorian chairs with mahogany moldings faced his desk. I looked to my right, and my Thank You card was posted on his corkboard.

"A lot has happened since I've been gone," I said. "Congratulations on your promotion, Dan."

He looked a bit surprised, crossed his hands and leaned forward. "Promotion?" he asked. "Do you know something that I don't? Spill your guts, Demeter. Come on."

"Well," I said, looking around the office. "You have this office."

"You have been gone too long, Demeter," he said with a laugh. "You forgot about us already? My office has been in this spot for the last two years." He leaned back, crossing his arms behind his head. "Is that what this is about? You feel that Directors should have offices too?"

"What?" His question caught me off guard.

"Well, I know how you feel, being out there with your staff, working along side of them," he said. "We'll work something out."

"Where's Patricia's office?" I asked.

"Who?" he asked.

"Patricia ... the one who had this position before you?" I reminded him, but he gave me a blank stare in return.

"Patricia ... Patricia ..." he said as if trying to recall the name. "I don't remember her. She must have left the company long before I came on board."

"Oh," I said, getting up to leave. Hot flashes ran rampant through my body, as tiny sweat beads formed on my head. "Well, I just wanted to stop by and say hello." I started to feel a bit light-headed, so I braced myself against the wall.

"Are you all right?" Dan asked, rushing to my aid. "Are you sure you're ready to come back to work, Demeter? You can have as much time as you need. We just want you to get back to one hundred percent. I admire your dedication to the project and all, but if you need more time just let me know."

"All right, Dan," I said. "Thanks."

He must be playing a joke on me, I thought. I assumed that something drastic had happened to Patricia and my imagination ran wild with ideas.

Perhaps she was fired and Dan wasn't at liberty to discuss the matter. I shouldn't have pried.

Trevor and Marcus were deeply involved in a hushed conversation in the aisle between our cubicles when I'd arrived back at my desk. They were probably talking about me because the whispering stopped as soon as I sat down.

"Hey," Trevor said as Marcus walked away. "I'll catch you later."

Trevor gave me a curious look. He grabbed a pen and pad in one hand, and a cup of coffee in the other, and started for the aisle.

"Trevor," I called.

He stopped dead in his tracks, backing up to my cubicle. "What you got?" he asked.

I looked around, as if to see if anyone were in hearing range. "What happened to Patricia?" I asked. If anyone knew what happened, it was Trevor. He knew everything about anyone and anything in the company.

"Who?" he asked.

"Patricia," I said. "You know, the one who Daniel Batchelor replaced. What happened to her?"

He gave me a blank stare. "Patricia ... Patricia ... lemme seeee ... lemme seeeee ...I don't remember nobody named Patricia. Dan replace ... ummm ... ummm ... " he said, tapping his feet and looking up and down as if that would make him remember something. "Oooohh. Her name wasn't Patricia, you must be thinkin' 'bout somebody else. Her name is on the tip o' my tongue too ... ummm ... Dewey! That's right. Her name was Cynthia Dewey. Nice lady too."

Oh, oh! I thought. *There goes that name again. Are the Cosmos playing some joke on me?* Hearing that name sent hot flashes through my body, knotting my stomach in the process. But I kept cool, well to Trevor anyway. "Cynthia Dewey?" I asked. "What happened? When did they decide to get rid of her?"

"Who?" Trevor asked.

"Cynthia Dewey," I said. "The one who replaced Daniel Batchelor."

A strong feeling of déjà vu came over me. The room suddenly became gray and fuzzy. I blinked my eyes a few times when Trevor turned his back to position his chair in place, and the scene became clear again.

Trevor looked at his watch, "Oh, you mean Patricia. I got to be at the meeting in two minutes and it's gone take me five minutes to walk there, but I'll make this quick."

Good old Trevor. It's a good thing he couldn't resist a good piece of gossip. He put the pad and pen in his chair, then rolled it over to my cubicle, still holding the cup of coffee in hand. When he got completely over, he placed the coffee on my desk and removed the pad and pen before sitting down.

"Honey, let me tell ya," he said, looking me straight in the eyes. "That was when we was over there in the Perimeter Center off o' I-285. Patricia had foundt out that they was gone merge three divisions into one, and they was gone be layin' off some o' the executives. She foundt out that they was gone move all o' us to either Downtown Atlanta or Buckhead. She live up in Dunwoody, about two minutes from where we had worked at, and ain't want to be drivin' all over town in that traffic. You know how bad Atlanta traffic can be."

"Who you telling?" I agreed with Trevor.

"Well," he said, then took a sip of coffee. "They had offered her a buy-out package, so she took it. Can you blame her? Girl, people say she went out o' here in a golden parachute. That was right befo' our division had merged with this one. And right befo' we moved in this building two years ago."

"When did Dan get the job?" I asked.

"When we had moved in this building. Two years ago. You don't remember?" Trevor asked, then sipped some more coffee.

How do I explain that I don't recall any of it? I asked myself.

"Oh, that's right," Trevor said. "Dan was working in the building 'round near Underground Atlanta—Downtown—before he had got promoted. You was working up here, wasn't you? I forgot 'bout that. So you prob'bly didn't even know Dan back then." he said.

"Right," I agreed. I was relieved that Trevor had come up with a cover up story for my question. He was a gem when he wanted to be.

Trevor looked at his watch. "Ooo," he said, jumping up and grabbing his pad and pen. "I'm late fo' the meetin'. Girrrrl, let me get up out o' here." He stuck the pen over his right ear, pushed the pad under his right arm and rolled the chair back to his cubicle, holding the coffee in his left hand all the while. "Gotta run," he said, then dashed toward the elevators.

With Trevor gone, it sure was quiet. I ventured outside my cubicle, and everyone else was gone too. *They're at the meeting,* I thought. *Good. Now, I can get some work done.*

I definitely needed some of Chap's coffee before tackling that long list of e-mail messages. That's what I needed to light my fire. So I thought.

Chapter 19.
Nowhere to Turn

"Peace and quiet at last, Fern," I said. "Now, I can finally get some work done."

I scrolled through the long list of e-mail messages, opening each one in stride. Boring!

Meeting today to discuss budget...
Reminder: budget estimates are due...
Staff reviews are due...

"Later for e-mail, Fern," I said.

I worked on the budget spreadsheet for about thirty minutes, then started a few staff reviews.

"Fern, I have so much to do, I don't know where to start," I said.

"You need a break," Fern said, startling me.

"What?" I asked. "You got quiet on me earlier."

"I couldn't talk back then, 'cause I don't want certain people to know I can talk. They might try to kill me or somethin'. Don't tell nobody I can talk, either, Didi. Please."

Concern echoed through Fern's voice, as if he were afraid of someone or something. But who? Besides, I wouldn't dare tell anyone that my plant could talk. Who would believe me anyway? That's a sure way to get a one-way ticket to the funny farm.

"Who would want to hurt you, Fern?" I asked.

"I can't say right now. He not gone yet," Fern said. "When he gone fo' good, I'll tell you then."

"Who?" I asked, wondering who would harm a sweet, innocent plant. "Marcus?"

"No."

"Trevor?"

"No."

"D'Angela, Lou, who?"

"No, it's a man," Fern said.

"Dan?"

"No, not Dan," Fern said. "But, I still wouldn't trust 'im ferther 'an I can throw 'im."

"Then who?"

"Don't wurry 'bout it," Fern said.

"Well, why did you tell me, Fern?" I was so frustrated. Why did Fern tease me like that? Worse, why did I allow a plant to rile my nerves?

"Honey, you need to just chill out," Fern said. "You don't need to be workin' yo'se'f so hard. The job gone still be here. Go rest yo's'f."

"You're right," I told Fern. "You're absolutely right."

"Now," Fern began, "what you need is to go get yo'se'f a nice cold Coke, unwind, then start working' nice and refreshedt."

"That's a good idea, Fern," I said. I opened my bottom drawer and grabbed a few coins from my purse. "Be back in a few."

"Wait," Fern said.

"What?"

"Now I know you ain't gone use the el'vators just to go up one flo'. You could use some ex'cise. The walk'll do you some good ... clear yo' mind."

"You're right, Fern," I said, not even wanting to know how Fern knew about the breakroom upstairs and how best to get to it. I didn't want to know or find out. My sanity was hanging on by a thread and I dared not do anything to cut the cord. If that day were a book, it would be titled, *Journey to a Can of Coke.*

The stairwell was unusually dark and cold. *The light must have blown out*, I reasoned.

***

No one hardly uses the stairs, Dr. Iverson—except for fire drills—because it's at the far end of the building.

***

I started up the stairs. The clank of my black snakeskin pumps echoed through the air, but something else was there. I paused for a moment, but the noise had subsided. My heart began to pound faster and faster. Between two floors, I had to choose between facing the unknown above, or run like a chicken back to my cubicle. *Didi, it's just your imagination,* I told myself. *Go on upstairs and get your Coke. It's probably just the overhead ducts blowing air. That explains why it's so cold in here.*

The walls and stairs were solid concrete ... and concrete is known to hold heat in the summer and cold in the winter. That day was kind of cool, but not as cold as it was in the stairwell.

Only three more steps remained before reaching the platform connected to the second set of steps. I tiptoed slowly up each one, careful not to make a sound. I took one more step, enough to peek the second bend to the stairs that led up to the next floor. Shadows moved along walls—something or someone was in the stairwell with me. Just about everyone went to the round table discussion in the hotel auditorium, so no one should have been around.

My heart raced even faster, but I couldn't let fear defeat me. I took a deep breath, counted to three, then peeked over the gray guardrail, just below one of the stairs above.

Oh my goodness! Daniel Batchelor had his long, hard member standing at attention. Lou was on her knees licking him up and down and around and around as though his manhood were a lollipop.

Dan ran his fingers through her hair. He bit his lower lip while tossing his head back.

Up and down and around and around, Lou licked. I couldn't take it anymore. *I don't need a Coke that bad,* I said, then ran back down the stairs as quietly and quickly as my feet took me.

I violated a very personal part of Dan and Lou. They brought me into the midst of their privacy, a place that I did not care to be.

I couldn't believe it. My stomach began to churn; I was nauseous to say the least. Oh, Lou, how could you?

I stopped in the bathroom just down the hall to throw water on my face. Would that have taken away the yuck factor that I had just witnessed? No, probably not, but I never got a chance to find out.

Reaching the restrooms, I plumped down in the lounge area, not caring if anyone were around. The two red-and-blue paisley-print sofas were drab and worn. They were ugly as heck, but as comfortable as heaven. I rested my head on the arm, intending to splash water on my face in a few seconds. Staring into the mirror to my right, I saw D'Angela performing Percy's ritual.

A clear spiral glass pipe filled with crystals sat on the countertop. She put a few more crystals in the pipe and inhaled the steam from the end. The most brilliant yellow and blue flame ignited when she flicked the cigarette lighter to cotton swabs dipped in vanilla extract. The fire instantly vaporized the crystals, making the most beautiful bluish-white steam. D'Angela looked so relaxed.

D'Angela took one long whiff then froze. It was as if she suspected that someone were watching, so she looked around and checked under the stalls—my cue to exit the premises.

I turned away, feeling guilty for invading her privacy. *What kind of therapy is that? Must be some new type of aromatherapy with vanilla extract,* I thought.

In desperate need of Chap's coffee to ease my nerves, I ran faster than fast straight to the elevators. *No more stairwells or bathrooms for me, thank you very much.* "Come on, come on elevator," I said, tapping my feet. I hoped that Dan or Lou hadn't seen me, and sure hoped that D'Angela hadn't seen me either. How embarrassing if either of them did. *Didi the peeping Thomasina.*

Finally, the elevator arrived.

"I want get wit' choo," a voice said during my ride on the elevator.

I looked around. It was the young fellow from the mailroom who I had seen at the party at Antoine's back in September. He was tall and slim with a shiny baldhead and gold teeth to match. Judging by the way his long white cotton

Fubu shirt and Fubu jeans hung loosely, they looked three sizes too big. A tiny goatee, if you can call it that, littered his chin chiseled face. He couldn't have been over twenty-four years old.

"Excuse me!" I exclaimed.

He licked his lips, before he spoke again. "I want get wit' choo."

I removed my jacket upstairs, forgetting that those black jeans fit a little too snug. *Percy was right, I shouldn't have worn that outfit to work. What was I thinking?* I was partly to blame for the young fellow's lewd comments. *I am the Director of Product Development. I shouldn't be wearing tight-fitting jeans to work!*

Luckily, the elevators opened. I quickly walked out, almost racing to Chap's. The young fellow quickened his pace and was almost on my heels. *Does he know who he's dealing with?* I asked myself.

"Hol' up, hol' up," he said. "Don't be like that, now." He caught the attention of passersby, embarrassing me in the process.

The more I ignored him, the more he ranted and the louder he yelled after me. What was I thinking?

Finally, I'd reached Chap's. But the young fellow followed me right on in, causing a commotion.

"Don't be disrespecting my woman, boy!" Mr. Chap appeared from nowhere behind the young fellow, startling both of us. "Are you bothering my woman?"

"Mr. Chap," the young fellow said. "Where you come from? I ain't see you standin' 'ere."

"I asked you a question, boy!" Mr. Chap said. His lips thinned and his hands slowly formed into two fists. "You are messing with my woman!" Mr. Chap neared closer and closer to the young fellow, step-by-step, until he was right in his face.

Other customers stopped in their tracks and looked on as if to see what would happen next, including me.

"I was just playin', Mr. Chap," the young fellow said with a laugh.

"Demeter is a lady," he told the young fellow, who was almost trembling. "You don't talk to a lady like that, boy! Do you understand me!"

"I was just pla ..."

"Oooh!" everyone yelled.

Mr. Chap cracked something in the air, alarming everyone in the store. I didn't notice him carrying anything before, but he held a cat-o'-nine-tails in his hand. From the looks of things, he wanted to use it on the young fellow. He stuck his index finger in the young fellow's face, poking him a few times.

"Ouch," the young fellow said. "That hurt, man. Come on now." He continued to laugh, but it seemed like Mr. Chap was serious.

"If-I-ever-see or even hear about you meddling my woman, your ass is mine. Do we have an understanding?" Mr. Chap shook his head yes. The young fellow followed suit. "Now go on and get out of here!"

Other customers in the store laughed, clapped or dog whistled as the young fellow left the store. The young fellow mumbled something on the way out, hanging his head down low. He must have been trying to regain what little pride he had left. It served him right, if you asked me, but I still felt sorry for him.

I looked around a spell, browsing the magazine rack near the cash register when I felt someone near me. I moved to the right, thinking that I was blocking that person's path. But no one was near the register except me. *Maybe that person left before I saw him ... or her.*

The presence had returned. That time, sending a chill up and down my spine. *I need to go upstairs and take my medicine,* I thought.

I went over to the coffee counter and got a cup of Chap's coffee. *Why don't I sit by the fountain?* I told myself. I started to feel a bit light-headed, so I paused for a second.

"Oooo, shake it, shake it baby!" I heard Mr. Chap say from the storefront.

Here he is telling that young fellow not to disrespect me and he's doing it too, I thought. I was feeling very queasy, and being meddled, as Mr. Chap put it, was the last thing I needed.

The presence became stronger and stronger, overpowering me almost. I sat by the fountain, the sound of the cascading water was magnified one hundred fold. My head started to spin, as the presence emanated a strange, hot energy. *What's wrong with me?* I asked myself. I sipped Chap's coffee, hoping it would ease my nerves. *That's it,* I thought. *I'm suffering withdrawal from the real Chap's coffee. I can't go a day without having the real Chap's coffee.*

I stood up from the water fountain and headed for the elevators. Looking behind me, there was Mr. Chap in the distance with his hands on his hips, watching my every move. The atrium was deserted. Just minutes earlier, the lobby was almost swarming with people. *Where is everyone?* I asked.

I pressed the *Up* button. I leaned on the walls next to the elevator to catch my balance. Everything started to sway back and forth, back and forth. Tiny waves appeared in the air, oscillating like fierce heat waves in the desert's sand. Mr. Chap came nearer and nearer, he probably saw that I was in trouble. *Is he going to rescue me again?* I felt so tuned out, that I didn't know or care.

Back and forth, back and forth ...

Chapter 20.
No Hiding Places

I blinked once, opening my eyes to complete whiteness, submerged deep within a heavenly cloud. Tiny waves vacillated through the air; a faint buzz grew louder and louder, its dull vibrations penetrating my body cell by cell, dissolving my essence. With racing heart, pounding ever so fast, pure terror saturated my being.

I blinked twice. Still in a daze with my back against the wall, I ran my fingers along the elevator panel, feeling desperately for the smooth roundness of the *Up* button. Far to the left, Mr. Chap approached, but something was different. With a straight back, head held high, he strutted toward me in a slow, steady gait, rippling through the faded corridor.

I blinked three times. A tide of an ocean's wave transformed the world around me. Drenched in peace and tranquility, I beheld that strange new place.

***

I walked down a long dim corridor. An occasional ray of light smiled through tiny cracks in the bare, black walls, lighthouses guiding me safely down that mysterious path. The floor was solid concrete with dark cracks and crevices along its surface. Every step I took echoed through infinity. What a lonely place, not a soul in sight. Elongated shadows of overhead ducts were my only companions. Absolute silence of a vacuum surrounded me, with air so thick and foamy, like my very first lucid dream.

Far ahead was a slightly ajar door, a barrier between my silhouette and the brightness just beyond its portal. A brilliant sliver of golden light pushed its way to my feet from the great beyond. Slowly, I walked toward the brightness, fascinated by its seductive charm, lured by the endless possibilities that waited on the other side.

I pulled the golden doorknob to me. Blinding, white sunlight poured forth into the hallway, revealing its vast multicolored electrical wires and water pipes once concealed in darkness. Straight ahead was a short hallway, at the end were two sets of golden elevators, beyond which was a large picture window. A deep, plush violet carpet covered the floor. Light from two golden sconce fixtures against the lavender wallpaper cast a magical glow before me.

The elevator doors sparkled so much until I saw my reflection.

"Oh my goodness," I said out loud when I noticed my appearance. People always said that I looked young, but I appeared to be about twenty-four years old. My hair was gently curled and hung down my back. I wore a black mini-dress that was so short, tight and low-cut that it left nothing to the imagination. The black fishnet pantyhose and black pumps with golden, six-inch, pencil-point heels were definitely home entertainment accessories. My fingernails were elegantly manicured to a nice round shape and medium length, but they were black with gold stripes!

I decided to go past the elevators. A golden guardrail overlooked a five-story atrium. What I thought was a picture window, was a massive crystal that revealed the skyline. Judging by the size of the other buildings and the tiny ants of people walking about, I was pretty high up.

The guardrail circled the elevator shaft, so I walked around for a few minutes. It wasn't like I had anything else to do.

A door slammed down the hallway. Footsteps crushed down into the carpet, coming in my direction. I was alarmed to say the least.

Wait, I said to myself. *This is my dream. Nothing can harm me.*

I walked toward the elevators.

"Shake it, shake it baby."

I turned around and it was Marcellus. He wore a black suit with tiny, red pin-stripes, black shirt, black tie, and mirror-polished, black shoes. His hair was slicked back with a part down the middle, giving a clear view of his clean-shaven face and baby-smooth skin.

A devilish grin crossed his face. He was up to something, and I was about to find out what. "Shake it baby," he said, slapping and squeezing my rear. "Give me some of that big ass, girl!"

He smelled so fresh and clean, and all so masculine.

The elevator dinged, inviting us into its midst. Polished mahogany panels lined the walls. Carved mahogany moldings trimmed the mirrored ceiling. Alternating chocolate marble and white porcelain rectangles patterned the floor. Tiny, golden streaks branched across each tile, flowing into its neighbor's domain like the river of life.

Marcellus backed me against the golden rails, a smirk covered his face the whole time.

"Going down," the electronic elevator voice announced.

The digital indicator flashed *72* before we began our descent. Marcellus turned around and pushed the *Stop* button, bringing the cab to an abrupt halt.

"Hello," a man's voice said over the loud speaker. "Are you okay in there, Mr. Angellel? Mr. Angellel?"

Marcellus looked me straight in the eyes, backing me into the wall, with his arms extended on each side, trapping me in his private jail. Lust covered his face, as I was his willing prisoner. "Come here woman!" he said, placing his big, strong masculine hands around my waist and drawing me close.

I felt the warmth of his body as he opened my mouth with his tongue. I ran my arms up his chest and around his shoulders, holding on for dear life.

Our tongues rolled up and down and around and around, stopping for an occasional whiff of air.

"You are my wife," he said, then kissed my forehead, "to have and to hold," followed by his tongue in my ear, "throughout eternity."

I cringed in delight as he nibbled every nook and cranny of my neck, up to my ear, then to my face, all the while he squeezed and tantalized my rear.

Someone continued to speak over the intercom system, but I was so engrossed in Marcellus, I just didn't care.

Marcellus picked me up by the waist with those big strong hands, and balanced me on the rear guardrail. Peeling my dress to waist length, he then playfully pinched my crouch.

In a snap, he reached under and behind me and pulled both my fishnets and panties down and beneath my bottom. Holding my garments tight, he tugged and tugged, as I wiggled my wetness on his big hard fist. Next thing I knew, he had ripped my fishnets and panties right off of me.

Hunger filled his eyes as he repeated over and over, "You are my wife, to have and to hold throughout eternity."

He unbuttoned his jacket, revealing the hard, firm contour of his chest. Marcellus stretched my legs apart, placing my heels on either side of his waist. Staring me straight in the eyes, he unzipped his pants and expertly exposed his rock-hard cock. He penetrated me with long, hard strokes, up and down and around and around, deeper and deeper, over and over again.

He had his way with me ... and I let him.

Each stroke sent passionate balls of fire to my face, arms, legs and deep within all at the same time. I desperately wanted to match his rhythm, but he teased and tantalized my rear, squeezing it in and out, almost tearing it apart. His big, juicy balls danced with my inner lips, sending a signal to my clit that it was time to come home.

Marcellus put me ablaze. I struggled to contain my moans of pleasure. *This is a dream,* I thought. *I can moan in a public place in my dream.* And that I did.

"Is it good to you?" he asked. Sweat rolled profusely down his face.

"Yes," I screamed. "Ooooh, yes. It's good, Marcellus! It's good. Give it to me. Give it to me!"

"Uhm," he moaned, continuing to pump harder and faster. "You're so wet and tight. You're so good, baby! You're so good."

Marcellus rolled my bottom around and around to his rhythm, crackling to his beat. Liquid flowed from deep within me, as I began to quiver.

"I'm about to come, baby," he said. On that note, the elevator began to move. The digital indicator changed to X, as we were on our way down ... and fast.

Marcellus quickly withdrew and quickly fixed his pants. He removed my shoes and ripped the legs of my fishnets—all that were left of them—off and put them in his pocket. Like a gentleman, he helped me down off the guardrail.

Removing his jacket, he covered my nakedness. With mere seconds to spare, the elevator doors had opened.

A young man and young woman dressed in gray maintenance uniforms stood right in front as the doors opened. They both looked frantic.

"Are you all right, Mr. Angellel?" the young man asked.

The young woman looked surprised to see my nakedness. Her mouth hung low as I pulled my dress down over my bare hips and put my shoes back on.

"We checked everything, but all the switches said the elevator was working. We had to go into manual override," the young man said. He was so concerned about pleasing Marcellus that he didn't even notice me, or pretended not to notice.

"My wife and I are fine," Marcellus said as we walked passed them.

I felt a bit uneasy, especially since that little dress kept inching up my behind. But those two just kept on talking like they didn't even notice.

"Let's go, let's go," the young woman whispered to her companion, tapping him on the arm. Not once did she take her eyes off me.

"We'll get one of the engineers on it right away, sir," the young man said.

"Come on, let's go," the young woman said, then grabbed her companion by the arm and pulled him away. "We're sorry," the young woman said as they walked back to the maintenance desk down the hallway. Strange, but in *real life*, the buildings have security desks. In that world, they had maintenance desks to make sure things ran smoothly. Interesting.

"We have some business to finish," Marcellus whispered in my ear, sending chills through my body as we walked through the lobby.

Slithering, golden arteries flowed endlessly through the solid chocolate marble floors and walls. Occasional prisms reflected colors of the rainbow off a large abstract painting near the glass panel entrance. The beautiful sights were heightened by affection for Marcellus.

"Where is all that light coming from?" I asked Marcellus.

He pointed up, without saying a word. Common language couldn't describe the crystal ceiling. It extended almost to heaven, fully capturing the sun's true essence.

"Have a good one," the same young man said as Marcellus and I passed the mahogany maintenance desk.

"You too," Marcellus said.

The young woman continued to stare after me. I couldn't tell if she was embarrassed or loss respect for me … or possibly both. It was almost as if she held me in high regard and I had shattered that image. Judging by the pitiful way she looked at me wrapped in Marcellus' jacket, I sensed that something troubled her.

A battle of sorts had ensued, and I wasn't winning. It had become a constant struggle to keep that clingy dress from inching up my thighs and exposing my bare flesh. If that were real life, I would have been so embarrassed, not just for myself, but also for the young woman. Then again, I wouldn't have allowed a man to just reach under my dress and rip my panties off with his big, strong hands just because it was thrilling … even if he were my big, strong, masculine husband … and no matter how good he smelled … and no matter how long I stared into his deep, dark, dreamy, lust-filled eyes. Yum! What point was I trying to make again? *Wait a minute,* I reminded myself. *This is all a dream. No one has feelings here. Well, except for me.* Maybe her character was a message from my subconscious telling me to handle my business affairs, like my e-mail and staff reports. Yes! That was the message. Boy, was I ever wrong. Not only was I off base, I was miles away from the ballpark.

To the right of the maintenance desk was another set of elevators that led to the executive parking deck. Back in reality, executives had special parking spaces, not their own deck, but what a noble concept.

"Going down," the computerized elevator said when Marcellus punched a button.

"Going down," Marcellus said, then dropped to his knees. He looked up at me with that devilish smirk again and proceeded to raise my dress. Before he could kiss my goodies, the elevator doors had opened.

"After you, my sweet," he said, raising to his feet.

An arctic blast gushed into the cab as the elevator doors opened. I pulled my dress back down before entering the garage; that was a good thing because it was freezing. Ice cycles hung from the steel beams above. Icy patches had begun to form in a dark corner beyond the up ramp. *Does it get cold in dreams?* I wondered.

The parking deck was rather ordinary. Large rectangular cement pillars supported the structure. The walls were made of plain gray cinderblocks. Silver pipes and ducts lined the ceiling, and the floor was just ordinary cement. Dull white, diagonal lines separated parking spaces. When the elevator closed its doors on the parking level, they were just gray and not gold like the ones in the lobby.

Out of the blue, Marcellus slapped my behind.

"You've been a very naughty girl," he said, then slapped me again. "You must be spanked."

"Stop it," I said. It was just too cold for playing around. "That hurt."

"Let's get out of this cold," Marcellus said, wrapping his jacket tighter around me, while at the same time shielding me with his body heat.

Numbness had set in my legs as a frigid breeze blew from above. A chilling cold like no other I've experienced before penetrated down to my bones. My whole body began to shiver, as I could barely put one foot in front of the other.

"We're almost there," Marcellus said as we continued down the ramp.

"Only in my dreams," I whispered.

"What?" Marcellus asked.

"Nothing," I said.

All the cars took me aback. Every model of Rolls Royce filled the parking lot: Corniche, Park Ward and Silver Seraph. I looked to my right on another down ramp, and a black sapphire Bentley Arnarge sat alone in a dark corner. In another corner was an amethyst Bentley Azure.

We paused at a Rolls Royce Silver Seraph with black tinted windows, one of my all-time favorite fantasy cars.

"Here we are, my sweet," Marcellus said, escorting me to the passenger side. He opened the door and I jumped in.

Only in a dream would anyone dare leave a car like this unlocked in a parking deck, I thought.

The seats were beige and soft like lambskin. Plush oatmeal carpet covered the floors. I watched as Marcellus walked around to the driver's side, the frigid temperatures didn't seem to faze him one bit. *He's a dream,* I said. *He can't get cold.* Dream image or not, he made me feel more real than life itself.

"We have some unfinished business to take care of," Marcellus said when he got in the car, pressing a red button on the dashboard that turned on the heat.

Looking into his deep, dark eyes pressed my little red button and turned on my heat.

He began to stroke my hair.

I noticed that my seat had begun to recline backwards.

Marcellus sucked my lips, licking them with his warm, moist tongue. Soon, we had engaged in a deep, hungry French kiss with his tongue halfway down my throat, as he freed his masculinity from its zippered prison. He over powered me as I fell back on the seat.

Pulling my dress over my thighs, Marcellus entered my womanly glory.

In and out and around and around he moved, as I wrapped my legs around his waist, stroking my feet along the coarseness of his wool pants. That big, strong chest was so warm and inviting, as his beating heart pounded in my ear.

"You're so good, baby," she moaned.

I was a hostage taken prisoner by that long, hard cock, dancing to its rhythmic beat. The thought of being caught on camera by the maintenance crew or by passersby magnified the chills that ran rampant through my body ten-fold.

In and out and around and around he thrust, rubbing my behind against the seat as my juices flowed. The silk lining of Marcellus' jacket felt so soft and sexy beneath my back and behind, adding an extra layer of sensuality to our lovemaking.

He paused for a moment, bracing himself on his fists. "Is it good to you?" he asked as he stared deep into my eyes.

"Yes!" I moaned, and he thrust so deep and hard inside sending me into lust-shock. "Yes, yes!" I moaned loud and from the gut; I had no choice.

"Is it good to you?" he asked again. Tiny droplets of perspiration rolled from his forehead, falling on my face.

My whole body was blazing from his calculated movements—my face, back, fingers and toes. Every cell in our bodies had merged into a single entity— one indistinguishable from the other. No one ever made me feel that way, not even Tish and she was a dream too. Marcellus had something that a woman could never offer me; he changed my whole outlook toward intimacy. What Marcellus and I had was sacred—holy. We made love; every other encounter up to the point of meeting him was just sex, nothing more. I never knew what I had been missing all those years. *Is a dream the only place for me to find happiness?* I wondered.

His thrusts became sharper and deeper, as those big, fat balls knocked at my door. He froze for a second, tossing his head back as his face tightened in ecstasy, fighting hard to contain himself, "Ooo, I don't want to come. Not yet, not yet. Don't move, don't move," he pleaded. His shirt was drenched.

At that point, sweat beads dripped profusely all over my face. I turned away to avoid more hits.

"Nnnnn," he moaned.

His big, juicy balls constricted and released over and over, spilling the stream of life deep within me.

Marcellus withdrew and collapsed beside me. We stared into each other's eyes as he ran his fingers through my hair.

What felt like the Atlantic Ocean flowed continuously from my loins, as my lower abdomen tingled with pure delight.

Marcellus helped me to an upright position and he returned the seat to its original setting. Once I was strapped in and comfortable, Marcellus pressed a silver button on the steering wheel to start the ignition.

My loins felt as though they had been smeared with mentholated ointment. Tiny bubbles tickled my insides, as I continued to throb from passion's thrashing.

I pulled the dress down over my thighs, trying to maintain some level of dignity as we drove out of the parking deck. Crowds of people clad in suits or business-casual attire walked along the cobblestone sidewalk. It looked like lunch hour in Buckhead, if I didn't know any better.

A stoplight sat at the end of the driveway. Tons of people crossed this way and that way in front of us as we waited for it to change. The lights weren't red, yellow or green. Instead, a single square black box flashed *Go, Stop,* or *Caution* in big, bold, red letters.

"You were incredible," Marcellus said.

"So were you, Marc," I said.

He just chuckled. "We still have some more business to settle," he said, tickling my stomach.

"Stop it!" I said between laughs.

The traffic signal changed to *Go.* "I love you, Demeter," he said, looking me straight in the eyes, melting my soul.

We turned left, pausing for crowds to cross the street. Half of the people didn't seem to care that traffic was heavy. It reminded me so much of Buckhead. People just walk right into traffic like they're made of rubber. Amazing.

I took Marcellus' hand in mine. Kissing each of his knuckles brought a big smile to his face. Sitting there holding his hand sent shock waves through my body. A feeling of contentment and belonging filled my spirit.

"What are you thinking about?" Marcellus asked as we drove along the freeway.

"Nothing," I said, admiring the tall buildings along the way. "Just how this is so wonderful. How you're so wonderful. Too bad it's not real. Too bad you're not real."

"I am real," Marcellus said. "Who says I'm not?"

I was shocked that he responded that way, as though he were a real person. "I'm just going to wake up and go back to my same old reality." I sighed, in frustration.

"You don't have to go back," he said. "You can stay here with the children and me."

Again, his response surprised me. My lucid dreaming had definitely taken on a life of its own.

We had just entered the countryside. I sat back and enjoyed the ride on that deserted road. It was definitely fall, as the leaves had changed to beautiful natural tones. The forest had dissected the afternoon sun into tiny slices of rays, each with its own sparkling personality.

The trees soon thinned, gradually revealing a vast sandy beach. A royal-blue ocean appeared in the distance. The sun looked down on the surface from the heavens, admiring its image as it rolled across the tumbling waves. Its charming, pristine water—so crisp and clear—was a fountain in the garden of the gods.

"Lovely," I said as we passed the ocean.

Marcellus pulled over on the side of the road, driving along the beach. The sand was whiter than snow. He turned off the ignition and pulled me near. We sat there for an hour, watching the waves splash against large black rocks and enjoying each other's company. A flock of gigantic, white seagulls—with songs so cheerful—flew overhead.

***

The scene reminded me of the *Sounds of Sea* tapes I got from you, Dr. Iverson. Splashing of the ocean waves and songs of seagulls is just how I had imagined the scene to be.

***

Anyway, we looked deep into each other's eyes before engaging in a hot, hungry French kiss. Marcellus paused for moment, then pushed a button to recline his seat back slightly.

"Come on," he said, exposing his rock-hard cock as he pulled me on top of him.

I straddled my knees on either side of him, then eased down on top of him. The whole time, we continued to lick and suck each other's lips. He tantalized my bottom, squeezing it in and out as if he were kneading bread dough. .

"Ooo," I moaned, as he bounced me up and down like a seesaw, my dress slid up to my belly button on its own accord. I groaned loud and hard from the gut as he hit my spots time and time again. *Can pleasure get any better?* I asked myself. Marcellus twisted and turned my bottom as he rotated his hips.

His big, fat balls rubbed against my inner lips, sending firecrackers to my clit. At the same, time he greased my walls to perfection. I had never experienced outer and inner stimulation like that … ever. *This can't happen in real life,* I thought.

"Oh shit, shit," Marcellus groaned. His stride increased faster and faster. He pressed my bottom firm to his hip as he arrived at his peak.

I eased from over him, as his semi-erect member slid from deep within me. A long glob of come oozed onto his wool, pin-striped pants. I returned to my seat, soaking-wet from pleasure.

Marcellus closed his eyes for a moment in an effort to catch his breath. "Was it good?" he looked over and asked.

I smiled at him. "Incredible."

He held me in his arms, kissing my forehead, as we sat there watching the dancing ocean waves. We chatted for hours about everything and nothing at all. I was in heaven and wasn't sure if I wanted to return to the doldrums that awaited me back on Earth. But what would that mean? Keston and Kevin would be well-taken care of: the million dollar insurance policy was more than sufficient to cover the remaining mortgage, car notes and college tuition. Daddy or Percy didn't need me, and I could rely on them to help guide the boys.

"No, Didi," a familiar voice said, coming almost from nowhere, startling me. It was so loud and distinct. Then, I realized that it was my conscience talking again in my head. "The boys need you to be there more than anything. Without you, the money means nothing."

"What's wrong?" Marcellus asked. "You look a bit distant."

"What?" I asked. I was still taken aback from the voice talking in my head. I didn't know what to make of it. "Oh, nothing," I said. "I was thinking of how nice this day has been."

"Let's stroll along the shore," Marcellus suggested.

It was freezing cold earlier. What was he thinking? "I don't know. It's a bit nippy to be out on the beach."

"I came prepared for this. I have some blankets in the trunk," he said. "We'll be fine."

"All right," I agreed … reluctantly.

"We can walk home from here," he said.

"Walk home?" I asked.

"Yes." He pointed to a structure about a mile to the left up a tall hill. "Our house is right over there on the hill."

During all my lucid experiences, I had never noticed that the house overlooked the ocean. All I ever saw was the forest and waterfall from the veranda. I had always fantasized about living in Hawaii or on some exotic island in the middle of no man's land. My dreams fulfilled so many pent up desires. *If only real life were so simple.*

He started to get out of the car, but looking at the come on his pants bothered me. Marcellus didn't seem to care. *He's just a dream image. It doesn't matter to him.*

"What are you looking at?" he asked, then glanced quickly at his come-stained pants. "Oh, that. It'll come out. It's kind of sexy looking at it. Like I said, we still have some unfinished business to take care of."

He pulled a tissue from a box under the dashboard and wiped the mess away. Marcellus walked around to the passenger side. Soon as he opened the door, a gush of wind flooded the car, causing me to shiver like heck. He helped me out of the car, shielding my body from the cold as best he could. It was even more frigid than before.

"Here," he said, pulling his jacket from the seat and motioned me to put my arms through the sleeves. "Wear this."

He rolled the sleeves up to my wrists. His jacket hung below my knees, but it sure felt warm. My calves were freezing, though.

I followed him around to the back of the car, even though my six-inch heels dug deep into the sand, making it hard to walk. I was anxious to see what the trunk of a Rolls Royce looked like. *Oh*, I thought. *It looks just like a regular trunk.* I stood there shivering, with my arms folded across my chest, jumping from leg to leg, in an attempt to keep from freezing.

Marcellus pressed a gold button, which was where a keylock should have been, that popped the trunk open.

"What happened to the lock?" I asked.

"Lock?" Marcellus froze in position as if I had offended him in some way. "People don't use locks here."

"They don't?" I asked.

"No," he said. "This is the Astral Plane."

"Oh," I said, not paying much attention to his words. What a mistake. Instead of dismissing him, I should have asked far more questions.

"Take your shoes off," he said. Marcellus retrieved three pairs of what looked like ski socks from a side compartment.

I kicked off my pumps and sat on the bumper. Balancing against him, I put on each pair of socks in stride. They extended over my knees and were ever so warm and soft.

Several blankets were neatly folded in the trunk. I stood up while he draped a white blanket over my head, wrapping me like a mummy, including my hands, and secured it at the ankles with what looked like two large safety pins.

A gentle breeze blew our way, the blanket and socks kept me cozy. Marcellus wasn't fazed by the chill, or so it seemed.

He pulled out a tartan-plaid comforter, folded it in half, and draped it over my shoulders. Then, he finally covered his head with a blue stocking cap and threw a matching blue scarf around his neck. He pulled a heavy wool coat that was stashed under the pile of blankets, and quickly put it on. Marcellus draped himself in a pale-blue comforter. He grabbed the last remaining blanket, which was canary-yellow, and threw it over his shoulders. After donning a pair of black leather gloves, he slammed the trunk.

He pulled me near and draped us both with the pale-blue comforter as we started down the beach. Marcellus was definitely prepared for walking on the beach in freezing weather.

"How about the car?" I asked.

"What about the car? he asked.

"Will it be all right overnight?" I asked.

"It's far enough back on the beach that the tides won't reach it."

"Someone could take it."

He looked a bit surprised by my statement. "Evil can't exist here for long. It's an abomination

"It doesn't?" I asked. "Interesting."

"Light and dark can't occupy the same space," Marcellus explained as we strolled along the shore, watching the tide wash in and out, splashing against the rocks occasionally. "There are several dark universes and one is … " he paused.

I didn't think anything of it; he was a dream image. Looking back, knowing what I do now, it was a good thing that I didn't pry further about the dark universe. But I still should have inquired more about the strange, new world that fascinated me so much.

Without the addition of heels, I reached below Marcellus' chest. We walked slowly along the shore nestled beneath the comforter, as he tucked me safely under his arm.

"It's all about balance," Marcellus continued.

"What do you mean?" I asked.

"Here, there's a place for everyone and everything, and everyone and everything has a place."

"Oh?" I asked.

"Yes," he continued. "Everybody uses his innate talents to the fullest here and fulfills his destiny."

"They do?" I asked.

"Yes. Everybody has a job that's just right for him that he enjoys doing."

"So, there are no lazy people here who don't want to work, right?" I was being facetious, but to my surprise, he answered my question anyway.

"In the absolute, there's no such thing as lazy."

"Oh?"

"No. Where you're from, people are taught to confirm to certain standards and live a certain way. There's no place for people you call *lazy*. Here, such people live on land that, without them, would be overgrown."

"What?" I didn't know what the heck he was talking about.

"There are places here that have natural hot springs, fruits and vegetables that people can't eat. Those so-called lazy people live there, eat the fruits and vegetables, and prevent the plants from growing wild. So, there's a place for everybody here. Everything is in balance."

"Interesting," was the only word I thought of to describe such a perfect world.

***

Dusk was upon us. Two half-moons filled opposite sides of the eastern sky casting light on the deep, dark, mysterious ocean below. Scattered twinkling stars sparkled brightly in the night.

"Red stars?" I asked, noticing a cross-shaped cluster of red stars.

"Red stars are baby suns," Marcellus said, kissing my hair.

"Oh," I said.

"Let's stop and look at the night sky," he suggested. "That's why I brought along this yellow blanket." He patted the blanket that he threw over his left shoulder.

"All right," I agreed.

Marcellus spread the blanket across the sand. "After you, my sweet," he said, gesturing for me to sit first.

He had secured the blanket so tight around me that I could hardly bend.

I struggled to the ground, with a little help from Marcellus, as we both laughed.

Soon, he joined me on the comforter, then covered us both with the tartan blanket. I reclined on my back and stared at the night sky, thinking back to times when I star-gazed with my father. He pointed out stars with a slightly blue tinge. "Blue stars are hotter and more intense than the sun in our solar system, Didi," my father said. My favorite, Deneb, was the biggest, brightest star in the sky— and it was blue. But I've never heard of a red star, well except Mars, but Mars wasn't big and crimson like these stars. *Didi, this is a dream,* I reminded myself.

I looked directly overhead in awe. "That can't be the sun, can it?" I asked Marcellus. "It's much smaller. But I guess it's not as bright because it's farther away at night, right?"

"That's a globular cluster," he said.

At the zenith was a bright, white light that faded at the edges. It looked as if someone had flopped a giant Alka Seltzer in the middle of the sky. Around the perimeter were scattered twinkling, orange and red stars, and beyond that were two brilliant, royal-blue stars and a few white stars.

"The center is made of thousands of bright white stars. They're so close together … well they're not actually that close together. But from where we are, their combined light makes them appear to be one giant star.

"The big blue stars are galaxies. The white ones around the perimeter are white dwarfs."

Far to the left, I noticed what looked like a firecracker that had burst into the shape of a single red rose. Each petal was lined with golden lights; its base was neon green and at the core was one tiny diamond of a star.

"How beautiful," I said. "It looks like a flower."

"That's a planetary nebula," Marcellus said. "It's light years away, yet looks so close. In the center is a white star, probably a white dwarf. The red and green formations are gases emitted from the star during explosions."

"Explosions?" I asked.

"Yes, I believe so," Marcellus said. "Don't be alarmed. It's evolving into another type of star.

"I recall how we studied astronomy back in school. White dwarfs eventually become black holes," I said.

"Well, they actually become black dwarfs. Nothing ends here. It just creates some other form of life. We have no black holes here."

"Oh," I said.

Marcellus rolled onto one elbow as we stared deep into each other's eyes.

"You know something?" he asked.

"What?" I asked.

"I love you," he said as he grabbed me in his arms and pulled me close.

"I love you too," I said.

We kissed the night away, as the heavens smiled down on us.

Thinking back, I fell in love with Marcellus on a starry sunset eve. It was twilight, that beautiful, peaceful hour between day and night. Pending nightfall gushed forth with the ebb tide, as passion surfed along its waves. *Love at first sight exists only in dreams*, I thought, *that mysterious world where fiction becomes fact, and reality fades into oblivion.* In that fleeting moment of time, I knew he was my flame, that lone soul destined to burn with mine for all eternity.

The warmth of his body was so comforting—so soothing. I wanted that moment to last forever. Then, my femininity had begun to itch. The insides felt as though they had been coated with mentholated oil. I had enjoyed Marcellus company, but it was time to return to my world. No matter how hard I tried, I couldn't wake up. Pinching myself didn't work. Closing my eyes and thinking about waking up didn't work. I wasn't sure what to do.

"What's wrong?" Marcellus asked.

"I'm itching really bad," I said. "I need to wash up."

"Let's go home," he said.

Marcellus helped me to my feet, then folded the blanket and comforter on which we lay. All was dark and still as we continued our walk down the sandy, deserted beach. Ocean waves splashed against the rocks as a steady breeze blew from behind, rushing us closer to home. The whistling wind brushed over the sand like a giant broom, keeping it low to the ground. A few grains spiraled around our feet as we continued along the shore.

The ocean receded far into the distance, exposing rocks, exotic shells and sea life. *Is the ocean going away?* I asked myself. In an instant, a giant thunderous wave rushed toward us. Marcellus swooped me into his arms. "We better get out of here," he said, running toward the house.

I looked behind me to face the shore, and a large wave headeded straight for us. It looked as if we were about to be draped with a giant, black blanket. I was overcome with fear, but somehow I knew that Marcellus' was my protector.

"Oh no!" I yelled.

The wave blocked out the stars and moon as it moved over us. All was still, dark and quiet as the ocean cascaded down on us, knocking us both into wet, slushy sand. The receding tide carried us a few feet closer to the ocean.

"Whoa!" Marcellus said, as he protected me from a few renegade waves that splashed against us in the aftermath.

Frigid water chilled me down to my bones. I shivered with each passing moment. The wet blanket wrapped tightly against my skin combined with the winter's wind was unbearable. I didn't know if it was better to remove the blanket and expose myself to the bitter temperature, or remain wrapped in hopes of drying out.

"Let's get out of here," Marcellus said. He removed the blanket—that protected both of us—and his coat, tossing them both onto a large black rock just ahead.

I saw the tide receding far off the coast once again, leaving a trail of shells and sea life along the way.

"It's absolutely freezing," I said. "Let's get out of here."

"Yeah," he agreed. Marcellus quickly untied the blanket from my ankles, looking up toward the receding wave.

I spun in a complete circle as he unwrapped the blanket. "Weeee," I said, giggling. It felt good to get out of that cold, wet blanket. But the night air against my wet hair and skin were no laughing matter, especially with another monster wave headed our way.

"Run!" Marcellus said as he grabbed my hand.

We ran up a hill in the knick of time. The monster barely missed us; a few spatters of water flew our way.

Marcellus led me up a rocky hill. The stones were cold to touch and slippery to climb. I had to use my bare hands and leg power to climb up. Marcellus went up first, then reached down to pull me up next to him. Moonlight and stars reflected off smooth rocky surfaces, navigating our course safely to the top. The wind became more brisk as we climbed higher. My hands and legs were numb; touching each surface became more painful. Frost had formed on my socks, chilling me beyond words.

"Almost there," Marcellus said as he pulled me up the last tier. "Hang in there."

I looked back and down after awhile and was surprised to see that we had climbed quite a distance. Sounds of the ocean's waves were faint and less distinct than before.

The black rocks were soon covered with thick blades of grass as we neared a white cobblestone path. I looked up to the balcony and noticed a dim, flickering light through the large French doors.

"Uhh!" I yelled. Walking across the cobblestone path shot ice bolts through my legs, numbing them further. It must be the worst feeling ever to be outside in freezing weather with wet hair. Goose bumps covered my entire body—even my scalp.

"What's wrong?" Marcellus asked.

"This stone is so cold," I said as I tiptoed behind him.

Marcellus swooped me into his arms again and ran along the path. His wet shirt felt like suede rubbing against my freezing arms and legs. But before long, the warmth of his body shielded me from the cold … well, partly anyway.

"Here," he said, placing me at the bottom of a spiral stone staircase. "Walk up slowly."

The steps were covered with a thin layer of ice. So, it probably wasn't safe for Marcellus to carry me. One by one, I carefully stepped up holding on to the wooden guardrail. It was dark, so I watched every twist and turn and gripped the rail as I continued to climb.

"Careful," Marcellus said.

I stepped on a slick spot and came inches shy of falling to my knees. He was right behind to catch my fall. I didn't know what was worse: being chilled from head-to-toe and inside out by the blustery air, or the thought of losing my footing on a slick piece of ice.

Finally, we reached the veranda, and it too was covered with a thin sheet of ice. Flickering lights from inside cast shadows of the French doors across the patio wall.

"I'll race you inside," Marcellus said, as he slid across the ice sheet, using his shoes as skates.

He was almost to the door when I slid across the ice right behind him. "No you don't," I said, laughing all the way, slipping and sliding. I grabbed on to the back of his wet, cold shirt when I finally caught up to him. An Arctic blast rushed through the veranda, knocking us both against the stone wall. "Oooo," I yelled, as an icy vapor rushed through my nostrils. My back hit the surface, sending a piercing chill down my spine and extremities. I parted my legs to keep from falling. My loins were damp and sticky with Marcellus' fluids. The cold air relieved the itchy-burning sensation on the outside, but the tingly-bubbling feeling deep within me grew stronger.

"Are you okay?" Marcellus asked as he caught me in his arms.

"Oooo!" I yelled. His fingers were like ten ice cycles that sent strong, nippy pulses down to my bones. I shivered and shook as even more goose bumps covered my body. The chattering of my teeth sounded like a skilled typist tapping on the keyboard of an old-fashioned electric typewriter.

"Whoa," Marcellus said. "Let's get inside and thaw out."

I peeked inside as Marcellus pulled the two French doors toward us; my frosty breath clouded the panes.

I began to shiver yet again; the inside was almost as frigid as the outside. Fading embers scattered in the fireplace saved the room from complete darkness, but did nothing to warm the place.

"Let's get some heat on in here," Marcellus said on his way to the fireplace. He rubbed his arms in a futile attempt to stay warm.

Marcellus pulled a pile of fresh kindling sticks from a large gold bucket near the back wall and mixed them in with dying embers and thick, gray ash. After carefully positioning each one with a gold poker stick, he flicked a white lighter to rekindle the dying fire. Raging yellow flames shot up high, drenching our private world in a soft, golden hue. The glowing red and amber logs that crackled through the eve served as music for a heated, passion-filled night with Marcellus.

"Get closer to the fire," Marcellus said as he pulled me closer.

"Oooo," I yelled. His hands were ice-cold and sent a chill through my body.

"Wait here," he said.

Yeah, like I was going somewhere half-dressed in a strange, cold world.

Marcellus disappeared into a dark hallway to the right of the fireplace. He opened a white shutter door and began to rummage around inside. It must have been a closet because the room didn't appear to have much depth.

I stretched my arms and legs in front of the fireplace to thaw out. The flames were hot and wild, so I was careful not to get too close. After walking along the beach and climbing the rocks, it was definitely time to sit for a spell. I was reasonably warm, so I decided to dive onto the white sectional—butt first—and enjoy the fireplace from afar.

I jumped up as soon as my tush hit the sofa. "Oooo!" I yelled. It was like sitting on a frozen toilet seat. Streaks of bitter cold shot through my body as I was covered with goose bumps from head-to-toe. Brrrrr. The sitting area was out of heating range for the time being. Suddenly, the room became dark, so I turned around to see what was going on.

"Come over here where it's warm," Marcellus said. He held a hunter-green and white plaid comforter stretched out over the fireplace that blocked most of the light. The fabric smelled of fresh lavender and lilac. "It'll take some time for the house to heat up." He turned the comforter so that the opposite side faced the fireplace. "This will keep us warm for now," Marcellus said as he spread the comforter on the floor about ten feet away from the fireplace. He picked up another hunter-green and white plaid comforter and began to heat it in front of the fireplace. Again, the room dimmed, which made my time with Marcellus much more romantic.

Oh, when my skin hit the comforter, I was in heaven. I felt a chill in that damp dress and decided to take it off. The thing was skimpy anyway, so what if I took it off? As I pulled it over my hips, another deep stabbing streak of coolness penetrated my flesh. "Oooo," I yelled.

"What's wrong?" Marcellus asked.

"This dress is so cold," I said.

He just chuckled and went back to warming the comforter.

I had a decision to make: keep the cold, damp dress on and be miserable for hours hoping that the fire would dry it naturally, or quickly yank it off and be miserable for a few seconds as I felt the coldness creeping up my body. I decided to pull it off on the count of three. *One* ... I said to myself as I inched it over my hips. Cold streaks penetrated my flesh for the umpteenth time. *Two* ... I managed to ease it over my breasts. Brrrr. *Three* ... I yanked it over my head, removed my arms and tossed it at Marcellus' back.

"Hey," he said when the dress hit his back. He looked me up and down. "Umm," he moaned as his eyes rested on my breasts.

"Oooo," I yelled as my hair scraped across my back. The ends were cold, damp and felt like iced needles against my skin.

"Oooo is your favorite word tonight," Marcellus said with a smug look. He joined me on the floor and covered us both with the freshly heated lavender-scented comforter. "That's all I'll have you saying tonight." He kissed my forehead and went back into that dark hallway again. A few seconds later, he emerged with a large hunter-green towel then joined me again between the two comforters.

Starting at the ends, he parted sections of my hair with his fingers and pressed each one between the towel to absorb moisture. He kissed and caressed my hair when he reached the scalp.

"That feels good," I said.

He twisted my hair and tied it in a knot at the base of my neck. Then, he wrapped another towel that he hid beneath the comforter and fastened it securely around my head.

"There," he said, as he tied a knot at the base of my neck. "Your hair is safe and sound."

I asked, looking straight into his dark, dreamy eyes, "What would I do without you, Marcellus Angellel?"

He pulled me closer. "Come here," he said, then we engaged in a deep, hot, hungry kiss. His arms were warm and toasty and felt ever so delicious stroking up and down all over my spine.

I eased my hands up his warm, hairy chest. He shuddered for a moment, long enough to break our kiss.

"Your hands are cold, Demeter," he said. "Let me warm them up."

He reclined on the floor and summoned me on top; my legs straddled his hips. The comforter slowly fell to the floor, allowing the sweltering fireplace to have its way with my skin. Marcellus gently kissed the palms of my hands. He nibbled around the edges, licked down to my wrists, then up to my fingers, sucking each one in stride. The sensual tugging of his lips and tongue sent shock waves up and down my arms twice over.

I looked at Marcellus as never before, examining his fine masculine features. His soft olive complexion appeared deeper and darker than before. Those deep, dark eyes had transformed into chestnut-brown spectacles under the fiery, yellow flames. Tiny, dark, squiggly dots surrounded his faintly dilated, black pupils as they contracted in and out, responding to the dancing flames. His hair was as black and wavy as ever. I ran my fingers across his thick, black eyebrows, and then up, down and around the stubbly five-o'clock shadow that covered his face. I rubbed my breasts across his eyes, down his nose, across his lips and cheeks.

He circled his tongue around one nipple, pinched the other with one hand, and stroked my clit with the other hand—what skills!

I rotated my hips to the rhythm of his skillful finger, as he continued to tease and tantalize my breasts. Without warning and just shy of reaching a climax, Marcellus plunged his hardness deep inside of me. My inner walls cringed with pleasure; waves of passion rushed down my arms and legs, shooting firecrackers to the tips of my fingers and toes along the way.

I gazed deep into Marcellus' eyes as he pounded my flesh in and out and around and around. He squeezed my lower cheeks, pulling them in and out with each of his movements. Those big, juicy balls bounced over and over against my outer lips, sending my clit into overdrive.

I was but a cowgirl riding the wildest, most dangerous rodeo bull. Marcellus' hips were the saddle; his hairy nipples were my reins. I tossed my head back and forth in pleasure and enjoyed the bumpy ride. "Oooo," I moaned, as I watched in pleasure as shadowy outlines of our entwined flesh flickered against the back wall.

"Oh, baby," he moaned, then pumped deeper and harder.

"Oooo," I moaned again.

"Is it good, baby?" he asked, then pounded my flesh even harder than ever.

"Yes!" I yelled. "Oh yes, yes! Give it to me, Marcellus. Give it to me!"

He closed his eyes and tossed his head back. "You want me to give it to you, huh?"

I remained silent.

"You want me to give it to you?" he asked, then pounded me three hard and strong times.

"Yes, yes!" I yelled. "Give it to me! Give it to me!"

"All right. Uhhh!" he moaned. "I'll give it to you!" Marcellus grabbed my rear tighter and tighter. He pounded one last time and froze in position. "Uhh, uhh." His breathing intensified as he gripped my rear tighter and tighter, as if he were welding our loins together.

Continuous shock waves penetrated the depth of my womanhood. I felt his big, juicy balls contract as the river of life spewed forth its harvest into my valley. Being with Marcellus was surreal. I was safe and secure in his arms. *Could carnal desires be fulfilled so completely in real life?* I asked myself.

"Uhhh, uhhh!" he moaned. Marcellus closed his eyes and panted over and over before collapsing on the floor. "Whew," he said, still out of breath. "You're something else ... whew!" He stretched his arms over the comforter, as buckets of sweat poured from every inch of his body.

I pulled away. A large white lump of Marcellus' juices dropped from within me as I sat beside him. I stung with bliss as his sticky, limp member fell on his leg. It looked as if it had been dipped in a vat of whipped cream.

"I'm tired," I said as I wiped my loins with the towel on the comforter. My inner loins were pulsing strong and hard, and felt as if mentholated oil had been shot deep inside more than ever before. "Can we go to sleep?"

"All right," Marcellus said. He sat up as if he were doing sit-ups; his legs were slightly apart as he stretched his arms forward.

Marcellus took my hand to help me up. He led me toward the back of the room; our shadows flickered across the wall. We passed the white sectional sofa on the way into a long, dark corridor.

"Oooo," I yelled. It was freezing cold once we left the sitting area.

"Ummm," Marcellus said. "I love to hear you say that word. That's all I have you saying tonight."

"It's cold in here, Marc," I complained.

Marcellus flicked on a light switch before we ascended up a staircase that was narrow at the top and widened at the bottom, giving the effect of a cascading waterfall. Each step was made of solid mahogany. A burgundy and black Persian runner lined the stairs. The banister consisted of a series of antique-white and shiny, gold braids. To the right, double, white doors opened into a formal dining room. I paused for a second to admire the opulence before me.

"Oh, that's just the dining room," Marcellus said. "We can see that later."

The table was rectangular and made of clear, sparkling crystal and stretched over twenty feet long. A large black-and-gold floral arrangement served as an elegant centerpiece beneath the dangling crystal chandelier.

The table was surrounded by twenty antique-white velour armless chairs trimmed in gold; on the table sat gold flatware and fine, white china trimmed in gold. A silky, white napkin trimmed in gold folded in the shape of a rose sat to the right of each setting. The water and wine goblets were sparkling crystal trimmed in gold.

To the rear was an antique-white china cabinet filled with fine, white china trimmed in gold. A soft, white light on the top shelf cast a dim orange tinge over the room. To the right of that was a large French window that looked into the darkness of night.

A large dormant fireplace sat to the right of the entrance. Three large logs and kindling sticks were piled in front. A golden poker stick with a white handle lay over the pile.

The floor was solid white marble with golden veins. It was buffed so smooth and clear that mirror images of the dining room furniture reflected off its surface.

"Let's go upstairs," Marcellus said as he pinched my left behind cheek.

"Ouch, Marc," I said as I pulled away. "Stop it."

I stood in position, fascinated by the regal dining area before me.

"Come on," he said again. That time, he stood several steps above me.

From the corner of my eye, I noticed his manhood standing at attention like a soldier awaiting his next command. Marcellus seemed impatient and started down the stairs toward me.

"We can look at that another time," Marcellus said.

Suddenly, a strong gust of wind blasted through a set of French windows beyond the rear of the dining room, causing the French doors to clatter against the back wall. The floral arrangement swayed back and forth. The chandelier clattered melodic tunes as dancing currents of air flowed through its midst.

I walked to the rear of the room as a gentle frigid freeze tossed my hair about. The house had begun to warm a bit, but I was still cold.

Beyond the French doors was a sunroom that extended the width of the dining room, but was not more than ten feet deep. It was dark, but the floor appeared to be white marble just like the dining room. In the distance through the French windows, trees moved back and forth to and fro as their bare branches whipped in the wind. Sparkling snow flurries whirled under the moon's beam, lighting up the night sky.

I heard a noise behind me and looked in that direction. Marcellus had started the fireplace and was headed toward me with a smirk on his face. Golden flames filled the room with a soft, yellow glow.

Marcellus enclosed me in his warm, hairy arms from behind cushioning my back against his warm chest. He rubbed his manhood up and down my back, teasing and tantalizing my spine in pure delight.

"Come on," he said.

Marcellus kissed me on the forehead. He ran to the sunroom to secure the clattering French windows, closed the French doors in the dining room behind us, then stood before me.

He kissed my face soft and long, while stroking me with his fingers. Marcellus removed the towel from my head and tossed it on the chair at the head of the table. He ran his fingers through my hair while hypnotizing me with his eyes. Over and over he kissed my face, down to my neck then my ears, sending balls of fire down my spine.

I closed my eyes and ran my fingers through his soft, black chest hairs, combing each strand.

Marcellus licked my ear lobe, then twirled my flesh between his tongue. He tossed my head back and nibbled down the side of my neck, around the front of my throat, up to my chin, then finally to my lips.

We licked and sucked each other's lips as our mouths collided, pausing every few strokes to gaze into each other's eyes.

Marcellus pulled away for a moment.

"Whoa!" I said as Marcellus bent down and put one hand below my knees and the other around my back. In one quick motion, he swept me off my feet and into his arms as though I were a rag doll.

He rocked me back and forth, then twirled me around.

I laughed and laughed as I gripped his shoulders tight.

"You like that don't you?" he asked, then twirled me around once more.

"Stop, Marc," I managed to squeeze out between laughs. "Stop, stop."

I was having the time of my life. What a pity it was a dream. I savored every precious moment with Marcellus. I knew I would soon return to my real life on planet Earth.

***

Wait a minute: Where was I? Was I still on Earth? I didn't know what to think anymore. Marcellus and everything around me was so real? Scientists believe that we use less than ten percent of our brainpower. So, did I really tap into some dark recess of my mind that lay dormant until now? Or, am I going insane? Am I so desperate to escape the stresses and strains of life that my mind has created a safe haven for me to runaway and hide? Oh, Dr. Iverson, too many questions and too few answers.

***

Anyway, Marcellus stopped spinning me around. We both laughed and laughed like nobody's business.

"You know something," Marcellus said as he finally caught his breath.

"What?" I asked.

He ran his fingers up and down my face and stared deep into my eyes."I love you," he said

"Oh, Marcellus," I said, then kissed his lips. All the while we stared deep into each other's eyes. "I love you too. If only ..."

"If only what?" he asked.

I put my head down, but Marcellus pulled my chin up with his finger.

"If only what?" he asked again.

Electric bolts darted to my soul, as I looked deep into his deep, dark eyes. Tiny mirror images of the flickering amber fire reflected off of his dilated pupils.

"If only this were real. If only you were real," I told him.

"Like I told you before," he said. "I am real. Why don't you think I'm real? This world is more real than your world."

"This world?" I asked. "What is this world?"

"I told you," he said. "This is the Astral Plane."

"Astral Plane?" I asked. "All I know about Astral is astral projection. Is that what this is?"

"Yes and no," he said as he stroked my hands. "The Astral Plane vibrates much faster than your plane."

"Vibrate?" I asked.

"Yes, vibrate," he continued. "All of life is energy and not solid like it appears. The purer the energy, the higher the vibratory frequency. So, your universe is a subset of this one. Higher vibrations can slow down to slower ones, but slower ones cannot speed up to higher ones."

"How did I get here?" I asked. I didn't know what the heck he was talking about, but he was fascinating nonetheless.

"You vibrate at a higher frequency than most people in your world."

"I do? How do some people vibrate differently than others?"

"Many ways. When a person masters certain universal or spiritual principles, they vibrate higher and can come to the Astral Plane."

"You mean like good people?"

"No. Mastering spiritual principles has nothing to do with good or bad. For instance, back in grade school, some children pass to the next grade and some are kept back. Being promoted to the next grade has nothing to do with good or bad, but rather mastering key concepts. And those who really excel can be put into honor's classes. It's the same with spiritual truths. So, just like with school, those who master certain principles—in this case, spiritual truths—move on to higher worlds whether or not they're good or bad. But only those who really accept God's ways go on to light planes. We're on one of the highest Astral Planes, so only positive vibrations exist here. So you can call us the honor's class. Honor students can exist in the other classes, but students in those other classes are not equipped for the honor's classes.

"Then, there are others who are masters and want the experience of what it's like to live on lower levels. Kind of like you."

"Like me?" I asked.

"Yes, Demeter," he said. "Like you. This is where you belong."

"Where I belong?" I asked.

"Yes, where you belong. When the time comes, everything will be revealed to you. This is only the beginning. But for now …"

Marcellus licked my lips, then stood me back on the floor. He removed three place settings—the one at the head of the table and the two on each side—and placed them on the china cabinet. Then, he spread the towel that he threw on the chair across the top edge of the table, then picked me up by the waist and sat me on the edge of the dining room table.

I ran my fingers through his chest hairs, stopping on occasion to pinch his plump brown nipples. I bent my knees against my chest, as Marcellus' big, juicy head pounded at my front door.

"Ouch!" I said.

"What's wrong?" he asked.

"Careful," I said. "It hurts." My femininity no longer itched or burned, but the touch of his manhood proved to be quite sore.

"I'll be gentle," he said and kissed my face ever so gently. His warm, moist lips against my skin released an avalanche of passion that chased away all traces of soreness. I welcomed him inside as I wrapped my legs around his waist. He pounded my flesh in and out and around and around, over and over again, sending me into ecstatic shock. Talk about higher vibrations—Marcellus shot sweet vibrations from the top of my head to the soles of my feet. That night, I experienced orgasms in every nook and cranny of my body; my scalp, teeth, ears, bellybutton, fingers and toenails were all afire. Marcellus had skills.

He wrapped his big, strong arms and held me near and dear to his heart. His pace slowed for a moment, then quickened again; slowed then quickened until I felt his big, juicy balls contract against my outer lips.

"Uhhh!" he moaned. "Oh, baby. Oh, baby."

My walls clung to him like a vise. He had difficulty withdrawing his limp member from deep within me. As he tugged to release himself, a strong suction held him securely in place.

"Oh, baby. You're too much!" he said, then finally freed *Big Willy*.

Marcellus' fluids gushed forth onto the towel beneath my hips.

My loins were tingling with pleasure, but the feeling of having mentholated ointment smeared deep within returned with a vengeance. I cleaned myself as best I could with the towel, but I needed relief.

"Come on," Marcellus said. "Let's go upstairs and relax."

He helped me down, removed the soiled towel from the dining room table and wrapped it around his waist, covering his private section.

Our reflections were crystal-clear in the rear French window. I looked so frail and demure as Marcellus towered inches above and around me.

We made our way into the hallway, slowly walking hand-in-hand.

"Wait right here," Marcellus said, then pecked me on the forehead. He darted upstairs and removed the soiled towel from his waist, exposing his nakedness. Marcellus disappeared into a dark corridor.

I took a few steps up with my eyes planted on the dining room. Something about that room fascinated me, I'm not sure what, maybe it was its charm and mystique. Or perhaps, it was all the sparkling crystal and marble floors.

It was dark as I neared the top of the staircase, so I held on tightly to the banister, taking one step at a time, to keep my balance.

"Oh, oh!" I yelled. I tripped on a step.

"Watch it," Marcellus said as he approached from the top of the stairway.

"Please turn on the light, Marc," I said. I felt around the dark until I found the nearest step and sat down. My loins were burning and itching something terrible. I felt as if I were ripped apart at the seams.

Marcellus stood over me, looking down with those deep, dark mysterious eyes. He placed one foot next to my thigh and tickled me with his toes.

"Please, Marc," I said. "Please turn on some lights. Please."

Marcellus looked down at me again with not much as blinking or saying a word. He was beginning to scare me. I tried to wake up, but couldn't. I was stuck in God-knows-where with God-knows-what. *Who or what could save me?*

"All right," he said.

It seemed like he sensed my apprehension and ran upstairs to turn on a light switch.

"There," he said on his way back. "Are you satisfied?"

I didn't answer as he helped me to my feet. His manhood danced before me as big, bulging veins throbbed along the shaft. Marcellus' virility was at full force; I, on the other hand, was ready to rest, so I pulled away slightly. *What I need is a big stick to beat this man off me,* I thought.

He tried to touch me once more, and again, I pulled away.

"What's wrong?" he asked. He sat one step below my feet.

"I'm sore, Marc," I said before sitting down next to him.

He pulled me close and we sucked each other's tongues. Nestled in his arms, I wanted to feel him once more before returning to my world, but my womanhood was tender. I caressed his manhood up and down, making it harder with each touch.

"Come on," he said, then stood to his feet. "Let's go upstairs."

His craving was far from being quenched, but I knew he didn't want to let on. I wanted to please Marcellus, but how? I scooted up two steps, putting his hot, throbbing cock at face level. I combed his silky, black leg hairs with my fingers, up to his thighs, around back and squeezed handfuls of thick, meaty flesh.

I kissed his head below, rubbing it around my lips. He ran his fingers through my hair, as I ran my tongue up and down the shaft, down to those big, juicy balls, then up again. Once more, I ran my tongue up and down the shaft, but that time, I devoured his big, juicy balls like they were grapes, sucking and nibbling one nut after the other.

"Oh, baby," he moaned. He ran his fingers through my hair, down my neck and began massaging my shoulders in circular fashion.

His cock was covered with a dry, white, salty substance, evidence of our day together. Oh, but he tasted ever so sweet as I sucked and pulled his manhood in and out, and around and around like a lollipop, as he cringed in delight. I circled his cocked with the top, bottom, sides and back of my tongue, constricting him between my palate and cheeks, carefully experiencing the depth of his masculinity.

"Oooo, baby," he moaned over and over again, rotating his hips to my rhythm as I continued to suck and lick his hardness. "Uhhh!" He grabbed my hair and held me in position as I twirled my tongue around his thick, swollen head.

Marcellus gasped for breath as goose bumps slowly covered his quivering body. Then it began. He strained to hold back, but the life force that dwelled deep within him could be contained no more. Marcellus shot off like a volcano blast and spewed his hot, flowing lava all over me, covering my hair and face with that gooey, white syrup. "Uuuuhhh, uuuhhh! Oh shit, oh shit, oh shit!" he repeated over and over, moaning and groaning.

I partook of that hot, salty, slimy richness, swallowing each drop in stride. His seed eased down my throat—smooth and silky as Louisiana oysters seasoned with just a hint of wild animal musk.

Marcellus smiled down at me, as I milked his cock dry. He rubbed his come into my hair, down to my neck and breasts, until it became a clear, sticky film.

"Oh, baby," he said. "Where did you learn to give head like that?"

I looked up at him. "It's instinctive," I said.

Marcellus chuckled. "Let's go upstairs," he said, then extended his sticky hand down around my waist to help me up. "I have something special waiting for you."

Special? I asked myself with a bit of apprehension. *This is a dream and he's here to please me,* I reasoned. *Enjoy!*

At the top of the stairway was a life-sized portrait of a woman draped in a long, flowing burgundy Victorian gown. She wore a sense of dignity and innocence; her hair was pulled up and long ringlets and curls fell around her face. The background was dark and the golden frame was hand-carved like those seen in a museum.

"Who's that?" I asked.

"Don't you know?" Marcellus asked.

"Know what?" I asked.

"She's the lady of the house. Don't you know that every manor has a painting of the lady of the house?"

As we reached the top of the stairs, I took a closer look at the portrait. "What?" I was surprised to see that it was a painting of me. *Only in my dreams,* I thought, *only in my dreams.* The collar was white with ruffles, and held in place by a large burgundy and white floral broach. My hands were gently folded across the banister; my nails were meticulously manicured to match my outfit.

"You seem surprised," Marcellus said.

"Well ... I ... "

"Why are you surprised?" he asked.

"What ..."

"You're the lady of the house." Marcellus gave me a blank stare as if to challenge my sanity in some way. It was if he and the world—well, the dream world anyway—saw me as the lady of the manor, but failed to understand why I didn't see myself in that role.

Can I lose my mind in dreams too? I asked myself.

I started to ask when the portrait was painted and by whom, but then I realized that it was all a dream. *What's the point?*

"Come on," Marcellus said. He placed his sticky, slimy hands across both my shoulders and pulled me away from the portrait.

Marcellus led me down a short, dark hallway to the right of the stairway. Two white double doors with golden handles opened into a fragrant paradise. Delicate hints of eucalyptus and spearmint permeated the room as we entered. The walls and floors were chocolate marble. The vanity and sink were black porcelain with sparkling, gold faucets. Straight ahead, massive French windows gave a clear view of the night sky. Three chocolate marble steps led up to a large oblong fizzling chocolate marble tub filled with bubbles. To the left, streams of water cascaded down a solid chocolate marble wall, creating more foamy, white suds in the tub below.

Three large white flickering candles—that sat atop a tall black porcelain divider that separated the bathroom and shower room—provided a source a light.

Marcellus helped me up the steps that led to the tub, and down three steps that were hidden beneath the bubbles.

"Whoa!" I yelled as I eased down. The water came up over my breastbone, a little deeper than I had expected.

"Careful," he said, then sat beside me.

Massaging jets lined the sides and bottom of the tub, circulating warmth of relaxation like I'd never experienced before that time.

"Come here," Marcellus said. He pulled me close to him, and then planted a wet, sloppy kiss on my forehead.

I let the ends of my curly mane fall lose in the steaming currents. Marcellus' masculine juices had begun to gel, emitting a fowl jungle scent in my hair. While still nestled in his arms, Marcellus reached around and poured handfuls of water through my curly locks, rinsing away any evidence of his violent eruption all over my landscape.

"The children will be here in the morning," Marcellus said.

"Children?" I asked.

"Yes. Hera and Marcel."

"Marcel?" I asked.

"Little Marcellus." The tone in Marcellus' voice suggested a bit of sarcasm, like I were a terrible mother who would do anything to be away from her children. "They're with their grandmother and ..."

"Grandmother?" I asked.

"Yes. They're with my mother ... Hera," he said sarcastically, as if I were pretending not to know his mother.

"Hera is your grandmother, right," I said, thinking back to when my sweet, little Hera was born. I distinctly remember Marcellus saying that she was named after his grandmother, not his mother. *I must be confusing my dream memories,* I thought.

"Hera, is the name of every first-born daughter, remember? Hera, my mother, will bring them back in the morning."

No. I didn't remember any mention of his mother before that night. And no, I didn't recall any mention of the children spending time with their grandmother. Then, it hit me, I had a second baby, but didn't think of his name until then. *Am I losing it in my dreams too?* I asked myself for the second time that night. I ran away to the world of dreams to escape stress. Was stress following me to my sacred place too?

It's just a dream, I tried to reason. *Dreams echo real life. Just enjoy the hot tub.*

I cuddled between Marcellus' arms with my back against his wet, hairy chest. Sounds of gushing jets and cascading waterfalls filled the room like a mother's lullaby, inviting slumber upon me.

Chapter 21.
For Curiosity Lured the Cat

Air quickly filled my lungs, jolting me in a sitting position. Gushing water behind me stirred a cool breeze through my hair.

It's getting cold in this tub, I thought. With eyes closed, I stretched my arms up and out, and wiggled my back to snuggle closer to Marcellus. All around me was a large open space. Marcellus and all his warmth were gone. "Oooo," I yelled as bone-chilling water drenched my arm.

"Careful," a voice said from behind, startling me.

Everything was white and hazy for a moment. I blinked a few times to gain my composure. The scent of eucalyptus and spearmint had suddenly transformed into the harsh smell of chlorine. I blinked a few more times. Relaxing sounds of gushing jets and cascading waterfalls that relaxed my soul as I submerged in the hot tub were replaced by grinding motors that powered the fountain in the lobby of the building at work.

"What?" I was surprised to see Mr. Chap sitting behind me on the fountain's edge.

"Looks like you can use some coffee," Mr. Chap said. "You've been sitting here for quite some time."

I glanced at my watch. *3:30! Couldn't be!*

"Come on," Mr. Chap said as he stood up and walked around in front of me. "I have just the thing for you."

The last thing I recall was feeling a tad light-headed on my way from Chap's. I pressed the elevator button to go back upstairs, then I saw Mr. Chap walking toward me. He probably saw that I wasn't feeling well and walked me over to the fountain to sit for a spell.

***

Good ol' Mr. Chap. He always watched out for me. Gosh, I sure do miss that old man, Dr. Iverson.

***

Anyway, we walked toward the coffee shop and the clank of my footsteps on the marble floors echoed through the atrium. *I need my medicine,* I thought as

I accidentally bumped into Mr. Chap. When he grabbed my arm to brace my fall, I thought that I had stuck a wet finger into an electric socket.

"Careful," he said.

He was surrounded by a white aura—well, it was dim and translucent, but white nonetheless. Mr. Chap emitted an eerie static electric charge that made my skin crawl. I looked at my arms as I watched the tiny hairs stand up straight. The air within inches of Mr. Chap was thick and foamy like in my dreams. *Where is everybody?* I asked myself. I felt a panic attack coming on as the lobby was completely empty. Especially that time of day, people would be either gearing up to go home, or stopping at Chap's for an afternoon snack. Then I realized that everybody attended the session that day. *Everybody probably went home after the session,* I reasoned.

"I have something for you to sample for me," Mr. Chap said when we entered the shop. He immediately ran to the kitchen area and retrieved a small white bag. "Try this," he said.

Mr. Chap always used me as his guinea pig to test his latest concoctions— from a new coffee blend to fudge brownies. I guess he trusted my judgment and valued my opinion. He opened the bag and the smell of fresh chocolate filled my nose. But, another distinct nutty aroma was mixed with the chocolate, but I couldn't quite place it.

"Ummm," I said. He knew I liked chocolate. Heck, Mr. Chap seemed to know what made me tick. "What are these? Looks like chocolate-covered peanuts."

"Ah-hah!" he said, then motioned for me to open my hand. "That's where you're wrong." He poured a few irregular-shaped chocolate thingies into my hand and gestured for me to try a few. So I did.

"Ummm," I said. "I've never tasted anything like this before. What kind of nut is it?"

"You'll never guess," he said with a grin.

It was firm and toasty on the outside like a roasted nut, soft and chewy on the inside, yet crunchy at the same time as if it were an acorn of sorts. *No,* I said to myself. *This can't be an acorn. Besides, an acorn probably wouldn't taste this good.* A bitter aftertaste remained, but it wasn't so bad, especially after chucking down one after another

"I give up," I said, then gobbled a few more. "What is it?"

He got up close to me—the electric charge had subsided—and looked me straight in the eyes. "Chocolate-covered coffee beans."

"I've never heard of chocolate covered coffee beans before. But these sure are good."

"Here," he said as he handed two more small white bags of beans. "You can have these."

"Thanks, Mr. Chap," I said on my way out.

I perked up after each handful of beans. Only minutes earlier, the lobby was dull and dreary, but it had suddenly become alive and vibrant. The marble floors were shinier and more brilliant than ever. The sunshine appeared brighter, and most of all, for the first time in weeks, I felt like going out to do something nice for myself. So, I did something that I never did before and never thought I would do: go to the mall and shop for pleasure. *These beans did the trick,* I thought. *Mr. Chap knows how to hit the spot.* Everyone was gone anyway, and I decided to catch up with work the next day.

I walked up the road to Lenox Mall. It was nearing rush hour for sure in Buckhead. Peachtree Road had already started to become a parking lot. Thank goodness for the South. I had forgotten my jacket upstairs in my cubicle, and it was almost December, but warm as heck outside. *Oh, oh.* Then I realized that I had forgotten to sign off the LAN, you know, the local area network. But, I didn't care. The sun looked so pretty and it was such a gorgeous day, especially for walking.

Amazing how Lenox Mall was bustling with people, especially on a Tuesday afternoon. Well, it was the Christmas season and folk just flocked to shop, shop, shop. I browsed a few windows, nothing special—shoe boutiques, department stores ... the usual places.

***

I even bought a little black dress from one of the petite shops, Dr. Iverson. It's not like I needed a new dress, I just bought it just because. Now that's a new one for me.

***

Anyway, I had never felt so relaxed just walking through the mall, munching chocolate-covered coffee beans, just enjoying the scenes. Office workers dressed in suits, seniors and mothers with strollers all seemed so carefree. Maybe I just enjoyed being around people again. Perhaps that's what I needed all along: to be around people instead of being cooped up in the house with Percy. Lord knows that woman drove me crazy.

Anyway, I noticed a commotion near the bookstore on the level above. A few women strolled down with books in hand, excited about something or the other. I just had to find out what all the fuss was about.

"What bookstore is he going to be at tomorrow?" I heard a woman ask another in front of me on the escalator ride up. "I hope there's not a long line because I'm not even supposed to be here, girl. I have some work to finish up. I may have to catch him tomorrow."

"I don't know where he'll be tomorrow," she told her friend. "He was at Nubian in Southlake Mall on Saturday. They told me he was going to be there from four to six, but he was there from one to three, so I missed him. But they said he was going to be here at Nubian Bookstore today, so I came on out. I don't care how long it takes, I'm going to wait and get my book signed. He's going to be here from four to six, and if I have to wait 'til six, then ... oh well."

Nubian Bookstore is definitely not in Lenox Mall, I said to myself. *She must be mistaken.* I looked up and noticed in big red letters—

Nubian Bookstore II

"When did he open another store in Lenox Mall?" I asked one of the women behind me. "How long has it been here?"

"He just opened this one up last summer," the woman said. "I usually go to the one in Southlake Mall, but I work across the street and come here at lunchtime."

"He also has one in the new Stonecrest Mall in Lithonia," the friend said.

"Stonecrest?" I asked. That was my first time hearing about Stonecrest. "I didn't know that there was a mall in Lithonia."

"Oooo, it opened around October or November," the woman said.

"Oh," I told her. "Thank you." *November*, I said to myself. *Why couldn't she just say this month. It is still November. It's November 30, but still November nonetheless.*

I strolled through Lenox Mall at least once a week last summer, and that was my first time seeing Nubian Bookstore II. How did I miss it? As often as Percy and I visited Nubian Bookstore in Southlake Mall, you'd think the owner would have advertised or told us about it or something. And what about that Stonecrest Mall? I was never a big shopper, but Percy probably heard of it.

Well, at least the owner should have told Percy, especially how she used to flirt with him shamelessly, embarrassing me to the nth degree. But did she care? Noooo! He graduated from Morehouse—a Morehouse man—and Percy sure loved her some Morehouse men. He was way too young for Percy. Did she care? Noooo! *Maybe Percy forgot to tell me*, I thought. *Like she neglected to tell me everything else.*

A new mall opened up that I never knew existed. A new bookstore opened up. Where have I been? *I've been so busy*, I thought. *When the Year 2000 Project is over, I'm going to catch up on the goingson in this town.*

Who's signing books? I asked myself. I had been out of touch with the world, so to say. Maybe something like that was just what I needed. So, I followed the two young ladies to the bookstore.

"Oh shucks. It's barely four o'clock and there's already a long line," the first woman said.

"Girl, let's get in line before more people come."

I took my place in line behind the two women from the escalator. The author looked up as I passed and we made direct eye contact. He was in the middle of signing a book and stood up as if to get my attention in some way.

Does he know me? I asked myself. *If he does, perhaps I can go to the front of the line.* I decided that was a bad idea. All the other ladies probably would have had my hide if I had jumped ahead of them. *He's Percy's type for sure*, I thought. He looked like a bodybuilder: tall, dark and weighed about two hundred pounds. Large, bulging muscles flexed each time he held that silver pen to autograph a book.

I stepped to the right of the line to gauge the wait. Inpatiently, I sucked a chocolate bean in and out of my mouth, then balanced it between my teeth. At that moment, the author looked up and we locked glances again. *Oh man!* I thought. *That man thinks that I have no manners, putting candy back and forth in my mouth.*

His head was bald and shiny; and his skin was just as deep, dark and chocolate as the covered coffee beans. *If only Percy were here,* I thought. A light bulb went off. I called the house on my cell phone, but all I got was the answering machine.

"Percy," I started the message, "if you're there pick up. This author is signing books at Lenox Mall. You need to come and check him out. He'll be here until six, so you better hurry."

Maybe she's out and about, I thought so I called her cell phone. A message came on saying that the number cannot be reached. *Maybe the circuits are busy,* I thought. *Maybe she's at her condo.* I hit the speed dial button for her home number and, to my surprise, a message played saying that the phone had been disconnected. *That can't be. I must have dialed the wrong number,* I said, then manually dialed the number. The same message played.

I'll try later. The circuits must be busy or something.

I continued to wait in line. I looked behind me as hundreds of fans were lined up to see the author. Conversations were going on about his previous books, and some of the ladies talked about the characters as though they were real people.

After waiting for fifteen minutes, it was finally my turn.

"How many do you want?" an attendant asked.

"One please," I said.

"Cash or credit?" she asked.

"Credit," I said then handed her my gold Amex.

So many people flooded the store that the manager probably decided that it was quicker to set up a portable cash register outside near the signing table. That was smart because we could have been there all night waiting in line.

"Hello," he said. His voice was deep and mellow; soothing almost.

"Hi," I said as the attendant handed him a book from the pile. "Could you autograph the book to my sister, Percy."

"Percy?" he asked. "You sure that's not your husband?" He winked at me.

"No," I said. "Percy is my sister. It's short for Persephone."

"Oh," he said, then began to autograph. "Just checking."

"Oh, wait," I said, then went back to the attendant. The two women behind hissed and rolled their eyes at me as if to say, *Look, bitch, if you want another book, get your ass at the end of the line. You're holding up traffic!* I didn't care.

"Excuse me." I got the attention of the attendant. "I'd like another book, please." I motioned for the two women behind me to go ahead and get their books signed while I paid for the second book. Of course, the woman behind me gave me a dirty look, but again, I didn't care.

"Back again?" the author asked.

The attendant handed him another book. "Make this one to me. My name is Didi. That D-i-d-i."

"Is that short for anything?" he asked.

"Demeter," I said.

"Demeter. Ohhh, like in mythology," he said.

"Yes," I said. I was surprised that he had heard of Demeter.

"She was Persephone's mother, so that must mean you're older than your sister, Percy, right?"

Some women behind me hissed and sucked their teeth. I didn't care. *Let them wait their turn.*

"No, actually I'm two years younger than Percy," I said. "I'm impressed that you know about Demeter and Persephone. Not many people know the story." *Of course he knows the story, he's an author. A well-read author at that,* I told myself. The intellectual type really turned me on.

"All right, Ms. Didi," he said. "Here you go. Enjoy!" He stroked my hand when I reached for the book, sending chills up my arm.

I shivered.

He noticed, because he smiled—pure evidence that he knew he had given me pleasure, even if it was brief.

I felt his eyes following me as I walked away. I looked back and, sure enough, his eyes were following me. He winked and smiled at me, then went back to signing copies of his new book, *Gold Diggers of* something or the other. Anyway, I stopped at a wooden bench in front of some trees and read the inscriptions in both books:

Percy,
Spread the peace and joy.

Didi,
May each word bring you as many hours of pleasure as I plan to bring you tonight.

Enjoy!

If I didn't know any better, I'd say he was flirting with me. I still hadn't really noticed the title of the book or his name. He was a bit charming, I must admit. I was never attracted to his physical type—he was too much of a pretty boy. But something about his style—the intellect, flare for words, and deep, dark eyes—was overtly sensual.

I sat there on the bench and, to my surprise, finished the second bag of chocolate-covered coffee beans. A faint buzzing noise whispered in my ears for a few seconds, as I became light-headed.

I looked up for a split second and the same old man from Underground Atlanta, the hospital, gas station and my dream with my cousin, Juanita, walked by. He appeared almost from nowhere and just moseyed along the mall at a snail's pace. I blinked once, and he was gone. I looked all around the corridor, peeked over the banister to the level below and the level above. The man was nowhere in sight.

Whoa! I thought. *I've had too much caffeine.*

I sat still for a few moments to regain my composure. The buzzing returned, but that time louder, as if two kazoos were ringing in my ears. *I need some water,* I thought and decided to go to the food court for a drink: bad idea. The mall spun around and around, over and over again, all colors melting as one, as the buzzing grew louder and louder. I tried in vain to grab on to the trees behind me, waving my hands frantically through the air in hopes of catching a branch. *Someone help me!* I thought, but the words were trapped deep within my throat. My heart raced faster as I was stricken with panic. The buzzing became more intense—unbearable. A kaleidoscope snared me into its midst, spinning around and around as the floor introduced itself—top indistinguishable from the bottom; up and down became as one until …

***

A thick, white fog surrounded me, as a faint buzz echoed in the distance. All my senses and body faded into one, uniting with the universe—a pool of matter drifting through eternity on a journey to infinity, defying laws of time and space.

Soon, the buzzing grew louder, gradually transforming into distinct voices, one competing against the other—an argument of sorts. The energy field that comprised my body spontaneously condensed into a solid mass; I felt each organ and every limb form into the body to which I had grown accustomed. The white cloud ignited my form with an almost orgasmic, electric shock, as I felt the warmth of my blood circulate through every vein.

Hidden beyond the smokey mist were carved mahogany walls. To the right, double mahogany doors opened to a conference room where several men clad in suits argued—one competing to out yell the other. I blinked a few times, and the room came into focus.

"Nice," I said as I admired my surroundings.

I was in a parlor. I sat in the middle of a mauve Victorian-style sofa. On either side were two matching chairs. The two end tables were mauve with antique Beckwith China lamps. On the floor in the sitting area was a large dark, multi-colored Persian rug. The remaining floor was mahogany.

Directly above was a vast skylight in the middle of the cathedral ceiling. The sun filled the room with a soft, white light, bringing out the sheen of the mahogany wall paneling and floors. I looked up and behind me and saw a large oil painting of Marcellus hanging on the wall. The gold inscription at the bottom read: *Marcellus Angellel, Founder.* He wore a navy-blue suit, blue-and-white striped tie, and white shirt. A serious, down-to-business expression covered his face. His eyes looked deeper and more mysterious than ever.

"Mrs. Angellel," A woman called, who apparently appeared from nowhere and shocked me out of my wits. Judging by her reaction, I frightened her too. "I wasn't expecting you."

I didn't know what to say. "Well," was all that came out.

"Mr. Angellel is going to be delighted to see you." She shuffled to the other side of the room and closed the double doors, muffling the loud voices from the heated argument that ensued.

I caught a glimpse of Marcellus seated at the head of the table before the woman closed the doors.

Far beyond the conference room was a huge desk and big black leather chair. In front of that were two smaller leather chairs, probably for visitors. Two more double doors led to the conference room, and across from that was another set of double doors that opened to another outside office. The entire area was larger than the bottom floor of my house in the real world.

Mounds of food were stacked on a table and wet bar to the far left near the conference room, most likely for the participants of the meeting. The woman brought over a golden tray of petit-fours and sat it on the mahogany coffee table in front of me.

"May I get you something else, Mrs. Angellel?"

"What?" was all I could say because I didn't know how to answer her question. Something about her was familiar, but I couldn't quite place it.

"Would you like anything else, ma'am?" she asked again.

I just stared at her, trying to figure out why she seemed so familiar. She was tall with long, kinky auburn hair. Her eyes were deep, dark and almost hypnotizing and contrasted with her pale skin and full, pale pink lips. Tiny, brown freckles dotted her cheeks and nose.

"Mrs. Angellel," she said, "are you all right?" She must have noticed how long and hard I stared at her.

"I'm fine, thank you," I said. I reached for the petit-fours, but couldn't decide which one to take. The tiny cakes looked too pretty to eat. They were arranged to resemble an ancient Egyptian pyramid—with alternating pink, white and brown layers—and sat atop white icing. Pink, white, and doce drizzle and sugary roses decorated the base. A small pink icing bow adorned each one. "Ummm," I said, after finally deciding on the brown one at the top. The doce icing was so rich and creamy. Inside was a light, buttery yellow cake filled with fluffy doce cream. I tried a white one, then a pink one and inside each was a light, buttery yellow cake filled with fluffy doce cream. Next thing I knew, I had eaten almost half the platter.

"How about some café to go with that, Mrs. Angellel?" she asked.

"What?" I asked. Her question took my attention away from the petit-fours.

"Some café," she said, and then walked toward a door far in the right corner.

Directly in front of me were blue-and-gold, paisley-print, velvet draperies, over which was a wide flowing matching valance.

"Would you like for me to pull the draperies, Mrs. Angellel?" the woman asked, shocking me yet again.

"What?" I asked.

"It's such a pretty day, Mrs. Angellel," she said. "Come and enjoy." She curled her index finger, motioning for me to stand by the window.

I joined her by the window.

She smiled at me before drawing the draperies apart at the center. More sunlight poured in as the curtains were completely drawn.

Ooooo.

She had unveiled a new masterpiece. Hidden behind the draperies were large French windows that revealed the metropolitan skyline. I became a bit light-headed as I looked far into the distance. The office towered at least one hundred stories above the city. It took a few minutes for me to regain my composure.

Short buildings, tall buildings, structures designed to look like rockets. The city was filled with magnificent edifices ... exactly like the ones I saw the night we danced in the rotating restaurant ... when he gave me flowers and doce candies. "Delicious doce-chocolate for a delicious chocolate," he said. Oh, and when he sucked remnants of doce-chocolate off my fingers ... I nearly hit the roof with spin-tingling passion.

***

If only he were real, Dr. Iverson. If only he were real. Why can't life be one long series of fantasies? Why can't we have everything we want—when we want it—and how we want it? Why can't life be simple and free each and every day? Why does life have to be filled with stresses and strains? As soon as we think we have life figured out, something comes along to throw us off track. When things are smooth and easy—wham—something happens almost as if destiny is saying, "Ah, ah, ah. You're not getting away that easy. Who do you think you are to have things that good?" Why can't the world be plain and simple? Why all the chaos?

***

Anyway ...

"You're probably tired, especially with the two at home," the woman said before exiting through the door.

What a strange thing to say, I thought, but then realized that she probably noticed I was a tad dizzy.

"Then, being five months along and all," she said.

I looked down at my slightly bulging belly. What? I was pregnant ... again. *Every time I touch that man I get pregnant. At this rate, I'll have a million babies,* I thought.

The woman walked in with a sparkling, gold café server set—kettle, cream ladle, a small pile of sugar cubes and tongs; a white café cup trimmed in gold; and one gold café spoon.

Ummm. The aroma of café captured my attention away from the scenic cityscape. *If I didn't know any better, I'd say that was Chap's coffee. I know his coffee anywhere.* Of course, it was only a dream—my fantasy. I craved Chap's coffee in real life, so it was only natural to dream about it too. Right?

Long clouds of steam rose from the kettle as she poured. She added a bit of cream, dropped three lumps of sugar, stirred until the café was tan in color, and handed the cup to me on a saucer.

"Ummm," I said after taking a few sips. *This is even better than Chap's coffee.* "This café is good. Thank you."

Both double doors flung open as the woman poured more café into my cup. A noisy flood of people exited from both directions—some went straight to the hallway, while others stopped at the bar, took a few petit-fours in napkins before leaving.

"Hi, Didi," a few of them said before leaving.

"Hi," was all I said. I didn't know any of them. Besides, they were dream images.

"Cynthia, could you get me a copy of the report," a man asked the woman.

I only caught a glimpse of the man. But from behind, he looked like Daniel Batchelor. He wore the same black wire-rim glasses, displayed the same mannerism, and even talked the same.

"Yes," she said, then walked to the hallway with him.

Cynthia? I thought. *Why do I keep hearing that name?* I trailed the remaining crowd to the outer office, trying to find out more about the Cynthia person and the Daniel Batchelor look-alike without being too obvious. *Too obvious? This is a dream.* Anyway, I had fun being on a mission to learn more about Cynthia and Daniel.

The outer office was light and spacious. Skylights from the cathedral ceiling cast soft, white lights on the carved mahogany paneling and floors. To the far left and right were large French windows that gave clear views of the vast skyline. I became a bit light-headed as I viewed the cityscape. Yet another set of double doors led to a single penthouse elevator. Jumbled conversations filled the room as everyone patiently awaited their turn to board the elevator. Cynthia and the Daniel look-alike disappeared amongst the crowd.

I'd seen enough and decided to wait for Marcellus back in the parlor.

"Oh my!" I was surprised.

The CEO's assistant's L-shaped work area was hidden in an enclave behind the double doors that led to the conference room. Her large mahogany desk was stacked high with neat piles of mauve manila folders and other odd gadgets. Of particular interest was her gold nameplate; a chill ran down my spine when I saw the name:

Cynthia Dewey
Executive Assistant

Is this some cosmic joke? I asked myself for the millionth time. *Why do I keep running across Cynthia Dewey?*

"Mr. Angellel's office, this is Cynthia," I heard her say from behind me. "How may I help you?"

"What the world?" I said as I turned to face her. She wore a pair of mauve eyeglasses. In place of regular lenses were black cubes. Attached to the frames were two mauve earplugs. She moved her fingers in the air as if she were typing on a keyboard. I didn't see a mouthpiece or anything like a receiver to speak into. *So how does the caller hear her?* Then, I realized that it was all a dream. *Anything is possible,* I reminded myself for the umpteenth time.

"He's in a meeting right now, Mrs. Angellel," she told the caller. "I'll put you through to his message system."

Mrs. Angellel? Wait a minute. I thought I was the only Mrs. Angellel? I don't believe in polygamy in real life and I sure won't tolerate it in my dreams. What's going on here?

Cynthia turned to face me and pulled the eyeglasses down on her nose. "That was your mother-in-law," she said. "I would have let you talk to her if I'd known you were still here."

I was sorry that I missed the opportunity to speak with my mother-in-law. What did she look like? What did she sound like? Was she prim and proper or laid-back? All those questions ran rampant through my mind as curiosity caught the best of me.

"Those are interesting glasses," I commented.

"You like them?" she asked.

"They're okay," I answered.

"These are the latest model," she said proudly. She motioned me over, anxious to show off her new toy. "Here. Put them on."

"Nice," I said. Looking through the glasses reminded me of an old View Master that my father gave me for Christmas way back when. It was a 3-D representation of the office from the perspective of being seated at Cynthia's workstation.

"It's intuitive," Cynthia said. "I can still do my work no matter where I am. It's like being here at work."

In front of me were a virtual keyboard, square mouse thingy, 25-inch color monitor and printer. I typed a few words—*This is a test*—clicked the picture of a printer at the bottom of the monitor, and the sounds of a printer rang in my ear. Amazing, but it actually felt as if I were typing on a real keyboard, and I actually saw the words appear on the monitor as I typed each letter.

"What are the floating buttons for?" I asked, referring to a red *Talk* button, blue *Flash* button, and a few others floating in mid-air.

"Oh, you hit *Talk* to answer the phone and to see and hear your caller. You don't really have to hit *Talk,* you can just say *Talk.* This is better than the old model because you see the caller and they see you as if you weren't wearing your optimizers. Then, just click *Flash* to hang up a call when you're done, or you can just say bye to hang up the call. The others buttons are self-explanatory. Nice, isn't it?" Cynthia asked. She held up a paper with my message *This is a test.*

"Where's the printer?" I asked. When I removed my glasses, I didn't see the paper anymore. All I saw was Cynthia waving her empty hand as if she were holding a sheet of paper.

She gave me a blank stare. "There's no *real* printer or *real* paper. You could create a whole book, but it only materializes when you click *Print.* You need your optimizer glasses or contact lenses to see anything you create in the virtual office." Cynthia gave me that you-need-to-keep-up-with-technology look—one that we techies back on Earth often issued to computer novices in other departments at work. It would be nice to have a truly virtual, paperless office in real life. We wouldn't need passwords to protect our computers and wouldn't have to shred confidential papers. *But what if someone were to steal your optimizer?* I thought. Then I remembered Marcellus said that stealing doesn't exist in that world.

"Thanks for the demo," I told Cynthia, then gave back her gadget.

I patiently awaited Marcellus in the parlor, but two other men had detained him in the conference room.

"How do you know it'll work?" one man asked.

"He's right, Marc," another man said. "How do you know it'll work?"

Marcellus angrily grabbed some papers off the table and neatly placed them into his burgundy briefcase.

"Because I'm Marc Angellel, that's why!"

"But ..." one of the men tried to get out, but Marcellus would hear no more.

"End of discussion," Marcellus said.

Both men soon left, leaving Marcellus alone in the conference room.

Marcellus wielded power like the wave of a magician's wand, which made me fall deeper in lust with him with each passing day. He was a mover and shaker in the corporate world, but I only wanted to move and shake him in the bedroom.

What a fine specimen of a man, I thought. Well, he *ought to be; I made him myself.* Or did I?

He wore a tailored, navy-blue suit covered with tiny burgundy M's. The pants were perfectly cuffed at the ankle, showing off his polished, navy-blue wing-tip shoes.

I walked over to the door of the conference room and peeked in. *My, my, my. Don't we look handsome?* Under the suit was a burgundy vest covered with navy-blue M's, starched white cotton shirt, and navy blue bow tie speckled with burgundy M's. He sported a chic faded haircut as if he'd just paid a visit to the barber. His nails had a slight sheen and the tips were pure white—evidence that he'd had a recent manicure.

Oh, no! A man who's prettier than me! I thought after realizing that my polish was chipped. *What?* I said to myself. My hands were perfectly manicured too. My nails were rounded and trimmed to corporate length. Each one was done in a creamy mauve polish to match my long mauve sarong skirt and mauve-and-white, squared-toed pumps.

"Hello," I said.

Marcellus jumped a bit, as if he were surprised to see me.

His face was clean-shaven, giving full view of his square jaw line and dimpled chin, features that I hadn't noticed until that time.

"What are you doing here?" His tone of voice and facial expression conveyed that you're-not-supposed-to-be-here look. He stopped arranging papers and walked toward me with a curious look on his face. "How did you ..."

Marcellus paused. His expression had changed to one of delight.

If I didn't know any better, it seemed like he wanted to ask how I got there. Truthfully, I didn't know what I was doing there, or how I got there. It was odd for a dream image to ask me how I got into my own dream. Marcellus had developed a life of his own apart from me.

For the first time, I felt out-of-place—like I didn't belong there. I sensed deep down in my gut that I wasn't supposed to be there at that time. *It's just a dream,* I reasoned for the trillionth time. *Stop thinking so much and enjoy.*

Cynthia poked her head half-way in the conference room. "Can I get you anything, Marc?" she asked.

Marcellus walked over to Cynthia and closed the conference doors behind him. Their conversation was hushed, so I couldn't hear what they were saying. *Why all the whispering?* I asked myself. *Are they hiding something from me?*

"That'll be all, Cynthia," Marcellus said as he re-entered the conference room. "Please close the conference room doors and hold all my calls."

"Yes, Marc," she said, then winked and smiled at him. Cynthia quickly closed the set of double doors leading to her office and walked around the perimeter of the conference room to close the ones that lead to the parlor, giving us complete privacy.

"Good seeing you, Demeter." Marcellus pulled me near with those big strong arms. He ran his hands under my white-lace maternity blouse, then caressed my bulging belly. "I made this," he said as we stared deep into each other's eyes.

The warmth of his hands combined with that ultra bass voice sent shock waves through my body. He smelled so warm and earthly—like that of lavender and jasmine potpourri.

He ran his hands up my back, pulling me closer.

I inched my fingers up his chest, feeling the silkiness of his vest; that coarse, white shirt; velvety bowtie and smooth face.

He picked me up by the waist and put me on the conference room table.

Our lips met, as he opened my mouth with his tongue. But, that green-eyed monster had taken over me.

"Marc?"

"What's wrong?" he asked. Lust covered his face. I looked down for a moment and noticed the outline of his manhood protruding through his pleated pants.

"Why does Cynthia call you Marc?" I asked. Then it hit me: Cynthia was the same woman who had seduced me during an earlier lucid dream, and Marc urged her on. She looked different that time—probably because she was wearing clothes and her hair was longer. *What gives Cynthia the right to call him Marc?*

"What?" Marcellus asked.

"Is something going on between you?"

"Honey." He took my hands in his. "I love you, Demeter. I love our family. What would make you think such a thing?"

The large, firm cock that rubbed against my leg had gone limp. "I noticed the way she winked and smiled at you."

"Demeter," he said with a whimper. "Adultery doesn't exist here."

"Is that so? Marc, we've both been with her."

"Yes, Demeter," he said, rubbing my hands frantically. "It's not adultery then if we both had her. It's only wrong if one of us doesn't approve, honey. Where you're from, people marry those who are not right for their lifestyle. Here, you're born for the right mate. When it's time, you meet each other and fall instantly in love. That's what happened to us, remember?"

"Yes, Marc," I said. "I remember."

He took my chin in his hand as we gazed into each other's eyes. "You like to be with women, right?"

I didn't know how to respond. I never thought of being with a woman until that lucid dream with Tish. "Yes," was all I could think to say.

"All right then," he said. "It turns me on for you to be with women because you're the one for me. Back where you're from, you were married to someone who fooled around, right?"

"Yes," I answered. *Are my dreams drenching up the past?* I wondered.

"You didn't approve because you were the wrong person for him. The right person for him would not mind at all. Now do you understand?"

"But do you fool around with Cynthia without me?" I asked.

"No, Demeter. I don't. You're the only woman who turns me on. Being with someone else without you being there wouldn't turn me on."

"How about fornication?" I asked. It didn't make sense. Okay, so it's not adultery if a married couple agrees to a threesome. But how about the other party?

"What?" he asked as if I had caught him off guard.

"Didn't Cynthia fornicate by being with us?" I asked. *Let's hear him get out of this one.*

"No."

"How so?"

"Because, Demeter..." he sighed. It was hard to tell if he was frustrated because I didn't understand the new world system, or because he needed to think of a clever lie. "It's only fornication if someone is hurt because of the arrangement or one party doesn't agree to the arrangements. It wasn't fornication because Cynthia didn't expect anything but pure pleasure from us. She didn't expect a relationship with you, and she didn't expect a relationship with me. Back where you're from, people fornicate all the time because one person always expects more than the other is willing to give. Or, someone has children out of wedlock."

"But, people could have children out of wedlock here too," I said.

"No, Demeter." He was thoroughly flustered with me. "No they can't."

"Why not?" I asked.

He tried hard to keep his cool. "Because, when a man is born, his sperm can only fertilize his wife. If he's a polygamist, then his sperm can only fertilize his wives."

"Polygamy?" I asked. That man was lying more with each passing moment. Or was he?

"Yes, Demeter." A gold water pitcher and water goblets were on the far corner of the table. Marcellus walked over and poured himself a drink, probably to erase his frustration with me.

"You're not making sense," I told him. He was beginning to frustrate me also. Was the man of my dreams having an affair? *A man just can't be faithful, not even in a dream.* Or could he? I had decided that it was my dream and if I didn't want him to be unfaithful to me, then he wasn't going to be. Besides, all I had to do was replace him with a new and improved imaginary playmate—that's all there was to it.

"A person's chemistry at birth determines if he will be single, monogamous, a polygamist, bisexual or homosexual. We don't get into all of that here like you do where you're from. All I can say is that everyone and everything is at peace here. Everything is in divine order."

He put the goblet back on the table and walked over to me with a devilish smile on his face that sent chills down my spine.

It's just a dream. Enjoy. I told myself again as he took me in his arms.

Marcellus parted my lips with his tongue as we engaged in a heated, throaty French kiss. He sucked and licked my lips, then twirled his tongue around mine over and over again. His mouth was still cold from drinking the icy water, which cooled me off a bit.

I felt one of his ice-cold hands on my thigh. For a moment I shivered, but it added to my excitement that much more. In one calculated slip of the wrist, Marcellus had untied my sarong. He parted my legs, wrapping them around his waist. Next thing I knew, he had unzipped his pants and penetrated my womanhood. In and out and side to side he moved, making me wetter and hotter with each stroke of his cock. He pumped me a lot slower and softer than previous times—and he didn't penetrate as deep—but firecrackers shot to the top of my head to the souls of my feet nonetheless. Marcellus was so loving and gentle; I wanted that moment to last forever.

What if someone walks in? I thought. *Just enjoy the moment. It's just a dream.* But the thought of being caught sent adrenaline soaring and blood pumping to my loins, making the experience much more sinful.

"I love you so much, Demeter," he whispered soft and low in my ear. "I can't wait for you to be with me always. It's not too much longer now."

I held my head close to his chest and heard the thump of his beating heart and breaths of his lungs. *He has a heart ... and he's breathing! It's just my imagination,* I told myself.

"Uhhh," Marcellus moaned soft and low. He closed his eyes, then withdrew his manhood from my glory. A gush of white, sticky fluid saturated my panties. "Let me get that up."

Marcellus grabbed a few white paper napkins at the far end of the conference table. He ran over to me as if I were about to leak all over the place—which I was—and sopped up his moisture from my undergarments.

"Well, at least I won't get pregnant this time."

Marcellus laughed. I didn't know if that meant that I could get pregnant in that world while I was already pregnant or if he admired my sense of humor.

"No," he said with a smile. "You can't get pregnant while you're already pregnant ... not even here."

"Every time I touch you I get pregnant," I said, then slid from the table.

"That's not true," he said as he straightened his clothes. "You just don't recall the other times." His expression changed from humorous to serious. "You just don't remember. When you shed your skin, you'll forget matters of the flesh and remember everything."

"Shed my skin?" I asked. *Why do I keep hearing something about shedding my skin?* I wondered.

"You'll find out in time," he said. "You can't remember anything with your skin is still on."

Marcellus plopped on one of the chairs and motioned for me to join him.

"Come on." He extended his arms for me, then slapped his lap.

I accepted the invitation to sit on his lap.

Marcellus cradled me in between the silky softness of his burgundy jacket lining, as I wrapped my arms around his shoulders. I removed my shoes to get more comfortable, then I ran my toes along the bottom of his pants leg. Dabs of lavender and jasmine oil behind his ears were so fragrant and relaxing. *Aromatherapy in its highest form.* I hadn't a care or concern.

Something caught Marcellus' attention. "Wait, wait," he whispered, patting me on the thigh to get down.

A red light flashed near the conference doors that lead to Cynthia's office. I wondered what was wrong because Marcellus raced to the door. *Not a fire drill in my dream. Can't be.*

Marcellus and Cynthia moved the conference room chairs behind the door near the window. Next, Cynthia cleared the tray of water and ice from the table and carried it into the hidden room. I hadn't noticed the opening before because the door blended in with the mahogany wall paneling.

Marcellus pressed a button on the conference room table and it began to fold—accordion-style—unto itself. When the six pairs of legs were compacted together, Cynthia and Marcellus picked the thing up and placed it into a small black trunk. I watched in amazement as Cynthia carried it away. The trunk must have been lightweight because she carted it to her office under her arm like a big, bulky bed pillow. The more I saw of the strange new world, the more it fascinated me.

"After you, my sweet," Marcellus said from behind.

I paid so much attention to Cynthia and the table, that I didn't notice that Marcellus had spread a tartan comforter on the floor. Cynthia came back with a large white wicker picnic basket and what looked like a chilled bottle of sparkling water.

Marcellus helped me to the floor.

"Can I get you anything else, Marc?" Cynthia asked.

"No," Marcellus said. "That'll be all for now. Just hold all my calls."

"Yes, Marc," she said, then quietly closed the doors leading to her office.

Marcellus had removed his shoes and walked over to open the mauve vertical blinds. Soft, white light beamed in and brightened the dim, dull conference room. Again, I became dizzy as I beheld the spectacular view of the metropolitan skyline.

I opened the top of the picnic basket and two wine goblets were securely placed in the lid. Other goodies were neatly stored in clear plastic containers: finger sandwiches, doce cubes, black grapes the size of lemons, strawberries the size of small oranges, and a few other delectables that I didn't recognize.

Marcellus removed my shoes then massaged my feet to perfection. Starting at the heel—with my left foot in his left hand and right foot in his right hand—he kneaded my flesh with his fingers. I leaned back on my elbows and enjoyed the experience.

He moved along the length of my soles up to the balls, then each individual toe.

"You like that?" he asked.

"Yes, Marc," I said. "I do."

"Don't mind me," he said. "Go ahead and eat something. I know you're probably hungry."

He was right; I was so hungry. Pregnancy can give a woman the most voracious appetite. I reached over and pulled out the container of giant grapes and strawberries.

"Ummm," I moaned.

"Sweet, huh?" Marc asked with a smirk on his face.

"Yes," I said after biting into a giant grape. The fruit was so fleshy and juicy like a ripe plum, but tasted like a grape. I bit into the giant strawberry and thought I was in heaven. It tasted like a sweet, ripe strawberry, but had the texture and juiciness of a ripe, red watermelon. "What are these? They're so good."

Marcellus paused for a second and gave me a dumb look. "Those are black grapes and those are strawberries."

"I knew that," I said.

Marcellus continued to massage my feet up to the ankles, calves then back to the toes again.

The experience was very relaxing, so I decided to recline on my back. My eyelids grew heavy as sleep was upon me. I dozed for a few seconds…

***

My lungs quickly filled with air, jolting me in position. Grunts of snorting hogs rang loud in my ears, bringing a strange sensation of being shot back into my body by a silver bullet. Marcellus cuddled behind me with his arms wrapped around my shoulders. With my eyes still closed, I turn to face him and snuggled a little closer—what a mistake. Something was different about the long, warm body next to me. Those once silky-fine chest hairs were coarse and scratchy.

The scent of lavender and jasmine oil had transformed into stale perspiration of a hard-working man—one that longed a shower and a can of Right Guard. Those delicate, masculine hands had become callous-covered sheets of sandpaper. Once fresh, minty breath wreaked of a two-day-old garbage pale with each hog-grunting, teeth-grinding snore.

Was I unsatisfied with Marcellus and so insecure with thoughts of him betraying me with Cynthia that I had conjured up another imaginary playmate? Or, did I create another image of Marcellus—one that was so rough, tough and undesirable to other women that not even I longed for him? Was I so insecure—even in my dreams? I needed to know.

I slowly opened my eyes—not knowing what to expect—afraid to behold yet another strange, new world that awaited me. Was I leaving behind a place of opulence and splendor for one of squalor and chaos? Unprepared to face my new unreality, I counted—one … two … three … and popped my eyes wide open.

The room was dim and smothering hot. Straight ahead was a door leading to a hallway. Green and gold paisley-print wallpaper covered the walls; deep teal carpet blanketed the floors. A gold trimmed mirror sat between two white sconce fixtures trimmed in gold; directly below was a small antique secretary. *How can anyone sleep with such bright lights?* I wondered.

Two brief shrill toots sounded between the loud snores. It sounded like beeps from my cell phone when I had a message waiting. On a nightstand to my right was a small black digital clock. In big, bold, red numbers read *11:15*. To the right of that was an entertainment center with stereo system and a forty-two inch TV. I wanted to hear the news and weather report, but the snoring was so loud.

In front of the entertainment unit were two white antique chairs and coffee table covered with several copies of *Black Enterprise* magazines and *The Wall Street Journal*. I looked again and noticed that my clothes were draped over one of the chairs; my purse and shoes were tucked underneath. I knew without a doubt that I was on Earth, but where? *Where in the world am I?*

I looked around more and more, desperately searching for clues of my whereabouts. Ahead—next to the door leading to the hallway—was a mirrored dresser. I sat up and my hair was tossed about as if I had been fighting. My heart began to race as I began to panic. I wasn't at home or at Percy's condo. It was too personal, like someone's home, so I wasn't in a hospital.

A royal-blue comforter covered the oak wood sleigh bed. Two firm mattresses were piled high; an oak wood bed stool sat at the side of the bed. An empty Trojans box sat between the mystery man and myself. Three used condoms littered the sheets beside me. My femininity felt dry and scratchy—almost like that dreaded visit to the gynecologist.

Oh-my-goodness. What have I done? I had to know, so in one quick swoop, I yanked the comforter from the mystery man. I couldn't believe it. What was I doing with the author from the book signing? I didn't know his name or anything about him.

Drool had run down his mouth, forming a flaky, white crust. The sandman had covered the cracks of his eyes with thick, yellowish-white goop. He had turned onto his stomach and air escaped his gut like a giant balloon, leaving a long trail of putrid fumes burning in my nose, charring my nostril hairs.

"Enough is enough," I said as I nudged his shoulders.

"Huh, huh?" He smacked his lips in a stupor, and glanced over at the digital clock. He looked up at me with those snotty eyes. "Whoa!" he jumped to his elbows, as if knowing the time shocked him awake. "It's damn near midnight. Do you want me to take you home? You're welcome to spend the night if you'd like."

"What?" I was shocked he asked such a question. *Spend the night with Mr. Warthog? No way.* "I need to get home."

"Fine," he said, and pointed over his shoulder. "If you want to wash up, the bathroom is over there."

I dashed up out of the bed in lightning speed, almost missing the stool, and grabbed my belongings from the chair. He followed my nude body with his eyes all the way to the bathroom. I felt a bit embarrassed and scared of what I had done. I had never had a one-night stand before. That was Percy's style, not mine.

***

It was that night I knew I needed your help more than ever, Dr. Iverson. I had lost it ... really, really lost it.

***

It was one o'clock in the morning when we arrived at my humble abode. A light went on upstairs followed by a parting of the curtains from Keston's bedroom window.

"I had a wonderful time," he said, then turned off the ignition and headlights. "I'd like to see you again soon."

A sick feeling churned in my gut realizing that I had given my glory to that mysterious stranger. He was a famous author, but an alien to me nonetheless. "I'll see." I looked away into the shrubs along the roadside too bashful to look him in the eyes.

"Your phone has been ringing and beeping all night," he said. "Who's that spying on us?" he asked and pointed with his head to the second floor. Seconds later, the curtains closed and all was dark. "That's not your husband is it? Is that who's been calling you all night?"

"No." I chuckled to keep what remained of my sanity.

"I don't want him coming out here after us," he said.

"We'll get together," I told him.

We looked into each other's eyes, as he reeled me closer to him. Something was special about that man. Only an hour earlier, he was a smelly Neanderthal and snorting hog with thick gobs of drool oozing down his cheeks. But at that tender moment he smelled so fresh, clean and all so delicious. "No." I pulled away. I detected a sense of disappointment in his expression as he withdrew his embrace. "It's late."

I reached for the door; he reached for my hand.

"Didi," he called.

I turned to face him. A look of infatuation covered his face. Looking deep into his full, dark eyes sent a chill spiraling down my spine.

"It's late," I said once again. "I really must be going."

"Let's have dinner sometime," he insisted. "I can't explain it, but it was like magic all evening. Please, I'd like to see you again."

It was indeed magical being with him too, well, the little that I remembered anyway. *This is Earth,* I reminded myself. *Love at first sight doesn't exist here.* He wore a tight, red T-shirt that outlined his strong chest and buffed, muscular arms. The scent of fresh mint filled the air as he spoke. His face was cleanly shaven, and his lips looked so kissable—soft, moist and glistening—like morning dew. *Amazing what a shower and a little toothpaste will do for a brother,* I thought.

He got out of the car and walked around to the side. His arms were solid muscles and that butt, was high, tight and right. The slamming car door and clanking soles of his wing-tip shoes against the pavement started the neighborhood dogs—including that mutt, Sampson, Keston and Kevin brought home—barking up a storm.

Nice. He was just as fine as his black gold-trimmed Lexus and soft lambskin seats. But a fancy car and sexy body weren't enough to wash away tawdry feelings of worthlessness and humiliation that drenched my soul.

"We should have dinner tomorrow night," he said upon opening my door and helping me out of the car.

"I'd like that," I said, but wasn't sure if I really meant it. I looked up at him and chills ran through my body. He reminded me so much of Marcellus in size and build. Perhaps it was because he, too, was six-two and weighed roughly one hundred eighty pounds. Maybe it was his ultra bass voice. Or, perhaps it was his deep, dark eyes, or big feet or big hands … I didn't know.

A deep feeling of shame and anxiety grew stronger with each passing second. I had opened my glory to a nameless stranger, violating my hallowed ground.

"Good night." He pecked me on the cheek light and tender.

His lips were so soft and supple; shock waves ran rampant, igniting every nerve ending in my body. I watched in awe as he drove off into the night; our paths never to cross again.

***

Oh, so good to be in my own bedroom, I thought. Without bothering to flick on the switch, I threw my purse, shoes and shopping bag into the closet. Street lamps were plenty to light a dark house.

"Why are you getting home so late?" a voice said from behind, terrifying the daylights out of me. "It's almost one o'clock in the morning. We've been trying to reach you all night."

How dare Keston scold me for getting in late. "I need to get some rest. I'm tired," I told him, then headed straight for the garden tub to draw some water for a hot bath. Frankly, I just wasn't in the mood for another shouting match with him.

I stopped in my tracks because what he said struck me hard and cold. We tried to reach you? What "we" was trying to reach me? Keston, Kevin and Percy?

I sat down as my heart sank low. A sense of urgency filled his voice. Amazing. That was the first time I didn't bother to answer my phone or listen to voice mail, and I missed an emergency.

"I've been trying to call you all night," he said.

I wondered if something had happened to Kevin, but I looked around and he had turned on the bedroom light and joined his brother.

"Who was that man?" he demanded.

"A coworker. Aunt Percy took me to the MARTA Station this morning, so I didn't have my car to drive home. I couldn't catch up with her."

"That's what I called to tell you," Keston said. "I called to tell you about Aunt Percy."

"She's gone," Kevin said.

My heart raced faster and faster. "She's gone?" I asked, too afraid to hear the answer. I wanted her to leave me alone, but not permanently. "What do you mean?"

"She packed all her stuff and left," Keston said.

Keston and Kevin walked me to Percy's room. Not even a single piece of lint was left in the chest, dresser or closet. All her personal effects were gone from her bathroom too. Well, almost everything. *Good. That heifer finally went home,* I thought.

"But look what she left behind," Keston said.

Kevin held up a clear plastic bag. Inside were a small bottle of vanilla extract, cotton swabs, a white cigarette lighter, tiny clear crystals and a glass pipe like the one she used in her ritual.

"So," I said.

Keston and Kevin both looked with puzzled looks on their faces. "So?" they asked in unison.

"What's the big deal? She'll be back for it." I turned for my room, too tired to be concerned about Percy's aromatherapy supplies.

"I don't want this stuff around," Keston said.

"Me either," Kevin said. "We should flush it down the toilet."

"I know that's right," Keston agreed.

I was getting a bit annoyed with them. Did they think that the crystals were some *female product?* I wanted to take a hot bath to wash my sins away, then retire to bed to sleep the pain away. Percy's crystals were the least of my worries, or so I thought.

"Do what you want," I told them. "Whatever, I'm going to sleep."

They stood there with mouths hung low as I made a date with a hot, bubbly foam bath.

December
Nowhere to turn
No hiding places
For curiosity lures the cat
With tricks and smiling faces
It's too late
Have gone too far
No more chances
For curious dances
In the dark

Chapter 22.
With Tricks and Smiling Faces

That was the night when my lucid dreams weren't fun anymore. I couldn't seem to turn them off.

I dreamed I was in the produce section of Kroger, but everything was so strange. I walked around the store for at least an hour before realizing I was lost. Everything looked different somehow, but I couldn't quite explain why.

"We better get her granddaughter," I heard someone say, but didn't pay attention. "She's in the check out line."

"I'll go get her," another woman said. "She really shouldn't let her grandmother roam around like that."

"Are you finding everything okay, Mrs. Williams?" someone asked, startling me. "Mrs. Williams?"

The young man appeared from nowhere and escorted me to the back office. He kept referring to me as Mrs. Williams. My hips and knees were stiff. A sharp pain shot through my body with each step I took. It was as I if I had been exercising all night long.

It was so bone-chilling cold in the store. *Must be the freezer section,* I thought. *They're cold even in dreams.* The young man was talking to me and kept referring to me as Mrs. Williams.

I was horrified when I glanced in a mirror as we passed the meat department. I looked twice just to make sure that what I was seeing was real. My hair was pure white and pulled back in a bun. I looked at my hands and they were frail and boney.

An older woman about fifty came along. Something was familiar about her that I couldn't quite place. She was tall with a smooth caramel complexion and hazel eyes. "Come on Grandma. Let's get you home."

"She was roaming around the store," the young man said as he handed me over to the woman.

"Grandmother?" I asked. My throat was so sore and scratchy that I could barely utter a word. "Who's your grandmother?"

"Oh Granma."

By that time, several people had crowded around me, laughing playfully at my question. As we neared the front of the store, a young man who looked a lot like Keston, came along.

"I put the groceries in the car, Ma," he told the woman.

"Keston?" I asked. The young man was about eleven with the same red-bone complexion and hazel-green eyes as Keston, but he was a bit shorter and stockier in build. I had wondered if others could visit my dreams and be aware of the experience. "What are you doing here? You look different."

The young man and the woman claiming to be my granddaughter looked curiously at each other.

"Grandma, sweetie," she said. "This is Christopher, your great-grandson."

"She always forgets my name," the young man said to his mother as if I weren't there.

"Boy," she said impatiently, "go wait in the car."

"But she always ... " he tried to say, but his mother cut him off again.

"Boy, just go wait in the car," she demanded. "Go get her wheelchair."

The woman held my hand as we slowly walked to the parking lot. "You should have waited in the car, Gran." She spoke to me slowly, as if speaking to a child. "You shouldn't have come out without your wheelchair, sweetie. Especially after dark."

The cars in the lot looked funny. They were in these odd shapes and colors like Popsicles. And another thing, people weren't walking, they were going around on these motorized scooters.

We drove along Hwy 74, but everything had changed. Tall, beautiful trees were replaced by strip malls and restaurants. Cow pastures and farmland gave way to condominiums and houses.

"What happened to the gas stations?" I asked, not thinking that anyone had heard me. Two restaurants stood in place of gas stations that were near the corner of Hwy 54 and Hwy 74.

"Gas stations?" the young man asked from the back seat. "What's that?"

"Gas stations were where people went to fill their cars with gasoline around the turn of the century," the woman said.

"Gasoline?" The young man was curious. "What's gasoline and why would people fill their cars with it? Wouldn't that ruin the seats?"

The woman laughed. "No, no," she said. "Cars had special tanks to hold the gasoline."

"Don't cars run on gasoline?" I asked.

"Oh, Gran," the woman said, then laughed.

I noticed that she was steering the car, but there were no pedals on the floor.

"How do you run this thing?" I asked. "Where are your brakes and gas?"

They both laughed.

"Oh, Gran." She laughed so hard that she almost ran off the road.

"Everything's on the dashboard, Great-Gran," the young man said. "Cars don't run on gasoline."

"They don't?" I asked. "Then what do they run on?"

"Nothing," he said.

We finally arrived home. Everything looked the same. Fern was planted in the front yard, but had grown into a big tree taller than the house with long, waxy leaves.

"Hey, what's up, Didi," Fern said.

"What's up with you, Fern," I said.

"She's talking to that tree again, Ma," the boy said.

"Boy, hush up," the woman told him.

Inside, over the mantle were pictures that were taken over the years of Keston and Kevin with their wives and families. Some pictures of younger families that looked like Keston and Kevin.

"Let's get you to your room," the woman said.

I started up the stairs, but she pulled me away.

"Where are you going, Gran?" she asked.

"To my room," I said.

"Your room is downstairs," she informed me.

The sunroom had been converted into a master on the main—large bedroom and master bath. Royal-blue wallpaper with golden dots covered the walls, and plush royal-blue carpet covered the floors. Burgundy velvet draperies covered the length of the windows. If I didn't know any better, I'd say that someone had moved my bedroom downstairs to make it easier for me to get around.

The bathroom was small, but cozy. The walls and floors were done in small powder-blue tile; even the tub, vanity and commode were all powder-blue. To the left was a white shutter-style door that opened to the linen closet; inside, royal-blue towels of all sizes filled the shelves. I opened the oak medicine cabinet to my right; sundries, medicine bottles and men's grooming accessories littered the place.

"What's all this?" I asked.

"Oh, those are Big Daddy's things," she said. "Oh, that reminds me. They're bringing him home from the hospital tonight. I bet you can't wait to see him."

"Big Daddy?" I asked.

She gave me a sorrowful look, as if to pity me for not knowing who Big Daddy was. Tears welled in her eyes as she fought desperately to regain her composure.

"Just rest yourself, Gran," she said, holding her head low, sniffling her nose. Tears rolled down her cheeks as she wiped each one with her fingers.

"What's wrong?" I asked. My heart sank low as I heard her sob. She was hurting and I could do nothing to make it right. Somehow, I had caused her such deep and dark sorrow.

"I'll be all right, Gran," she said, struggling against the tears. She pulled back the blue satin comforter and helped me to the bed. After removing my white loafers, she tucked me in bed.

The blue-and-white plaid flannel sheets were so soft to touch and smelled of fresh eucalyptus. I rested my head on the pillows and fell fast asleep.

***

I didn't like that dream, Dr. Iverson, and hoped to awaken back in present time, present place. They're not fun anymore, Dr. Iverson. Please do anything to make them go away.

***

I was abruptly awakened by glass smashing on the kitchen floor. *I wonder what those boys broke,* I thought. *I hope it wasn't my good china.* My joints ached something terrible as if I had slept in a fetal position all night. I struggled long and hard to sit up on the side of the bed. It felt like I had been sleeping in a knot all night. The room was still and dark, but there were voices in the living room. I looked at the digital clock on the nightstand and *8:15* blinked in big, bold, red letters.

"Go get Gran," I heard a woman say.

"Yeah," a man said. His voice was hoarse and crackling like that of a senior. "Go get my woman. Bring her here."

Laughter burst forth as footsteps neared the bedroom. Someone tapped on the door.

"Gran," a woman's voice said. "Guess who's here?"

The same woman who called me Gran earlier that day entered the room. *What's the use of knocking if you're coming in anyway?* I thought. "Who's here?" I asked.

"Good, you're up. Big Daddy just got back from the hospital, Gran," the woman said. A high degree of excitement filled her voice.

She disappeared into the bathroom, then returned with a warm, wet towel. "Let's clean you up, Gran."

"Whoa," I said as the woman knocked me off balance.

She rigorously wiped the corners of my eyes, mouth and nose. I knew she was crazy when he got on her knees and looked inside my nose and cleaned my nostrils with the towel. She loosened my hair, then brushed it back into a ponytail before pinning it back into a bun.

"There," she said. "Now you're nice and pretty to see Big Daddy."

She helped me to my feet. Each time I moved, every joint in my body felt as if it had been hit with a sledgehammer.

"Oh-my-goodness." I exclaimed when we passed the dressing mirror. "I'm old! I'm old!" I thought nothing of waking up in my own bed, young and refreshed. But I checked the mirror once more, and I was still old.

"Oh, Gran," the woman laughed. "You're so funny."

"You don't see me laughing," I told her. "And why do you keep calling me Gran anyway? I'm I supposed to be your grandmother?"

That look of pity flashed across her face. "Let's go see Big Daddy in the living room. Everybody is in the living room."

"Gran is having another episode, Big Daddy," I heard a man's voice say. "She may not recognize you."

"That's a'ight," Big Daddy said. "She still my woman. We been together over fifty years. I took a vow to love her for better or worse, in sickness and in health, 'til death due us part, and I mean that."

That dream wasn't fun. I couldn't seem to wake up no matter how hard I tried. I was curious, though, to know who Big Daddy was. Who could he be: Marcellus, the author, some other imaginary playmate? Curiosity had the best of me.

Hand-in-hand, the woman and I navigated through the kitchen. Dishes were stacked in the sink and two small gray pots rested on the stove. We made our way through the hallway, then finally to the living room. A man who looked like an older version of Keston laughed and joke with Big Daddy, who sat in a wheelchair with his back turned to me. He looked so frail with all those tubes running beneath his pants and small green oxygen tank by his side.

The woman ushered me to the sofa. My knees were almost too stiff to bend, as I faced the mysterious man.

"Hey, Gran," the man said who looked like a forty-five year old version of Keston.

"Keston?" I asked as I looked up at him. "What are you doing here? Why are calling me Gran?"

"Oh, Gran," he said. "It's me, Dewey. Keston is my daddy. You know that."

"Shhh," the woman said. She slapped Dewey's leg, indicating her annoyance with his comments.

"Stop it, Cynth," Dewey said. "The doctor said to correct her. That's the only way to stimulate her memory."

They talked about me as if I weren't there. I pinched myself over and over, trying to wake myself up from that nightmare. I didn't budge. *Why do I keep hearing the names Cynthia and Dewey over and over? Is this some cosmic joke?*

"Are you all right, Gran," Cynthia asked. "Do you need something?" She must have noticed me pinching my leg.

"Hey sugar," Big Daddy said. "Give Big Daddy a hug."

I turned as quickly as my aching neck allowed to face him. I was shocked to learn who he was. "Big Daddy? Marcus?"

"In the flesh," he said.

Big Daddy was a much older version of Marcus. Fine gray fuzz covered his head and face. His face and fingers were but skin and bones, a fragile image of a man. He looked thin and sickly, not anything like the robust Marcus I know today.

What was he doing in my dream? Did I secretly desire Marcus on some subconscious level? I pleaded with the cosmos to wake me from that nightmare.

Dewey helped Marcus out of his wheelchair and next to me on the sofa.

"We'll be right back," Cynthia said, then set off for the kitchen.

Marcus took my hands in his. "Didi," he said, rubbing my hands as we gazed deep into each other eyes. "I'm not long for this world, but I want you to know that you've given me the best fifty years of my life. I loved you the first day I laid eyes on you, but you wouldn't give me the time of day."

I didn't know how to respond. It was all a dream anyway, so I listened attentively.

"We were smart," he continued. "We skipped the raising kids part and moved right on to the grandchildren, great-grandchildren, and great-great-grandchildren part." He began to laugh. "We let our children have the children for us."

He wasn't making sense. "What do you mean?" I asked.

"Your son, my daddy, Keston married his daughter, my mother," Dewey said sarcastically, as if he were making fun of me.

"Stop that." Cynthia popped him on the arm. "Here, Gran," Cynthia said, then presented me with a large white photo album.

I flipped through the pages: photos from my childhood with my two brothers and Percy; pictures of me in that navy-blue and silver marching band uniform, pretending to blow my flute; pictures of me walking across the stage at Spelman and Tulane during graduation. So many memories flooded my mind: good times with my father as we gazed the night sky, special moments with Percy and Tish, the birth of Keston and Kevin. All the pictures in the album reflected the highlights of my life.

Most photos I didn't recognize: Keston and Kevin looked so handsome in their burgundy-and-gold high school graduation gowns. Keston's graduation from Morehouse then Morehouse School of Medicine; interesting to know that he followed his grandfather's footsteps; his marriage to Marcus's daughter, the birth of their two children—Cynthia and Dewey, and three grandchildren. I ran across a picture of Cynthia's wedding.

"I didn't know you still have a copy of that, Gran," Cynthia said. "Turn the page." She ran away upstairs, as tears welled in her eyes.

I became light-headed for a few seconds as my temples began to throb. Pressure of an invisible band tightened around my head as memories of Cynthia flooded my mind: her husband was in the military on assignment when Christopher was only two years old. He didn't make it back and Cynthia never quite recovered from losing her husband so young. The family deemed it best for her if she moved in with Marcus and me. The arrangement benefited her financially and emotionally, and Marcus and I had someone to care for us in our old age. It was Marcus's idea to build the master on the main a few years ago.

"Come on back," Dewey said as he ran after his sister. He whispered something in her ear. I heard him mention "Big Daddy" and that was enough to bring her back to the living room.

"Look, there's uncle Kevin," Cynthia said.

"Oh, my, my," I said. All the scenes were quite fascinating.

Kevin's graduation ceremonies from Morehouse and Howard looked like such fun. The whole family was there: Daddy, Keston and me. Where was Percy? Everybody was all dressed up, sipping Champagne and toasting the occasion. I flipped a few more pages and discovered newspaper articles of Kevin's patents and inventions. He was quite the scientist. Pictures of his wedding—he married a Spelman girl—way to go, Kevin. Pictures of children and grandchildren were quite spectacular. *What time did he have to make babies?* I asked myself when I counted the number of children Kevin and his wife had.

"What's this?" I asked. The next five pages were filled with articles of a famous scientist who had formulated theories of inter-dimensional time travel.

"Oh, those are articles about Uncle Kevin when he got the Nobel Prize for quantum physics."

My Kevin, a famous Nobel Prize winning scientist.

This dream isn't so bad after all, I thought. My babies will have fulfilling lives. What more could I wish for?

Keston retired from his private medical practice ten years before. Kevin moved to Maine and retired as a research scientist. I flipped some more, and learned that the grandchildren and great-grandchildren lived all over the world: Greece, Spain, Nigeria, Canada, Bolivia and too many other places to name.

"Look, Gran," Cynthia said, then gave me a burgundy photo album with gold trim.

All the pictures were of me with a few of Marcus: pictures of my retirement party as CIO, Chief Information Officer; travels to exotic parts of the world— New Zealand, Zimbabwe, Egypt, and Kenya. What a blessed life. *If only my future could be so bright,* I thought.

"Now this is my favorite one," Marcus said as he flipped to the last page.

It was our marriage license:

State of Georgia
Fayette County
September 2, 2011

"We've been married over fifty good years," Marcus said.

Me marry Marcus? Probably not, he's very happily married. My son married his daughter? Perhaps.

Fifty years? I asked myself. *Let's see, in 2011, I'll be fifty. So, in this dream, I'm supposed to one hundred years old. What a life to look forward to. What a fulfilling life.*

"Big Daddy," Cynthia yelled.

"Big Daddy," Dewey yelled.

"Call the … " Cynthia yelled to her son.

Everybody was frantic and yelling up a storm. I couldn't make out what she said. Their voices began to fade and became no more than faint whispers echoing through one big open space. My vision began to blur and I became a bit light-headed. White and lavender fog surrounded me as I floated aimlessly into no man's land.

Tiny lavender and silver pulses flared from the clouds and high above like a New Year's Eve fireworks display. The blasts formed a brilliant, white light at the pinnacle that grew larger with each explosion. A strong feeling of peace and tranquility overtook me; the scene was so incredibly beautiful. What started as a faint buzz vibrated through my core, growing louder and more intense as the light source continued to expand.

I was pulled to the light by a magnetic force as the buzzing grew louder and louder. The buzzing had become unbearable until …

Chapter 23.
It's Too Late, Have Gone too Far

I fell from great heights and was jolted to a sitting position. The alarm clock beeped over and over again. I blinked a few times and observed my surroundings. "Thank goodness," I said, realizing that I was back in my own home ... in Peachtree City, Georgia ... submerged in my own bathtub. I had fallen asleep in the tub overnight and was freezing something awful. The alarm clock—with all that loud beeping—drove me batty, that's for sure.

It was daylight, but looked a bit overcast. *I hope it doesn't rain today.* Thick, green mucous dripped from my nose as I went into a sneezing and coughing frenzy. I felt like heck, probably from falling asleep in the tub, but I had so much to catch up on at work that I couldn't take off another day.

I dragged myself from the tub, brushed my teeth, washed my face ... you know the routine. Searching the closet for items fresh from the drycleaners, I found a burgundy pantsuit and white cotton blouse. *This'll do nicely,* I thought, then threw the garments on in lightening speed.

"Oh that damn alarm clock," I said on my way to turn the thing off. "Why can't it stop on its own after a certain time?" I pressed the black *Off* button, then noticed the time: *9:30. I'd better call in.* Still groggy, I fumbled through the medicine cabinet for my little blue pills. The big pink ones affected my ability to concentrate, so I stayed away from those.

Can't forget this, I thought. I threw a pill in my mouth. The thought of boning a complete stranger lingered. What if I was pregnant or contracted some disease. Worse, what if he were a lunatic and had harmed me in some way? My nerves really needed calming, so I threw two more pills right on in. That chalky, bitter aftertaste remained even after gulping two glasses of water. They were so cute and small—like little blue diamonds—too cute to taste so nasty. Gosh, I really hated taking those pills.

I looked around my bedroom for the phone, but it was nowhere in sight. *That Percy,* I thought. *That bitch moved the damn phone again!*

I went to Keston's room, thinking the phone would be there, but it wasn't. I went to Kevin's room, but still no phone. Something was odd about their rooms: the beds were perfectly made without as much as a wrinkle, the floors were freshly vacuumed, and the closet doors were closed. I went into their bathroom, and it was just too spotless: the shower stall and sink were dry. Personal hygiene items—like toothpaste, hair-filled razors and soap, things that they usually scattered about the sink and floor—were nowhere in sight. For once, clothing and underwear didn't litter the floor. If I didn't know any better, I'd say they were away at summer camp.

I went back into my room, grabbed my burgundy purse and shoes—to match my suit—and briefcase then headed downstairs to use the kitchen phone. *Well, at least traffic should be light this time of morning.*

First, I dialed Daniel Batchelor's line, but reached my voice mailbox instead. I tried twice, carefully punching each digit as I dialed, but each time I was routed to my voice mailbox. I assumed that he was out and forwarded his calls to my line, or maybe the lines were crossed. In either case, I didn't want to waste time so I called Trevor. His line rang several times and voice mail didn't pick up. As a last resort, I dialed Marcus.

"QA, this is Marcus," he answered.

"Finally," I said. "Someone answered. I tried calling around the office, but no one answered."

"Demeter?" he asked.

"What?" I asked. Hearing his voice sent chills down my spine. I was at a loss for words and couldn't explain the feelings that flooded my system. Maybe it was because I had dreamed about him the night before. Did I harbor some deep-down buried emotions for Marcus that were brought to light?

"Hey Demeter. What can I do for you?" he asked.

"I'm running a tad behind and will be in about eleven-ish."

"You do remember that it's *Bring Your daughter to Work Week*, right?" he asked.

"Oh, yes, yes, Marcus. I remember," I lied. I had no clue of what he was talking about.

"You're not trying to get out spending time with my daughter are you?" he asked.

Right, Marcus. Your daughter. "Now why would I do that, Marcus?" I was being playful because I didn't know what the heck he was talking about. "When is she coming in?" I asked.

Marcus was silent for a moment. "Oh, I need to talk to you about something when you get in." Marcus said. "Personnel sent over some paperwork for you to sign for Trevor. I left it on your desk since you were off yesterday."

I wasn't off the day before. If Personnel left something, it was when I had gone to the mall. I assumed everybody went home after the session, but apparently I was wrong. And another thing, Marcus didn't sound like Marcus; his language was—how should I put this—a bit more formal than usual. Was I in another dream?

"What's up with Trevor?" I asked Marcus.

Again, Marcus became silent. "It's something we can't talk about on the phone. It's confidential."

Curiosity had the best of me. I knew for sure that I had to go to work just to find out about Trevor.

Before leaving, I tried to call Percy to find out why she left so suddenly. Not that I cared because I was glad that she had gone. What pissed me off, though, was the fact that she didn't bother to tell me.

I tried calling her cell phone without using speed dial. I dialed several times, making sure that I keyed in the numbers correctly, but I kept getting someone else's voice mail message. I dialed her at home, again making sure that I keyed the numbers correctly, but the phone had been disconnected. I tried five times, but each time a recording indicated that her phone was disconnected. Silly me, I assumed that she had changed her number and failed to inform me. I was even more pissed than ever. I planned to visit dear Miss Percy before going to the office and give her a piece of my mind—well, what was left of it. What a bad idea.

***

I was right. Traffic was so light at ten o'clock in the morning. *It should be this way all day long,* I thought. It was so bright and sunny, but only an hour earlier it was so gloomy and overcast. At eleven-fifteen, I arrived at Percy's building. A few new faces worked the security desk, but I didn't really pay attention.

"How ya doin' Ms. Pickens," the concierge said.

"Hey. I'm fine. How about yourself?" I asked.

"I ain't seen you in these parts in a long time. How ya sister doin'?"

"She's fine," I said.

Everyone else had to present their residence badge, but he let me in the security gate leading to the elevators. *I don't recall a security gate or passkeys before. Must be new,* I thought.

"Tell her I said 'hello' next time you see her," he said. "It's been a long time."

"It has been just too long," I said. I'd never seen him before. There's no way I or anyone else could miss a man like that. He was over six-six and weighed at least three hundred pounds. On top of that, his deep, dark, delicious, chocolate skin and big bulging body-builder muscles … mmmm … made him stand out like a sore thumb. He had probably seen me around the building and knew I was Percy's sister. It was a good thing because he let me through the security gate without a fuss. *Yeah, he is Percy's type,* I thought. *She probably flirted with him too.*

I got off the elevator and the carpet was a deep shade of wine. The paisley-print wallpaper had been removed and the walls were painted a deep rose hue. *Maybe I'm on the wrong floor,* I thought. I glanced back at the elevators and *14* appeared in big, bold, black numbers across the doors.

I made my way to Percy's condo, but a small black and neon red *For Sale* sign hung on the door.

For Sale
Contact Peppermint Management at 404-555-5555

The door was slightly ajar, so I took the liberty to walk right on in. Straight ahead, the living room was bare. I peeked in the laundry room to the left, and it was dark. *Maybe the light blew out,* I thought. I flipped the light switch and the room remained dark. Percy's washer and dryer, ironing board and laundry products were gone. I snooped through the kitchen cabinets and refrigerator; they were clean as if no one had lived there for several months. Not even a single piece of lint remained in the bedrooms and closets. The bathroom cabinets were empty, and the fixtures were dry as if they hadn't been used in a while. I strolled out to the balcony, but all the patio furniture was gone.

"Hello!" someone called from the living room.

I didn't recognize the voice, but hoped it was Percy. *I'll give that bitch a piece of my mind. How dare she leave without telling me!*

I walked back to the living room where a strange woman waited. She was tall with short auburn hair and pale-green eyes. Two black cats with yellowish-green eyes quickly ran to her feet. With backs hunched and tails erect, the creatures hissed at me the whole time.

"Are you thinking of buying this place?" the woman asked. "Some of the neighbors have been hearing strange noises. It's rumored to be haunted."

Buying this place? "Haunted?" I asked. I knew for sure that I was in the wrong condo. "I'm sorry," I said. "I must have the wrong place. I'm looking for 1419." I had to leave because that woman creeped me out. *What she's been smoking?*

"This is 1419," the woman said. "Back Pepper, back Sebastian." She kicked the cats under their bellies with her foot and tossed them back a few feet. The cats returned with backs hunched and hissed louder and more aggressively.

"I'm looking for Persephone Pickens," I said, thinking that I had the wrong place—even though I had been there a million times before—and perhaps she could help me find Percy. It seemed that I had trouble remembering things.

"Oh," the woman said. "She used to live here, but moved out some time ago."

"When?" I asked in disbelief. *This must be a joke,* I thought.

"I'm not sure," she said. "I moved in two years ago, and she moved out a few months later. I think. You might want to check with the management office downstairs. They might be able to give you a forwarding address."

You've been here two years and don't know when she moved out? I started to ask, but decided to leave well enough alone. "Thank you," I said, then high-tailed it to the elevators.

I didn't know what to think. Was Percy trying to avoid me because I was sick and the only way to free herself of me was to run away? I decided it was a waste of time to check with the management office. With a stack of work with my name on it, I decided to go on to the office and think about Percy later.

Besides, that woman didn't seem to have all her marbles anyway. *Why should I believe her?*

***

Twelve-fifteen, and I had finally arrived at the office. A crowd of people gathered around outside the building, as I drove into the parking deck. *I wonder what's going on?* Flashing orange and white lights glared in my rearview mirror, almost blinding me as I drove into the parking deck. I found a spot on the second level, which was the lobby level. *Lucky me. I could stop by Chap's before going upstairs.* I heard sirens—awfully loud sirens I might add—as I crossed the bridge from the parking deck to the building. Next thing, an ambulance rushed away, veering in and out of Buckhead's lunchtime traffic.

Ooo, I hope everything is all right. I started to worry and knew for sure that I needed to get upstairs—well, after getting a cup of Chap's coffee and a blueberry muffin.

Hundreds of people flooded the lobby—some sobbed, while others shook their heads in disbelief. The lights were out at Chap's as I passed by. I took a few more steps and the silver security bars were also drawn. A few of the workers were still inside, so I assumed they hadn't fully prepared for the lunchtime crowd. *I'll stop back a little later. Everybody is out here because Chap's isn't open for lunch yet.* I assumed the commotion from whatever happened prevented Chap's from preparing for lunch. I was indeed highly pissed—and I mean highly, highly pissed—at whomever or whatever prevented me from getting my coffee and muffin.

"That's a damn shame," I heard a woman say on her way to the elevators.

"It sure is," another woman agreed; she held her head low as tears fell from her eyes.

The elevators were crowded, but something was strange; everyone was quiet. I thought nothing of it. I had just too much going on in my life to figure out why nobody was talking.

"Hey, Demeter." It was Marcus walking with a young lady dressed in a black-and-white houndstooth suit. She was average height with the most beautiful, smooth deep-dark bronze complexion. I hate to admit it, but she looked like a young female version of Marcus with tapered black hair. "I want you to meet my daughter."

"Daughter?" I asked. My mouth dropped to the floor.

Marcus wore a brown plaid jacket, beige turtleneck, brown slacks and brown wing-tip shoes. *He probably wants to look nice for his daughter.* I hate to admit it, but Marcus was looking mighty fine; not just any fine, fancy fine—p-f-i-n-e—pfine.

"Nice to meet you, Ms. Pickens." She extended her hand and planted a very firm handshake. "I've heard so much about you."

"I'm looking forward to working with you," I said.

I headed for what I thought was my cubicle, but Marcus' name was displayed in big, bold, black letters—*Marcus Williams, Director.*

What the fuck is going on here? I wondered.

I looked behind me and saw what used to be Trevor's cubicle. "What's this?" I asked. Trevor's cubicle was completely empty.

"That's what I need to talk to you about, Demeter," Marcus said.

"Wait here," he told his daughter. "I have business to discuss with Ms. Pickens in her office. We'll be back in a few minutes."

So, that's why Marcus is speaking more formal. His daughter is here, I thought. Then, it struck me. *Whoa! Office? When did I get an office?*

"After you," Marcus said, motioning with his hand for me to lead the way.

"No, after you," I teased. "I believe in reverse chivalry."

We both laughed. In all honesty, I didn't know that I had an office or where it was. I let him lead the way. *Is this another dream? If it is, I don't want to wake up!*

Marcus led me to Daniel Batchelor's old office, but the nameplate was different:

Demeter Pickens
Vice President/New Product Development

All of my personal effects were there; my blue technical references lined the mahogany bookshelves; my crystal clock with the gold face—the one Percy gave me for my birthday a few years ago—sat on my desk; and Fern, who was only a small houseplant the day before, had grown into a small tree. *This can't be real.*

Marcus closed the door behind us and made himself at home in one of the black leather swivel chairs facing me. I went ahead and signed on to my computer, while he called down to Personnel.

"Hey," Marcus said to the person on the other end of the phone. "Glad I caught you. Yeah, it is a shame what happened. I'm going down to the hospital later on to check up on him. Uh, uh … uh, uh … Could you bring Trevor's file up? Uh, uh, Demeter is right here. All right, see you in a little bit."

I finally got into my e-mail and the dates were strange—January 15, 2002. *We're still testing the Year 2000 date software,* I reasoned. *Where did someone get a 2002 calendar?* I asked myself when I saw a 2002 Dilbert daily calendar on my desk turned to Wednesday, January 16, 2002. Again, I reasoned that we were getting in the mood to test Year 2000 dates, so I dismissed it.

My chest began to tighten and I coughed uncontrollably. That's what I get for sleeping in the tub … and taking three blue pills instead of one.

"Are you all right?" Marcus asked, then pulled a tissue from the golden receptacle on my desk.

"I'll be fine," I said between coughs.

A strange young woman wearing a red pantsuit tapped on the glass outside my office. Marcus motioned for her to come in. She presented him with the file. "Hey, Demeter. Love that suit," she said before leaving.

Do I know her? I asked myself. If I was Vice President, what was Daniel?

My inquiring mind needed to know. "By the way, Marcus. Where's Daniel Batchelor?"

"You're too funny, Demeter," Marcus said. "No one has seen or heard from him or Lou in about two years?"

I knew I was in a dream because I was in that very office talking to Daniel the day before. Or, was it the medicine? *Maybe the blue ones affect my ability to concentrate too.* "Two years?" I asked. "They should call somebody and at least say hello."

"Would you call somebody and say hello if you were caught in the stairwell giving your boss a blow job?"

So, someone saw them. I wonder who? What if it was me? I had to find out. "It's been a while and so much has been on my mind. Refresh my memory of what happened."

"That li'l fellow in the mailroom caught them and started spreading rumors. Some of the Board members got whiff of the rumors and confronted old Danny boy. They threatened to fire his ass, so he just up and quit. Lou up and quit, too, because they were about to fire her ass too. The only reason she got that job was because she was screwing old Danny boy. Till this day, nobody has heard from either one of them."

That was a good enough explanation for me. I didn't need to know more. Besides, they were dumb for airing their dirty laundry in public, especially with all the hotels along Peachtree Road. Anyway, all I cared about was being Vice President, even if it was an illusion. So much supposedly took place in the office; I didn't know if it was all real or imagined, but I didn't care. Those pills clouded my mind and gave me a "don't care" attitude. That's the way Percy described drinking hard liquor. "It makes you feel like you don't care about anything. The house could be on fire and you're burning in it, but you just won't give a shit," she always said.

"Your copy of Trevor's short-term disability papers are in that manila envelope in your inbox," Marcus said. "I also need for you to sign off on his long-term disability papers."

"Long-term disability?" I asked, then opened the envelope in my inbox.

"It needs a vice president's approval for it to go through. If you don't approve it, then he can sue us. If you ask me, I don't want us getting hit with a lawsuit."

"Lawsuit?" I asked. *What the hell is going on here?* "How you figure that?"

Marcus scooted closer. "Usually, most people only get sixty percent of their salary when they go on long-term disability. Right?"

"Right," I agreed.

"But Trevor got one of those lawyers you see on TV who specializes in accidents and workman's compensation claims. His lawyer is trying to get him one hundred percent of his salary. They're trying to prove that it was our fault he's injured."

"How do they figure that?" I asked.

"Because we supposedly created a hazardous, unsafe office environment."

"What?" I was appalled. That was absurd; the office was cleaner and more organized than a hospital nursery.

"He's not satisfied just being here only two days a week and working from home three days. Oh, and he went to one of those chiropractic-type doctors. His doctor says he's getting to the point where he won't be able to even work part-time. If you ask me, I think he's faking."

"What's supposed to be wrong with him?" I never thought I would be concerned for for Trevor. Sure, I didn't like him, but I didn't wish him ill either

"Some boxes supposedly fell on his back, so now he can't sit down for eight hours and work."

"And when did all this supposedly happen?" I asked.

"About three weeks ago."

"Three weeks ago?" I was shocked.

"Yep," Marcus said. "And he's walking with a cane and wearing a neck brace and wrist braces like he's really hurt."

Trevor's belongings were at his cubicle the day before. Not only that, he looked fine—well, you know, fine as in okay—to me the day before. He sure wasn't walking with a cane. And he sure wasn't wearing any braces. Did I miss something?

"Wrist braces?" I asked.

"Yep. Oh, and get this, when he tried to get up from under the pile by bracing himself against the door, more boxes fell on his arms. Now he claims he has carpal-tunnel syndrome." A look of disbelief crossed his face. "So, he has a cracked spine, crooked neck and carpal-tunnel syndrome. That's what's wrong with him."

I leaned closer to him and crossed my arms. "Yeah," I said, sarcastically. "No way!" I was surprised—kind of anyway.

"Way! Somebody put about twenty boxes of printer paper on the top shelves. I don't know why, but somebody did. The rumor mill has it that he put them there himself just so they could fall on him and he could collect worker's comp. Whether that's true or not, I can't say. But I can say that sooner or later, things come to light."

"That's so sad!" I said. "Trying to get over. Is Legal involved yet?" I asked.

"Yep," Marcus said. "Looking into it as we speak."

I had pushed Trevor's foolishness aside for a moment and was curious about that young woman who delivered the paperwork. "Is she one of D'Angela's new people?" I asked.

"I know, I do it too," Marcus said.

"Do what?" I asked.

"You know, call D'Angela's name. She's been gone almost a year, and I still find myself calling her name."

"I wonder how D'Angela is doing?" I asked, trying to get information from Marcus. I hadn't a clue that she was gone or why. Well, I knew why; it was the medicine. Those pills clouded my mind sometimes. Frankly, I didn't care for that bitch D'Angela anyway. It was a relief knowing she was gone, even if it was a dream.

"She's still in rehab the last I heard. Crack is a hard substance to break free of."

"Crack is hard ...?" I asked, still fishing for answers.

"Yes ma'am, it must have been a hard habit to break. She couldn't control herself enough not to smoke it at work."

"What a shame." I said, still fishing for answers.

"Common sense should have told her not to smoke dope in the ladies' room. She should have known better. But crack takes away a person's sense of reasoning."

I thought of the time when she performed that ritual in the bathroom, the same one that Percy did every morning. *Surely, that couldn't have been crack.* "Who caught her again. I don't remember."

"The cleaning lady reported her to security, and security called the police."

Sharp pains like pins stabbed my left side, as I coughed hard and strong. I was shocked beyond belief hearing news about D'Angela. *I'm not liking this dream too much.* I tried to pinch my arm to awaken from the nightmare to no avail.

"Are you all right?" Marcus gave me a strange look.

"I'll go downstairs to Chap's in a minute and get something for this cough," I said.

"You didn't hear?" Marcus asked.

"Hear what?" I asked. I had heard enough bad news for one day and couldn't stomach anymore bad news.

He put his head down as if to think of the right words. "Mr. Chap had a heart attack about a half-hour before you came in today."

My heart sank. "What!"

"He was sitting down reading the newspaper when he collapsed on the floor. They took him to Piedmont Hospital down the road. A few of us are sending flowers and a card to him later today. Oh, almost forgot. " Marcus gave me a get well card—which was as big as a book—to sign. I added my Joan Hancock—

Get well soon. I miss you.

Demeter

"All right, Marcus." I signed Trevor's disability papers, stuffed them in the envelope and gave them back to Marcus along with the card.

"I'll send my daughter over about two o'clock tomorrow, if that's okay with you," he said then stood up.

"Fine," I said. "Why can't we do it today?"

"All the girls are in the auditorium for a leadership session today. They let them out for a lunch break until one-thirty. It's over at about four or four-thirty.

If their parent is still at work, they're welcome to stay and watch them work."
He headed for the door, anxious to join his daughter in the hallway.

"Oh," I said.

"Catch you later," Marcus said, closed the door behind him, then joined his daughter.

My chest tightened more and more. I inhaled tiny puffs of air as breathing became almost unbearable.

"Psst," someone whispered, but no one was around and the door was closed. "Psst, Demeter. It's me, Fern."

"Fern?" I asked.

"Yeah, it's me," Fern said. "You went lookin' fo' yo' sistah today, heh?"

"Yes," I said, but wasn't sure how to answer. *How did Fern know?*

"Well, she done skipped the country," Fern said.

That was absurd. Why would Percy leave the country? But look who was talking—a plant. "How do you know that, Fern?"

"I knows ever'thang," Fern said.

"Why?" I asked. I was pissed at all I had heard that day, on top of that, I had the worse case of indigestion and my chest had begun to burn.

"She was in the black-market pharmaceutical trade. She had owed some folk some money, she ain't paid them folk they money, and they came lookin' fo' her. She done skipped the country.

"You think she was at yo' house 'cause you was sick and she had wanted to help you. She was hidin' out at yo' place so them folk wouldn't find her."

"Oh, Fern," I said in disbelief. My chest ached to the point that I could barely speak or move a muscle. *Could I be having a heart attack too?*

"You don't believe me, but what was them li'l white rocks she had left at yo' house?"

"Fern, those were crystals. She did this meditation ritual every morning."

"Chil', I don't know where you done come from. Them wasn't no crystals, thems was crack cocaine rocks. The pipe is what she had smoked it from."

"Oh, yeah," I said, and didn't know why I was arguing with a plant of all things. "Well, if it wasn't a ritual, what did she use the vanilla and cotton swabs for?"

"Chil', crackheads… "

"Don't call my sister a crackhead." I was upset that a plant would call her that, even if it was a dream.

"They dip the swabs in pure vanilla 'cause it got al'hol in it. When they light the swab, the al'hol make the flame hotter so they can get a mo' better, mo' quicker high."

"Look Fern," I was upset, my chest hurt more and more.

"That's why she was so skinny," Fern said.

Come to think of it, Percy was thinner than usual when she moved back from New York. I assumed it was because she watched her diet more carefully. Before she moved to New York, Percy was what men called fine. Back in the '70's, men whistled and sang the Commodores' "Brick House" as Percy walked down the street. Percy was a bit emaciated lately, and she had the audacity to call me skinny. What nerve! Not only that, her personality had changed. Before moving to New York, Percy was so feminine and demure. Lately, she had been abrasive and could out-cuss and out-drink the rattiest sailor. I assumed that rude New York mannerisms had rubbed off on her.

"It ain't her fault," Fern said.

"How you figure that?" I asked.

"She had foundt out what y'all daddy had done to y'all. She knew it was her turn to go first, and she couldn't take it. She thought that if she defiled herself 'nough, they wouldn't come get her. But they came got her anyhow."

"What?" Fern wasn't making sense. But, I was in a bizarre dream talking to a bizarre plant. What did I expect?

"I got to talk fast 'cause my time almost out too. I gots to go back from where I came from. When he go, I gots to go. He had no bid'ness uprooting me from my home and bringing me here. But I'm here. At least I got a chance to know you, and I'm glad fo' that."

"Well, I'm glad I know you, too, Fern," I said. Fern was babbling again, so I didn't ask about the other stuff. Perhaps I should have.

"Back in '58, y'all daddy had likeded this girl name Pearl-Elizabeth Youngblood," Fern said.

Fern caught my attention. I never cared for that woman, but never knew why. "Go on," I said, not questioning why or how Fern knew of that woman.

Marcus knocked on my door, breaking my almost hypnotic spell with Fern. "Talking to your plant again, huh?" he asked. "That why it's grown so much. Anyway, we're running out to the mall for lunch. Want me to bring you something back?"

"No, I'll get something later," I said. Fern's words were interesting, so I didn't want to be distracted by lunch or anything else. "Thanks."

On that note, Marcus closed the door behind him then left with his daughter.

"Well, they had got engaged, but Pearl-Elizabeth had likeded somebody else."

"Who?" I asked.

"Let me finish my story," Fern said. "Well, Pearl-Elizabeth was friends with Ernie. Her and Ernie used to go ever'where together: to the movies, play pool, drink beer, you name it. She even took Ernie to her grandmomma's house for Sunday dinner. All the while she was seeing yo' daddy."

"So, she was two-timing Daddy?" I asked.

"No," Fern said.

"But if she was dating Ernie and my daddy…"

"Now, I didn't say she was dating Ernie. She and Ernie was friends," Fern said.

"But," I said, but Fern cut me off.

"Pearl-Elizabeth started having these feelings fo' Ernie, feelings she ain't knowed how to 'plain. She ain't even knowed that she could have feelings fo' somebody like Ernie."

"Why not?" I asked. "What was wrong with Ernie?"

"Well, if you let me finish," Fern said with frustration. "Ernie's name was Ernestine."

"Ernestine? That's a woman's name. So his name was Ernestine? What kind of parents named their boy Ernestine? Why not Ernest?"

"Did I say somethin' 'bout a boy?"

It clicked. "Ernie was a woman?"

"Yep. Pearl-Elizabeth had done run off to Atlanta to be with Ernie. Ernie was a pharmacist and was startin' a bid'ness in Atlanta wit' one o' her uncles."

"What?" I was surprised. "What happened to Ernestine? Did my daddy break them up this time?"

"No. They done broke up long befo' yo' daddy and her had got back together. Honey, Pearl-Elizabeth and Ernestine was together fo' a real long time, until her oldest …"

"Her oldest what?" I asked.

"Oh nothin'," Fern said.

"What?" I asked.

"Oh nothin'," Fern said. "That ain't 'portant no way."

"Well, why did you mention it?" I asked. "Tell me … please."

"Honey, that's a 'hole 'nother story. If you really want to find out what had done happened between them two, you gots to read the next book."

"All right, Fern," I said.

"Anyhow, when yo' daddy had foundt out, he went to see a old man name Bot who lived in the woods of Morgan City, Luz'ana to get Pearl-Elizabeth to come back to him."

"Did she?" I asked. "Percy looks a lot like Pearl-Elizabeth. Did my daddy marry one of her sisters or cousins?"

"Boy, boy," Fern said in frustration. "Do you know why you got two ears and one mouth?"

"Why?" I asked. I knew Fern way pulling my leg all along.

"So you could listen twice as much as you talk! Now let me finish my story. I ain't got much time."

"All right, Fern," I said. "Don't get so huffy."

"Well, Bot had told yo' daddy to get three things that belong to Pearl-Elizabeth. All he had was a long strand of hair that had got caught up in one o' his jackets, the engagement ring, and somethin' else, I can't 'member. Anyway, he told yo' daddy to come back in a week wearing a tuxedo with a ring, ready to get married. Then, his bride would be waitin' fo' him. Like a fool, yo' daddy told yo' Grandpa 'bout it. You see, yo' Grandpa always thought Pearl-Elizabeth was too wild fo' yo' daddy, so he sho' ain't want him gettin' Bot to get her back."

"Too wild?" I asked.

"Yes, too wild," Fern said. "Pearl-Elizabeth had a child out of wedlock back in '45. Nowadays, that ain't nothin', but back then havin' a child out of wedlock was downright scandalous. On top o' that, Pearl-Elizabeth used to go out drinkin' and smokin' and hangin' out in barrooms all night long. She could cuss up a storm and got in many a fights. That ain't nothin' today, but back then ..."

"She acted the way Percy acts now," I said.

"They is a reason why she act like Pearl-Elizabeth, if you let me finish my story!"

"Don't get so huffy," I told Fern.

"And, yo' daddy wasn't no saint neither. He was what people today call a pimp daddy, mack daddy and was into dope and ever'thing else under the sun.

"Anyway, yo' daddy went back to Morgan City in a week. Yo' Grandpa went wit' him against his better judgement.

"It was a full moon in the middle of the woods. Bot came out wearing a long white robe. Behind him was the bride, with a long white veil over her face. They stopped under a big oak tree. It was real dark and creepy, 'specially with all them crickets churping, bull frogs croakin' and fireflies flyin' all o'er the place.

"Anyway, Bot read the vows and all that good stuff, but he never said her name. Yo' daddy ain't even pay no mind. But they had a catch: before yo' daddy said 'I do,' Bot made him promise the souls of the daughters conceived by the union—the older one to his brother and the other one to him. Then, he made yo' daddy promise the souls of his sons to take the place of him and his brother. Well, they wasn't really brothers, they was just brother souls. But, brothers souls is too complicated to 'plain, so let's just call 'em brothers."

"Oh come on now," I said. The story was so farfetched. I was thoroughly entertained.

"You think I'm lying. You need to ask yo' daddy," Fern said. "Bot and his brother was dark Ascended Masters a long, long time ago

"Dark Ascended Master? What's that?" I asked.

"Now how can I put this fo' you to understand? A Ascended Master is the spirit of a person who once was human. They reincarnate over and over again until they earn the right to leave the Earthly plane. Instead of going on to a higher level, they keep hangin' 'round the Earthly plane and used they powers fo' worldly pleasures. Bot used to take human form to lay up with women. After he had got him some, he disappeared. His brother, on the other hand, used his powers to take human form to conquer kingdoms and have folk bow down to him.

"That mess went of fo' 'bout a thousand Earth years, maybe mo'. They was not only on Earth, but they went to other worlds too, worlds higher in vibration than Earth, but was just as evil as Earth. They did that one time too many when they messed with a true man of God, one who honor His ways. You can't go messin' wit' God folk and get 'way wit' it.

"They learned the errors of they ways and wanted to repent to God. God had cast them back down to hell, this thing called Earth, in a hellified prison fo' one thousand Earth years. They punishment was to use they powers to do petty favors fo' mankind on Earth, like love spells and other junk like that. To them Earth was just a playground. They was Ascended Masters and thought they punishment was beneath them. But, they punishment was 'nough fo' them to change and see the errors of they ways."

"Wait," I said. "You're talking about hell and being sent back to Earth and all. So, what you're saying is that they died and went to heaven, but decided to visit Earth?"

"No, no, no," Fern said in frustration. "You been on Earth so long that you 'came ig'nant like the rest o' 'em."

"Wait, who are you calling ignorant!" I said. Fern was getting a bit out of line.

"No, no, no," Fern said, apologetically. "Ig'nant in terms of heaven and hell. They is mo' to it than that. Earth is one of the hell planes. People think if you is good, you go to heaven; and if you is bad, you go to hell. That's part of the story, but it ain't that simple. To move out of the Earth plane, you got to learn certain truths of the spirit. Good people and bad people can learn the truth, then move on to a higher plane. That's what Bot and his brother had did."

"What?" I asked. That went against everything I had been taught about religion.

"Fo' 'xample, in Georgia, chil'ren gots to pass the high school graduation test to get they diploma, right?"

"Yes," I said. What else could I say to a plant that knew everything?

"Well, would you agree that good chil'ren and bad chil'ren can pass the test?"

"Yes," I said.

"Would you agree that good chil'ren and bad chil'ren can fail the test?"

"Yes," I said.

"Same thing with the spirit and movin' on. It's not how good you is o' bad you is, it's whether you learn what you need in order to move on."

"That makes sense," I said. Fern's tale sounded plausible.

"Now, to move out o' the hell planes, like Earth, that's a whole 'nother story."

"How?" I asked.

"Take high school again fo' 'xample. To get a scholarship, you gots to have certain credentials, right?"

"Yes," I said.

"Thems the chil'ren who made sure they did the right thing to get that scholarship. Not just anybody could get a scholarship. Them chil'ren was disciplined and did what they had to do to get it, right? But, if they mess up, they could lose they scholarship. It's the same thang with movin' out of Earth and hell planes. The folk who disciplined on the word of the Lord and don't make 'xcuses as to why they don't obey His word, move on up to something better. When you on a high spirt'al level, you obey the word 'cause you want to. Them things o' the world don't matter no mo'."

"All right, Fern," I said. "What does any of this have to do with this Bot person, my daddy, Percy or me?"

"Well, being in prison made them repent fo' they sins. The ways of the world been knocked out 'o 'em. They learned God's way fo' doin' things. God look inside a man's heart to know if he's fo' real or not. They goin' on to somethin' higher.

"Bot was cast in the body of a old man, never to touch a woman in one thousand years. His brother was cast in the body of a decrepit old man, left broke and penniless to live among the poorest of the poor for one thousand years.

"Wait, they was 'nother brother I forgot to tell you about. He don't matter though,'cause he ain't movin' on. He stuck on Earth fo' 'nother thousand years 'cause he ain't learnt his lesson. He gone be here 'til God knock the world out of 'im."

"Why hasn't he learned his lesson?" I asked.

"Well, I guess because out 'o all the brothers, he the only one who was stuck in the body of a young man."

"That doesn't seem like punishment to me," I said.

"But, he was older and viewed as wiser back in the day. He was a wizard that ever'body came to fo' healing. Now, people don't give 'im the time o' day. He can't stand that. But he love him some women though.

"Anyway, them other two time is about up and they is goin' on to a higher level. Nothin' evil can even make it where they gone live 'cause they world is so high up on the spiritual plane—almost as high as God himself. Folk there don't get sick or old and they live fo'ever. Don't nobody have to worry 'bout goin' hungry, 'cause all they food grow on trees or in fields. Don't nobody worry 'bout folk cheatin' on 'em, 'cause from birth, ever'body got they own mate made just fo' 'em. They ain't got no wars or famines and other plagues that make folk mis'ble on Earth. Envy and jealousy don't exist 'cause ever'body in they right place doin' what they was born to do. Don't nobody beg, steal or borrow 'cause ever'body blessed with God's best."

"Come on, Fern," I said. "That place sounds too good."

"Anyway, back to the weddin'," Fern said. "When yo' daddy done lifted the veil, he saw that it was kind of Pearl-Elizabeth."

"Kind of?" I asked.

"Yes," Fern said. "Just like Pearl-Elizabeth is kinda yo' momma."

My blood shot cold thinking that woman could be my mother.

"Kind of?" I needed clarification. "Either she is my mother or she isn't."

"Yo' Grandpa named the bride Constance 'cause he liked the name. You see, Constance was a clone of Pearl-Elizabeth that Bot pulled down from another world. It was a soul confused between worlds, almost like Bot and his brother. It needed direction befo' movin' on to somethin' higher.

"Yo' daddy got the clone body of Pearl-Elizabeth, but the soul of a free spirit. She didn't belong here, but was promised to yo' daddy fo' a short time. Again, yo' daddy agreed to them terms 'cause he ain't think nothin' of it.

"Yo' daddy was always a slickster back in the day. But he ain't knowed that when it come to matters of the spirit, they ain't no being slick. Yo' Grandpa tried to warn him 'bout foolin' round with what he ain't understand, but he ain't listen. So when it came time fo' yo' momma to leave, Karma came got her and yo' two brothers and took them to where they belong."

"Karma?" I asked. "Like in reaping and sowing?"

"Yes, but Karmas is spirits that always was, always is, and always will be. Yo' daddy used to take you and Percy by two o' the Karma spirits. Y'all used to spend a lot of time wit' them. They been preparin' y'all fo' y'all journey. That was a long time ago, but that wisdom is still buried in you and gone come out at the right time. The Karmas been wit' you all yo' life, but you just ain't know it."

"Yeah right," I told Fern. Now that was just too much. The only people my father took us to see were Great-Gran and Great-Aunt Ruby. People used to say they were witches, and I didn't believe that story.

"I know you don't believe me," Fern said. "Here you is, all this time thinkin' yo' momma done run off wit' yo' brothers 'cause she ain't love you. But them three was promised to yo' daddy fo' a short time, now they back in another world where they belong."

"Come on, now." That story was a bit fantastic, but entertaining nonetheless.

"And 'nother thing," Fern said. "About what had happened to yo' friend Tish."

"What?" I asked. *What does Fern know about Tish?*

"She ain't commit no suicide," he said. "Percy lied when she said Tish daddy had found a note. They was no note. Karma came to get her and they was nothin' nobody could do. Why you think her daddy was by her house that time of mornin'? And why you think Tish was so depressed? She had started havin' dreams too and foundt out what was goin' on. Percy knew."

"What?" I asked in disbelief.

"Yes, ma'am," he said. "Karma had came to get her. It was her time to go. Yo' daddy and her daddy was in the same secret fraternity."

"Secret?" I asked. I knew that Daddy and Dr. Dewey were part of the same organizations, but I wouldn't call them secret.

"Well, Tish daddy had went to see Bot too," he said.

"Why?" I asked. Curiosity got the best of me. "Is Mrs. Dewey a clone too? Is that how Dr. Dewey got her to marry him?"

"No," Fern said. "He wasn't interested in no love stuff. He wanted to be a big-time doctor.

"Back in the day, Tish daddy was the oldest of fifteen chil'ren. They was dirt po' and lived down in the Miss'ssippi swamps. He wasn't too bright, and peoples used to say that he was slow and could barely read. He had told folk that he had wanted to be a doctor, but the teachers and ever'body else laughed at him.

"Anyhow, one o' his aunts was a teacher in New Orleans and believed in him and was gone pay fo' his ed'cation. So, she had took him down to the Bayous in Morgan City to see Bot 'bout makin' him be smart 'nough to go to college—not just any college, but to Morehouse. Ever'body just laughed and laughed when he had went off to Morehouse and they said he wasn't gone make it. But he did.

"When he had went to Meharry, that's when they had stopped laughin'. Anyhow, that's when he had met yo' daddy, when he had went to Meharry Medical School. And, that's how yo' daddy had foundt out 'bout Bot.

"So, what does that have to do with Tish?" I asked.

" 'Cause," Fern said.

"Because what?" I asked. I hoped that Fern wasn't playing with me again. Because that time, it just wasn't funny. It was too painful to think of Tish.

"In order fo' him to get them smarts, he had to promise to let a lost soul from the black void come to Earth through his first born. It wasn't just any ol' lost soul, it was the soul of a friend he lost back in Sodom."

"Sodom?" I asked.

"Yeah, like in Sodom and Gomorrah," Fern said.

"Yeah, Fern," I said.

"You don't got to believe me," Fern said. "The two of them used to get into a lot of stuff back in the day. She was married, but he ain't even cared."

"So, what does that have to do with Tish?" I asked. Fern was beginning to annoy me.

"'Cause, that lost soul was Tish, only her name was Zoa back then. She and her husband and daughters was 'bout to leave the land of Sodom when he called to her. Then, she had looked back and had turnedt into a pillar of salt. He felt guilty and had blamed hisself."

"Who is this 'he' you're talking about?" I asked.

"Him … Marcellus," Fern said. "Chil', pay 'tention. Anyway, to make a long story short, Tish used to be Zoa back in the day and had got turnedt into a pillar of salt. Then, she was cast down in the black void and was born into the body of yo' friend, Tish. In other words, that hot, li'l thing called Cynthia Dewey in yo' dreams is the soul o' yo' friend Tish. That's why she seem so familiar to you." Fern said.

"No, that can't be," I said. "She doesn't look like Tish."

"No, she don't," Fern said. "In fact, she don't 'member nothin' 'bout being Tish. She shed her skin and paid fo' her sins, so all her memories of life on Earth is gone. And the reason she don't look like Tish is 'cause she went back to lookin' the way she did back in Sodom."

"So, if she can't remember anything, why is she using the name Cynthia Dewey?" I asked.

"Out o' 'spect fo' Marcellus," Fern said.

"What? Out of respect for Marcellus? That doesn't make any sense."

"Yeah it do," Fern said.

"How?" I asked.

"Don't nobody know this, but Dr. Dewey name used to be Charles Jackson. Bot ain't like that name and said it had sounded too po', so he made 'im change his name to Charles Dewey. Bot had said that the reason peoples thought he was dumb was 'cause his name ain't match the year, day, month or hour he was born."

"What?" I asked.

"Yeah, chil'. Life is like a recipe; ever'thing gots to be mixed up just so or the things you want to make won't come out right. Bot told 'im that Dewey had matched his birth time and would make him rich. Dewey is a rich man's name, so he made Dr. Dewey promise to name his first-born Cynthia."

"But Tish's name was Letitia," I reminded him.

"Yes, that's 'cause Dr. Dewey's wife was stubborn and named her Letitia. Now, if she woulda listened to her husband and named the girl Cynthia Letitia Dewey, then Tish woulda had a better life while she was here. You see, Cynthia is a power name ... a name fo' a wise woman. But Dr. Dewey ain't think nothin' of it and named that girl Letitia, which is a spoiled housewife's name.

"Anyway, Marcellus had brought her back to the Astral World after she had shed her skin. All she had 'membered was being in the black void. She had asked Marcellus how she had got out that hellhole and he told her that he used the body of a woman named Cynthia Dewey as a vessel to clear her soul. Since she was so grateful, she kept that name out of respect for her long-time friend, Marcellus."

"I'm confused," I said.

"Confused 'bout what?" Fern asked.

"How can Bot be Marcellus? How can he be on Earth and on the Astral World? Why can he remember everything? Or will he forget everything once he sheds his skin?"

"He is a Ascended Master and will remember ever'thing, so he can't shed his skin. A Master's job is to learn about life and guide other folk on they way. Right now, he half-way between worlds 'cause he being punished. When his time is up, his earthly body will die and then fade away a few days later like it was never even there.

"Oh," I said. "So, is anything going on between her and Marcellus?" I asked. I needed to know and put my suspicions to rest.

"Naw," Fern said. "Even back in the day, she had likeded women mo' than men. She had men other than her husband from time to time though. But her and Marcellus was just real good friends ... real good."

"What do you mean by *real good?*" I asked.

"They used to go pick up women together and had a good time," Fern said. "They had what young folk today call *ménage a trois.*"

"Fern," I said in embarrassment.

"You know you like it too," Fern said. "He made you that way."

"What ... Fern ..."

"That's right," Fern said. "Don't be 'shamed. Marcellus made you just the way he wanted you."

"Now Fern," I said. That couldn't be true because I made Marcellus. Or did I?

"Why you think you don't look like nobody in yo' fam'ly?" Fern asked.

"That's not true. I look like my daddy," I said.

"No you don't," Fern said. "Don't nobody in yo' fam'ly got no nappy hair."

"Fern," I said. He sure was flip at the mouth for a plant.

"And you the only one in the family who got that nice brown, mahogany skin," Fern said.

"Now that's not true, Percy…"

"Percy was black and beautiful like yo' momma," Fern said.

"So, you're saying that I'm not pretty?" I asked. I always felt insecure about my looks and always knew that Percy was prettier than me. I didn't need a plant to drudge that up in my face.

"Chil', you sho' 'nuff prettier than Percy … hands down. He made you that way."

"You keep saying he made me …"

"Check it out. Marcellus daddy was a travelin' merchant back in the day and sailed all o'er the world. One day, he had went to Greece, that's where he had met Marcellus momma, Hera. They got married and moved back to Egypt. You see, his daddy was Egyptian and his momma was Greek.

"When he got grown, Marcellus was a travelin' merchant like his daddy and went all o'er the world. No matter where he went, he had to have him some Egyptian women. Honey, let me tell you, Marcellus had likeded him some Egyptian women, ooo boy! So, he made you to be a Nubian goddess, a queen of the Nile.

"Honey, you his imaginary playmate. All the while you thought he was yo' imaginary playmate. He gave you that nice soft brown Egyptian skin; them big, dark Egyptian eyes; that long, kinky Egyptian hair; and that big, juicy Egyptian booty. Boy, boy, boy!"

"That's just too much." *Fern's story can't be true,* I reasoned.

"Just ask yo' daddy," Fern said.

Ask my daddy? Truthfully, ever since I separated from what's-his-name back in the '80's, Daddy stopped speaking to me. In his mind, I was an embarrassment to him. No daughter of the great Dr. George Pickens would be a divorced single mother making it on her own. Oh, it didn't matter that I had degrees from Spelman and Tulane. And, he overlooked the fact that I earned fifty-two thousand a year working as an engineer for South Central Bell back in the '80's. No, all he and my grandfather saw was a "struggling, single, female head of household," as they put it.

He really hurt me and I never quite forgave him until now. I knew for sure that my grandfather poisoned his mind against me, rubbing it in how my cousin—his precious Juanita—had married two big time doctors—her first husband, then my ex—and lived on the New Orleans Lakefront. Then, there was me, a woman who couldn't hold on to her husband. I was the victim, but they made me feel like it was all my fault.

Juanita was wrong; my ex was wrong. In truth, they would have been together whether I had pursued my master's degree or not. The only difference was that my education got me the life I deserved. With no education or husband, my life would have fared like Juanita's. In my eyes, I'm the lucky one.

One weekend back in '90, I attended an alumni function at Spelman. I ran into an old professor who was a manager with Georgia Power. Later that night, we had dinner and she interviewed me on the spot. I was looking to make a change at work, so I always kept my resume with me. When I got back to New Orleans, lo and behold, I was offered the job. Needless to say, I accepted; it was too good to pass up.

That was perfect timing; it was summer and the boys were out of school. I needed to get away from New Orleans; too many painful memories. Juanita and my ex had already married; she had given birth to their "supposedly" second child. Percy had already moved to New York years before. With Daddy at bay, no close friends or family ties, there was no reason to remain in New Orleans.

The company offered to pay my moving expenses, but I was determined to start a new life and leave the past behind. So, I sold all my furniture and any reminder of New Orleans. I packed what remained in my '89 Chevy and set off for Georgia with Keston and Kevin—never to return again.

***

You know something, Dr. Iverson, I hated my grandfather with a passion until ... well, until he cleared his soul on his deathbed. Come to think of it, I hated my cousin, Juanita, too, until I dreamed about her that day. Somehow—and I can't explain it, Dr. Iverson—my soul was cleared after I woke from the dream.

***

"Ain't you ever notice how you felt out of place, like you didn't belong? Like you was always different than other folk, but just ain't know how?" Fern asked.

"Well, maybe," I said. It was true. All through school, Percy and I didn't quite fit in, so we clung close to each other. We assumed—*there's that word "assume" again*—that people in our community and our so-called kinfolk didn't like our mother because she was darker than the proverbial "paper bag." Even as an adult, I was always different somehow, but never figured out how.

"Well, maybe nothing'," Fern said. "That's because you don't belong here on Earth. This ain't yo' world. You belong with Bot on yo' own world. Well, his name ain't really Bot, but folk starting calling him that 'cause he always kept all kinds o' fancy bottles 'round: li'l ones, big ones, you name it, he kept it."

"What happened to Bot?" I asked Fern.

"Honey, he right here in Atlanta. He somebody you know too."

"Who?" I asked sarcastically.

***

Okay, I was being playful, but you must admit that Fern was pulling my leg, Dr. Iverson.

***

"Well, I can't tell ya just yet. But I'll tell ya tomorrow."

"Whatever, Fern," I said.

"They takin' they brides wit' 'em real soon. They preparin' they worlds right now and can't wait to shed they skin."

"Shed their skin? I thought you said they don't... " My head began to spin as a faint buzz rang in my ears.

"Yes," Fern said. "They skin is they Earthly body and they prison. That's what hold 'em in bondage to the Earth plane. They been creatin' they own world and livin' in it, but they can't fully enjoy the fruits of that world 'til they shed they skin. Once they do that, then they can never return to Earth because they skin gone just evap'rate like steam. And honey, they don't never want to return to no Earth."

The room began to spin, top and bottom blended as one. An invisible force, like that of an elephant, weighed heavily on my chest, pinning me to the floor. I blinked once. Three white lights flashed before my eyes. I blinked twice...

Chapter 24.
No More Chances

My senses came into focus as I sat there, startled by my own reflection, brushing my hair across my shoulders. I viewed that strange, new world as a casual observer, scrying into that magical looking glass seeking answers to the problems of mankind. Even in my dreams, life seemed more exciting, grandeur on the other side. But as mirror images—reflections of reality—Marcellus and his world, too, amounted to nothing more than grand illusions.

I had awakened to a familiar place, one of splendor and beauty. That room represented the most glorious experience of all my dreams; the night Marcellus and I enjoyed each other on the beach, exploring every nook and cranny of each other's body, one enjoying the other as fully as two beings can explore and enjoy one another.

Just as I had remembered, three large pale-green candles on my right filled the room with hints of eucalyptus and spearmint. The walls and floors were chocolate marble. The vanity and sink were black porcelain with sparkling, gold faucets. Far behind me down a short, dark hallway a dimly lit fountain flowed down into a grand chocolate marble hot tub. French windows behind the tub gave clear view of the night sky—a large, white half moon with all its gray craters amidst scattered bright, twinkling stars.

"Come to bed," Marcellus said. Big, strong hands massaged my shoulders, as a big, hard stick caressed my spine, sending pulses through my body.

I saw his nude reflection looked ever so sinful, as I watched him rub that rock-hard cock up, down and around my neck over and over again. He slid his hot hands between my silky, black negligee, as it fell to the chair, exposing my splendor.

I stood up to face him, craving his manhood more than ever. He pulled me closer as I ran my fingers around his belly button, through his silky, black stomach hairs, sliding up his big, strong, masculine chest. He cringed in delight as I teased and tantalized his nipples, sucking one while pinching the other between my fingers.

Picking me up by the waist, Marcellus cushioned my bottom on the chocolate marble vanity as my feet dangled off the counter. He ran his hands up and down my back as we engaged in the hottest, juiciest French kiss; our tongues collided around in a frenzy, as we licked and sucked each other's lips.

Marcellus grabbed my hair, pulled my head back, and nibbled every nook and cranny of my neck, making my body sizzle to his beat. He licked my nipples, one-by-one, sending firecrackers to my clit. I craved him inside me as my nerves seared in pleasure.

He wrapped my legs around his waist and entered my slippery haven. Mercy! Marcellus slid in and out, around and around, and side to side. I held on tight, my arms secured around his neck, and enjoyed the bumpy ride. He was so caring and tender; his love flowed to my soul with every lustful stroke.

Marcellus, King of the Jungle, growled and roared as my loins crackled through the eve. I moaned deep and low from the gut, as he stroked deeper and deeper. Then he stopped, pulling his long, firm come-covered cock from inside me.

"What's wrong, Marc?" I asked. I grabbed his cock to ease him back inside. Oh, it was warm, hard, and sticky to the touch. Mercy!

Marcellus put his big, strong hands around my waist—oh, I loved it when he did that—and stood me up before him. He towered over me like a giant specimen of a man. I felt so weak and helpless as I ran my fingers through his chest hairs.

He turned the vanity chair sideways. "Bend over," he said, then motioned for me to climb on the chair.

I balanced on the chair seat, then stepped onto the countertop. One leg with knee bent remained on the countertop, while the other dangled over the side of the chair. Marcellus plunged his hot, throbbing manhood deep inside. Mercy!

In and out, and around and around he moved, sending balls of passion to the top of my head, down my arms and legs, to the soles of my feet. My palms began to sweat; my nipples stood at attention.

"Is it good to you?" he whispered in my ear between jungle-roaring moans.

"Yes! Yes!" I screamed. "It's good, Marcellus. Give it to me, give it to me."

And that he did ... he gave it to me long, hard and strong. Looking at Marcellus in the mirror sent chills to my face; squeezing his eyes closed, the circular motion of his hips, distorted facial expression, biting his lower lip—just knowing that my body pleasured him sent me further into a frenzy.

Marcellus' touches were unbearable to the point where I screamed and moaned loud enough for the whole universe to hear me. The more I screamed, the harder he pumped. The harder and deeper he pumped, the louder I screamed. Mercy!

A baby cried in the background, probably awakened by my moans of passion.

"Uh, uh!" Marcellus moaned. He tightened his face and grabbed my hips, locking himself inside me. The sea of life flooded my loins as he pulled away. One big white glop of come dangled from my womanhood, swaying back and forth before falling down on the vanity chair.

I always felt so safe and secure in Marcellus' arms; nothing or no one could harm me. Tish, Percy, Daddy, the stranger in the night, those little blue pills or nothing else mattered. In that moment in time, it was only Marcellus and the unearthly pleasure he bestowed upon me. That was my haven. Too bad it can't last forever. Or can it?

"What's wrong, Mommy?" Hera asked.

I was startled and quite embarrassed. It was Hera dressed in a long pink nightgown with little pink bows around the collar, holding a small brown teddy bear. *She's just a mirage,* I thought. *I shouldn't be embarrassed.* But I was; looking into her deep, dark eyes and sweet, innocent face brought a sense of shame to my soul.

"Go to bed, sweetie," Marcellus told her, as he put on a silky, blue robe. He quickly covered me with a silky, mauve robe and helped me down from the countertop.

I sat on the vanity chair.

"I heard Mommy screaming," Hera said. She looked to be about five years old, a bit older than in my last dream. "What's wrong with Mommy? Is she still shedding her skin, Daddy?"

Hera was frantic, jumping up and down in a tantrum in her concern for me. A tear rolled down her little cheeks, melting my heart. I reached for my little girl, but Marcellus whisked her away. All the while, the baby screamed louder and louder in the background. It needed comforting that only a mother could give.

"The baby," I said. "Where's the baby?"

"Mommy's okay, sweetie," he told Hera, then walked her toward the hallway, completely ignoring me. "Be right back." He winked at me.

"Is Mommy okay?" another child asked Marcellus. It was definitely the voice of a boy. "Is Mommy shedding her skin, Daddy?"

"Daddy said no," Hera told the boy.

"Awe," the boy whined. "When is Mommy coming home for good, Daddy? You said…"

"Shhh." Marcellus interrupted the boy. "Let's not disturb Mommy."

"But Daddy," the boy said.

"Let's go, Marcel," he said. Their voices grew fainter and fainter, so I knew they were headed to another room. The baby screamed at the top of its lungs, desperate for care.

I peered down the hallway to get a glimpse of the boy, but it was too dark to see much. He wore dark plaid pajamas and looked to be about three years old. His hair was thick, wavy and jet-black just like his father.

My loins were afire, and tiny energy pulses rang through me. *Am I pregnant again?* I wondered.

Finally, the baby stopped crying. *Thank goodness!* Except for the cascading fountain and the hot tub jets, the place had become quiet.

With Marcellus gone and the children calmed, I decided to venture to the hot tub and enjoy a long, hot soak. Fresh jasmine and lilac scents guided the way, teasing and taunting my nose.

All lights were off. "Oooo," I moaned. Sharp, cool pulses shot through every bone in my body as I neared the tub. Sure, marble can be cold, but the floor felt like a solid sheet of ice. Frigid wafts of air blew from some unseen vent high above, tossing my hair about and instantly chilling every cell in my body. Brrrr!

Crimson and deep violet glowed from the fountain wall. Frothy pink and blue tinted bubbles fizzed around the tub, inviting me into its midst. I shivered to say the least, especially with that silk bathrobe wrapped around me. I was almost too cold to move. Large goose bumps covered every square inch of my body.

I inched closer and closer to the tub. Eucalyptus scented steam rose high into the air, as warm vapors thawed my body. *What am I waiting for?* I asked myself. I removed the robe and eased into the hot, steamy bubbles. Soothing, warm energy flowed through me as I relaxed against the back wall. The French windows gave a clear view of the heavens above, clearer and more magnificent than I remembered.

I blinked once and slowly opened my eyes to a small meteor shower; occasional orange-tinted stars shot hither and thither through the cosmos—tiny needles weaving majestic beauty for my pleasure—bestowing the gift of art on my soul for a few fleeting moments before passing on to the great beyond. *Why can't this be real?* I wondered.

I sat back to admire the night sky, wiggling my toes under the warm fountain. Gushes of water massaged my feet, sending vibrating pulses through me. I gently closed my eyes; sounds of cascading waterfalls and turbulent water that circled around and around the tub lulled me to sleep.

***

"I still don't understand why she can't stay right now," Marcellus yelled, waking me from a peaceful sleep. "That just doesn't make any sense!"

An argument ensued in another room between Marcellus and at least two other people. Their voices suddenly came to a hushed whisper, so I couldn't make out if they were men or women. Curiosity got the best of me; I just had to find out what was going on. What a mistake.

Reluctantly—and very reluctantly—I emerged from that hot, relaxing whirlpool. The arguing continued, but the voices blended into one mass of confusion. I patted myself from head to toe with the mauve towel beside the tub. Oh, that towel was so soft and fluffy that it practically drank the water from my skin. It smelled sweet, too, like fresh rose petals. *Even the towels are better in this world,* I thought.

I put on my silk robe and headed down the hallway to find out what was going on. The bedroom was cold and dark, and the bed looked as though it hadn't been touched all night. The draperies were drawn, as moonbeams cast shadows of the French windows along the walls.

The hall was dark, but a bit warmer, as I followed the banister to the stairway. *It's just as I remembered,* I thought. Looking at my portrait gave me a sense of pride. Sure, it wasn't real, but I deserved to shine and gloat nonetheless.

Slowly, one-by-one, I eased down each step, holding tightly to the guardrail. The carpet was so soft and cushiony between my toes. Light from the dining room to my left brightened the otherwise dark foyer, making it easier for me to find my way.

"I just don't understand why she can't stay," Marcellus said again. A level of frustration filled his voice, as if he were trying to convince someone or something to see things his way.

"It's not her time," a woman said. Something was familiar about her voice; it was deep and raspy, yet smooth and sultry like that of a jazz singer.

"But she served her time in limbo," Marcellus continued. "I served my time in the depths of hell. She didn't serve time like I served time, but she served her time. Why can't she be free?"

"Right," a man said in a stern tone. I didn't recognize his voice. Determined to find out what the fuss was about, I hastened my pace to the parlor. "You served *your* time, and *you* can be set free. She still has more time to serve."

"But that's a long time," Marcellus said, almost pleading. "You know I can't go back to hell to be with her once I cast my skin aside. She won't be able to come here anymore without me there. How much longer must she remain in hell? How much longer will it be before she sheds her skin?"

"Until the one hundred year agreement has been fulfilled," the man said.

"Even a short time in hell is punishment enough," Marcellus said. "That's too long."

"What's time anyway?" the woman asked. "That's a long time in prison, but time is nothing here. She'll be here in a blink of an eye."

"Didi!" Marcellus jumped off the sectional when he saw me standing at the door.

The woman turned to face me and to my surprise it was …

"Great-Aunt Ruby!" I said. "What are you doing here?"

Greant-Aunt Ruby didn't answer for she, too, was nothing more than a mirage. She sat there on the corner of the sectional, staring at me without as much as blinking an eye.

Marcellus made eye contact with the stranger almost as if to say, "Please don't look at her."

Slowly, the man stood up and turned to face me. From afar, his skin looked deep and dark like Mississippi mud. He wasn't very tall—perhaps five-five or five-six with a stocky build. His ears were small with pointed tips. As he neared me—closer and closer—his eyes sparkled silvery-green in the darkness like that of a cat's.

"Didi!" Marcellus shouted. Great-Aunt Ruby held Marcellus' arm as he tried to run to me.

Only two feet before me, the strange man held out his hand for me. His skin was deeply cracked as a reptile's. His eyes were set deep within his head, surrounded by several round layers of flesh; the irises were light brown and glassy, completely filling the sockets. The pupils were but … wait …his eyes had no pupils. I stood there—paralyzed—unable to move as that mysterious stranger came within inches of me. He exuded a feeling of peace that touched my soul as I peered deep into his bright, catty eyes …

***

Entrenched in blackness, thunderous roars echoed all around me. I fell from great heights—falling faster and faster, spinning out of control. Roars grew louder and louder. I spun faster and faster unable to free myself from that horrid merry-go-round. Hurling down a bottomless pit, unable to scream—couldn't break free—I was but a spiraling soul on a journey to nowhere.

Out of the darkness, small dark whirlwinds danced all around me; disembodied souls trapped in limbo—belonging to no one. I felt their pain, we struggled as one, in desperate search of peace and serenity in that cold, dark, empty prison. Roars—wails for help to universal powers—pleas to God— begging forgiveness and mercy for past transgressions unknown.

"Didi," someone called deep within the void—perhaps another trapped soul struggling to free itself. The voice was indistinguishable; garbled—male or female—I couldn't tell which. "Didi," it called again.

***

I was jolted in my seat as air quickly filled my lungs. "What?"

"Oh," Marcus said with smile. "I didn't mean to startled you. Looks like your mind wondered a million miles away."

"Yeah, right." We both laughed. Marcus didn't know how right he was; my mind had wondered a million miles away. So much so, that my vision was blurred and doubled. Sounds of vacuum cleaners echoed down the halls, evidence that the cleaning crew was near—and the cleaning crew always started their rounds at five-thirty.

"Are you okay?" Marcus asked.

"Yes, Marcus." Except for the computer monitor, my office was dim. I turned to face the window. I was surprised to see that the mini blinds were open and the sky was dark. All I could see were lights from nearby office buildings and taillights from Georgia 400 traffic below.

A deep sense of panic overtook me. The last thing I remembered was sitting down at my desk talking to Fern. That was at about one o'clock. I looked at my digital desk clock. "Six-thirty!" I said. "No way!"

"Way. Time flies when you're busy," Marcus said. "Give me about five minutes. I have a few things to wrap up before we leave."

"Where's your daughter?" I asked before he raced out of my office. "Did she enjoy today?"

"Oh, my ex-wife works down the street. She went home with her today because she knew I wanted to attend the services tonight."

"She went home with your ex-wife?" I asked. That had to be a dream because Marcus talked about his wife just too, too much. Come to think of it, he didn't mention her one time that day. *This must be a dream.*

"Yeah, so," he said. "My ex and I still communicate."

"How long have you been separated again?" I asked, fishing for answers.

"We've divorced over eighteen months now," he said.

"Oh," was all I could say. I wanted to know why they divorced, but I didn't want to appear to be too nosy.

"Oh, but my daughter really enjoyed it a lot. She said she had a really good time. Be back in a few."

Marcus practically ran back to his cubicle. *He must have something special planned,* I thought. He wore a black suit and white shirt, quite a change from what he wore earlier.

I glanced at the digital clock display on my computer screen—*6:32.* I opened my e-mail window and the dates were off—*Friday, January 18, 2002. Still testing Year 2000 dates,* I thought. *I'll be glad when Year 2000 testing is over.*

I grabbed my purse from the bottom desk drawer and noticed that I was wearing the little black dress I had bought a few days ago from Lenox Mall, black stockings and black pumps. *When, how and why did I change clothes?* Feeling nervous and queasy, I scrambled through my purse for my medicine bottle and quickly tossed two of those blue pills into my mouth, then washed them down with a bottle of water stashed away in the second desk drawer.

I scrambled through my purse once more and retrieved my two-way pager. It read *6:33.* Again, I looked at the digital display on my computer. It too read *6:33.* Frantic, I walked to Marcus' cubicle, which was three stations down from my office. He kept a digital clock radio on his desk. It read *6:34.*

The cleaning crew was busy emptying waste paper baskets and dusting venetian blinds. Yellow caution markers appeared outside of the restrooms.

"You still here?" Trevor asked from his empty cubicle, almost appearing from nowhere and frightening me. "The get-together is at Antoine's. What you workin' on now? I came back 'cause I forgot my car keys in the QA lab. Everybody else is at the party."

What party? I started to asked, but just wasn't in the mood. *Isn't he supposed to be on disability?* I asked myself. *I guess he's not too disabled to party.*

"Why you still here?" Trevor asked.

"I was just checking the time," I said. "What happened to all the clocks?"

"What you mean what happened to all the clocks?" Trevor asked.

"They all say six-thirty-five," I said. "It can't be past two o'clock."

Trevor gave me a blank stare.

"I'm just..." I started, "oh, nevermind."

I ran back to my office. Knowing that I lost track of time made my head spin. I opened my bottom desk drawer and fumbled through my purse in search of my little blue pills. *Oh no!* I couldn't find the bottle. *Pills are pills,* I reasoned as I located the bottle of big, pink, horsey pills. Grabbing for the bottle of water in my second lower desk drawer, I popped one in and swallowed long and hard. Yuck!

"You always be workin' all the time," Trevor said, shocking the heck out of me. "You need to be home taking care o' them chil'ren. Don't you need to be home cookin' supper or some'n?"

"Not today, Trevor," I said. "Oh my God!" I gasped. I glanced at the digital computer clock and was horrified to see the time. "Six-forty-five!" The room began to spin as I balanced against my credenza to keep from falling. I gained my composure, looked up and he was still there.

"You always be trippin' up in here. You better lay off them drugs." Trevor stood at the opening to my office with his arms stretched apart, almost as if to stop me from leaving. *If he were truly injured and disabled, he wouldn't be able to stretch his arms like that,* I thought. *He's faking for sure.* He wasn't walking with a cane, but he was wearing a neck brace and wrist braces.

"Whatever, moth' fucker," I said as I continued to log off my computer. The network was sluggish, so I became a bit agitated because it took a little longer than usual. I pushed him out of my path and proceeded to the window on the other side of the hallway just to make sure that I was seeing correctly. All I saw were streetlights along Peachtree Road and fleeting red brake lights from cars that passed along Georgia 400.

"What did you say?" Trevor demanded, as he followed me down the hall. He got so close to me that I smelled the strong scent of Bourbon that saturated his body. "I know you ain't call me outta my name!"

"Whatever," I said, without paying much attention to what he actually said. I continued to stare out of the window. My nerves were frayed, and he was but a mosquito.

"You make me sick. What you supposed to be anyhow? You one of them strong, ind'pendent black women, heh. Y'all think y'all too good fo' the black man. Think y'all too educated fo' us! But don't nobody want y'all sorry asses no way! Y'all don't know how to be no woman, how to take care o' no man, and y'all wonder why the black men date outside his race!

"What you need is for a man to lay you down and give you a real good fuckin'. You think you fine, don't you? But don't nobody want to fuck yo' ugly, tired ass anyhow..."

"What *you* need is for a man to give *you* a good fucking," I told him. "Now I told you to leave me the fuck alone!" I grabbed a black stapler from a nearby desk and whopped him upside the head. I was more disturbed by my complete lapse of time than by that idiot. Trevor was inconsequential, a mosquito that buzzed endlessly around my ear. *Damn!* I thought. *I wish I had a fly swatter!*

"Wh ... uh ... uh ... " He jumped back in horror, as if I had offended him in some way. "You crazy," was all he could say, as he stood there with his mouth hanging open.

I ran back to my office to turn my computer off, but decided to start for the elevator instead. Trevor, his loud mouth, and the sounds of vacuum cleaners were left staggering behind.

"I was just about to come and get you," Marcus said as he got off the elevator. "I had something to take care of on the eleventh floor. What's wrong? You look upset."

Trevor strutted himself down the hall, rolled his eyes at me, then got on the elevator going down.

He would probably try to get me arrested for assault and battery, but I didn't care.

"Oh," one of the cleaning men said as he emptied the trash can next to the elevators. "Excuse me, Miss."

"Oh my goodness!" I said in shock. It was the same old man from Underground Atlanta, the hospital, the gas station, and the dream with Juanita, only he wore a dingy, gray cleaning uniform.

"I ain't mean to scare you, Miss," the man said.

I needed a Coke ... and fast.

"Where are you off to?" Marcus asked as he held the elevator door.

"To the snack room upstairs," I said, then raced on the elevator.

I passed at least three clocks on the way to the snack room, all of which read *6:45. Finally, the snack room!* Three white walls combined with the large windows gave it a light and airy feel. I passed the long black counter with the two large white microwaves and toaster oven. The clocks on the two microwaves and coffee machine all read *6:46,* and so did the large round black clock on the rear wall next to the vending machines.

I got a Coke, then walked to the rear of the room to enjoy it. Immediately to the right was the conference room. The doors were closed, but I heard voices. *What's going on? A late meeting?* I opened one of the doors—quietly—to sneak in. The room was cold and dark like no one had been there for the night. *Creepy!*

I raced back to the elevators, threw the empty Coke can in the white recycle bin, then wondered back to my office downstairs. Oh, those vacuum cleaners were just roaring, roaring, roaring. *Now we want clean floors, right?* I took a backward glance out of the windows to Peachtree Road. Both Peachtree Road and Georgia 400 were gridlocked, pure evidence that it was in fact rush hour.

"Knock, knock," Marcus said as he entered my office. "I don't want to leave without you."

"Leave without me?" I was confused. Was there an office party or meeting that we were attending?

"We could ride together since you don't know where it is. I'll bring you back to your car after the services. Or..."

"Or?" I asked.

"Or, we could get some dinner afterwards."

Why does Marcus want me to meet him for dinner? I was indeed curious. *Maybe the medicine is kicking in.* "I'm just..." I started, but Marcus interrupted my sentence.

"You're always working all the time," he said as he took my hands in his. Our eyes locked in an almost impenetrable stare, looking deep into each other's eyes. "You need to be taking care of," he said as he stroked my hair.

"Marcus," I said, then pulled away. Marcus came up behind me, and unmistakably, his hardness rubbed against my rear. "Oh my God!" I gasped.

I turned to leave, but Marcus stood at the opening between my desk and the door almost as if to stop me from leaving. I tried in vain to push him out of my path and proceed to the door. As he held me in his arms, all I saw were the street lights that lined Peachtree Road and fleeting red brake lights from cars passing along Georgia 400. We engaged in a deep, hot, hungry French kiss. His arms were so strong, as I let him have me. I inched my fingers up his big, masculine chest on way around his broad, strong shoulders.

We licked and sucked each other's lips, twirling our tongues up and down and around and around. "Oh, Marc!" I whispered between kisses. *What if someone catches us? There goes my reputation.*

"What did you call me?" Marcus asked. He got so close to me that I smelled the strong scent of Lagerfeld that saturated his body. "Who's Marc?"

"You're Marc," I said, hoping he wouldn't suspect more. Besides, Marc-ell-us and Marc-us are almost one in the same except for the "ell" in the middle. Ironic, but my ex's—what's-his-name—name was Mark too. What's-his-name was just plain old Mark; not fancy Marc like Marcus or Marcellus. *Is some form of the name Mark a prerequisite for being involved with me romantically?*

"I like Marc," he said. "No one has ever called me that before." He held me in his arms as we admired the Buckhead skyline. "Do you know what you need?" He turned to face me.

"No, what?" I asked.

"What you need is for a man to take you in his arms," he took my hand in his, "and pamper you silly," followed by nibbling my fingers in his hot, juicy mouth, "and treat you like a lady."

Hearing those words sent balls of fire traveling to every cell in my body. Only one person sent me into a tizzy like that ... Marcellus. *Maybe I can have heaven on Earth after all.*

I was no longer disturbed by my complete lapse of time. Marcus calmed my nerves—or—was it the medicine? Was it all a mirage? Was I dreaming or was that night real? *Damn! I can't live like this anymore.*

He closed my office door as we headed for the elevator. "Remember what Mr. Chap said in the hospital when we went to see him the other day?" Marcus asked as we boarded the elevator.

"No, what?" I asked. First of all, I didn't remember seeing Mr. Chap in the hospital. Last I knew, he was taken away in an ambulance only a few hours earlier. My big pink pill had started to kick in, so not much fazed me. Or, was it the little blue pills that I had taken earlier in the day?

"He said that I should take care of his woman until he gets back," Marcus said.

"Oh, yeah," I said.

"Chap had a thing for you," Marcus said.

"Had?" I asked. Why was he referring to him in past tense? Mr. Chap was in the hospital after all, nothing else. I didn't think much of it. *Bad English,* I thought. *Marcus has been hanging around Trevor too long.*

***

"Where's your car?" I asked as we entered the parking deck.

Sounds of our footsteps clanked like jackhammers on the concrete floors. Only six cars remained on that level and none was an old Ford like the car Marcus drove.

"The black one over there," he said.

Only two black cars were parked in the area where he pointed: a Mercedes Benz and an Expedition. Marcus clicked his remote door opener and lights flashed on the Mercedes.

"When did you get this car?" I asked.

"Don't you remember?" he asked. "I got it last year around this time."

I knew for sure that he was joking. *Maybe he borrowed the car. Maybe he rented the car.* "Whatever you say, Marcus."

"After you, my sweet," he said, then opened my car door.

I don't know what got into Marcus, but he was so different. Maybe it was the pills; maybe it was a dream.

We drove through Buckhead listening to sounds of Norman Brown. I was so relaxed, without as much as a care in the world. Well, until we arrived at the funeral parlor.

"Why are we stopping here?" I asked, just realizing that we were both wearing black. It's a good thing those little blue pills killed any trace of anxiety, because my nerves would have been frayed to high heavens. Excitement and surprises of the negative kind were two things I definitely did not need. News about Tish and Percy were too much to swallow. It was a good thing I had those little blue pills to dull my pain.

Anyway, the place had the eloquence and charm of an old Southern home. It was a white Victorian style mansion with tall white columns and black shutters, kind of like my Great-Aunt Ruby's house back in New Orleans. Out front was a porch swing that seemed to be more for show than sitting. To the right side was the parking lot; it was so packed that night with only one or two more spaces hidden between the myriad of cars. The owner had quite a bit of landscaping done with all the shrubs, trees and thick, plush grass.

Marcus pulled a pale-green announcement from his coat pocket. "This is the place."

I started to snatch the paper from him, but decided not to. *Maybe I should be surprised this one time.*

A strange smell greeted us at the foyer entrance. It had the odor of pine, potpourri and another pungent aroma like that of a veterinarian's office blended together. Buffed, white tiles with golden specks covered the floors. The walls were antique-white and a single chandelier hung from the ceiling, its crystals chimed through the night each time guests entered the parlor.

The services had already begun as Marcus and I sneaked in. The place was packed with familiar faces from work—standing room only. It was so crowded that I couldn't make out the décor. Far in a corner to the left, Lou and Daniel

Batchelor—both dressed in black suits—attempted to hide from view. D'Angela stood along a wall far to the right; she was frail and thin as if she'd been ill, and looked a tad on the rough side. Her hair was plain old nappy as heck; she wore an old, raggedy, Goodwill, hand-me-down, black dress; black stockings with a big gaping run down the side; and scuffed, black shoes. D'Angela had let herself go—big time. We didn't get along, but I must give it to her—she always made sure she was looking good from head to toe.

A familiar redhead sat toward the front row, turned at an angle. *Something's familiar about her,* I thought. *Patricia!* Amazing, how sad occasions bring people from the woodworks.

Marcus finally let me see the program.

"What!" I was shocked to see the name—

Marcellus Angellini Chapperonne
??- 2002

"No one knew how old he was, so that's why we put two question marks when we got the announcements printed."

"Oh," I said. I was so curious about the name. Did I see that name somewhere at work and buried it in my subconscious? Is that why I dreamed of an imaginary playmate named Marcellus Angellel?

"Come to find out, Dan Batchelor was his nephew or something like that."

"Interesting," I said. I didn't want to let on about my memory. Letting anyone know that I was breaking down was a sure bet to losing my position as vice president. That was my secret, a burden for me to share alone. Plenty of people, including Marcus, would be glad to take my place. Sure, I was starting to become close to Marcus, but I still didn't trust him yet. Then it hit me: *Could Marcus be responsible for my condition?* I thought. *Could he have poisoned me in some way? Is that why Patricia and Daniel Batchelor disappeared so mysteriously?*

I looked at Marcus as he remained focused on the services. *Are you out to get me, too, Marcus?* I asked myself. I needed an excuse to leave. No way could he take me back to the parking garage. I needed an escape ... and fast.

It was time for the viewing. Daniel and Lou sneaked away without anyone—well except me—noticing.

"Let's wait until the crowd thins out," Marcus suggested.

Why should I trust him? He wants us to be the last ones here so he can do whatever to me. No Marcus, you can't have me. Rage toward him grew deep within me. "No," I said. "Let's go now."

"But ..." he said.

"Now!" I insisted.

"All right, all right," he said.

Marcus took my hand as we squeezed and prodded through the crowd, making quite a few guests pout and frown. I didn't care one bit.

Front and center, surrounded by wreaths, floral arrangements and individual long-steamed roses was the mysterious, real-life Marcellus Angellini Chapperonne. The casket was some sort of wood, mahogany perhaps. White silk lined the inside. Submerged deep within his eternal home, hidden from sight was the guest of honor. Who could he be? A member of the Board of Directors who I only met in passing? One of the cleaning crew? Surely, he couldn't be the young fellow from the mailroom? Soon, my curiosity would be quenched, and the real Marcellus Agellini Chapperonne would no longer be a secret.

The room began to dim as I neared him. "Oh my goodness." The room began to gray before my eyes as I beheld Marcellus Angellini Chapperonne. He looked so peaceful in that blue, pin-striped suit and arms folded over his lower abdomen. I stepped a little closer. "Oh Lord!" He looked like an older version of my imaginary playmate—Marcellus. I felt so ashamed. Did I secretly lust for Mr. Chap, even on some remote, subconscious level? It was him without a doubt. How could I lust after such a sweet old man?

My stomach churned hard as all blackened before me. All the conversations melted as one giant sea of confusion. I felt my legs give way beneath me.

Chapter 25.
For Curious Dances in the Dark

I had the strangest dream when I blacked out that night, Dr. Iverson.

Strange? How so?

Well, I'm not sure if it was a dream or the medicine. Either way, it was strange. They weren't making any sense.

Who wasn't making any sense?

Daddy and Percy.

***

"Didi," a woman's voice called, waking me. "Didi."

I slowly opened my eyes to a white, fuzzy room. "Percy?" I couldn't move and everything remained hazy, probably from a sedative. "Where am I? In the hospital? Which hospital?"

She didn't answer.

I saw her face clearly, but her body was a blur. She had put on a few needed pounds since the last time I saw her. Frankly, she needed the extra weight. Percy looked a few years younger too.

"It's almost time for you to go home," Percy said.

"Are you coming home with me?" I asked. I was happy to see Percy and didn't want to argue about where she'd been or what she'd been doing. Besides, she probably had a good explanation.

"No," she said. "I have a new home of my own."

I knew it. She had moved without telling me. Once Percy got settled in, she'd invite me over. She just got too busy to tell me. "Where? Where?" I asked.

"Oh, far away from here. It's beautiful," she said. "No crime, no envy, no jealousy, and the streets are paved with gold."

"Oh, I can't wait to see," I said. She was so silly at times.

"This is my husband, Adonis," she said. "He went by Victor when he lived here."

Husband? Lived where? I asked myself. *Who finally made her settle down?*

"Hello, Didi," her husband said. "Good seeing you again."

I didn't know what to say or think. It had to be a dream; everything was just way too weird. Percy's husband was the old man from Underground Atlanta, the hospital in North Carolina and the gas station; only he was young like I had seen him in the dream with my cousin, Juanita.

"You have some visitors," she said. "Daddy has something to tell you." She and her new husband stepped away. I assumed that they were just outside the hospital room.

I was expecting Daddy, but Marcus came in first. He looked a bit fuzzy and his voice was raspy, like that of a much older man.

"I just came to say good-bye," he said.

"Bye?" I asked. The sedative made my vision blurry because I could barely make out his face.

"Yes," he said. "It's time for me to be going on. I promised Mr. Chap that I would take care of his woman until it was time, and I kept my promise."

"You're so silly, Marcus," I said. I thought his comments were strange, and a little bit in bad taste. We had just lost Mr. Chap and there he was joking around about him.

He started for the door. That's when Daddy came in, but something was odd. My eyesight had improved slightly, but my body was still frozen. Daddy looked much younger; maybe it was because his hair was black instead of gray. I was sure I needed glasses—that or the sedative had affected my vision. All I saw were faces, but the bodies were like clouds.

"Daddy?" I asked. I was glad to see him. He smiled all the way to my bed, so he must have been glad to see me too.

"Didi," Daddy said as he neared me. "They didn't give me much time, so I apologize for rushing. I have to get straight to the point."

"Okay, Daddy," I said. I assumed that when he said "they" didn't give him much time, he meant that visitor's hours were almost over and "they" referred to the nurses.

"I never told you this, but when I was a young man, I was in love with Pearl-Elizabeth."

I must have been doped for sure because hearing that woman's name didn't bother me one bit.

"Oh," I said.

"Yes," he continued. "One day, she just up and left me. That hurt me really, really bad."

"Oh, Daddy," I said, trying to be sympathetic.

"Well," Daddy continued. "I went down to Morgan City to see this old man named Bot. He told me to get three things that belong to Pearl-Elizabeth. So I did. I took him the white picnic basket she used to pack our supper in when we used to sit out on the levee. Then, I took the engagement ring she left—that was a beautiful ring—three carats you know. I couldn't find anything else. I searched and I searched and couldn't find anything. Then, something told me to reach inside my jacket, and I found a single strand of her hair. I took those things to him. He said within a week we would be married and for me to come on down ready for a wedding. So, I did what he said. I didn't think anything of it.

"Bot told me that I had to promise my children to him. But he was more interested in the girls. He and his brother wanted brides. So, I said okay, not thinking much of it.

"Your mother was soooo beautiful. She looked so much like Pearl-Elizabeth. She even smelled like her, all fresh and sweet like roses." A smile lit his face as he reminised.

"Daddy," I said. "I'm curious."

"Yes, Didi," he said. "Curious about what?"

"I'm curious about why Pearl-Elizabeth and Mother looked so much alike. Were they sisters?"

He put his head down as if to conjure up an answer. "Well, it's like this," he said, looking at me. "Your momma was part of Pearl-Elizabeth."

"Part of?" I asked, remembering back to my conversation with Fern. Still, I wasn't sure if I were dreaming, drugged or what. "You mean like a clone?"

"Yes," he said with a look of surprise on his face. "How did you know?"

"Just a lucky guess," I said.

"Anyway," he continued. "I didn't think much of it. Your momma and me were doing okay. Everything was going well, except that day ... that day she left with your brothers. Mother Ruby came and took them to their rightful places, which were in their world, not this one. In truth, your momma was never happy being taken away from her world. I don't blame her. Who wants to leave streets of gold for hell?"

"Mother Ruby?" I asked, knowing that everybody used to call Great-Aunt Ruby Mother Ruby. "Do you mean Great-Aunt Ruby?"

"Yes," he said and lowered his head once again. "You see," he raised his head, "she wasn't really your aunt. She was ... she was ..."

"She was what, Daddy?"

"She was one of The Three Sisters. And Great-Gran was her mother, but she wasn't your great-grandmother."

"So, Grandpa was right about them not being kin to us, right?" I asked.

"Yes," he said. "Yes he was."

"So, why did we go by their house all the time?" Percy and I really enjoyed visiting with them, until they just up and disappeared.

"Well, Didi ... it's like this," he said, standing up.

My limbs were frozen, so I couldn't sit up and follow him. All I heard was his voice behind me.

"Percy was promised to Bot's brother. You ... you're promised to Bot. I'm... I'm sorry, Didi. But I'm being punished for messing around with things I didn't understand. I'll spend eternity in hell, one incarnation after the other without escape until I repay my karmic debts. You and your sister, on the other hand, will flee this place and will never return. That's the only part I don't regret; you and your sister will spend eternity in a better place."

All was silent, as if no one were around.

"Daddy?" I called, but he didn't answer. "Daddy? Percy? Marcus?" Still no answer. Sunlight poured through the windows as pure, white light blinded me...

***

"Daddy? Percy? Marcus?" I called.

Every joint and muscle in my body ached to high heaven. It felt as if someone had beaten me silly with a giant sledgehammer. My head, muscles and places I didn't even know I had, ached something awful. *Must be the medicine wearing off,* I thought. I tried to move, but I couldn't do as much as wiggle a toe without my body going into painful spasms.

"Great-Gran is still calling for her daddy and sister. She's still living in the past," a young man said. "Didn't her daddy die right before she married Big Daddy, Momma? And didn't they find her sister dead in the woods almost sixty years ago?"

"Go wait outside, Chris," a man said. His voice sounded familiar, but I couldn't quite place it.

I mustered up all the strength I had, but I called out for help. "Marcus?" I called. "Is that you Marcus?" I managed to open my eyes, but everything was a blur. Three fuzzy images floated before me.

"Doesn't she know that Big Daddy has been dead for eight years?" the young man asked.

"Just shut up, Chris," the woman said. "Just … just … leave Chris."

"But, Ma," the young man said.

"I don't want to hear it. Just … just go," the woman insisted. "Get him out of here, Dewey! Get him out, Dewey," the woman shouted in frustration. "I don't even know why you came. Go check on the ambulance. They should be here any second."

"Let's go, Chris," the man said. "Let your momma tend to Great-Gran."

I saw two shadows leave the room; one returned to the foot of my bed. Who was it? Was I in another dream, or was I in a drug-induced stupor?

"She says they all come to visit her," the woman said.

"Who comes to visit her?" the man asked.

"Her daddy, her sister and Big Daddy," the woman told him.

"You shouldn't be encouraging her, Cynth," the man said. "She's hallucinating again. The doctor said that's common with Alzheimer's. Besides, she's one hundred eight years old. Her mind is not that sharp anymore."

Everything came into focus as I lay helpless beneath a lilac scented, white comforter. My granddaughter, Cynthia, held my frail hand in hers. My grandson, Dewey, sat on the foot of my bed, leering at me. They spoke as if I weren't there.

"It's okay, Gran," Cynthia said as tears rolled down her cheeks. "Hold on a little longer. Just hold on."

My chest tightened, as if a giant rubber band were fastened around me. Sharp pains ran through my sides with each breath. Until that moment, I had never experience such grueling agony. It had to stop. I wanted the pain to stop.

"Gran!" Cynthia said. Dewey ran to her side.

The room began to gray, as I was pulled up by an invisible force. All pain quickly vanished. Cynthia, Dewey and Chris were but clouds hovering over my frail, decrepit body.

"Gran! Gran!" Cynthia voice faded as traveled faster and faster through that gray void.

Faster and faster I traveled. Up and down and left and right—one indistinguishable from the other—as I spun around and around, spiraling through space on a journey to...

***

I came to in the parlor of my dream home, sitting on that plush, white sectional. It was twilight as I watched the fading sunlight through the open French doors leading to the veranda.

Oh, it was sooo beautiful—with the birds singing and wind blowing scents of exotic flowers to tickle my noise—I just had to go outside.

I rested my back against the tall, white columns and admired the plush landscape—with all its rolling hills and waterfalls—from a distance. No one was around, but I felt a strong presence follow me as I walked along the veranda. I looked right, left and back ... nothing.

"What are your greatest accomplishments?" a deep, raspy voice asked, almost from nowhere.

I turned quickly, only to face that strange creature from one of my last dreams. The sun shined on its skin, giving it an oxblood hue. His eyes were brown and glassy, like that of an elephant.

"What?" I asked. *My dreams are becoming too weird,* I thought. *Why can't they all be fun anymore?*

"Come," the strange man gestured. "Sit."

He led me to a stairstep on the far side of the veranda. Oh, it was so lovely watching the sunset over the sea in the distance. The sand looked so white and pure. Marcellus and the three children walked along the shore. Hera looked to be about ten, Marcel was about seven, and the baby, whose name I didn't know, was around four or five. They seemed so peaceful and relaxed as they walked hand-in-hand, skipping over ebb tides.

"Now," the strange man said. "What have you accomplished with your life on Earth?"

What a strange question, but this is a strange dream. "What?" I asked, then I looked back at all the wonderful times in my life. That was an easy question. "Well. I bought my first house when I was twenty-nine back in '90. It was a townhouse, but it was mine. I was a single parent with two small children too. Then, I got my first BMW in 1991. I drove that for a few years. It was a reliable car. I bought my dream house in 1996 in Peachtree City. At first, it was a strain on the budget, but I got promoted to team leader, then project manager, then manager, then director, so it was easy to afford. Then, I got tired of my BMW and got an Acura in 1998. The boys and me traveled all over the world. So, I've accomplished quite a bit in my life. Yes indeedy."

The strange man looked at me as if to say, "So?" He opened a big white book trimmed in gold that he held on his lap. I didn't see him carry a book. "Honey, the Lord doesn't care about material things; they fade away. Anybody can get a BMW or a fancy house. The Lord cares about the heart, that which is eternal and of the spirit. What did you do to help make Earth a better place for yourself, somebody else; the creatures in the sky, on the land or beneath the sea is what the Lord cares about.

Then, I thought of all the animal rights activists and environmentalists.

"Look," he said and pointed to pages of pictures of Kevin and Keston from the time they were born to high school and beyond. I had never seen those pictures before. The boys smiled at times, but others seemed dismal. "These are the times when you encouraged your children to be the best they can be. Because of your pushing and prodding, their lives are full till this day."

"What's that?" I asked as he showed several pages of pictures of my times with Daddy. What memories he brought back: stargazing, private family barbeques, outings to Ponchartrain Beach and just sitting in the den watching television. Those were truly special times that I will always cherish—even if Daddy thought that I was an embarrassment to him by being a divorcee.

"You brought a lot of joy to your father's life. All these years, you thought he turned his back on you."

"Well, didn't he?" I asked. *Why should I argue with a mirage?* I asked myself, but his answers were very curious.

"No," the strange man said without an ounce of emotion in his straight, flat tone of voice. "You see, your father was slick in his day. He thought that he could get over on anybody. When it comes to matters of the spirit, there's no getting over. A deal is a deal."

Okay, is he going to tell me the same story Fern told me about this Bot character? I wondered. "What do you mean?" I asked, knowing the answer.

The next several pages were pictures of Percy back to when we were kids all the way to the times she cared for me when I was sick. I needed her and she needed me. Oh, how I missed her. Thoughts of never seeing her again pained my heart. Maybe after I passed out I really saw her in the hospital room. And maybe she just moved away and got too busy to tell me. Either way, I wanted my Percy back. I needed her in my life more than ever.

"Your father promised you and your sister to Bot and one of his brothers. When he learned what he had done, he couldn't face you or your sister. That was around the time when Percy started having dreams that she couldn't explain."

"Dreams?" I asked. He had caught my attention. I needed to know more. *It's only a dream,* I told myself. *Don't even worry yourself about it.*

"Yes, like the ones you started having."

"Oh," I said. My heart began to race, but instead of nervousness, a strong sense of peace overcame me. Again, I reminded myself that it was only a dream. The dreams weren't fun anymore. I wanted them to stop. Besides, I had had enough of Marcellus anyway, especially now that I had Marcus, who was real.

"Your daddy went to see Mother Ruby, who told him that there was nothing to be done."

"You mean Great-Aunt Ruby?" I asked.

"Yes. But she's not your Great-Aunt, she's not even a she or a he. On Earth, she is known by many names, but most call her Mother Ruby. She's a Karma. Your daddy used to send you and your sister to her so the two of you could enjoy your lives on Earth a bit longer; she prolonged your stay, but that's all."

"A Karma?" That was something for a dream image to pull my leg like that. But it was just that—a dream—and weird things happen in dreams.

"Yes," he said. "The Karmas keep the universe in balance. They keep really busy on hell planes like Earth. Where there's up, there must be down. Where there's wrong, Karmas make it right. Karmas, always were and always will be. There's truth to the saying, 'What's goes around comes around.' Karmas make sure there's balance in everything."

"Oh," I said.

"Look," the strange man said. "Your greatest accomplishment."

It was a large red-brick building with large white columns. A crowd of young adult men and women crowded in front to pose for the picture. In big, bold, black letters read—

The Letitia Cynthia Dewey
Development Center

"What's this?" I asked.

"Your greatest accomplishment of all," he said. "This is the career center that you, your company and others helped to sponsor."

"No," I said. "I've never seen this before."

"It's almost time," the man said. "Old memories fade fast."

"What?" I asked. *Oh, just another weird dream conversation,* I thought. *Conversations can be illogical in dreams; they're figurative.*

"Back in 2006, your children were grown and gone. You missed your sister. You missed Tish the most. That's why in the end, you saw her in everyone and everything. As a reminder of your legacy to the world, you helped hundreds of young people live fulfilling lives that they wouldn't have if it weren't for the Letitia Cynthia Dewey Development Center. Through the center, you exposed them to things they never would have seen, and made them see greatness in themselves that they never knew existed. You helped the young, the old, the homeless, the battered—no one was turned away."

The next several pages were pictures of Tish—from the time we met at Spelman to the last day I saw her alive. Feelings of glee and sadness filled my spirit.

"Just like your children, you pushed and prodded Tish to be her best. Since you felt you didn't succeed with Tish, you created the center in her honor, because you saw everyone and everything in her. You even named two of your grandchildren after her—Cynthia and Dewey."

Suddenly, a strong feeling of hope flooded my being. Bottled up emotions of Daddy, Tish and Percy vanished as soon as I owned up to the affects their actions or inactions had on my psyche. Forgiveness had replaced all traces of negativity in my soul. Hallelujah!

"My work is almost done here," he said. "Just a few more hairs to shave."

More illogical dream talk, I told myself.

All became hazy and periwinkle blue. My head began to spin faster and faster until ...

***

"Grandma," a woman called from deep within the fog. "Grandma."

Her voice echoed in the distance as I came to in a bright hospital bed. No aches or pains, just a bit groggy from the medication.

"Grandma, grandma," the woman continued to call.

I looked all around, then realized she called from a neighboring hospital room.

A nurse entered the room. She looked so familiar. *Where do I know this woman?* Her low-cut, jet-black, wavy hair brought out her heart-shaped face and smooth caramel complexion. The white uniform she wore exposed her ample cleavage, barely leaving anything to the imagination. Her pants were so tight, giving full view of her shapely rear.

I lay there, groggy and tired, watching the nurse gyrate in front of me as she took my vital signs. As she came near, I goosed her. *She thinks I'm crazy or drugged anyway.* Then it hit me: *what have I done? I wouldn't blame her if she slapped me silly.*

"You're a fresh one," she said.

I got a look at her name tag: Cynthia Dewey. She looked a lot like Marcellus' secretary, Cynthia Dewey, only with shorter hair.

Oh, my goodness. Not that name again. I'm really, really losing it. So what did I do, I goosed her again, only that time, I held on and fondled her flesh. The medicine made me groggy, but it also made me naughty.

To my surprise, the nurse closed her eyes, and rolled around and around to my rhythm as her pants dampened. She walked away to the door, as I heard the lock click. Her butt was so wide and juicy, my loins were moist just looking at her in anticipation of feeling her body next to mine.

She removed my blue-and-white, backless hospital gown, exposing my nude body, rubbing my breasts along the way.

"You have some nice, soft titties and a big, juicy ass, Ms. Pickens. I can't wait to lick your pussy 'til you come in my mouth."

She hungrily licked one breast, as she tickled the other with one hand, while grinding my wet cunt deeper and deeper with the other hand. Up and down and around and around she licked, from one breast to the other, while I lay there—helpless.

My womanhood was ablaze; my heart pounded, as the horny woman had her way with me. The possibility of being caught made the experience that much more exciting. Blood rushed to my clit, making it throb in delight.

She ran her tongue up and down my stomach, down to the belly button, making its way to my pubic hair, where she rubbed her face—around and around.

I caressed her breasts, teasing her hard, erect nipples and soft, supple flesh.

She parted my lower lips and blew cool air up and down and around my femininity, sending spine-tingling chills throughout my body. Without warning, she licked the length of me—from the back of my cunt to the tip of my clit— slowly, over and over again. Oooo. She penetrated my plug with her tongue, twirling it around and around, and she dug deeper and deeper, all the while pinching my nipples with her fingers.

She nibbled my outer lips, inner lips, licking skillfully inside and outside. Her fingers penetrated my soaking-wet walls, as I cringed in delight. She thrust in tiny, quick strokes, in and out—her finger becoming stickier with each dip— as she licked and sucked my clit between her teeth and lips.

My inner walls began to tighten as I rolled around to her rhythm. She grabbed both my cheeks in her hands, squeezing me in and out, continuing to lick and suck my clit between her teeth so long and strong, as if she were slurping my flesh through a straw.

A strange, warm energy flowed from my loins, up to my breasts and beyond. "Ooo, ooo," I moaned soft and low, as my body jerked to and fro, as I came to a most delightful climax.

A long white, sticky trail hung from the nurse's lips as she broke free of me. Her hot tongue savored my juices as she buttoned her blouse.

***

Noise of a busy hospital flooded in the room as someone slung the door wide open. "Beautiful flowers for a beautiful flower," a man called.

I looked in the direction of the door and the scene changed before my eyes, as if a giant bucket of water had been poured over the room. I came to with a thermometer under my tongue. The once hot, horny nurse had suddenly transformed into a diligent professional who held my arm and checked my pulse. A loud beep sounded in my ear, jolting me fully into reality.

Marcus sat a large bouquet of roses on the stand beside my bed.

"How are you doing," he asked, then pecked me on the cheek.

"Ninety-nine," the nurse said. "You have a slight fever, but you'll be okay." She smiled at me and was distinctly different; her name tag read *Swan Davis, RN.* She was average height with deep bronze skin; her complexion was much darker than the other woman's. Her long, black hair was pulled back into a ponytail, which brought attention to her broad heart-shaped face; the other woman's hair was considerably shorter. *No one had a face shaped like that except my mother and Percy,* I thought. The nurse was no more than maybe twenty-five years old, a tad younger than the one who had pleasured me so much.

"I'll be back later with your medicine," the nurse said.

As she left the room, I noticed how skinny she was. Actually, skinny was an understatement because her butt was flat, her chest was flat, and her little stick-bird legs were straight and shapeless. *At least she has a pretty face,* I thought.

"How are you feeling?" Marcus asked with such enthusiasm.

"Fine," I said.

"Well, you look great," he said.

We both laughed. How could anyone dressed in a hospital gown with a bunch of tubes sticking from her arm look great?

Then it hit me—my loins were dry, as if they hadn't been touched. That darn-awful, backless blue-and-white hospital gown was also intact as if it hadn't been removed. And I sure didn't remember an IV in my arm either. I knew for sure that the medicine had caused me to hallucinate the episode with the nurse. Marcus woke me from my dream when he burst in unannounced. Yeah, that's what happened.

Oh, the room was just so intense. The blinds were pulled up to the ceiling. All I saw was thick, white fog outside my window. The sun reflected its light off the clouds, making it just too, too bright. I could barely stand it.

But, Marcus looked so fine in that clingy, black turtleneck sweater; black jeans and black lizard skin cowboy boots. I sure hoped that he had nothing to do with my condition, because I had begun to develop deep-rooted feelings for him. Perhaps deep down inside—on some level—I always wanted him to divorce his wife and be with me. Maybe I had been attracted to him all those years—just lurking in the corners—hoping for the worse to happen. And, just maybe, it was him who I had dreamed of all along—my real-life Marcellus. No mistake, the names are too much alike for it to be purely coincidental. Forget about Mr. Chap, I couldn't have dreamed about him. Now, that was a coincidence—for his name to be Marcellus.

"Demeter," Marcus said as he held my hand in his. "I loved you from the first time I laid eyes on you. But, I was married and knew you wouldn't give me the time of day. When she finally left me two years ago, I was relieved, but still didn't have guts enough to let you know how I felt."

That woman in the next room broke my fixation on Marcus' words. Why wouldn't she shut up? She kept yelling, "Grandma, don't go. Grandma, don't leave me." She cried something terrible; probably her granny had just passed on. I felt her pain, for I never got to say good-bye to my Great-Aunt Ruby and Great-Gran. Perhaps, I shouldn't have been so selfish.

"Oh, Marcus," I said. Balls of passion flowed to every cell in my body, as we looked deep into each other's eyes. "I don't know what to say."

He ran his fingers through my hair, stroking my face, as our eyes locked. Marcus came closer and closer until our lips met. He stroked my lips with the tip of his tongue, then we engaged in a long, throaty French kiss, briefly pausing for an occasion whiff of air. We sucked and licked each other's lips; my loins moistened for sure as I wanted him inside me.

My head began to spin; he pulled away. The medicine started to kick in once more as all I saw before me was pure whiteness. That woman mourned her grandmother so much; her voice echoed through the clouds.

Marcus face blurred and his body faded into whiteness. He looked much older as he backed away from me. "Thank you for …" he said, backing away in slow motion. His words were garbled and slurred, as if he were speaking in slow motion.

Gradually, everything faded to white; all sounds were muted as I floated away into oblivion.

***

That's when I woke up in your office, Dr. Iverson.

How did you get here? You said you drove before.

Well, no. I was in the hospital. I couldn't have driven myself. Marcus must have driven me.

Are you sure, Demeter?

No. I'm not sure of anything anymore. Wait, this isn't your office, Dr. Iverson.

Where are you then, Demeter?

No. I can't be dreaming. This is the sectional in my dream parlor. This is the home I share with Marcellus in my dream world. Wait, that's Marcellus and the children waiting outside on the veranda. This can't be real.

Wait, you're not Dr. Iverson. You're … Great-Aunt Ruby.

It's real, Demeter. I'm not your Great-Aunt Ruby. I'm Karma like Fern told you. I'm here to help you get to where you belong.

So the stories were true? But, Marcus and the hospital and my grandchildren …

That was all real. You were one hundred eight years old.

Real? How about Mr. Chap?

All real, you just don't remember everything. All those memories will eventually fade away. You're still clinging to them by a thread. That life is gone. This is where you belong. You have to let go of that life. Let go of the memories.

That life is gone?

Yes, don't worry. Your family is fine. To them, five years have passed by.

Five years? So, Marcellus and the children are really waiting outside? Why don't they come in?

They can't.

Why not?

Because you must completely shed your skin.

How do I do that?

By letting go. Your memories of the past are fragmented. You remember enough to clear your conscience. You needed to make peace with those you thought did you wrong: your family, ex-husband, coworkers and friends. Now, you can shed your skin.

You must do one more thing.

What's that?

You must accept Marcellus now that you know he was Mr. Chap. By accepting him for who he ever was and is, then eternity is yours. The choice is yours, Demeter. Now that you know who Marcellus really was, do you want to be with him throughout eternity or would you rather go back to the bottomless pit? Soon as you say yes to him, all former memories will fade and he will be yours forever.

I love Marcellus so, so much. Why wouldn't I? I accept him for who he is and was—top to bottom, inside out, and upside down. I want to be with him more than anything in the universe. Yes! Yes! Yes! Yes, I'm ready to go home. Yes, I'm ready to take my rightful place by his side. Yes, I want to be his mate for all eternity.

End

Reader's Companion

Hello, readers!

I hoped you enjoyed *Imaginary Playmate*. I've included a list of discussion questions to make your reading experience much more memorable. For your convenience, answers are found at the end of the companion. Remember, no peeking.

1. What does Didi think is happening to her?
2. Is she really having a lucid dreaming experience like she believes? Or, is something else going on? What are some of the hints?
3. Where does Didi think she is throughout the book? Where is she really?
4. Why is the doctor taking her back to relive the past?
5. Which dream is her true reality? What are some hints?
6. Why does she lose track of time?
7. Why is she losing her memory?
8. Is Marcellus someone she knows in "real life," or is he truly an imaginary playmate? What are some hints?
9. Why does she continue to meet characters by the name of Cynthia Dewey?
10. Why does Didi's Great-Aunt Ruby appear in many of her dreams?
11. Why did she go shopping with her cousin Juanita?
12. What do the passages about "shedding skin" mean?
13. Who is Fern?
14. What's the significance of the name Mark, and why are the three husbands given this name?
15. What are some of the hidden philosophical messages of the book?
16. What's the overall theme of the book?

1. What does Didi think is happening to her?

    Didi has a stressful career and believes that she is having a nervous breakdown.

2. Is she really having a lucid dreaming experience like she believes? Or, is something else going on? What are some of the hints?

    a. Yes and no. While she's asleep, she's having a lucid dreaming experience. Lucid dreaming is the ability to control all aspects of a dream. Less than five percent of the population has this ability. Dreams are supposedly as "real" as real life.

    b. While awake, she's having an astral projection experience. In some spiritual circles, individuals have been known to have out-of-body experiences where the life force visits another realm called the astral world, hence, the name astral projection. In cases where we experience a falling sensation and/or jolting, then suddenly awakening, this is said to be an out of body experience rather than just a dream state.

3. Where does Didi think she is throughout the book? Where is she really?

    Didi think she's in Dr. Iverson's office. She's actually on her new world.

4. Why is the doctor taking her back to relive the past?

    Didi must forgive certain characters for whom she harbors ill-feelings. She must cleanse her soul by forgiving the transgressions they committed against her. The list includes: coworkers, family and friends.

5. Which dream is her true reality? What are some hints?

    The dream toward the end in which she's an elderly woman suffering from memory loss. The hint is when she looks through photo albums.

6. Why does she lose track of time?

    She's loses track of time because she has entered eternity where time doesn't exist.

7. Why is she losing her memory?

    Didi is entering another level of existence. To do so, she must shed all ties to the past. She only remembers the people and events that must be cleared away for her to move on to a higher level of existence.

8.   Is Marcellus someone she knows in "real life," or is he truly an imaginary playmate? What are some hints?

Marcellus is actually Mr. Chap incarnate. Long ago, he was punished for violating spiritual laws. He was sentenced to prison on Earth to spend one thousand years in the body of an old man, never to touch a woman.

Things that she liked in real life and in the dream world were somehow tied to Mr. Chap. These include: references to black-and-white diagonal tiles, coffee, spearmint and eucalyptus scents and the dream mall being named after her favorite star, Deneb.

9.   Why does she continue to meet characters by the name of Cynthia Dewey?

Didi misses her friend Tish, whose name was Letitia Cynthia Dewey. She wished that Tish would have lived her life more fully by living up to her potential. As a result, she saw anyone who appeared to have fulfilled her dreams as Tish.

10. Why does Didi's Great-Aunt Ruby appear in many of her dreams?

Great-Aunt Ruby is a Karma who sees to it that spiritual laws are enforced. Didi's father dabbled too far in matters of the spirit; Karma was there to guide her to where she really belonged.

11. Why did she go shopping with her cousin Juanita?

This relates in part to Question 4. She needed to clear up past issues before going on to a higher level of vibration. Didi had deep-rooted hatred for her cousin that needed to be forgiven.

12. What do the passages about "shedding skin" mean?

Shedding skin refers to getting rid of matters of the flesh: hatred, sorrow, unforgiveness, lust and other unresolved issues of a secular nature.

13. Who is Fern?

Fern is a talking plant. On a deeper level, Fern is Didi's spirit guide.

14. What's the significance of the name Mark, and why are the three husbands given this name?

On page 307, Didi made the distinction between plain old Mark and fancy

Marc. Mark, Marcus and Marcellus; the names represent an evololution to a "fancier" level of existence.

The marriage to Mark was filled with misery, which can be likened to a hellied existence. The marriage to Marcus lasted fifty years and though not discussed in the book, was successful. The marriage to Marcellus was the ultimate in existence and would last throughout eternity.

15. What are some of the hidden philosophical messages of the book?

   Several meanings are hidden in text:
   a. Forgive and forget
   b. More to life than what the eyes can see
   c. Material things fade away, but matters of the heart live forever
   d. Unforgiveness blocks blessings
   e. The past must be cleared to make way for a brighter future
   f. Karma
   g. The universe is filled with unlimited possibilities
   h. Responsibility; every action has consequences
   i. Happiness is for the taking
   j. Live life to the fullest

16. What's the overall theme of the book?

   Forgiveness; letting go of the past.